The
Polymath

The
Polymath

Bensalem Himmich

Translated by

Roger Allen

The American University in Cairo Press
Cairo   New York

English translation copyright © 2004 by
The American University in Cairo Press
113 Sharia Kasr el Aini, Cairo, Egypt
420 Fifth Avenue, New York 10018
www.aucpress.com

First published in Arabic in 2001 as *al-'Allama*
Copyright © 2001 by Bensalem Himmich
Protected under the Berne Convention

Dar el Kutub No. 7690/03
ISBN 977 424 821 X

Designed by AUC Press Design Center
Printed in Egypt

Contents

Translator's
Note

Albert Hourani, with whom I had the good fortune to study Middle
Eastern history during my time at Oxford University, used to admit
that he often found it very hard to dissuade students who came to
study for graduate degrees with him from writing about Ibn
Khaldun. This was particularly the case with students from the
Middle East itself. The number of studies devoted to various
aspects of the life and thought of this great Tunisian-born scholar,
our 'polymath,' is certainly large, but there can be little doubt that
his status in the world of history and historiography is fully
deserved. For not only were his works written from the unique perspective of someone who was born, raised, and educated in the
Western parts of the Arab-Islamic dominions (the Maghrib—the
Arabic word implying the place where the sun sets, the West), but
also his penchant for theorizing about the phenomena that turned
the region into such a turbulent place in which to live and work has
traditionally been viewed as the beginning of what has since
emerged as the social-scientific method. And now Bensalem
Himmich has taken the interest one stage further by turning this historian and his historical surroundings into the topic of a novel.

Himmich, born in 1949, teaches philosophy at the University
of Muhammad V in Rabat, Morocco. He himself has written an

academic study of Ibn Khaldun's philosophy of history, *al-Khalduniya fi daw' falsafat al-tarikh* (1998, 'Khaldunism in the Light of the Philosophy of History'). One can perhaps surmise that the process of preparing for and writing such a study provided at least part of the impetus for following it up with a novel devoted to the same basic subject. For *The Polymath's* focus assumes almost vertiginous proportions: a university teacher of the history of philosophy and historical novelist here presents his readers with a novel about a historian, Ibn Khaldun (d. 1406). Exiled from his native region of the Maghrib, Ibn Khaldun (or 'Abd al-Rahman as he is described for much of the novel, using one of his forenames) spends his latter days in Egypt. In a tremendous personal tragedy his family—his wife and children—have been drowned at sea in the process of joining him in the Egyptian capital. The aged and lonely historian lives in Cairo, now controlled by the Mamluk dynasty, and ekes out a modest living by teaching and serving as judge of the Maliki school of law—whenever, that is, he is not being dismissed because of the rigor that he brings to his judicial functions. To compensate for his loneliness and disillusion, he decides to revisit his earlier works on history and its science and to rework those sections of them that are in need of either revision or complete rewriting in the light of the tumultuous events involved in his own experiences with rulers and tyrants in North Africa. A historical novelist and philosopher of history is here writing a novel about a historian rewriting his own historical record and his theoretical conclusions based on an analysis of its contents. In brief then, neither the topic, the sequence, nor the technique of this novel link it directly to the more familiar strands in novel writing, whether on the local Arab-world stage or within the larger perspective of world fiction. Therein, for me as translator, lies its primary interest and importance.

At this juncture, I have to acknowledge that the process of translating this Arabic novel into English has presented a number of challenges. Translations from other languages have always served the valuable function of introducing to literary cultures fresh and strikingly new ideas and modes of expression. In the realm of art and culture of English expression, for example, the impact of the various translations of the Biblical text—and perhaps most notably the King James Version—on style, imagery, and proverbial utterance has been incalculable. Within such a context of cultural transfer, translators thus find themselves regularly operating along a spectrum of choice between the familiar and the strange. My own preference as a translator has always been to give the latter quality its fair share, not least because the process of familiarization to an English-speaking cultural milieu, if taken too far, runs the risk of being viewed as a somewhat undesirable form of cultural hegemony whereby one culture perceives itself as 'stronger' than another. In the case of Bensalem Himmich's *The Polymath*, these principles and choices come up against the realities of a work of fiction ("a novel of historical imagination," as the author himself terms it) that is firmly grounded in its indigenous tradition, a work in which the principal character is a renowned historian who provides ample illustration of his ideas from his own life experiences. The narrator of this novel—whether it be the third-person, external narrator in certain chapters or Ibn Khaldun in the first person in others—assumes a great deal on the part of the reader's knowledge regarding Islamic beliefs and institutions and the history and geography of Spain, North Africa, Egypt, Syria, and Central Asia. The resulting montage of geographical detail and historical information is not a little daunting, not only for the reader of its translation, but also for native speakers of Arabic. It is that fact that has brought the scholarly side of me—somewhat reluctantly—to bear on the translation process and its adjuncts.

As a consequence, this translation is provided with a glossary in which I have tried to provide historical, geographical, and cultural details for those who feel a need for them. Those readers of translations (of whom I myself tend to be one) who prefer not to be interrupted by such external information will not be distracted by note numbers in the text and can confront this narrative on its own terms. All dates in the text appear in their Islamic (Hijra) form. To make an approximate calculation of the equivalent Gregorian year, the reader can add 620 to the Hijra date. One other change has been made in an effort to make the text more accessible to readers of English: book titles that were of course in Arabic in the original are now rendered in English. More complete information on many of these book titles and important dates will be found in the glossary. Finally, Qur'anic quotations are peppered throughout the narrative. These appear in italics and their exact location within the Qur'an can be found in the concordance after the glossary.

The
Polymath

Preface

The life of the world-renowned historian, 'Abd al-Rahman ibn Khaldun (who hailed from the Maghrib), was often affected by the ups and downs of politics, events that, more often than not, were triggered or terminated by a deterioration in the relationship between himself and the ruling authorities. Unlike most scholars and politicians of the era, he was inclined to make light of the consequences of such upheavals; rather than give way to resentment and despair, he welcomed them. That is why the siren call of scholarship would often rouse him to seek opportunities that would allow him to retire to the privacy of his own quarters for indeterminate periods.

'Abd al-Rahman had no experience in the various arts of subterfuge and intrigue nor was he savvy when it came to political infighting. That was because he adamantly refused to involve himself in the political life of his times. Where facts and learning were concerned, he refused to accept anything that was either flimsy or unrigorous. Had he been willing to condone either category—God forbid—he could simply have been categorized as yet another 'jurist of darkness,' judge of iniquity, and agent of evil—one among many human foxes and wolves who thronged around the cupboards and kitchens of government in those days.

One of the last of these dark circles that brought our revered Master into contact with the rulers of the time saw him, garbed in his Moroccan attire, appointed by Sultan al-Zahir Barquq in 786 as Maliki judge in the Salihiya College on Bayn al-Qasrayn Street in Cairo. From such a vantage point, our Maliki judge was in a position to assess the other side of Cairo life. Upon his arrival there a mere two years earlier, he had described the city as "the center of civilization," "the garden of the world," and "the very portico of Islam"; he had compared the River Nile with the river of paradise. But by now he had discovered Cairo's other side: the utterly corrupt practices and customs, the overwhelming power in the hands of wealthy and influential people, and the suffering of the poor and indigent. He himself describes the situation in his *Information on Ibn Khaldun and His Travels East and West*, with a combination of certainty and frustration:

> I assumed the responsibilities of this lofty office and made
> every effort to implement God's law as entrusted to my care. In
> the interests of what is right, I ignored all potential sources of
> reproach, refusing to be deterred by either rank or influence. In
> so doing, I endeavored to treat both parties on the same footing,
> siding with the weak against the powerful and steering well
> clear of all efforts at influence-peddling from either side. I paid
> particular attention to proffered evidence and checked the probi-
> ty of people charged with offering testimony. There was a
> bewildering mixture of the pious and the brazen, a veritable
> mélange of the good and the wicked. Judges would habitually
> overlook the foibles of rulers and refrain from negative com-
> ments since they were keen to display their close connections
> with the ruling elite. The majority of them, including Qur'an
> teachers and imams who led the prayers in mosques, used to
> mingle with the Mamluk amirs. They would make a big show of
> their sense of justice so the rulers would think well of them and
> share a little bit of their prestige with the judges who had
> certified their probity. As a consequence, this plague of judicial
> corruption went from bad to worse; forgery and swindling
> became the order of the day.

In coping with such a situation 'Abd al-Rahman found himself between a rock and a hard place. On one side were God's own laws and the need to apply them just as required by the shari'a and his own Maliki school; on the other, the political powers of the time devoutly tied to their own particular beliefs and interests. These two sides were like polar opposites, only coinciding in a noisy clash involving contradiction and discord. Anyone caught in the middle had to make whichever choice most closely matched his own sense of self and creed, no matter what the tiresome consequences might turn out to be. Thus it was that 'Abd al-Rahman from the Maghrib chose the first of the two, absolute and sublime. Once decided on that course, he pursued it doggedly and used it to triumph over evil, relying, of course, on the One Who Never Sleeps. He always kept all necessary documents and keys close at hand. How could it have been otherwise when his excuse for coming to Egypt in the first place had been a yearning to perform the pilgrimage to Mecca— that being a pretext that would allow him to escape the clutches of the Hafsi sultan, Abu al-'Abbas, who habitually made the great historian accompany him on his travels as a kind of badge of honor?

But how difficult and trying it was to maintain a posture of equity in dispensing justice! How our Maliki judge found himself buffeted by fierce gales, all of them blown up by clerks, agents, landed gentry, and the elite in general, resorting as part of the process to all manner of scum and swindler. Among the worst things he was accused of—apart, that is, from the most scandalous derelictions he was rumored to have committed—was that he was completely ignorant of the concept of common law. He would never compromise, come to understandings, or 'cut someone a deal,' as the saying went. For such people as these, it seemed as if there were two kinds of justice: one was real or authentic, which was completely useless for their purposes; the other was figurative and based on convention, something commonly accepted and practiced throughout the land. It was this latter type that judges were supposed to rely on in dealings with people's needs and desires.

Even before our Maliki judge arrived in Cairo, he had described the city in the following terms: one who has never seen Cairo cannot appreciate the glory of Islam. Once he finally got there, he did indeed come to appreciate its culture, its wonderful architecture, and its ceremonies. But then he started to penetrate beneath the outer surface in the process of attending to matters of justice of which he was the upholder. It was at that point that he was able to gauge the distance that separated Islam's glories from the habits of Cairo's grandees. He came to regret the way justice had been turned into a series of clever tricks and secular deals while the rights of Muslims had been crushed beneath piles of sheer fraud and iniquity.

Our Maliki judge was patient and stubborn by nature. He employed both traits in setting himself up in opposition to the gales of rampant iniquity that now confronted him. He would proclaim the truth loud and clear, even if it meant being dismissed from his position and censured for his conduct. However, there came the time—in the middle of 787—when he was devastated by a totally unanticipated disaster: his small family was drowned at sea. Sultan Barquq had managed to intercede with Abu al-'Abbas, the ruler of Tunis, and to get him to let 'Abd al-Rahman's family leave Tunis and travel by boat to Egypt. As was usually the case when describing personal misfortunes, 'Abd al-Rahman only refers to this tragedy in the briefest and tersest of passages; almost as if the very words were like a knife twisting in the wound:

> I caused a great deal of controversy, and the atmosphere between
> myself and the authorities became worse and worse. This situation
> coincided with a personal tragedy involving my wife and child.
> They were coming to Egypt from the Maghrib by ship. There was
> a storm, and they were drowned. With them went existence,
> home, and offspring. The pain of this loss was enormous, and a
> less complicated life beckoned. I decided to step down from my
> position.

So he petitioned the rulers of the time to give him what in his heart of hearts he was terming a 'sabbatical' (invoking here his own local usage). Such a break was something he really yearned for so that he could take a deep breath and nurse his colossal sense of loss. It meant turning his back on the petty concerns of daily life and instead aspiring to a yet greater learning and the Most Learned of

All. After a great deal of insistence he managed to achieve his wishes and retired to his house close by the Salihiya. From his roof he could look out on the River Nile. The only person who came to see him was Sha'ban al-Sikkit, someone who looked after him and did everything for him, including getting his food supplies and his share of the revenues from the al-Qamhiya College endowment.

'Abd al-Rahman realized that the only real cure for his grieving heart involved undertaking the pilgrimage to Mecca. However, his nerves were so shattered that he did not have the necessary energy to plan for the journey; the hardships involved weighed heavily on his heart. Thus it was that, whenever the season arrived for the fulfillment of the solemn obligation of the pilgrimage, 'Abd al-Rahman used to perform all the rituals involved in his own imagination, sitting in his own house in Cairo, just as al-Hallaj and other holy men had done before him. He stayed in this state of retreat for the remainder of the first lunar year and into a second. He would pass the time performing the ceremonies of a 'mental pilgrimage' in every aspect. Between one pilgrimage month and the one the following year, he would spend his days performing continuous litanies and reading Sufi texts. All these activities had the cumulative effect of bringing him ever closer to enlightenment; he would only allow himself to be diverted from them for short periods. He might occasionally welcome an insistent guest, take a nighttime promenade along the river, or visit the al-Azhar or al-Husayn mosques. Sometimes he used to walk through alleyways to various markets, scurrying along, enveloped by the din of humanity and the steam and smells of spices, perfumes, and various types of food and drink.

One bright, moonlit spring night during this period when he used to go out for walks to his favorite spots, 'Abd al-Rahman decided to go down to the river like a new visitor to the city. He hired a boat and sat down in the back; his servant, Sha'ban, whom he had brought with him, was a good rower and steersman. Before too long, he had wrapped himself up in his burnous and stretched out. The serenity of the night and the lapping of the waves made him feel that the boat was moving of its own accord and his silent servant had somehow vanished beyond the oars. Relaxing in the back of the boat, 'Abd al-Rahman spent a fair amount of time half awake; those moments seemed for all the world like glimpses of eternity, when the entire creation was at hand. He felt as though he himself had bathed in the blood of martyrdom and taken root by the stone of truth along with the Prophet's Companions from Islam's earliest days and the messengers of purity and justice.

Just as dawn was breaking and first light appeared, 'Abd al-Rahman woke up to find his servant staring at him, eyes twinkling. Sha'ban, with his ruddy complexion, cheerful face, and modest demeanor, kept uttering prayers of thanksgiving and devotions, as he told his master, "You dozed off. While you were asleep, you kept repeating some holy phrases, some of which I've memorized. 'Lord,' you said, 'how can I hold the scales of justice in one hand and a sharp sword in the other? Now my bones are feeble and my anger is at its peak. Lord, shower this country with Your mercy, or else cauterize the wound.'"

With that 'Abd al-Rahman sat up. He asked his servant what else he had said, but Sha'ban excused himself, saying that he had not heard anything else clearly.

'Abd al-Rahman continued his questions. "How long have you been in my service, Sha'ban?" he asked.

"Almost two years, Master. When I first came to you, it was with an angry heart and eyes filled with despair. You took one look at me, gave me the keys of your house, and put me in charge of your domestic affairs."

"All that I remember, Sha'ban. But do you realize I know almost nothing about you? All I can recognize is your name and face. Why have you never told me anything about yourself?"

"Because people like me are the plebeians, simply not worth bothering about. You, Master, have more than enough to worry about, without my burdening you with the details of my life. In any case, it's one long catalogue of misery."

"In the heart of every true Muslim, Sha'ban, there should be room for the tribulations of other people. So tell me about the things that trouble you. It may well help relieve some of your distress."

The servant stopped rowing and sat up in his seat. "I have just one major concern, one that towers over everything else. I don't want to go on about it or stir up painful memories, Master, so I'll tell it to you in brief. I opened my eyes on this world of ours in the house of the Shafi'i jurist, Siraj al-Din al-Fayyumi, who was as well known among folk as my own Master is for his proper administration of God's holy laws. I grew up in his house in Fustat and was fully honored and respected till I reached adolescence. At this point my master informed me that he had in fact purchased me from a slave trader when I was just four years old; he knew nothing about my father or family. He manumitted me, then told me I could either remain in his service or go to work for someone else. I begged him to allow me to remain in his household, especially since he had recently become a widower and had no children of his own. When he felt that his own end was fast approaching, he wrote a clause into his will in which he gave me half an acre of land in Upper Egypt, fully a third of what he owned there. However, I was never to benefit from that inheritance and for reasons that are repeated day by day in your court here in Cairo."

"Various heirs appeared from every conceivable direction," 'Abd al-Rahman commented, "and either challenged the will or else simply grabbed it with the cooperation of corrupt judges. So you simply acknowledged reality and entered your period of suppressed, silent rage."

"That's exactly what happened, Master. But, compared with the dreadful things that happen every day to the property of orphans, it's trivial. But I won't pretend, Master, that when I realized that my rights had been denied me, I spent many hours in cafés or houses of God, muttering to myself things like, 'Barquq and Baraka have set a trap for the world,' 'They're eating chicken, while the rest of us cluster by the gates,' and other things that I don't dare repeat. And I won't deny either having vivid dreams in which I was sometimes transformed into heroes like 'Antara or Sayf ibn Dhi Yazan or in others into 'Umar ibn al-Khattab—the drawn sword of early Islam—and launched a savage attack on iniquity and wrongdoing. I would leave them all dead on the battlefield or else rouse every oppressed person to fight them to the end. When I woke up, I would find myself pounding my pillow and coverlet, then burst into bitter tears because of my sheer weakness."

Sha'ban suddenly fell silent and rowed toward the embarkation point on the shore. 'Abd al-Rahman was reciting some verses from the Qur'an, among which were: *God will never oppress even a tiny atom,* or *Faces will be submissive to the Living, the Eternal; and whoever brings injustice will have failed.* It was as though he were trying to erase from his memory images that were so disarmingly close to his own, while realizing that, when matters of injustice and extortion were involved, the anger that his servant was keeping suppressed was considerably greater than his own.

When the two men left the Nile and returned to the house, they both performed the morning prayer and, for the first time, ate breakfast together from a single plate. That finished, 'Abd al-Rahman poured over some accounts of Sufi divines and told Sha'ban to get some of the sleep he had missed. Close to the reader's eye were *The Path to Eloquence, The Epistle of Qushayri,* and *Sufi Categories.* Stretching himself out on his bed, he started flitting from one snippet and tale to another. As he continued with the process, he kept culling fascinating and delightful details and relishing the impact they had on his heart and mind. Little by little, he felt himself being drawn in by the relentless onward momentum. As he read, he felt as though he were turning into a hallowed vessel, putting to sea on a voyage toward the port of his dearest wishes, to have the time to devote himself entirely to higher learning. However, it was only a short while before the vessel came to a halt; the passenger had placed the book over his forehead and eyes and surrendered to memories of the retreat that he had spent with devotees at the monastery of Wali Abu Madyan, the renowned Spanish mystic. At the time, he had been escaping continuous harassment from Sultan 'Abd al-'Aziz and rulers in general. This was before the Marini sultan had released him from his oversight and charged him with the task of establishing friendly relations with the Riyah tribes. 'Abd al-Rahman recalled that during his retreat he had experienced some truly extraordinary times, moments of genuine independence and illumination. By then, 'Abd al-Rahman had come to regard the Maghrib as a source of scholarly learning. Its valleys, plateaus, and mountains all provided direct, visible evidence of the presence of God's devotees and holy men. The snow-white domes scattered across the landscape radiated a sense of the luster to be found in the more glorious world beyond; around what looked like enduring flights of the spirit, they hung small segments of the hard lives people led, an ongoing record of their dismal suffering and copious aspirations. The person entranced by the spell of such visions would see before him the faces of gifted and generous people, those who kept at a distance this world's political leaders and others who indulged in speculative or denominational subjects. Before his eyes 'Abd al-Rahman could see the image of Abu Madyan standing in front of his cave amid the ruins, accompanied only by a tame gazelle and other friendly animals. Even before this particular ascetic, 'Abd al-Rahman could recall another illiterate hermit, named Abu Ya'za, who could tame lions, walk on water, and perform wonders in curing illness and removing distress. Then 'Abd al-Rahman called to mind his contemporary, Ibn 'Ashir, the wali who lived in Sale and whose heart was filled with the concerns of that city's inhabitants. It was he who had pointed out the huge abyss separating Sultan Abu 'Inan from Sale's citizens. The wali had refused to meet the sultan, taking to his heels on a famous day when the latter had come chasing after him on foot.

It was nighttime or close to it when 'Abd al-Rahman woke up from this daydream. He lit a candle and continued reading the *Path to Eloquence*:

> From Nawf ibn al-Bakali: One night I saw the Commander of the Faithful—peace be upon him. He had left his bed and was observing the stars. "Nawf," he said, "are you still asleep or are you watching the stars?" "I'm awake, Commander of the Faithful," I replied, "and watching the stars." "Nawf," the Commander of the Faithful continued, "blessings on those ascetic folk who deny this lower world and desire the world to come! For such people the earth is a carpet, its soil is a bed, and its water is sweet perfume; for them the Qur'an is a beacon and prayer a coverlet. Just like the Messiah they cut themselves off from the world."

'Abd al-Rahman's reading was interrupted by a knock on the door, followed by the sound of his servant Sha'ban's voice.

Thinking the worst, he assumed that the sultan's aides had come to ask him about something. He sprang up and rushed to the door, only to find a man and woman requesting to speak to him, while his servant was trying as best he could to stop them. 'Abd al-Rahman welcomed the two visitors and invited them to take a cup of tisane with him. They both gratefully accepted, albeit with a show of reluctance. As they came in, he could not avoid noticing how tall the woman was and by comparison how short her companion.

"My apologies," he said, "Sha'ban was rude to you. He tries to keep some people away so as not to disturb my peace and quiet or else because he is worried that a high-ranking official might have his eye on this house. You two are obviously either married or relatives. So is there something I can do for you or some advice I can offer?"

The man was utterly astonished at 'Abd al-Rahman's modesty, but after a moment's pause he plucked up the courage to speak.

"Great scholar and upright judge, I came to visit you more than two years ago to offer my condolences on the death of your family—may God keep watch over them and bring them into His paradise. Today I return to introduce myself to you and to acquaint you with my problem with this woman who, as the document will testify, is my wife. My name is Hammu al-Hihi. I am forty years old and emigrated to this country two years ago along with this wife of mine. I had married her less than a year earlier in the city of Fez, the place where she was born and raised. We have spent the intervening years in reasonably good circumstances, although we have not been earning much nor have we been blessed with children. My wife stays at home and cooks, and I never object to anything she does in the house. I try to earn a living in honest professions, of which the most significant is writing and copying. In recent months, my wife and I have started to squabble about something where only the opinion of a judicial expert such as yourself will be of any help. I would like to ask you to listen to the issue from my wife's perspective so that you can solve the problem in accordance with the doctrine of Anas ibn Malik."

The woman now lowered her veil as far as her mouth. 'Abd al-Rahman stole a glance at her face and noticed what beautiful eyes and features she had.

"No," she said in a voice that managed to blend bashfulness with a certain coquetry, "you talk first. Our Master the judge can then decide."

"So here's the argument we are having," the husband went on. "My wife wants me to take her out for walks along the banks of the Nile. She would like us to walk side by side. But, my lord, I find it impossible to agree with her request. My short stature means that the whole idea is out of the question. Quite apart from the fact that religion forbids it, I can't imagine that any faith would choose to threaten a man who refuses to walk alongside a wife who is much taller than he is. Now it's your turn to speak."

"My lord judge," said the wife, "I'm getting depressed spending all my time inside the house. Going out would give me some fresh air. But, if I go out on my own, young and even middle-aged men stalk me and made lewd comments. I have to return home in order to keep my honor intact and avoid having people make insinuating remarks about the Maghribi woman who is Salih al-Tazi's daughter. My husband and I have been living happily together, and I very much want to go on living as we have been, but on condition that he take me for walks beside the Nile."

"I won't go outside the house with you or accompany you on walks. If the house gets too much for you, then go up to the roof and walk around up there. A curse on these Egyptian women who flaunt themselves and take strolls along the river!"

"Every woman is accompanied by her husband, Hammu. There's nothing wrong with that. Ask the judge. He'll tell you that when it comes to judging men, it's the sense of manhood that counts, not how tall they are."

"On two occasions now, Umm al-Banin, I've accepted your ideas on that. I've accompanied you across streets and along riverbanks. It's been sheer torture, with women giggling and men giving me derisive looks. So, by the glorious career of Mawlay Idris, spare me such indignities! Why can't you be the way you were in Fez, a gentle, compliant wife?"

"In Fez, Hammu, I had my own family and loved ones. I could ask any of my brothers to take me out for a walk in your place. But in Cairo you're all the family I have. There's no one else to care for me."

She began to cry, and tears mixed with kohl fell from her eyes. Hammu hugged her bashfully and promised he would hire a servant girl to accompany and watch over her. 'Abd al-Rahman looked at the married couple, but said nothing. He had no idea what to say, nor could he come up with an opinion based on the Maliki school's interpretation of the problem. He did manage to recall a legal opinion that had been pronounced in Kufa during a similarly knotty issue. In that particular case, a man had told his wife that if she wore such and such a dress, he would divorce her; he went on to say that if he didn't have sex with her in that very dress, she was divorced as well. The jurist's solution to the problem was to say that he should put the dress on and have sex with her in it. He would not be breaking his oath, nor would she be placed in an insoluble position. An appropriate solution to the current problem, 'Abd al-Rahman thought to himself, might well involve making an analogy with the current dilemma. Should he give an opinion suggesting that the couple go out for a walk disguised in each other's clothing? He immediately abandoned any such idea because it seemed utterly frivolous. Just then, he heard the wife, who had by now wiped her tears away, take up the topic again.

"Tell the judge," she said, barely suppressing a giggle, "what that other judge had to say—may his guts rot in hell! He suggested that, every time we go out together, we should swap clothes. He quoted us a verse from the Qur'an, but you said that everything he said about it was a falsehood. Recite the verse for us, Hammu—may God himself remind you of our creed."

"'*Women are clothing for you, and you are clothing for them,*' from Sura 2, 'The Cow.'"

"Woe is me! May my Lord paralyze him!"

"Shut up, woman! Don't advertize the opinion that man gave regarding our peculiar situation."

"Now we'll hear what the judge has to say. But I'll state outright, Hammu, that your suggestion about a servant girl won't work. Only men can protect women against other men. Tell me, people, have I said something bad?"

This was the point at which 'Abd al-Rahman decided that he should tell the couple how concerned he was about their situation.

"Enough!" he interrupted impetuously. "I've heard enough. Here's what I have to say, and God forgive me if I go wrong and speak in haste. I'm not speaking as a judge, since I do not hold such a position any more, nor am I giving either a legal opinion or even advice. It is merely a proposal for you both to think about. My servant, Sha'ban, is over seventy years old, but he's strong and observant and fully understands the need for discretion and security. He can accompany Umm al-Banin on her walks. In return, Sidi Hammu will agree to compensate me accordingly, if he is as accomplished an amanuensis and scribe as he says, by being available at the end of every month until the time arrives for me to go on the pilgrimage to Mecca. Let me repeat that this is only a suggestion."

Al-Hihi beamed with pleasure, his expression a mixture of delight and surprise. "Dear sir," he said, "I never expected such kindness. I accept your offer and will undertake the task before you leave on the pilgrimage, even without compensation. It will be enough of an honor to sit with such a scholar, listen to his views, and record whatever he wishes."

"So then, we are agreed. But I still wish to hear what your wife thinks of it."

The wife gave 'Abd al-Rahman a look of love and admiration. "But for my sense of modesty," she said, "I would launch into trills of joy or express my views by doing a Fez dance for you."

"Well then all is agreed. Sidi Hammu, our appointment is for the end of this month, in other words, in twenty days' time."

"Time enough, God willing, for me to take another look at the *Introduction to History*, the crown jewel of your writings. We've agreed on the terms of your offer, sir, but I must also tell you that Umm al-Banin and I have agreed that she can go to the public baths whenever she wishes, but only to the ones in our street. She can go for a walk with Sha'ban, but only once every two weeks."

'Abd al-Rahman leaned over to al-Hihi. "Make it once more," he whispered in his ear. "You can take a boat ride with your wife, and Sha'ban will row for you."

"Agreed. I've no objections to taking a boat ride with her."

"So then, madam, remember that a wife should make every effort to please her husband."

"Did you hear the wise words of this eminent judge, Umm al-Banin? I'll explain the details to you when we get home. Now let's leave before we take up more of the judge's time than we deserve."

Everyone stood up and walked toward the door where Sha'ban was stationed like an immovable statue. Al-Hihi kissed 'Abd al-Rahman's shoulder in gratitude. Umm al-Banin in turn kept kissing his hands and rubbing her cheeks against them, while he made futile efforts to stop her. Finally she looked up and put her veil up again before following her husband out, stumbling and sighing.

'Abd al-Rahman had to struggle hard to overcome his emotions at the warmth of this feminine presence. "Come back after the noon prayer, Sha'ban," he said. "For the time being, prepare your own food and heat me some water."

1

Seven Nights of Dictation

[Ibn Khaldun was] a man of virtue, combining all the finest qualities, highly esteemed and rock-solid in repute; revered in assemblies, high-minded and steadfast; exceptional in both the intellectual and narrative arts; many-faceted, a rigorous researcher, possessed of a prodigious memory, forthright in his concepts, skilled in penmanship, and wonderful company—in sum, a veritable paragon of the Maghrib region.

Lisan al-Din ibn al-Khatib,
Comprehensive Work on the History of Granada

During Ibn Khaldun's retreats many people came to see him. He would welcome them all warmly and put them at ease. He himself would frequent the halls of influential men and act humbly in their presence. For all that, he never changed his Maghribi attire or put on the preferred judicial robes of this country; that was because he loved being contrary about everything.

Shams al-Din al-Sakhawi,
Gleaming Light on the People of the Ninth Century

Two Notes
Note One: Hammu al-Hihi who became 'Abd al-Rahman's amanuensis can be compared with Ibn Juzayy who served the same function

for Ibn Battuta of Tangier. They were both small, ugly to look at, and squint-eyed from reading and writing so much. However, truth be told, the former can be distinguished from the latter by his quickfire intelligence, wit, and perseverance.

Al-Hihi was not one of those amanuenses who automatically records everything he hears, blesses his employer's longevity every time he opens his mouth, and composes sentences and paragraphs, or writes down what is dictated even though it may be a series of meaningless ramblings or be embellished with a whole load of unintelligible phrases and images. For example, if al-Hihi had happened to be in Ibn Juzayy's position or else was deputizing for him, he would certainly have been very reluctant to write down the story Ibn Battuta related about pearl divers in the deep cleft between Sayraf and al-Bahrayn. Al-Hihi would have showed a much more lackadaisical attitude as he listened to such an implausible account.

> Whenever a diver decides to make a dive, he puts some tortoise-shell on his face, bends it into a scissors shape and puts it over his nose. He ties a rope around his middle, then dives. People have different ideas about how long divers can stay under water: some can stay there for an hour or something under two hours. Once they get to the bottom, they find the pearls in tiny oyster shells stuck in the sand. They either gather them by hand, or else cut them with a knife that they keep handy for that purpose.

The account that Ibn Juzayy provides of Sultan Abu 'Inan standing alone against the Banu 'Abd al-Wad during a battle close to Tilimsan is so absurd that Hammu would have trashed his papers and broken his pens in two rather than record such nonsense word for word. He would have cursed all purveyors of flattery and twaddle and gone his way, never to return. Here's what was reported:

> Our lord—may God support him—had learned that everyone else had fled and he alone was left to fight. With that he advanced on the enemy accompanied only by his own noble spirit. This move caused shivers of fear in the enemy ranks, and they all turned and

fled. That such a force should turn tail when faced by a single person was a genuine wonder.

It needs to be pointed out that, in adopting such a posture toward reporting, al-Hihi's motivations were neither stubbornness nor insubordination. For him, the profession of scribe was something to enjoy, to cherish, rather than a means of employment or gain. That is why he only agreed to work for the person whom he termed 'the teacher' or 'the great master' after reading his way through the *Introduction to History*, which he greatly admired—at least, the parts of it that he could understand.

Note Two: 'Abd al-Rahman usually met his scribe in the office in his modest abode. He had furnished it in the Maghribi style, only adding shelves and stepladders on the walls to house his most precious books. The meetings would occur one hour after the evening prayer and would usually go on till an hour after midnight. It's worth mentioning that these monthly sessions were not all devoted to dictation and recording texts. The two men would often chat about a variety of topics. Al-Hihi would always bring a tray of Maghribi food cooked by his wife. When appropriate, he would talk about the harsh lives people led and by contrast the extreme luxury that the sultan and his coterie enjoyed. He also told 'Abd al-Rahman how happy his wife was now that she could take walks with Sha'ban and how she insisted that she would make all the food for his Master. For his part, 'Abd al-Rahman spent part of his time asking his scribe about conditions in Egypt or listening to him as, in response to his request, al-Hihi read him a chapter from a book.

The Night at the End of Safar
During the first dictation session, 'Abd al-Rahman and al-Hihi sat opposite each other with a jug of coffee and a plate of dates and sweetmeats between them. The amanuensis's papers and pens were illuminated by lamps of various sizes and candle power. After a somewhat gloomy conversation, the two men worked together copying out extracts from al-Mas'udi's *Golden Prairies* and others from the manuscript of Ibn Battuta's *Travels*.

Once they had finished, 'Abd al-Rahman asked al-Hihi a question. "Can your mind conceive, Hammu, the possibility of Alexander descending to the bottom of the sea in a glass box, just to get a picture of the satanic beasts that were preventing him from building his city? Or that he then had statues of them placed on the bottom to scare them away?"

Al-Hihi immediately replied in the negative with a shake of his head and a hand gesture. "I never believed Ibn Battuta's story about Abu 'Inan's single-handed victory over an entire army nor his tale about the same ruler to the effect that it was easier to kill a lion than a sheep. So how can I possibly accept a story that is even more implausible?"

The master was delighted with his amanuensis's response. "Forget about the two stories you mentioned involving Ibn Battuta," he continued. "According to the text they come from the witticisms of his amanuensis, Ibn Juzayy. You should be aware that Ibn Juzayy was appointed as recorder by Sultan Abu 'Inan in person; the rest you can supply for yourself."

"I didn't realize that. Even so, it doesn't entirely exonerate Ibn Battuta."

"Forget that for the time being. Write this down: In deciding between what is possible and impossible, as in all matters of disputation, there is no avoiding an empirical approach. Anyone who disagrees with us about the statue of the starling should be asked to build one like it and wait for the oil to emerge after the starlings have brought it some olives. Similarly, with Alexander's construction of the city, anyone who disagrees with our position should be asked to repeat what Alexander did: could he have breathed inside a glass box lowered into the sea and would he have resurfaced still alive and breathing? This is the only way to deal with all these implausible myths that go against the natural order of things and impede the advancement of knowledge."

Whenever Ibn Khaldun broached serious topics, one of his habits was to lower his head in thought, then ask his amanuensis to record his observations and comments. On this particular occasion he told al-Hihi to write these thoughts down. "Record them, Hammu," he said, "so that no one will think I'm one of those academic types who is always gloomy and cantankerous or else thinks in circles or squares—a person who can only comprehend the world in terms of equations and numerals. Record that I never disregard stories simply because they are amusing. I only declare them insignificant once I have come to see them as mere appendages to major historical sources, available for citation without any proper investigation or detailed critical analysis. However, beyond those kinds of contexts, I think it's wonderful to be able to read such tales when we feel aggravated or downhearted; and how often that happens in these dark days of ours! We can read them and regard them as sources of pleasure and enlightenment; they may well be the only sources of fresh air and moderation in our troubled lives."

Al-Hihi's skill at taking dictation was without parallel. Proverbs were struck on the basis of his skill at keeping record of what was said. On this occasion, however, such was his companion's excitement and intensity that he found himself forced to postpone the process of correction and organization. This is what he heard him go on to say: "Hammu, record what I say—that is what I have commissioned you to do. So record that on several occasions, whether asleep or awake, I have dreamed of being turned into a starling, a bird that would carry olive after olive to the mouths of starving people across the breadth of the region where I live.

"Then note down that I have sometimes dreamed of seeing the City of Brass in the desert by Sijilmasa. I made my way inside the city through one of its walls. I neither cried out from the top nor did I throw myself down, and all to avoid vanishing inside the city for evermore. Instead I called to Him of the Beautiful Names, and then bargained with the stalwart guards of the city to give me a tour. They accepted, on condition that afterward, when I was leaving the city, they could make me forget everything I had seen. That's the way it happened. I saw the city teeming, with innumerable wonders and miracles. Of beauty and justice I witnessed things the eye has never seen, the ear never heard, and the hearts of men never sensed. Do not ask me for details. Everything was erased from my memory. What remains is the purest of fragrances.

"Now Hammu, record that sometimes when I have a headache or feel depressed, I sit down facing the river. All sorts of fantasies clog my mind, leading me into a glass cubicle that takes me to the bottom of the sea. The idea is not to hunt satanic beasts, but rather to encounter the netherworld of sea creatures and plants and to observe them from close up. I must confess to you that my innate curiosity leads me to imagine a descent to the depths, not merely for observation, but also to investigate in detail both their marine leaders and statesmen and their general populace. That is even more the case since my own knowledge of such matters is inferior to that of Aristotle and al-Jahiz. But please make it clear that the reason for my interest in the application of the imagination to the sea-world is not to prove that the hippopotamus, for example, has two penises and that its flesh can cure sexual impotence; nor to observe other amphibians, horses, dolphins, dogs, pigs, or other denizens of lakes, valleys, rivers, and canals. Our knowledge of such phenomena is reasonable enough, and further information serves to match our facilities in such topics. To the contrary, my own postulates on the subject concern the depths of the sea: I am anxious to find out whether the absolute, never-ending silence engenders group identities and clashes of leadership intentions among groups of mammals, fish, and crustaceans. It may well be that faulty equipment and weak will may be overwhelmed by such an all-pervasive silence. But, if such be the case, then I shall put my suppositions, albeit with broken wings, into a drawer and continue to stare, as long as God wills, at the magical tableaux of organic and inorganic entities beneath the surface of the sea. The dynamic and static elements will be explained as part of God's plan for the universe or else as random products of a frivolous universe. Are you following me, Hammu?"

"Master," replied Hammu, sweat pouring from his brow, "I am with you, with pen and paper, beneath the sea's surface!"

"In that case," 'Abd al-Rahman continued, "conclude the record of this session by noting that I am not one to deny the essence of dreams and the miraculous. Far from it! In the right circumstances I fully approve of them. Nor do I reject strange and fanciful tales with both ancient and modern implications. As contributions to the world of imagination and fancy I welcome them warmly. They offer an opportunity to blend norms and yardsticks and to consider initiatives and problems on a different level, one that is rid of the Bedouin mentality so deeply rooted within us, the habits of those good old nomads with their addiction to subterfuge and mayhem. Our way of thinking can never be truly free unless we purge ourselves of such notions and the modalities that they impose. There is much more to say about this."

At this point Hammu felt the urge to ask 'Abd al-Rahman why he was so keen to explore things in such depth, but he stopped himself—or rather, he postponed the question. He was afraid that if he extended the session 'Abd al-Rahman had already declared over, his hand would be aching even more.

'Abd al-Rahman was now left on his own. He stretched out on the cushions and started reciting to himself his favorite *muwashshah* poem, by Lisan al-Din ibn al-Khatib. This is how part of it went:

> *On nights when, but for the dazzling suns,*
> *Darkness would conceal love's secrets,*
> *When the star of the wine-cup inclined, then set,*
> *Its path straight, its trace felicitious,*
>
> ......
>
> *When sleep brought us pleasure,*
> *Or as morning light assailed us like nightwatchmen,*
> *Then did meteors take us downward,*
> *Or perhaps the eyes of the narcissus left a mark on us.*

Footnote

Once al-Hihi had returned home and had something to eat and drink, he nestled in with his wife as he usually did. He described to her in great detail the traits of his new employer: his penetrating intelligence, his extraordinary ability to discriminate and to take a straightforward approach to things, and his resort to a wonderful sense of ambiguity that al-Hihi's wife kept trying to get her husband to explain, but in vain. He tried to tell her that it lay in his willingness to wade into the arcane details of his own era but then to pull away whenever he felt the need to regroup and adopt a more detached perspective. When he noticed that his wife was not paying attention anymore but was busy delousing his head and rubbing his left hand (the one he used to take dictation), he told her that he might well continue in 'Abd al-Rahman's employ even without pay. She scoffed. "So what are we supposed to live on?" she asked. "On his blessings and emanations?"

When Hammu went to bed, he started thinking. "Why is the Master so intent on examining everything so closely?" he asked in an audible voice. His wife gave him a hug and blew out the candle. "You need to ask one of his most devoted lovers that question," she replied.

The Night at the End of Rabi' al-Awwal

At the beginning of this session, the two men started talking. 'Abd al-Rahman asked his scribe to write some of it down, but suggested that the rest of it should be left out, as they were mere passing thoughts with no enduring value.

It was al-Hihi who initiated the conversation. Putting aside any residual hesitancy, he plunged ahead with the question that he and his wife had failed to answer for themselves: Why was 'Abd al-Rahman so bent on exploring things in such detail?

"My response to your question, Hammu—write it down if you like—is something I've thought about a good deal. The only answer I can come up with is that a desire to explore things in detail—in other words, the world of the intellect, of bases and principles—is what really attracts me the most. Without it, all that would remain are superficialities, mere froth, a veritable desert of banality and fancy.

"Just imagine for a moment that I was totally unaware of the profounder issues or chose to ignore them. Do you think I would be able to go beyond the realms of the superficial? I'd be spending my time on all sorts of leisure activities and binges. Were that the case—God forbid—I would be just like thousands of so-called 'legal experts' in this territory of mine, playing games with my particular school of law, stuffing my mind full of legal briefs and commentaries. Or perhaps I'd be writing accounts of the glorious exploits and deeds of the ruling elite; in which case, I'd be using gold ink to describe the lords of time and men, their official activities and leisure, and the way they fill their days and nights. Were that the case, I might well be a world traveler, collecting tales and marvelous exotic images on my way."

"Master," Hammu interrupted, "shall I refer the reader to Ibn Battuta's *Book of Travels* at this point?"

"No," Ibn Khaldun replied, "don't bother about cross references. Watch your step with Ibn Battuta, and you'll avoid making mistakes."

"Tell me what you mean so that I can understand what your objections are."

"The author of those *Travels* and I, Hammu, both have had good reason to bemoan the hardships of a grim era. Both of us have tried to depict it as best we can. Ibn Battuta did it by leaving his beloved family behind him and taking off on a long journey across the breadth of God's world. For my part, I undertook a journey of a different sort, into the profundities that I've talked to you about. In other words, I've gone on a tour of a very particular and specific region, something totally human without at the same time being merely ordinary, something that is utterly different without being barbaric. Thus, each of us carries our own walking stick, which offers us support as we pursue faint glimmers of hope or imagine a life of ease along with all the difficulty and escape after hardship. I suggest that you come to terms with these facts and take note."

"Master," Hammu responded, "God creates what He wishes. In any case, I find myself more inclined to your kind of journey and recitation, even though I have to admit that when I was out of work I did consult the tales of the traveler from Tangier. Some of them made me laugh, they were so peculiar. I'd tell them to my wife, and she would keep saying 'heaven help us!' over and over again or else hurry away in distress. The one about Sudanese tribes, for example, who roll in the dirt as a sign of respect for their ruler—amazing; or another tribe using salt as currency; yet another that eats dog and donkey corpses and even human flesh—all of it amazing!"

"For sure, Hammu, mankind is a creature of habit and even perhaps a product of his environment. I wonder how many of the things we do would seem extraordinary to black- and yellow-skinned peoples!"

"The details provided by Ibn Battuta about those regions are certainly unforgettable: things such as the view among certain tribes that eating white people is harmful because the flesh is not ripe, while eating black people is fine because their flesh is."

"In that case, Hammu, you have nothing to fear if you fall into their hands."

"Then there's the statement that the tastiest part of human flesh are breasts and hands. He goes on to record that during the month of Ramadan he saw with his own eyes servants, slave women, and girls stark naked with their pudenda showing. There are two reasons why that is amazing: firstly that they are naked; secondly that an inquisitive visitor is able to observe it. Wouldn't it have been more appropriate for this Maliki legal scholar to avert his gaze, particularly in the month associated with personal abstinence?"

"Amazing indeed!" 'Abd al-Rahman replied with a smile. "But why don't you remember any other stories about Ibn Battuta's journey that might serve a more beneficial function in your religious and secular life?"

"Are there any such stories?"

"There certainly are, provided you can forget about stories about nudity and eating human flesh. I'll tell you one, so that you can take note. It's the one Ibn Battuta tells at the court of Sultan Abu 'Inan, the one in which he describes the generosity that the king of India, Muhammad Shah ibn Taghlaq, shows to his people, something quite extraordinary. Whenever he went on a journey, he used to compute the number of inhabitants of Delhi and give them all half a year's pay from his private funds. Upon his return he would order catapults to be set up in fields so that sacks of dirhams and dinars could be tossed to the poor and needy."

"An amazing tale indeed! Not least because it shows quite how preposterous the whole concept of India was in the Maghribi context. But Master, how was this story received by the sultan's coterie?"

"With a good deal of nodding and winking. Actually, people were twiddling their fingers at their temples, and there was a fair amount of guffawing and raucous laughter as well."

"The entire court is mean and despicable. It thrives on corruption and bribery! How else could such people respond to a tale of such generosity than with sarcasm and disbelief? But what is your feeling about this story, Master? It's one that involves profound reflection, no doubt."

"I've checked on it, then weighed it in the balance. I'd say that it's probably more likely to be true than false."

"What about Sultan Abu 'Inan? Did he stay cross-legged on his throne as usual, or did he fidget and lose his temper?"

For a moment 'Abd al-Rahman looked somewhat uneasy and stared at the ground.

"If you don't want your response written down," al-Hihi hastened to add, "then there's no harm just telling me, and it will remain a secret."

"You're rubbing salt in the wound, Hammu!" 'Abd al-Rahman replied. "The Commander of the Faithful neither disapproved of the story nor punished its teller. No, he pondered its implications humbly, as though he realized the gap between what his eyes could habitually see and what his hands used to dispense. Or perhaps he envied the king of India and realized that he was unable to imitate such behavior. But let's stop talking about such distractions and return to dictation."

"I'm listening, and my hand is ready to traverse the page from right to left, till dawn if you so desire."

"Well then, busy your pen with this correction: It has always been my genuine desire to explore in depth the knowledge of realities and the materiality of objects and to observe the laws of change and transformation. In the process, however, I've stumbled so often and failed to get beneath the surface."

"You mean, Master, that someone of your caliber can stumble and be superficial?"

"Don't interrupt me, Hammu. Note down that, at all events, I'm a child of my own era, even though I can easily dodge and leap about in time. Yes, a child of my own era; in other words, of its benefits—how tragically few they are!—and of its faults as well, and sadly how many they are, particularly when we look at the extent of political disintegration and lack of willpower.

"On the subject of faults, to which I'll devote a passage, many's the time when, faced with sheer reality, I've allowed emotion to sway my intellect and blind my perception. Just to give an example, I went too far in my defense of the 'Abbasi caliphs against the charge of drunkenness, immorality, and fornication, when it would have been better for me to say nothing or else leave the judgment in such matters to God the All Knowing. That's particularly the case since I developed the theory that such lapses in behavior are a natural product of civilizations that rely on pomp and splendor—that being precisely the case with the 'Abbasi caliphs. Another example is when I waded into the topic of differences among Christian sects over the birth of Jesus (on him be peace). It was as though I were writing as a Muslim from the earliest days of conquest rather than someone who has witnessed the loss of al-Andalus at the hands of overwhelming Christian force. There's a passage in my *Introduction to History* (how I wish I could take it out!) where I accuse all these sects of unbelief. Here's what I say: 'On this matter there is nothing to discuss or debate. The resolution involves either conversion to Islam, the poll tax, or death.'

"Those words, Hammu, are totally inappropriate for their time and context. They most closely resemble the kind of logic used by a pig-headed defeatist.

"I have undoubtedly stumbled and been too superficial in other areas too. In so doing, I have gone against my own principle, which demands that one reflect on events and judge them in accordance with sound rules so that they can be properly vetted. In all this I've failed to heed the advice of 'Ali (may God honor his countenance): 'When you hear some information, reflect carefully on its implications rather than simply reacting literally; after all, there are many purveyors of information, but very few critics.'

"Another area in which I have gone astray, Hammu, is in my dogged insistence on the importance of group solidarity by raising it to paradigm status. It allowed me to perceive some things, but it blinded me to others. The kinds of things that it did not allow me to realize were of a kind that no historian can afford to despise or ignore. By way of example, there is the matter of unsuccessful revolts, and revolutionaries and religious reformers whom I depicted in the most derogatory and insulting terms. By adopting such a posture I was on the side of the more powerful victor and keeping history confined to records written according to the logic of conquest and power. Left outside the picture were the masses of conquered peoples and those unsupported by the solidarity of a group.

"My worst offense involved some of what I had to say about pious Sufis. For that reason one is fully justified in characterizing my epistle, *The Cure for the Petitioner,* as naïve and worthless. It stands condemned for responding to the call of politicians to launch an attack on the spread of popular mysticism and Sufi hostels and to regulate the rules governing all Sufi devotees so that they would fall within the confines of Sunni educational practice. Anyone who wants to know why I have not referred to this work previously should realize that it's because I've come to despise a study that resulted from an ill-conceived topic, one that is already steeped in a good deal of hyperbolic discourse. In fact, it was a problem that finally led me to legitimize violent means in dealing with authoritative Sufi texts. I issued a fatwa of which I am ashamed. Its text stated.

With regard to volumes that contain such fallacious beliefs and those copies that people possess—such as *Bezels of Wisdom* and *Meccan Conquests* by Ibn 'Arabi, *Temple of the Knower* by Ibn Sab'in, and *Removal of Sandals* by Ibn Qasiyy—such books and their like, whenever found, are to be consigned to the fire and washed with water so that any trace of writing disappears. This decree is issued in the public interest regarding religion by eradicating faulty beliefs. Those in authority are enjoined to burn such volumes so as to remove all public corruption as are all people who have the means to undertake such burning.

"Today my only desire is that anyone reading this decree should either burn it or wash it with water. Then all trace of it will vanish, and I'll be rid of its sinful implications.

"I have also made a number of mistakes and wrong judgments in the realm of politics and its machinations. In the midst of so many clashing interests and complexities I can hardly blame myself for being a child of my generation, manipulating the strings of its contradictions just like everyone else and adopting the hue appropriate to local conditions and alignments. I have moved from one circumstance to another, either reconciling or estranging myself, all based on the demands of the situation or the sheer instinct for self-preservation. In the Maghrib, the entire era has been crippled by the rule of conspiracy and murder and rent asunder to such an extent that to escape the clutches of one ruler inevitably leads you into a trap set by another. The only thing that someone in my position can do is to acknowledge the situation for what it is and sail with the breeze. That involves responding to the orders of the rulers of the era by courting tribal chiefs and winning the allegiance of tribes, taking full advantage of the pilgrimage season or time spent out in the desert. No, it's not these things that make me fault myself. Rather, it is the way I find myself fascinated by the thrills of power and craving those lofty positions that I have watched my inferiors in both knowledge and competence achieve through influence, graft, and highly developed conspiratorial skills. While I was at Abu 'Inan's court, I found it so easy to reach an agreement with his imprisoned guest, Abu 'Abdallah, the deposed ruler of Bougie, the one that involved my helping him escape to his own country and then accepting the post of *hajib* there once things had settled down. (Note: In our country in the Maghrib, the word *hajib* implies exclusive control of the state and the process of mediation between the sultan and his people—a task that he performs alone.)

"I accepted this secret deal because the ruler's Hafsi forebears and my family had long been close friends with each other. However, it took no time at all for the entire scheme to be uncovered, whereupon Abu 'Inan threw me in prison for about two years. It was during that time that I came to realize how much I hated the sultan in spite of his courage and resolution. Examining my own motives, I attributed them to two factors: first and most immediate was the fact that the Marini sultan had only ever appointed me to the most general and broad-based positions such as the one for which he recommended me to Ibn Tafrakin, the *hajib* who had exclusive control of Tunis right at the beginning of my involvement with administration; secondly there was the fact that the sultan had wrested the throne from his own father, Abu al-Hasan, stabbing him in the back and exiling him to the Masmuda mountains. That happened after Abu al-Hasan had failed in his bid to revive the Almohad movement and had tasted the bitter fruits of defeat in Qayrawan at the hands of an amalgamated force of Bedouin. As I wrote in my *Book on the Lessons of History*, following this disaster he returned to his native Maghrib. As long as I live, I will never forget the wonderful treatment I received from the religious scholars who were part of this great sultan's coterie. It was they who fostered my ambition and my devotion to learning.

"The ruler of Bougie remained in prison until the last days of Abu 'Inan. For my part, I received a promise of freedom in light of a poem of some one hundred lines in which I lodged a protest and begged for mercy. Fortunately I've forgotten most of it. However, I was only released when the amir was strangled by his own *wazir*, al-Fawdudi. When Sultan Abu Salim appointed me as private secretary I found myself returning to Granada and the Banu Ahmar. Once there, the amir, Muhammad V, and his minister, Ibn al-Khatib, afforded me the warmest of welcomes and the best possible hospitality. In 756, the amir commissioned me to travel with a ceremonial gift to the all-powerful king of Castile, Pedro Alfonso, in Seville, the city of my forebears. The purpose of the trip was to cement the agreement between the local amirs and the king so that he could act from a position of strength in his war against Aragon, they being enemies of the Muslims. While I was in Seville, I was welcomed and honored. There I encountered Ibrahim ibn Zarzar, a Jewish physician I had met before at the court of the Marini sultan, Abu 'Inan. I recall that he confided to me stories about the ingrained cruelty of this king, Pedro, and the utterly debauched life that he led. He was able to confirm for me all the stories I had heard previously about the increasing level of violence that the rulers of both Aragon and Castile were wreaking on Muslims and Jews under their authority and even on people who had made a public gesture of converting to Christianity. A nasty and capricious tyrant, that was the picture he provided of Pedro the Cruel! How could I possibly fail to respond to him with a certain reluctance and with all kinds of genuine and contrived excuses when he offered to return to me the property of my forebears in Seville on condition that he be able to include me in his retinue?

"What's the point of recording all this information? You can explain it, Hammu, by starting with a deterioration in my friendship in Granada with Lisan al-Din ibn al-Khatib and the fact that I was the only one assigned to such a lofty mission on behalf of the amir. Add to all that the fact that I went to Bougie in search of a more senior post, basing my hopes on the fact that I had previously supported its amir, Abu 'Abdallah, during his own trials. In fact, no sooner had I arrived than I got exactly what I wanted. From Jumada al-Awwal in 776 till Sha'ban of 777, I was exclusive occupant of the post of *hajib*. I used the opportunity to the fullest, lording it over everyone, so much so that my tone of voice hardened, my demeanor became totally pompous and inflated, and my every gesture was decisive and arrogant. How could it be otherwise when everyone kept haunting my door from early morning; heads and backs bowed and scraped before me, and the pomp of my station governing my every move?

"Fortunately for me, this self-delusion did not last more than a year and a half. It all went up in smoke when Abu 'Abdallah was murdered by his nephew, Abu al-'Abbas, the sultan of Constantine. As a result, I found myself compelled to align with the victor and acknowledge his authority at Bougie. However, as soon as the opportunity presented itself, I absconded and took refuge with various tribes, first the Dawawida, then at Biskra with the Banu Muzni.

"From this failure I drew two conclusions, the one practical, the other more theoretical. The first led me some two years later to refuse another offer of the *hajib* post at the hands of the sultan of Tlemcen, Abu Hammu. All I needed to do was to remind myself of the old proverb 'The believer is never stung twice from the same hole.' The second took the form of an idea that I promised myself to commit to paper just as soon as I found the free time and could manage to avoid any further involvement in the affairs of kings: 'Of all people, scholars should stay as far away from politics and its machinations as possible.' That's exactly what I wrote on the front of a sheet of paper. On the other side I wrote the following: 'The position of king is noble and much coveted, encompassing all worldly benefits, bodily pleasures, and psychological comforts. More often than not, it is the object of rivalry, and it is rare for anyone to ascend to it without first conquering someone else. As a result, enmity is fostered, and the end product is war.'"

"To sum it all up then, Hammu, where scholarship is concerned, I've certainly made mistakes. On the other hand, in the political sphere, I've spread myself far and wide but have gone wrong on the details. But then, how can anyone expect to achieve anything satisfactory in an era so rampant with corruption?"

Al-Hihi paused for a moment. He was trying not only to rest his hand but also to alter the topic to something that would not involve his companion in so much self-criticism.

"Master," he said, "infallibility belongs to God and His Prophet alone. Ordinary people are endowed with just a tiny portion of such qualities. Actually, your own particular portion is considerable. Any faults or slips of the tongue that you make are simply the product of your admirable quest for profundity."

"You're just trying to make me feel better. May your hand never be paralyzed!"

"Were that the case, I would not have allowed one baffling question to stay floating around inside my mind ever since I met you. It concerns your interest in your own family tree. Forgive me for asking you this, most especially because I know absolutely nothing about my own—maybe I don't even have one. I do not dispute that you hail from the Hadramawt and trace your origins back to an Arab chieftain, a companion of the Prophet named Wa'il ibn Hajar, who was blessed, along with his offspring, by the Lord of Mankind. After he had been killed by the [Umawi caliph] Mu'awiya, among his descendants was Khalid Khaldun, your grandfather, who came to Andalus from the East. All that I do not dispute, but just for argument's sake, I still ask myself what might have happened if you had not been born with such an illustrious heritage, with no family tree to bolster you. Do you think your overall prestige and intellectual ability might have been somewhat diminished?"

'Abd al-Rahman fell silent for a moment and took off his turban. Then he gestured with his hand for al-Hihi to start writing.

"Note down that the only reason for mentioning my family tree at the beginning of *Travels East and West* was to quote the words of reliable genealogists. By no means did I intend any kind of arrogant boasting. How could that be when I've already penned a work about the way people's basic traits go through transformations over time? Not only that, but I have also written things like 'Honor and lineage come through a sense of rootedness. Such qualities are a reality to people with group solidarity, whereas to others the concept is more symbolic,' and 'Honor and lineage among converts and fake gentry have nothing to do with their lineage, but are only a consequence of their conversion,' and so on. Furthermore, if I were somehow convinced that lineage conveyed some sort of distinction or prestige either on individuals or ruling dynasties, I would never have lamented the spread of artificial prestige, nor would I have recorded the way in which the Zayani amir Yaghmarasin shunned a group of sycophants who kept trying to convince him that he had *sharif* origins. His response to them (in the Tamazight language) went something like this: 'Whatever gains I have made in this world have come through the sword, not lineage. Whatever advantage either of the two will bring in the world to come is for God alone to decide.' What an eloquent and totally appropriate response that is! So, Hammu, have I managed to dislodge some of the questions that were preying on your mind?"

"Indeed you have. Your answer is comprehensive and detailed."

"Just make it clear that in the Maghrib I am usually known as being from the Hadramawt, whereas in the Mashriq people called me 'Maghribi.' In these contentious times I can serve as a living reminder of the ties that bind."

With that 'Abd al-Rahman stood up and headed for the door. Saying farewell he repeated his usual phrase: "More to follow."

The Night at the End of Rabi' al-Akhir

On this particular night, no sooner had the two men sat down and exchanged greetings than 'Abd al-Rahman immediately started talking without even asking his scribe to write anything down. Even so, al-Hihi, bent over his pages and started writing.

"If God grants me a long life, Hammu," he said, "the time will come when I'll tell you about certain phases of my career that were unsettled and exhausting, some of them in the Maghrib, others in the Mashriq. There may be aspects of life here in the Mashriq that I forget about, but I can never forget the occasions when I've clashed with government authorities who have managed to exploit all manner of deceit, conspiracy, and falsehood to their own ends. While dealing with the Maghrib, my memory may again prove faulty, and yet I'll never forget the indignities I had to suffer at the hands of the tribal leader who hid his real intentions under the guise of an amir, minister, or legal expert. In both regions, violence is a reality, the law of the land, although its modes of planning and implementation vary greatly. But this isn't what I want to talk to you about. My subject tonight is something that has been completely preoccupying my mind during my time alone.

"Write this concept down, Hammu, and in big strokes: the word is 'history,' and don't overlook its derivative concepts of change, conversion, transition, overthrow, and transformation. The idea besets me, Hammu. It fills my days and my working hours. Sometimes I even dream of changing sides and resorting to its opposites; or, at the very least, joining the ranks of those who have written travel manuals or geography books. How pleasant and relaxing it is to let ourselves by lulled by the delights of peace and quiet! The idea of starting things from scratch or of having everything nicely settled and in order is extremely attractive.

"But how am I supposed to reconcile man's nature and conduct with his posture toward this globe he inhabits?

"How do I school my own tastes to gravitate toward the marvels of creation?

"How can I devote myself entirely to making a record of routes and cities, all the while disregarding all the variables engendered by petty disputes and avoiding reference to revolutions and the general chaos they cause—leaving all such things aside with a frown of displeasure?"

"Master," al-Hihi observed at this point, "you once described to me in passing the way al-Bakri, the biographer, completely overlooks Yusuf ibn Tashufin, the principal figure of the Almoravid movement. If you agree, I'll include it in the footnotes as an example."

"You can make it a footnote if you like," replied 'Abd al-Rahman, "but be sure to note down as well that Abu 'Ubaydalla al-

Bakri, who can describe a Maghrib that he never even saw, may have some kind of excuse since 'in any particular era, peoples and generations do not see a great deal of change or transformation.' For my part, note down that there is no conceivable way that the period I have lived through, one so replete with major events and significant historical trends, could baffle me to the extent of blunting my mind and senses. My dear Hammu, any decision to remain silent in such circumstances would require of me a very particular ability to indulge in mystical abstraction or to suppress those very senses; either that or to resort to the realms of the moribund and static. No indeed! The powers with which I have been endowed are the exact opposite of these. Where history is concerned, I've tightened the belt and gone out to meet it head on. I shall put it to the test in innovative ways. Not for me silly games with reports about events and vice versa. No, I prefer to contemplate the ways in which the two elements relate to each other without having to compromise on the ability of my intellect and intuition to make judgments. Looking at life from the vantage point of a process of bidding it adieu or rupturing all linkages with it, that is the basis of my method, the approach that I adopt in my published works, as long, of course, as I remain alive and life continues to course through my veins. Please don't assume from what I've just said that I'm laughing at the concept of eternal life or somehow trying to disparage it. Far from it! What I intend is to place it in its own lofty position, one where there is neither change nor history."

With that, 'Abd al-Rahman stopped abruptly, almost as though he were aware that his words had brought him to the edge of a very deep abyss. Al-Hihi seized the opportunity to rub his fingers and scratch his head. All the while, he kept thinking about how difficult it would be for his wife, Umm al-Banin, to comprehend the concepts being used by 'Abd al-Rahman. He kept coming up with a whole series of questions of the kind that she might well ask when she came out of the kitchen after chatting with the womenfolk. She too might wish to participate in a theoretical discussion about history aimed at identifying its benefits, lessons, and concepts. It was thus with a good deal of hesitation and humility that he now addressed 'Abd al-Rahman.

"Ever since you appointed me, Master," he said, "you have generously opened your heart and mind to respond to my comments and requests for clarification. Indeed you've often encouraged me to pose such questions, even though they were not a little simplistic. Such is the sign of a true scholar, correct?"

"I'm sure, Hammu, that you have a whole collection of them now, don't you? Very well, ask away and get ready to record my answers."

"At the moment I'm thinking of Umm al-Banin. To me, her awareness of the past and a total blank are one and the same. Even so, her ignorance of such matters doesn't stop her arranging her own life as it comes or relishing the present and even enjoying some of its moments. She might well say that dumb beasts seem to inhabit some kind of absolute temporality, one in which they have no knowledge of the past or interest in the future. And yet, were I even to suggest that from such a perspective she can be placed into the same category as beasts, she would rightly hurl abuse at me, and that would be followed by a veritable earthquake in the kitchen and a boycott of a month or more. When it comes to extolling history or convincing my wife of its merits, I find myself at a loss. Beyond that, Master—font of all wisdom—I find that my own knowledge, feeble though it may be, is not sufficient to prevent me from preferring to linger with the present and to remain ignorant of the rulers of the past."

For a moment 'Abd al-Rahman remained silent, his head lowered. Then his face broke out into a sympathetic smile.

"Hammu," he said, "your observation confirms the fact that the mouths of the simple and innocent will often pronounce truths that academics waste much energy learning. The questions posed are often as legitimate as they are perplexing."

"And your own modesty, Master, is itself something remarkable. But how can I record it in my documents?"

"Umm al-Banin—may God prolong her life—belongs with the majority of people. There's no fault in the fact that she's ignorant about the past and satisfied with the present moment. But in your case, Hammu, your knowledge is greater than you imagine. You're a fully cognizant transcriber, someone who can deal with the strange and exotic and use your habitual skill to force me to address important issues.

"Now you're asking me to venture into the complex topic of history's lessons. So write down that my thinking on the topic has gone through at least two phases. The first was the longer and coincided with my youth and the early stages of middle age. I believed then that history held a number of advantages; it was, I thought, a repository of major concepts and source of exemplary lessons. The second phase, lasting right up to today, is one in which I have come to question the ability of rulers and authority figures to delve into history and to consider its ramifications as I have described them. Expressed differently, I have doubts about their readiness to do so. Whether the brand of authoritarianism they apply is effective or atrocious, to me they all seem to be ruling with no memory, almost vying with each other either to forget the errors and calamities of past eras or to grab on to them. It's as though, Hammu, they're refusing point blank to listen to history—in other words, to the past—as being an authoritative source of object lessons and cautionary tales, as a veritable anthology of standards and yardsticks that stands totally in opposition to warped and crooked desires and instincts. And it is precisely here that the primary issue resides: the vast majority of people ignore history because it specifically goes against current trends and necessities. It is particularly rulers of countries and regions who choose to ignore history so that the past cannot become something that causes them to remember and ponder what has happened in the past, indeed something that through deeds and conflicts will inevitably become their own past as well. What is left for a historian? What is he supposed to do?"

Al-Hihi assumed that these two questions were being posed to him, and hurriedly pursed his lips to indicate that he had no answer to them. His expression relaxed however when 'Abd al-Rahman started talking again.

"Write down, Hammu, that, when confronted with this dilemma, historians fall into a number of categories. The first consists of people who are not even aware that there is a problem to be addressed. They wander aimlessly about without going beyond the basic information they have or contemplating its significance so that they can apply sound principles to its analysis. Then there's a second group of historians who realize that there is indeed an issue at stake, but still choose to ignore it for fear of its impinging on their habits and way of life. A third group continues to recognize the issue. They look at it with a patient eye and work consistently at it, all in the hope of witnessing some improvement in the mental abilities of rulers and of raising the profile of history and knowledge of civilizations among the younger generation and legal authorities."

"Master, you are someone who, in spite of everything, continues to cling to a glimmer of hope. Don't you think that the majority of historians are themselves undeniably at fault for the way in which their discipline has seen such a decline from its lofty goals?"

"Most certainly they are at fault, and what a fault it is! A story tells that one of them, a slimy sycophant like so many others, was asked once why he was such a fixture in the palaces of rulers. His response was that his consciousness was steeped in the cups of their coterie, while his stomach only found its ease at their tables."

Al-Hihi managed to suppress his laughter by invoking the name of God against such hypocrisy and hypocrites. That was soon followed by the voice of his master continuing his dictation.

"The demise of the discipline of history," 'Abd al-Rahman went on in a bitter and weary tone, "can be attributed directly to its practitioners. Just like soldiers, scribes, and spies, or even court littérateurs, astrologers, and other functionaries, they're all engaged in profitable employment. For such historians, truth is not something that we can only broach after a good deal of effort and exhaustion; it's whatever the prevailing authorities and powers state that it should be. They're always with the majority, glorifying its version of reality as the truth and advocating its logic as exquisitely rational. Even so, are we to blame them alone, the assumption being that they can choose their own mode of behavior? Or should we be looking for some kind of excuse in the extreme cruelty of this era and the total power of the ruler? Tell me, Hammu!"

"That's a tough question, Master. I cannot possibly answer it. Let me toss it back to you. After all, you know more than I do about the profession and the people who practice it."

"Then write down—God grant you a long life—that my condemnation of historians is neither total nor absolute. I single out for

blame those who cling like glue to the bootstraps of authority, purveyors of information and rumor, willing servants of the ringing
dinar, and denizens of the havens of luminaries. They are the ones
I am referring to. Keeping their spittle dry, as the saying goes, they
willingly allow themselves to follow the paths of coercion. The
blindness and vertigo that grip them as a consequence make them
lose their ability to discriminate. They find themselves incapable of
comprehending reality or staying in touch with the daily life of
God's people in the country concerned. Hammu, many are the
forces that resort to rapine and oppression. Some historians relish
the idea and are motivated by sheer greed, but there are others who
prefer to flee from the very notion or else deal with its contradictions by following the lead of those who are truly concerned about
the probity of both their soul and discipline."

"You clearly belong in this second category, Master, people who
examine the issues in depth and avoid the contamination of worldly
pleasures."

"I can't function as both advocate and arbiter. I'm not the one to
say whether your judgment is correct or not; that lies with other
people who will have to examine carefully the way I've transferred
from one capital city to another in the Maghrib and al-Andalus. But
you can certainly record one constant in my life, something from
which you may be able to make useful deductions: my dogged insistence on slipping away—like extracting the proverbial strand from
the dough, and on walking on tiptoe. That way, whenever I've
noticed dark clouds of malice and anger gathering round me with
their implicit threats of arrest and death, escape has always been my
primary resort. When that did not work, I could always use travel
for the purposes of learning or pilgrimage as my excuse. No one can
find fault with people who, when faced with the fickle forces of
tyranny, seek safety and peace of mind."

With that, 'Abd al-Rahman brought the session to a close. He
still had the lingering sense that he had not adequately addressed the
issue of change and the lessons of history, nor had he really exam-
ined all its aspects. He left for the night in the hope that he would
come back to the topic some time in the future, aided and abetted by
the spontaneous and intelligent queries of his amanuensis.

The Night at the End of Jumada al-Ula

Once the master had sat down with his amanuensis, the servant brought in a pot of coffee and two bowls of yogurt. As usual, the room was quiet; this time the ambience had been enhanced with extra candlelight and a newly hung lamp. It was al-Hihi who started the serious conversation between the two men; he was always ready and eager to acquaint his master with the latest news about God's people and the sultan. He portrayed the latter as always standing idly by while all sorts of illicit means were being used for personal gain. With regard to the latter he would record how people made do as best they could, bolstered by jokes at the expense of politicians and notables and relishing to the full all kinds of malicious rumors. All of a sudden Ibn Khaldun perked up, as though he had just remembered something.

"That comment you just made, Hammu," he remarked, "struck a chord. Now I realize that something I've regarded for a long time as being purely secondary is of crucial importance. So here's the import. If the territory of the Kinana tribe consisted purely of ruler and people and possessed no other subgroups, and yet they were no weaker or more dispirited than any other Maghribi tribe, then one cannot ascribe every calamity to the concept of group solidarity, nor can one generalize the application of the term and use it to either manipulate or constrain the formulation of events. Remind me about this piece of documentation later so that I can make use of it at the appropriate point.

"What's most on my mind this evening is a hankering I feel to broaden the scope of my perspective to an extent greater than I've done before. These new lights are a sound investment, presaging a favorable outcome. But more's the pity! At my age, the body starts to turn dull and heavy; there's a tendency for it to blunt the acuity of ideas and make them insipid and uninspired. That's why you'll notice that I'm making do with yogurt for my meals, in the hope that the mixture of milk, honey, and bran will protect me from noxious diseases and help me avoid other foods that might provoke my ulcer and upset my stomach. Have some of my yogurt now, then you can thank the person who made it, namely Sha'ban, and discover how successful he's been in producing a wonderful medicine. If only I

41

could discover a similar compound in the realms of politics and society that could provide a cure for some of the thornier problems and fissures in life's path!"

'Abd al-Rahman finished eating his yogurt, and al-Hihi wished him a long and healthy life. The master wiped his mouth, then started a dictation which was interspersed with sips of coffee made Maghribi-style.

"In terms of my own lifespan," he said, "I'm now broaching old age. Even so, I still feel a burning fire inside me that stops me from adopting an old man's retrospective view on the world. To be sure, life needs the freshness of youth, otherwise it's nothing but chaff and scum in equal measure. That's why, in spite of my advancing years, I can't see myself pitching my tent in those domains where all understanding and contemplation of the fate of mankind would be avoided.

"Last time, Hammu, I told you about the flaws involved in the concept of group solidarity. I revealed to you my current inclination to search for the best possible alternative. As I wait for the concept to ripen and for idea and reality to coalesce, that quest is still in process. Even so, I continue to interrogate my own field by making any necessary references to mistakes that I've made in criticizing the authors of books on principles of governance and advice to rulers, not to mention philosophers like Plato and al-Farabi in discussing utopias and political ideals. How easy it would be for me to elevate the level of discourse and seal it with all the necessary trappings of history! How simple to stuff the contents with relics and to encrust it with nuanced fragments culled from Persian sages like Buzurzumhur and al-Mubdhan, others from India, wisdom handed down from Daniel and Hermes, or ideas on organization and rulership drawn from the various schools of Hellenistic thought. But that's not what is needed, most especially since those scholars who have decided to ride the hobbyhorse of this specialization and have taken upon themselves to harangue us about it have gained absolutely nothing from the science of civilization, nor have they managed to use their homilies to change world affairs in any meaningful fashion. Instead they have mouthed off without showing the slightest subtlety; their fantasies have been utterly useless.

"The method to which I aspire involves establishing rules for what needs to be. I do not intend to preach from pulpits of ignorance about what actually is, but rather to make my way through a portal that I've traversed before, a procedure that has led me into whole fresh areas of knowledge about the nature of civilization and reality—fields where I've spent an entire lifetime and achieved as much as can be by invoking the intellect and the five senses. In so doing I've made use, to the extent possible, of my own judgment and insight. As a result, I feel that I can now make use of this experience of mine to concentrate on ways of throwing off the yoke of these perilous times and emerging from the dizzying whirl of ever-recurring tyranny.

"Today I can glean materials from all around me. I see evidence and linkages of all kinds. From such things all I can conclude is that ethics and manners are in a precipitous decline. As a group, city-based peoples are still just as I described them previously, namely that 'among their prevalent traits are debauchery, malingering, nonsensical ideas, and a determination to earn a living by hook or by crook. As a result, people think about nothing else, and concentrate all their energies on fraud and trickery.' But we still need to ask whether people are to be blamed when they find themselves utterly exhausted and totally overwhelmed by despair and hopelessness. Those feelings lead them to adapt to their circumstances by using whatever undesirable means may prove necessary; in that sense they are just like animals, motivated purely by the instinct for self-preservation. But from all this I choose to deduce something that is yet more subtle and bitter in that it combines all the factors involved. The conclusion I come to is that within the very structure of today's rulership there is a relentlessly creeping indolence and abandonment of responsibility. I am referring to those regimes whose sole power comes from the unjustified subjugation of their people, giving human beings free rein in exercising their desires, harassing visiting merchants with fines and outrageous taxes, and other kinds of oppressive behavior, all of it bound to eradicate people's feelings of hope and contentment. It can all be seen as the harbinger of civilization's destruction as a curse is once more visited on the corridors of power.

43

"I've already drawn attention to all this, and in considerable detail, in the *Introduction to History*. All I want to add here are a few bitter appendices concerning the way time is proceeding to our own disadvantage. It's almost as though it is working actively against us and planning yet more fiascoes and false steps.

"Hammu, just take a look with me at the Hafsi, 'Abd al-Wadi, and Marini regimes in the Maghrib. Join me in an assessment of the way they compete with one another to see which one can be the most fractious and disorganized. Keep doing it until, like me, you reach a stage at which you start to yearn for the days of the great Almohad empire before al-Nasir's defeat of al-'Iqab and its eventual demise in the time of al-Ma'mun. How puny and pathetic the sultans of this era are by comparison, despite their displays of tyranny! They have no competence in public affairs and politics. The only thing they are good at is hatching plots and indulging in intrigue.

"As I contemplate these sultans of today, I might adjust my previous statements by suggesting that tyranny comes in two kinds: the first involves the ruler monopolizing power, then successfully blending the physical and ideational aspects of authority into one; the second sees the ruler losing all sense of self-respect due to personal weakness or else the domineering effect of his own ministers, all of which leads him to treat his people with unadulterated violence. The first type brings beneficial consequences and is normally encountered during formative phases in a dynasty's course, whereas the second is both futile and deleterious and is a feature of all subsequent phases. In my opinion, Sultan Abu Salim, in whose chancery I used to work and composed some sycophantic verse, can serve as a primary example of what I've today termed 'futile tyranny.' Once he had recovered his throne thanks to the support of Pedro, king of Castille, he started practicing tyranny in its starkest form: his brothers, cousins, and all male relatives in the larger ruling family were all tossed overboard at sea. He then came under the direct influence of the jurist al-Khatib ibn Marzuq, and began to follow his advice, even though he had hired me as one of his senior secretaries. When he started losing his nerve, he asked Ibn Rudwan to write him a manual, namely *The Flashing Meteor Concerning*

Effective Government. During the reign of Abu Salim, people 'were so overwhelmed by fines and other exactions that no sowing or planting was possible,' as my dear colleague, Ibn al-Khatib, put it. Circumstances so willed that it should be this sultan who received a number of gifts from Mansazata, the king of Mali, including a giraffe that astonished everyone and duly impressed the poets of the era. This incident showed me just how prosperous the region of black Africa was in comparison with the collapsing power in the Maghrib. Eventually another minister named Fawdudi succeeded in getting Abu Salim's head into a basket, thanks to help from the Christian army commander, Garcia ibn Antun. As a result, that minister became the effective ruler of the country in the name of the insane prince, Tashfin, who was followed by a pseudo-prince, Abu Zayyan. The dynasty was only rid of the latter when he was murdered at the hands of Sultan 'Abd al-'Aziz who managed to restore authority to the Marini house, if only for a short period.

"So why have I let myself to be distracted by these details? What, for heaven's sake, have we established? What I've wanted to demonstrate is that, when a state follows the various stages on the downward path toward outright despotism, it reveals its flaws for all to see; in fact, with its untutored infant rulers it becomes a genuine laughingstock. Here's what Lisan al-Din Ibn al-Khatib has to say about being a guest of the infant, Sultan al-Sa'id ibn Abi 'Inan: 'I hear a voice but see no one. All I know about him is that he toddles his way from the minister's presence to the congregational prayer mosque. During parades he sits there like a stuffed chicken, all daubed, tail tucked under, clasping a handkerchief or knife for all he's worth; the turban encircles a moonlike visage. And there he stays, sitting atop his throne and glowing like the wicks in his own lamps, a model of brittle nobility.'

"By my life, Hammu, that quotation reveals for us just a minute segment of the dire consequences of rapacious rulership."

With that Ibn Khaldun stopped deliberately with the intention of giving his amanuensis a bit of a breather. He yelled out to Sha'ban to bring in some fresh coffee, then adjusted his sitting position. Sometimes he stared at the floor, at others the ceiling. For his part, al-Hihi was doing what he normally did during breaks in dictation, namely tapping his fingers by way of apology and checking on his pens and ink.

"Fine, Hammu," said 'Abd al-Rahman, "let's go back to where we were . . ."

"You mean, finding a way out of the genie's magic time-lamp which is constantly working against us?"

"That's a fine way of putting it. I've no doubt that some rulers have tried to escape from the bottleneck or to break the cycle of history with its inverted impact. One may have developed a sensible system of taxation and put in place some principles of justice and civil society. Another may have tackled the profit sectors and utilized their revenues to boost the exchequer. Still another may have tried to suppress feelings of tribal solidarity by creating a professionalized and multiracial army as a substitute. All these constitute different options, and, in spite of any number of obstacles and roadblocks on the way, other rulers will come along and try their hand at giving greater weight to the factors involved. Among such rulers, highly principled reformers will adopt the loftiest principles of the Islamic caliphate to effect such transformations. But what I envisage is a powerful ruler in the Maghrib, someone who can appreciate that the way ahead is blocked to the north and east and who can then order the army to march southward into the lands of the Africans, all out of a desire for the good things they can provide. I can also imagine another ruler who thinks that the best solution for controlling his entire country and all its people is to create a slave army that will only respond to his commands, and no one else's.

"All that said, the moral is always to be found in results and consequences. When it comes to the question of reform, what history tells us is that at the start of a particular reign it may last for a short period but it remains fragmentary. Before long, however, the winds of tyranny and personal whim sweep it all aside.

"What history tells us about eras of expansion and campaigns beyond borders is that every such extension of power and influence is followed in the vast majority of cases by an era of waning power, the disruptive effects of which may have a negative impact on the functions of the power center itself.

46

"What we learn from history about the creation of a tightly organized slave-army with all its concomitant force is that such soldiers rapidly become part of the gentry themselves, members of the ruling elite, and occupiers of the regal throne. I am firm in my conviction that the fault in this process does not lie in the fact that manumitted slaves become rulers of mankind, but rather that their reliance on esprit de corps is no less erratic and capricious than that of any other group. Just consider the situation with the Burji Mamluks of our generation and with their predecessors, the Bahri Mamluks; the problem is there for all to see. Their paranoia regarding the intentions of other Muslim communities leads them to give prominent positions in the chancery and treasury to Jews and Christians. Every dispute that breaks out within their coterie is settled with the sword, and as a result, many of their rulers and senior officials are murdered. Then consider how often the lives of judges and teachers are disrupted when they keep being appointed and then dismissed, something that will soon happen to me, no doubt. That's because the Mamluks prefer to deal with legal scholars who thrive on conspiracy theories and an atmosphere of gloom and doom, the kind of people who were directly responsible for the trial of Taqi al-Din ibn Taymiya.

"So then, the vague glimmerings of explanations for it all do exist, but the question still remains with us as to how to escape from the bottleneck of history as it continues to operate against us. I can recall, for example, that Ibn 'Arafa, someone utterly loathed and detested, once sent a messenger to convey some advice to me face to face: 'You're looking for a solution all over the place, when it's closer than your own nose.' What this Tunisian sage implied by the word 'solution' was a look into the past, the era of the Rightly-Guided Caliphs. At this point, I have to pause so that I can point out some of the errors committed by extremists and lay to rest other remarks made by people who have only succeeded in confusing the issue. I broached this topic in the *Introduction to History*, but no one read it carefully enough or took sufficient notice.

"The course of history demands of us that we make a clear distinction between the pure form of Islam, the foundational model on the one hand, and the current and normal sectarian Islam on the other. The former was a full-scale historical whirlwind, one that shattered the laws of nature and the rules of empirical history. Its power was derived essentially from the doctrine of the truth and the inimitable qualities of the Qur'an. However, that kind of Islam did not last for more than four decades. It was followed by the Umawi dynasty, and with that, the restraining factor of religion disappeared to be replaced by another kind of Islam, one divided and fragmented, with its own firmly established practices, dominated by conflicts between sects, parties, and separate community interests. Didn't the Prophet himself (upon him be peace) state: 'After me the caliphate will last for thirty years. Then it will turn into a rapacious monarchy'?

"While noting this dire split within the fabric of Islam, I will nevertheless refrain from laying the blame on the people responsible. Instead of dreaming about a return of the impossible—a pure, early form of Islam—I will endeavor to come to grips with a reality that can hardly be denied, and to comprehend a process of change dictated by the logic of historical methodology. Thus, when I am confronted by the knotty and sensitive issue of the caliphate, I prefer to adopt a more legalistic tack, examining each choice from the viewpoint of the degree of truth it contains. Behind it all, I see emotion and desire as being two vital forces operating in the clash of politics and history.

"In brief, and as I suggested earlier, 'The incipient religion of Islam dissipated once its miracles had disappeared and the Companions of the Prophet who had witnessed them had all died. That special quality that the early religion possessed changed bit by bit. As the miracles vanished, the system of governance reverted to its former status.'

"In making such a statement I am relying purely on the realities of the situation. To remove any ambiguity on the matter, I will clarify things by noting that on questions of belief, the religion of the Islamic community is still the orthodox version of Islam. On questions of personal status, inheritance, and endowments, the law is also based on the same religious foundation. However, in these spheres and others it is individual interpretation that controls the decision-making process. That is in accord with the principles of necessity and the public interest of the times, operating along the lines laid out for us by the pioneer figure in Islamic jurisprudence, Abu Hanifa al-Nu'man, my own personal imam. This is what he has to say about our predecessors: 'They are men and so are we. They made their own decisions, and so we should act in exactly the same way.' A fine statement indeed, and the essence of wisdom and good sense!

"Now, when it comes to those obscurantist legal authorities who strive to outsmart us or other obsessive manipulators who insist on arguing with us, proclaiming for all the world to hear that the solution to the problem is right in front of our noses, we have every right to stand in opposition to their opinions, and for three reasons. Firstly, every single Islamic government—Arabs, Persians, Turks, Berbers, Mamluks, and Mongols—has claimed to be protecting the basic essence of Islam and to being directed by its guiding light. Even so, such claims have utterly failed to prevent a mounting sequence of crises and errors. Secondly, true Islam has only come to grief when it has found itself tossed back and forth within the corridors of power or as part of professionalized politics. It is there that we find the clash of wills, desires, and lusts, all working in opposition to each other. It was that very clash that led to the murder of all the Rightly-Guided Caliphs of the earliest days of Islam, with the exception of the very first one, Abu Bakr, who died in his own bed. Thirdly, the fire of pure Islam can only be kept burning among the people themselves. They are the ones who need to make full use of its dicta in order to remonstrate with those authority figures who make decisions and maintain control over the chancery, the army, and the treasury. They will have to rely on its strength when it comes to arousing people's consciences and reinforcing humanity's awareness of the Islamic religion's values and truths.

"Politics, Hammu, is a matter of trust and delegation; there is no way of avoiding the processes of accountability and explanation. No one has the right to utilize political methods solely for the purpose of converting the recorder into some kind of authority figure or else in the name of some notion of divine succession. If that were the case, then history would find itself confronted only with accounts of authority and political power, something that is completely contrary to the laws of tradition and reason. That's how I look at our current era. *Our Lord, You know that which we hide and that which we proclaim.*

"I wonder, have I managed to discuss this sensitive topic with sufficient clarity and detail? It's certainly one where people regularly toss brickbats at each other and accuse each other of heresy. On this particular topic there's more to be said. . . .

The Night at the End of Jumada al-Akhira

Right at the beginning of this session, al-Hihi suddenly came to realize that 'Abd al-Rahman was a particularly cerebral being, someone who was continually thinking and debating with himself. His brain cells were permanently busy, a process of engagement that only sleep could interrupt. For that very reason, al-Hihi decided to try to steer the conversation toward lighter topics—life's trivialities and minor issues, things that would not require so much thought and concentration. Actually, he had a question on the tip of his tongue about the quest for change in history, something that he was proposing to attribute falsely to his wife, Umm al-Banin. But the whole plan had to remain poised in the air, because he found himself greeted by the following words from his interlocutor:

"Well, Hammu, I suspect that what I had to say earlier about the lessons of history and the processes of change did not satisfy your thirst. Isn't that so? With your dear, innocent wife's comments as corroboration, you may well comment that, since history seems to be a corpus in which the lessons of the past neither illuminate matters nor play a useful or significant role, then what is the function of variables and transformations in different periods and phases? By God, that is a very tricky question, one that has preoccupied my mind for a very long time. It's one that I cannot put aside, and neither the passage of time nor the course of events can offer me any help in resolving it."

Al-Hihi thought that this might be the appropriate moment to distract the master with some pleasantries, by relating to him some of the latest jokes he had heard from Umm al-Banin. He therefore suggested that 'Abd al-Rahman relax for a bit and listen to some diverting samples of humor. But 'Abd al-Rahman gave his amanuensis a piercing stare.

"Jokes have a short lifespan, Hammu," he said gloomily, "but the problems of history stay with us. The number of people who think seriously about fate and the future is minute, so it's not right for me to leave them high and dry, particularly when I watch today's rulers, those devotees of rampant egotism, exerting no restraining influence on anything and scoffing at the mayhem they're causing. I have no choice but to investigate matters persistently and in depth. I must train my mind to be patient and obdurate, the supposition being that there will indeed be light at the end of the tunnel. Day and night I will make myself repeat, 'Our Lord, You did not create all this for nothing, nor did You create us in vain.' But before we start supposing and hoping, Hammu, make a note of the way things really are, along with all their unpromising characteristics. Write it down, remembering all the while that knowledge of such issues is a solemn obligation of any genuine reformer. I've confronted the mass of detail on this subject in my books and pursued it as far as I can. But now that I've reached this stage of my life, all I can do is to stand by the outlets and take stock of things. My dear Hammu, how beset and fragmented everything seems! How many signs there are that point to a lack of aspirations and precipitous decline.

"Even though there may be a difference in degree, the basic features of plunder and decay are always the same: a ruler who behaves tyrannically or contemptuously. Soldiers and scribes alike surround him, and his universe is one enveloped by the interests of real estate, commodities, and livestock. This is the way matters proceed from one dynasty to the next and for as long as the instincts of group solidarity remain in place, like some phoenix rising up from its own ashes, bringing in its wake the same tribulations and sequences. Meanwhile the suffering populace . . . oh, dear! They have to suffer through gruesome times and the abuses of uncontrolled armies. In trying to exercise their own humanity the only discretion they have requires that they follow the dictates of reckless officials and the untrammeled tyranny of their overlords. In spite of the odd, fleeting glimmer of change, the internal structure is in ruins. How, then, how can I possibly be anything else but scared to death when I think of attacks from Christians in the west and Mongol hordes in the east?

"My expectations—and a pox be on them!—give me little cause for optimism. How could it be otherwise? As I keep an eye on events and gather information, everything presages dire consequences—and for the long term at that! I watch as our ports become subject to foreign monopolies and our vital regions fall prey to European penetration. Gangsterism is rife in our midst, and a general impotence is the order of the day. When I see all this, my heart breaks and I turn to God Almighty for deliverance.

"So, Hammu, that's the general situation as I see it. Even so, I've only provided a summary. If I were to go into detail at this stage, I might find myself indulging in predictions even more far-reaching than the one I recorded previously, when I said 'The past is more like the future than water is to water.' But whenever I make predictions—God will reward you well for making this much clear—He makes me (may He be exalted) feel vigorous rather than weak. I feel myself being propelled forward rather than backward. So, in spite of all the handicaps involved, I remain deeply concerned about the question. So, Hammu, remind me once again about the precise nature of the issue so that I can address it properly."

"The question as you have formulated it tonight, Master, is the following: If indeed history is a record in which the lessons of the past are not accorded their proper place and fail to fulfill their useful function, then what precisely is the significance of variables and transformations in different historical phases and eras?"

"In the *Introduction to History* I composed a number of specific sections in which I endeavored to subdivide the topic in accordance with contrasting principles. I made every effort to organize and enumerate them as clearly as possible. By way of example, I chose to problematize the blending of positive and negative in urban culture as being at one and the same time the goal of civilization and the principal indication of its fragmentation and corruption. This problematic was in fact based on my knowledge of the Maghribi region. Since it is much closer to my own experience, I was able to avoid indulging in sterile generalizations or rash judgments about the more eastern regions where I now reside and about which I am still in quest of the necessary knowledge. But, now that I've achieved a great age, I find that I cannot abandon this question and shut off discussion, relying merely on what I wrote earlier about the total inapplicability of the exemplary past in the light of the tensions caused by unfair taxation and the tyrannical control of sultans and ministers, or more generally the corruption of mankind's sense of humanity. It's as though the factors I've identified are in fact simply part of the surface layer of things, such as the Bedouin or the blight caused by the Great Plague; as though such things only serve to conceal other factors or even a single factor that is more comprehensive and encompassing. Whenever my intuition confirms such circular continuities and allows me to subject them to more intense scrutiny, I find myself spending untold amounts of time confronting a drastic irony: societies neither benefit in any significant fashion nor progress as a result of the passage of time or the sequences of generations. From one perspective, civilization stands as a concept for the life of history; but an equally cogent version sees it as a sphere within which that very idea wanes and falls apart.

"For more than two years now—to be exact, ever since the sea swallowed up my wife and children—I have actually lost all desire to take a fresh look at the complex and knotty questions we're investigating today. I've actually started depriving myself of the sole pleasure that remains for old folks once the delights of food, drink, and sex are denied them, namely listening to fabulous tales, both those that are of heavenly origin—tales of locust swarms and eclipses, and those that are earthly—plagues, earthquakes, fires, and drought. When I receive information now, it all fits into a never ending process of recycling and repetition, an orphan to novelty and self-interest, victim of that similarity I referred to above between water and water, a kind of eternal law carved in stone until such time as God inherits the earth and the people on it! That's what I used to chant to the words of the great mystic, al-Shibli: 'A thousand years past, a thousand years to come, that is the essence of time. And the phantoms shall never deceive you!'"

'Abd al-Rahman kept saying the words 'and the phantoms shall never deceive you' over and over again, like a chant or litany. As he continued chanting the words with a profound fervor, he kept his eyes closed. Al-Hihi sat there, pen poised, not knowing what to do next. Then 'Abd al-Rahman stopped abruptly, and the whole house was enveloped in complete silence. The evening session seemed about to end, and al-Hihi broke the awesome silence of the moment by rustling and folding his papers. Just then, he heard the voice of his master resuming his recitation in a calm but clear voice.

"Record it all before you leave, Hammu. Write down the major parameter that governs all other principles before it gets away from me or else I find myself dazzled by its distinctive clarity. As I see things now, the most significant factor in invalidating the lessons of the past and the pointless accumulation of periods involves the corruption of the very germ of history, the forward thrust of its different phases. I can see it in the ingrained flaws to be found in this stubborn and intertwined principle that is forever causing the same calamities and historical ruptures. In a word, Hammu, I see it clearly in that unmitigated disaster that is called group solidarity, along with all its defining characteristics."

That statement made al-Hihi's hand shake.

"Forgive my reaction, Master," he said. "Don't worry about the mess on the page. But that last statement of yours has left me thoroughly confused."

"Never mind, Hammu," 'Abd al-Rahman replied. "There's plenty in that statement to confuse its speaker as well. But what are we supposed to do when confronted with such a torrent of information amid the accumulated piles of error and tradition? We can't afford not to accept it all with open hearts and analytical minds, can we?"

"Indeed we can't, Master. But how can you now abandon a concept that occupies such a capstone position in your writings? To be sure, group solidarity involves struggle and conflict, but the major purpose of its innate vigor continues to be leadership and rule. In this ephemeral world of ours I can see no viable alternative to such a principle."

"To the contrary, that's precisely what needs to be changed. History must develop a better, more refined seed, one that will enable it to change its skin and its course of development. Failing that, the lessons of the past will have no function within its frame of reference, and all aspirations to progress will be in vain. Luqman's house will remain as it is, but it may well suffer ill should the instincts of group solidarity remain a cogent force among peoples and retain discretionary control over popular discourse. With regard to my previous writings on the subject, you should record that the status that I have given it as a concept is not based on any notion of sanctity or adulation, but merely part of a process of observation and description. Its value is purely procedural, no more.

"If you look at the dire consequences of group solidarity, you'll see what I mean. The first of them is that, when a dynasty attains a sufficient level of luxury and easy living, it finds itself confronting an imbalance between the ever-increasing costs of a life of ease and of the armed forces and administrative sector on the one hand, and on the other, static or dwindling tax revenues. In redressing such an imbalance, it is completely useless to raise taxes and duties as long as the extent to which they exceed normal expectations leads inevitably to civil unrest, abandonment by peasants of their usual work practices, and a general withdrawal from public activities. The second of these consequences is that when the treasury suffers a drastic fall in tax revenues because people refuse to pay and collectors resort to armed violence, the sultan decides to place the burden of revenue collection on commercial taxation, an action that turns the state into a gigantic market. He then moves to exploit merchant shipping fees to the maximum extent by giving foreign merchants special privileges in commercial transactions and freight. However, these two methods of reducing the treasury's shortfall in tax revenues by monopolizing the commercial sector lead to inevitable consequences: the boycott of commerce by local merchants who abandon the business altogether, and the aggravation of those people who take seriously the task of protecting the Muslim community. Perhaps the worst of all these consequences is that the state embarks on one final act of reform, one that rapidly reveals itself to be an even greater contradiction than all the others. It proceeds to reduce the number of soldiers in the armed forces as a way of confronting the rise in military expenses; soldiers thereby turn into mercenaries whose only business is to sell their services for whatever price suits them. This procedure is no less harmful than the others in that it weakens the military might of the state and as a direct result, exposes the security apparatus to genuine dangers from within and without. The state's fundamental weakness is exposed in broad daylight.

That dynasty is then destroyed by another group, with its own sense of solidarity, a group whose only role is to repeat the same cycle of civilizational phases and calamities, albeit with variations in resources and modes.

"I don't think I've added anything particularly original to what I wrote earlier. However, for now I'll make do with simply restating that this phenomenon of group solidarity is the root of the entire problem, whether the instinct is natural or contrived. The tribal basis of power and political life, that's the crux of the problem.

"Hammu, at this point you or someone else may well wish to pose the question: 'Assuming we accept your opinion that group solidarity is the root of the problem, what substitute is there to oil the wheels of history?'

"To tell you the absolute truth, that is the question of all questions. It's been flashing through my mind for a long time and disturbing my sleep. Many things have managed to distract my attention, and I don't think I have a grasp on it. Actually, I still feel somewhat distressed at the loss of my family, and I've yet to fully recover from it. Even so, you can record that I now have a burning sense of the need to put an end to whatever fails to serve life itself. That will inevitably and eventually guide me to a thin, thin thread of logic, one that will enable me to come up with a more practical and fruitful alternative to the concept of group solidarity. Among factors that fail to assist and enhance life are a number of defects, of which I'll mention the following as just a few among countless possible examples. The restraining influence of blood ties in gaining power is one such, as is the utilization of mercenaries and clients as a means of steering the rudder of state. Tyranny, whether effective or terrible, is another defect, as is a reliance on old men and corrupt officials thrown up precooked by the prevailing political system. It's a further defect to give preference to sycophants over competent bureaucrats in making chancellery appointments, as is any display of pomp amid a veritable ocean of poverty and nakedness. Reducing civilized society till it is as supine as a woman on her back is yet another. And I could go on and on with this litany, one that must inevitably be eradicated for good and all. With that in mind, I'll simply repeat what I wrote in the *Introduction to History*: 'When genius grinds to a halt, ambitions are quashed, and all aspirations vanish into thin air, then all light disappears, hopes are dashed, and the dead rule the living.'

"I think I've managed to grasp at least part of the thread of that loftier alternative theory I mentioned earlier, but not all of it. Some aspects of it I can understand, but as yet I don't have the entire picture. I shall have to rely on God to relieve my personal distress so that I can concentrate on the matters that are of interest to me: the Muslim community, one characterized by consultation and appropriate decision-making; government based on a proper balance of justice; and the role of ethics in all aspects of behavior and interaction. These are all Islamic concepts that need to be firmly established, even if it involves providing right guidance for an unavoidable disaster, a dynastic ruler for example, with his accompanying support group, who needs to be constrained by such principles so that he will not behave in a tyrannical fashion. I ask God Almighty to grant me an audience with such enlightenment in a fruitful session that resembles in every way the one that I can recall from several years ago in the castle of Ibn Salama. The atmosphere there was one of a serene tension, and it served to stimulate and give focus to the evidential materials that I was working on at the time: the state of civilization and urban culture, and the individual circumstances to which human society finds itself exposed. I ask God to grant me an untrammeled atmosphere, a private space suffused with an elemental spirit, so that once again my current interests can be poured like showers into words and concepts. With that, the cream will be churned and the production will be that much easier. Amen!"

This prayer was a sign that dictation and session were drawing to a close. Hammu drank the rest of his coffee and as usual, tucked his papers and pens into the sleeve of his coat. After saying farewell, he departed.

The Night at the End of Rajab

At the beginning of this particular session, 'Abd al-Rahman and Hammu had a conversation about the plague of locusts in the Fayyum region and the fact that it was uncomfortably close to Fustat and Cairo itself. They also talked about the low level of the

Nile and the drought situation. Both men raised their palms in supplication to God, asking Him to show mercy and forgiveness. Afterward there was a period of silence, during which Hammu indicated that he was ready to listen and take notes.

"I'm afraid your papers may remain blank tonight," 'Abd al-Rahman said. "It's almost as though the locusts in the air have assaulted my mind and severed the synapses. The low level of the Nile seems to be reflected in a negativity inside my mind. Until such time as God relieves us of this distressing situation, there's simply no scope for leaps of logic and intellect, and no way of overcoming drought and aridity.

"In times past I've witnessed dreadful calamities in the lands of the Maghrib. During those times I have observed people with large egos and crooked minds. When there have been famines and droughts, they have monopolized the storage of grain, oil, and other foodstuffs or even exported them to other countries. I have also witnessed a wide variety of terrible atrocities, but at the time, my age gave me sufficient strength and enthusiasm to protect me from the twin evils of indifference and depression. Today, my braincells, which are in any case naturally inclined to self-absorption, react to news of dynastic turnovers and disasters by becoming still more withdrawn and depressed. Capitulation and truce, those are the only ways of coping with the situation; either that or silent withdrawal."

"May God protect my master from all evil! But there are still two matters that you are obliged to address: firstly the penetrating proof; secondly, the escape from the bottleneck."

"Remind me about the first of the two, but leave the other one till, God willing, I return from the next pilgrimage."

"The gist of the first one is as follows: If the territories of the Kinana tribe know of no rivalries for power, but simply consist of ruler and people, and yet their people are no weaker or more withdrawn than in other Maghribi countries, then it's not possible to attribute all political misfortunes to the instinct of group solidarity, nor can the principle be generalized and brought to bear in order to either endorse or counteract the record of events."

"One of the main reasons why I have settled in this particular region is that I want to learn more about it both by reading and observation. I don't feel the process is complete as yet; I have not delved into it enough. So don't write anything down until I've had a chance to refine my thoughts. At this point, my thinking is that the reasons why Egypt is free of armed groups of the kind that cause so much turmoil in the Maghrib give it—in principle, that is, and to a greater extent than other regions—a measure of social stability and all the benefits that accrue therefrom: relatively light taxation levels, the boon of the Nile waters, and the infrequent occurrence of riots and religious dissent. However, the current Mamluk regime in Egypt, one that relies on both kinship and loyalty and eliminates any opposition within the country itself, has a mistaken notion of reform that only manages to retard it. That is the consequence of conflicting interests and a widespread institutionalization of scare tactics and preventive assassinations, all of which manage to distract the regime's attention from the rights and interests of the people. Things carry on in this fashion until the system is demolished by forces that, like some swollen destructive flood, sweep in from the outside. That's all I can say in my current state of exhaustion, but there's more to follow."

'Abd al-Rahman glanced at his amanuensis and gestured to him not to write down any more.

"There's something else," he went on, "something that mars the picture. I might just as well talk about it in the hope of improving my mood."

"Go ahead, Master. My heart is still open to your words, if not my papers. My only hope is that I may be able to offer some comfort and alleviate your feelings somewhat. As regards what you've said already and may still say about the Mamluks, rest assured that the contents will find inside my heart a tomb and impenetrable veil against those forces that are so swift to commit murder."

'Abd al-Rahman's expression revealed signs of trust and reassurance. "As you know, Hammu," he went on, "I have taught at the most illustrious universities and colleges, al-Zaytuna, al-Qarawiyin, al-'Ubbad, al-Hamra', al-Azhar, al-Qamhiya, and today in al-Barquqiya. I have never finished a class without 'eyes watching me with deference and respect and hearts appreciating my qualification for high office; elite and populace were both alike in their reception.'

"But in the middle of this past week two strange men showed up; I've never seen them in my class before. They took turns bombarding me with provocative questions and biased objections. As I recollect, it followed my presentation on *The Smooth Path* of Malik ibn Anas.

"'Master,' one of them asked, 'if there is just one truth regarding God's word and that of His Prophet, then how does it make sense for the imams of the four schools of law each to follow their own path and to give varied and contradictory interpretations of their tenets?'

"'What you're doing,' I responded, 'is to rehash what you've memorized. With a greater degree of profundity you would be able to appreciate that the differences between the leaders of the schools of Sunni doctrine only occur in tangential matters, not in the basic tenets of the faith. Such differences are in and of themselves a sign of mercy, a reflection of the ways in which people differ in the various regions of the Islamic world with regard to their livelihood and lifestyles.'

"'Professor,' the second of them asked, 'you have justified the success of the Maliki rite in the Maghrib as being based on two factors. Firstly, that the pilgrimage to Mecca and the additional visit to Medina, Malik's birthplace and the cradle of his particular school, permitted the people of the Maghrib and Spain, in your view at least, to have direct contact with Maliki jurisprudence and as a consequence to ward off any influence from the schools of Iraq. Secondly, you pointed to the similarities in lifestyle between the Hijaz in Arabia and the Maghrib, something that makes people here more receptive to the Maliki school with its greater lenience. My question: is there some other factor involved, one that is more profound and genuine?'

"'In a previous class,' I replied, 'one where I didn't see either you or your companion, I discussed yet another factor that is just as valid as the two already mentioned. It resides in the important status that Malik accords in his juridical writings to the twin concepts of action and custom, also and more precisely in the way in which he expresses his frank objections to the sale of dates on a barter system, since the entire process involves unacceptable levels of loss and deceit . . .'

"'There are any number of claims,' the first man interrupted, 'and all sorts of false stories extolling Malik. The truth of the matter is, however, that the prevalence of the Maliki rite in the Maghrib is entirely and exclusively due to the sultan's authority, something that has been pointed out by the great master of that region, someone who knows the region well, namely Ibn Hazm of Cordoba— may God give us all the benefit of his learning!'

"'What Ibn Hazm has to say is far more complicated than what you've just pointed out. But if it's the truth of the matter you're after and you already know it, then why ask?'

"'We can indeed see that truth,' the second interrupted, 'and we can also see another one yet more lofty and all-encompassing. Muhammad, the Lord of Mankind, was the seal of the prophets and transcriber of faiths. Ahmad ibn Hanbal God be pleased with him—is the one who has put all other preachers and claimants out of business. He is the seal of the schools of orthodoxy, the one who has incorporated their tenets in whole and in detail. Such is the import of the teachings of the revered and pious scholar of the faith, Imam Taqi al-Din ibn Taymiya—may God bless his spirit!'

"At this point he took a piece of paper out of his sleeve and started reading from it in a sarcastic tone. It was an extract from my *Introduction to History*:

The judge, Abu al-Faraj al-Isfahani, composed his *Book of Songs* as a collection of historical accounts of the Arabs, their poetry, the genealogies, their great battles, and their dynasties. The system of organization was based on one hundred tunes that singers had selected for Harun al-Rashid. In my view, he was completely successful in his project. By my life, it can serve as a record of the Arabs, an anthology of the very best passages culled from their poetry, history, singing, and other crafts. I know of no other work to rival it, since it represents the very acme to which the littérateur may hope to aspire.

"'That concludes what you have to say, Professor,' the reader continued. 'You're extolling to the heavens a text which is full of debauchery and fornication. Such opinions render you unworthy of the trappings of scholarship; indeed of judicial office, too. God preserve us from evil words that should be suppressed rather than recited out loud and acted on.'

"With that the two men stood up suddenly. One of them threw a piece of paper at me, but, when my students started threatening them, they rushed out. I sent the students on their way, advising them to show all necessary restraint, but not before I had promised to give them a class on *The Book of Songs* so that they could see for themselves what I was writing about. Then I took a look at the piece of paper. Never before in my entire life have I read the kind of abusive language that it contained; you can gauge the level of slander and sheer stupidity from the following short extract: 'Stripped naked of all legal competence, that's you. You lounge there in your house down by the river and spend too much time listening to songstresses and entertaining young people.'"

That made al-Hihi cringe. He prayed earnestly to God to offer His protection against the calumnies of the rabble.

"Time has become so corrupt," he said, "that professional character assassins and purveyors of errant falsehoods have taken control. But my master, a scholar who stands far above such mundane matters, is not someone to be bothered by the wagging of evil, contentious tongues."

"Those tongues have managed to get me dismissed from my post as judge. Even as we speak, they're trying to get me fired from my teaching position as well. Even so, God be praised in the face of every conceivable misfortune. The good news is that before too long I will be united with the Lord of the Universe."

'Abd al-Rahman took a deep breath and remained silent for a moment while he once again adopted his normal smiling visage.

"The incident I recounted to you a moment ago had the same impact on me as another incident that happened a while back with some students in Fez. Rather than write anything down, I would ask you simply to listen to the story of what happened.

"No doubt you recall, Hammu, what I wrote in the *Introduction to History* about people selling fancies and charms, and traders in all kinds of magic and mumbo-jumbo. I've always given two classes on the subject. The first has been on alchemy, where I've shown that it consists of a series of procedures and routines which, its practitioners claim, can turn material extracted from base metals into gold and silver. To do so, they make use of animal remains and bits of egg, blood, and hair, all in order to manufacture the necessary mixture that, when converted into a potion (at least according to their bogus claims), can turn heated silver into gold and heated brass into silver. The second class has always been devoted to treasure seekers, those stupid idiots among whom we find lots of Berber students in the Maghrib who are incapable of making a normal living.

"What happened was that these two classes provoked a strong reaction from three students, one that hit me just like an obscure syllogism or analogy that left me completely baffled. Here's what they had to say: 'Great Master, all matter, including precious metals, can never actually disappear, but rather, remains behind even after its owners have died. Among the Copts it is the custom to bury the dead in all their finery. Other peoples—Greeks, Persians, Byzantines, for example—have their own rituals when it comes to preserving their heritage and valuables. As a consequence, the treasures of this world still exist, but they are buried underground.'

"'Noble teacher,' the second of them went on, 'since excavations conducted blind get us nowhere, we inevitably come to the conclusion that treasures have their own guardian spirits to keep watch over their secrets and the seals that keep them protected. We have to know how to communicate with such spirits through the language of magic charms—incense, drugs, incantations, and mediums—so that they will hand over the keys to those treasures or else show us how to get to the places where the riches are buried that will provide us with a life of luxury.'

"'Authoritative teacher,' said the third of them 'whenever we fail to find the treasure, it does not imply that the act of searching is wrong but merely that either the charms have been wrongly read or else the guardian spirits are being recalcitrant.'

"I can clearly recall what these three students had to say (I heard later on that they were treasure seekers), but I can't remember what I said by way of reply at the time. The next week however I received a letter, the main part of which read as follows:

From the students who are treasure seekers to the illustrious Master: You have made use of the vilest of terms to describe us—may God forgive you—not the nastiest of which is that we cannot earn a normal living. But you're the one who has provided us with the means to deal with that very weakness, when you say: "Happiness and profit will normally come only to those who behave humbly and are prepared to flatter."—"People involved in matters of religion—judging, giving legal opinions, teaching, leading prayers, giving sermons, announcing the call to prayer, and other functions, do not as a rule make a lot of money."—"It is peasants who lead a humble life; it is among the Bedouin that genuine well-being is to be found." These are just a few quotes from your writings on this topic. With them in mind, revered teacher, it is the very fact that we are unable to earn a living by normal means that forces us to concoct fantasies of wealth and chase after impossibilities, even though such activities may cause us all manner of difficulties and dire consequences.

"I must tell you that this letter made me realize that I had not paid enough attention to the practice of the occult and magic. Had I given it any thought at the time, I could have begun by asking myself about the function of these practices in the context of society and humanity in general. Which of mankind's expectations and concerns were expressed and answered by them? With more thought, I might have realized that in this quest for precious metals lay a desperate effort to force the earth to surrender its treasures to people who spend their entire lives dreaming of copious, inconceivable riches. With more thought, I would have seen that the entire thing provides us with a yardstick for the genuine poverty that exists, not to mention the scarcity of precious metals; and that is exactly what makes them the target of both dreams and plunder. Even so, I did record that this social phenomenon was spreading during a period when the regime was in decline and had decided to go after these treasure-seekers so that they could be taxed."

'Abd al-Rahman looked over at al-Hihi and caught him surreptitiously making notes.

"I told you not to write anything down, Hammu," he scolded him with a smile, "and yet I see you're still writing. Are you so keen to record every single thing I say, digressions and all?"

"Indeed, Master, they are all pearls. I have to note them all down in rough form so that I can make a complete version at home."

"Stop that for now. Bring over that stew so that I can taste some. By God, I haven't eaten for a few days, so I need some food."

"Here's Umm al-Banin's stew. She makes it for you with all her affection and respect."

"God preserve her handiwork and lead her to what pleases His will."

'Abd al-Rahman tasted some of the stew, scooping up a piece of meat covered in beans and artichoke, all of it garnished with olives. He took a piece of bread, dipped it in the stew, and took it out slowly and carefully. With each mouthful he extolled the woman who had made it and blessed the way in which this wonderful dish was settling so well in his stomach. He recalled previous meals that Umm al-Banin had cooked for him. All of which led him to ask her husband a question.

"How is it, Hammu, that your wife's stews, filled as they are with fat, still manage to settle in my hypersensitive stomach without the slightest problem? For example, the stew we had before this was sinfully rich in eggs, all of which led me to expect the very worst consequences, and yet I had no bad aftereffects. What's the secret?"

"That's a good question, but the only answer I can give is that Umm al-Banin is a wonderful cook; all her relatives in Fez admit as much. She always uses the right amount of oil and spices, and absolutely refuses to use anything but the freshest and best produce. However, as far as I am concerned, the real secret lies in the oregano oil she uses. It's known to have beneficial properties, and I get my relatives in Ighilinghighil to bring it with them when they pass through on their pilgrimage to Mecca and Medina."

"The oregano of the al-Hihis, not to mention their honey, their pride, and their intelligence, these are all things that, God willing, I'll talk about some time, not to mention Ighilinghighil and its famous tableware."

At this point 'Abd al-Rahman wished his amanuensis and his wife health and happiness. That was the cue for the session to come to an end.

The Night at the End of Sha'ban

When al-Hihi entered 'Abd al-Rahman's house, he took up his usual position and waited for the master to finish his prayers and intercessions. It was only when al-Hihi greeted his master that the latter was even aware of al-Hihi's presence. With that he went over, sat beside him, and returned his greetings, rewinding his turban as he did so.

"Prayer is a cure for the weary soul, Hammu," he said, "so never stint on it or cut it short."

"Sometimes I pray with the congregation, Master, at others with my wife. I will not hide from you the fact that my very greatest delight is when I can persuade my wife to perform the prayers behind me."

"But for books, I would spend the majority of my time in prayer, in the hope of relieving my distress and erasing sad memories. At my great age and in the current circumstances, prayer becomes sheer pleasure. I can forget earthly matters and focus instead on a universe where one is made aware of the atoms of the eternal, repeating along with the poet:

> May God never bless me should I not focus my soul on what
>   matters most,
> And may He multiply my concerns if my goal should be other than
>   salvation.

"As I confront my immense sorrow, my consolation lies in the fact that I am about to embark on a journey to the Holy Places. I express my hope to God that He may come to my aid in ridding my mind of its spotted vermin and my soul of its melancholy apprehensions. My greatest wish is that those holy sites in Mecca and Medina will manage to expel all the foul humors that have possessed me and heal the wounds of my memory. I am so anticipating the advent of the middle of the fasting month and the opportunity to undertake a striving for God. I can barely stand the wait till the time comes to grab the pilgrim's staff and be on my way. But, for the time being, let's go up to the roof so we can look out on the Nile and reminisce as much as we can."

Once up on the roof, the two men sat on a padded bench with a large candle in the middle. The weather was dry and warm, and the Nile waters reflected the heavens above with their brightly shining stars.

"If it weren't for the availability of this roof, Hammu," 'Abd al-Rahman said, "I would certainly not have been able to stand living in this house for the past three years. Spending an hour or two up here in the evening or at night always provides me with a quiet atmosphere, and how much I have needed that! It gives me access to the whole of creation, one whereby I can direct my thoughts to a consideration of the four elements and the Creator of All Things. No sooner do I go back downstairs than my traumatized memory starts functioning again. The only way I can lighten the heavy load it imposes on me is to block it off with a barrage of books. So now start noting down some of my memory's red-hot irons so that I may soon be released from them and feel the welcoming arms of my Lord.

"When my entire family was drowned at sea, the impact on me was, needless to say, so severe that the sheer misery of it drove me to a silence more eloquent than any words could express. Something I've never told you before, something that has haunted me throughout my various travels and journeys, is that I am desperately afraid of being murdered or attacked. The feeling has stayed with me throughout my time in the Maghrib. Actually, it still affects me here in Egypt, although not so strongly since at this stage of life, my own instinct for self-preservation is of minimal importance. On the other hand, in earlier days I stared death straight in the face in so many Maghribi countries with their petty regimes. I have sensed the sword of death hovering threateningly over me. The occasion when it all came closest to execution was when I was imprisoned by the Marini sultan, Abu 'Inan, something I referred to earlier. My dear Hammu, I really felt I was inevitably going to die that time. In a vain attempt to overcome my despair, I composed a hundred-verse poem that I sent to the furious sultan as a plea for mercy. All I can remember of it today are two verses that certainly confirm my mood at the time: 'For what circumstance should I blame the nights, in what adversity wrestle with time? That I am far distant brings sorrow enough, removed as I am from the claims of my witnesses.'

"From today's perspective I have a much clearer appreciation of the reasons for this fear of death. The factor involved is both more general and more dominant, so record it carefully so that other scholars devoted to scholarship may take note of it.

"The sultans and rulers of this era are the primary cause of this calamity; sometimes they are its victims too. Be they major figures or simply petty tyrants, their major goal is to force religious scholars to work as their functionaries and to provide for their needs and desires, all in return for salaries and real estate that they give such scholars in accordance with their talents and abilities. Too bad for any scholar who either objects or panders too much! As a result, the image of the ideal ruler is based on a combination of conditional generosity and outright violence, a thought that finds expression in a verse of poetry attributed to Sultan Abu al-Hasan al-Akhal: 'My wealth I hand out as I see fit, while necks are severed by the sword.'

"In the kingship business, loss of either throne or life is truly the greatest danger of all. As a result, every ruler has to confront such a likelihood in order to maintain control over his position as suits him best. That's the way he manages to enjoy his sovereign power and its delights. For that very reason he is permanently on edge and suspicious of all those around him, even his closest confidant. He pays close attention to stories put about by rumormongers and scandal peddlers. His gifts and talents are focused on matters such as debts, preventive killings, and death threats to others.

"The covert aspect of this particular realm finds the person forced to tread on coals, often in spite of himself. Occasions for error and downfall appear at every turn, and conspirators and manipulators never take their eyes off him. Thus, every time the atmosphere between him and them deteriorates and the political fissure widens, he is forced either to use the obligation of pilgrimage as a pretext for leaving his territories for a while or else to shift his favor from one group to another in accordance with the dictates of the moment. By my life, when the religious scholar is faced with a system like this, one that so cheapens the normal order of things, he has no other tricks up his sleeve that will enable him to avoid all the pitfalls and stay focused on the scholarly life which allows him to devote all his energies to learning and writing.

"In this era of ours, politics has become a danger area, a kind of orphanage—and an appalling one at that! Just take a look at the *Book of Lessons* or histories by people other than me, and you'll see how many chapters and accounts there are concerning the evil ends of prominent rulers, ministers, counselors, generals, and scholars. Our age, an age of truly excessive brutality, is dreadfully replete with methods of torture and oppression: butchery, drowning, impaling, garroting, strangulation, poison, quartering, and execution. It's no wonder my book should be full of terms such as downfall, disaster, rebellion, deposition, abdication, aggression, destruction, murder, raid, sortie, devastation, siege, and the like.

"This is how politicians and luminaries of intrigue and manipulation behave these days. The genuine scholar has no place in such a scheme and certainly no status. Just consider any number of examples. The most glaring is what happened to my own shaykh, Muhammad ibn Ibrahim al-Abili, who fled from the court and Hammu al-Zayyani, ruler of Tlemcen, and went to live in Marrakesh where he could live with the scholars there and learn from them. Then there's the case of my dear friend (in spite of everything) Lisan al-Din ibn al-Khatib who was murdered in his prison cell at the hand of agents of Muhammad V, ruler of Granada. He had been handed over to this ruler by the Marini sultan, Abu al-'Abbas, in exchange for a commitment of support for his own throne. Just imagine, Lisan al-Din, amazing scholar, intellectual, and poet, has his life terminated as part of a sordid pact between two rulers! My younger brother, Yahya, is yet another example of the sheer brutality of this age of ours. He too was murdered by a bunch of thugs on orders from Prince 'Abd al-Wadi who chose to believe the tissue of rumors and lies that had been concocted against my poor brother.

"With all that in mind, shouldn't I be just as worried about the dire possibilities of imprisonment and a grisly death?

"The other thing that keeps preying on my mind like a malignant tumor is plague. As I discussed it before:

The pestilence that beset civilization east and west in the mid-fourteenth century decimated communities and wiped out the mountain people. Many of the beauties of civilized society were swallowed up and erased. As mankind diminished in size, so too did the earth's civilization. Garrisons and workshops were destroyed; pathways and landmarks vanished. Entire regions and houses were emptied; regimes and tribes were weakened. The entire population changed. The same fate befell both the eastern and western regions, the difference being only matters of degree and the extent to which the region was urbanized. It was as if the entire discourse of existence had pronounced the words apathy and gloom, and the response had come in a rush. God is indeed the inheritor of the earth and all who inhabit it.

"I was just sixteen when the plague hit Tunis, an age when my senses and desire to learn were at their sharpest. When the plague came (and I think it actually played a role in the downfall of the Marini, Abu al-Hasan, in Qayrawan), what terrible things I witnessed!

"It exacted a terrible toll from me in that both my parents died along with a number of my shaykhs—may God have mercy on them all. Becoming an orphan in this way was to have a profound effect on both my sense of lineage and my scholarly career. Even though I was still in the prime of my youth, I could feel in my bones the onset of middle age. The sheer feeling of dejection that affected me manifested itself in both my heart and outward expression.

"The very sight of death in general and of wanton carnage in particular serves to remind people of the fact that they will all inevitably die. Every single day they are alive is potentially their last.

"My dear Hammu, I have seen things that no tongue can describe. I have seen graves overflowing with corpses too many to be encompassed by the eye. I have seen cities turned into wastelands peopled only by piles of rotting bodies, places populated only by the spirits of men crushed and resigned. I have seen terror writ large on faces and bodies cowering behind arches and walls. I have watched as tame animals and even predatory birds have fled from living and dead as fast as they can. And I have seen other unmentionable things that my memory has forever suppressed, silencing my tongue and its language faculties.

"I can recall that from the bottomless pit of terror I used to beg God to give me the power to put a stop to so much death by performing miracles and wondrous deeds. During my dreams, by night and day, I would feel myself granted this gift. I would set spirits free, put an end to misery, and devise cures. It was only when I woke up that I found myself ranting away while my soul returned to its habitual weakness.

"People of the time give this plague names associated with terror and rage: 'the great perdition,' 'the dreadful disease,' 'the epidemic,' or 'fatal,' or 'mighty plague.' So, Hammu, note down now some details about it that I have not been able to include in my previous writings.

"God knows best, but it appears that everything started in the region of the Mongol tribes and of the Great Khan. A series of wars there about a decade or more ago led to the accumulation of horrifying numbers of corpses, and the putrefaction they caused was carried by the winds to European territories, both east and west. Tunis was infected by commercial sea traffic from Sicily, aided and abetted by caravans over land and shifting wind patterns that spread it from one region to another.

"As far as I'm aware, there exist no records of effective specifications or official legal procedures aimed at counteracting the symptoms of plague or maintaining any kind of normal life in countries that are affected. The reason is that regimes in the Maghrib, and I suspect in the eastern regions as well, are, unlike their European equivalents, incapable of intervening to control the spread of the plague and taking steps to prevent its spread, most especially when those regimes are in the latter stages of decline or almost so. As a result, the knowledge that we possess on this particular topic is of no use to us in assessing the enormous impact of the disaster or its extent across time and place.

"When we consider accounts from chroniclers and annalists, we are no better off. Figures that purport to compute the number of dead and descriptions that more often than not include biased and irrelevant impressions force us to make up for their patent deficiencies with speculative and approximate estimates of the full scope of the disaster.

"What is abundantly clear is that the loss of population resulting from the plague has its maximum impact on the poor quarters. It is the weakest and most downtrodden segment of society that is hardest hit. The primary reason, of course, is the foul air quality, but as Ibn al-Khatib noted, it is also the result of 'the fact that houses are cramped and built close together without any planning or attempts at proper preservation, due to rampant ignorance, and a complete lack of knowledge about such matters among the poorest classes.'

"On the other hand, wealthy people have fairly minimal exposure to the terrors of the plague, in large part because they stay inside their houses or else go to their estates in the countryside where they are far removed from the people most affected. Even so, they too are negatively impacted by the plague since the revenues from farming and estates diminish due to a fall in demand in the marketplace and the inflation of prices exacted by the rescuing hands of civilized society.

"My personal beliefs and the tenets of my legal school tell me that, absent a settled populace and incentives, there can be no real civilization. When a country is afflicted by plague, earnings, profitable employment, services, and all types of life support are negatively affected.

"At this point, Hammu, I have to mention the two postures that intellectuals adopt when confronted with plague and death.

"The first of them involves the implementation of basic medical procedures aimed at lowering the plague fever by using water and vinegar to freeze the blisters behind the ears and knees and under the armpits till they start to bleed and the noxious fluids dry up. This works only if the symptoms are external. However, if the fever hits the lungs, then there's nothing medicine can do about it. In all cases, doctors are agreed that prevention is better than cure. The intelligent Muslim is enjoined to protect himself against the likelihood of contracting the plague before it happens and to take all possible steps to prevent its spread once it has struck. In such circumstances it is absolutely essential to follow the advice of medical specialists, such counsel being a gift from God Himself. Such advice may include improving air quality by using fumigants to lower pollution levels, maintaining bodily health by eating appropriate foods, keeping houses well aired, and supporting the community's way of life by steering well clear of its more heedless and overcrowded activities.

"The second posture involves a resort to the consolation of faith, one that derives its effectiveness from the very weaknesses of the medical approach. This disease shows no discrimination in its hunger for death, and there is no cure. Faced with that reality, all mankind can do is to acknowledge it through the radical and absolute treatment that takes the form of faith. It is for that reason that a wide variety of judicial experts have opined that anyone who dies of the plague is a martyr in the path of God.

"This second posture is truly exemplary in the way that it provides support and comfort for the soul. It encourages people to read the Qur'an, to say prayers, and even to wear emerald rings embossed with some of the beautiful names of God Almighty: 'O God, Living, Prudent, Wise, Compassionate.' Even so, the wisdom of such measures in no way vitiates or challenges the efficacy of medicine."

"Master, shall I mention the advice that al-Tabari gives on this topic, namely putting an elephant's tooth on children as a way of keeping the plague at bay?"

"Don't bother with that. Note down instead that 'prayer is the preferred weapon of the believer.' But God Almighty has said: *Say, O people, act in accordance with your station. I am acting, and you will know.* The grounds for legalizing activity in this field associated with colossal disasters is to encourage the development of knowledge about the plague in its terrestrial aspects rather than its heavenly or other ones, and to prevent its spread among humanity as the result of ignorance and contagion. This should remain the case until such time as mankind can acquire the ability to overcome the disease or mitigate its effects.

"There are specialists in law and hadith who claim that the plague is caused by a pinprick from the jinn and who deny the possibility of contagion as being contrary to observation, feeling, experience, and research. Concerning such people I am reminded of an apt comment that Ibn al-Khatib made on several occasions: 'Ignoring the things that science tells us is an act of malice, a taunt against God Himself, and an insult to the hearts of all Muslims.'

"Just a minute more before we finish. It's not correct to attribute all the earthly causes of the plague to foul, humid air alone. Another factor involves symptoms of senility in a political regime, circumstances that are often characterized by unjust taxation and levies that oppress farmers and result in reduced activity and then total collapse. That in turn leads to food shortages, inflation, and rebellion, followed by famines and plagues. Politicians bear a large responsibility for this chain of events. That's why human beings should, to the extent that they can, take all possible precautions."

With that, 'Abd al-Rahman stretched out on a cushion, repeating his last phrase "take all possible precautions" over and over again. To that he added:

The world is a garden, with the regime as its fence. The regime consists of a ruler appointed according to custom. Custom is a policy controlled by the king, who is a kind of shepherd supported by the army. The army in turn consists of helpers who are compensated with money. Money takes the form of income collected by the people. The people are people of God served by justice. Justice is a known quantity, it being the mainstay of the world. The world is a garden, with the regime as its fence.

There was now an abrupt silence, and it lasted for a while. Sitting there on the roof, the two men were being wafted by the warm night air; their canopy was the entire firmament with its gleaming stars. Al-Hihi made sure that his master had fallen asleep, then called for Sha'ban and asked him to help carry their master down into the house. Sha'ban informed him that his master had given him instructions to leave him on the roof whenever he fell asleep there. The two men wrapped up 'Abd al-Rahman in a blanket, then went downstairs where for the first time ever they had a quiet conversation.

"Are you happy, Sha'ban, working for the Master?'

"Happy and satisfied. Thank God, he is the best of men!"

"Take this as an expression of gratitude for looking after my wife."

"My master pays me for that. I won't accept any more."

"But it's just between the two of us."

"And that's another reason for my not accepting it."

"As you wish, Sha'ban. But please tell the Master that I'll come to see him again before he leaves on the pilgrimage."

The two men bade each other a warm farewell, then parted company.

Two Notes

Note One: By dawn on the fourteenth day of Ramadan, preparations for the master's pilgrimage were all in place. His servant Sha'ban was sparing no effort rushing around and offering assistance. It was almost as though he were giving advanced expression to his delight because his master had promised to send him on the pilgrimage the following year.

Two hours after breakfast 'Abd al-Rahman had the idea of packing some books in his baggage, but he abandoned the idea, contenting himself with a copy of the Qur'an and of *Stations of Pilgrims on the Path to the Clear Truth* by al-Harawi al-Ansari. Just as he was thinking of choosing a third book, he heard a light tapping on the door and hurried over. As he opened it, 'Abd al-Rahman found himself face to face with Umm al-Banin, with Sha'ban standing just behind her looking aggravated and worried. Before even exchanging greetings with her, he asked how her husband was. Handing him two full baskets, she answered by saying that all she wanted was to give him some food for the journey and to ask him to pray during the course of his blessed pilgrimage that she might have a child. She also managed to stammer out that Hammu would not object if he knew that she had come to see him.

'Abd al-Rahman stood there, not knowing what to do. One moment he was looking at this veiled woman who clearly wanted to come inside, then he was glancing at his servant as though asking him for advice. When she grabbed his hand and kissed it fervently, he allowed her to come inside for fear that his neighbors might notice. He told his servant to take the gift and to stay close by.

'Abd al-Rahman now sat down on his bench, reciting verses as he did so, while his visitor sat on the carpet close to his knees. In a single rapid gesture she removed her veil.

"I have learned," she said, "that our Master is going on the pilgrimage. For that reason I have taken over the role of your late wife by providing you with some food for the journey: some local butter, honey, salted meat, and some sweets. Were I able to do so, I would have brought my Master all the gifts in the world."

"Umm al-Banin, may you be well rewarded for your thoughtfulness and may God guide you to what pleases Him."

As 'Abd al-Rahman mouthed these words, he had to make an enormous effort to keep his emotions under control. He kept snatching glances at the uncovered face of this beautiful and delicate woman. All of a sudden she grabbed hold of his hand and started kissing it on both sides with tremendous fervor. He told her to stop and begged her to do so, but nothing had any effect. When he gave up and surrendered to the reality of the situation, he had the strong impression that his hand was actually complying with the woman's wishes and enjoying the long, continuous kisses and the strokes of lips and cheeks it was receiving, mingled as they were with copious warm tears.

"Why are you weeping, Umm al-Banin?" he asked.

"Because, sir, my name is really not appropriate; I am called Umm al-Banin, mother of sons, and yet I have children only in my dreams. My desire for children has grown stronger than ever and occupies my every living moment. Neither distractions nor hugging other people's children are of any use when it comes to lessening the yearning I feel. Sometimes, sir, when I'm on my own, you'll see me grab a pillow to my lap and sing this nursery rhyme, crying like an idiot:

Pat-a-cake, pat-a-cake, baby,
Bringing baby nice din-dins,
Dada comes from the garden,
With peaches and pomegranates.

"I've been childless for so many years, it makes me worried. I'm scared I'll still be without children when menopause strikes—heaven forbid."

The woman was speaking in genuine pain. Once in a while she would raise her teary eyes to look at 'Abd al-Rahman who was lending a sympathetic ear to her tale.

"I beseech you, sir," she went on pleadingly, "in the name of the blessed aura of your scholarship and your love for God and His Prophet, please pray during the course of your pilgrimage that I may give birth. Do not forget me while you are clasping the grillework of the shrine, performing the circumambulation of the Ka'ba, running between Safa and Marwa, and standing on Mount 'Arafat. Ask the Generous Provider to give me a child, just one baby who will enter the world from my womb and suckle my own milk. If I have no chance to produce a child and bring it up, my nipples and womb will wither to nothing. Tell me, sir, am I begging God to do something of which He is incapable?"

'Abd al-Rahman grabbed the opportunity afforded by his annoyance at this inappropriate question and swiftly withdrew his hand so that nothing untoward should happen to him during this fasting month.

"Be reconciled to God, woman," he said, "and never despair of His mercy. I hereby promise to devote much prayer to achieving your wishes. Now go home to your husband and prepare his morning meal. Tell him that you have been to see me."

Umm al-Banin stood up, wiped away her tears, and put her veil on again. Eyes lowered, she left the room, compliant, yet happy. At first, Sha'ban hesitated to say anything, but when his master encouraged him, he spoke.

"Having accompanied this woman on her walks, I am convinced—and God knows best—that she is undoubtedly both devout and loyal. But she likes to show herself in public and enjoys listening to the admiring comments and flirtatious gestures aimed at her. On our walks she has often told me not to stop the young men by the Nile or in the streets when they say such things to her. Her excuse has always been that in such places the breezes soon waft away such amorous expressions. There's something else as well.

All the time she keeps asking me for news about you and your activities. As God can attest, I only respond in the most general of terms, nothing specific. I tell her that you steer well clear of any involvement with women. But when she insisted that I escort her to your house tonight, there was absolutely no way of stopping her."

'Abd al-Rahman gave Sha'ban a sympathetic smile. He asked his servant to recheck the baggage, heat some water for the solemn ritual of purification, and then go to the cameleer to check on the departure time next day after the noontime prayers. Once 'Abd al-Rahman was left alone, he offered thanks to God that Umm al-Banin had not paid him a visit before the breaking of the fast had been announced. If she had done so—heaven forbid, she would assuredly have invalidated his fast and ritual purity. Praise be to the Arranger of Times and Matters!

Note Two: On the morning of the middle day of Ramadan, 'Abd al-Rahman was shaken awake by a strange dream he had had. In it he saw himself saying farewell to Umm al-Banin who had become his wife. He was on his way to a Middle Eastern city close by where he was about to meet the descendant of Genghiz Khan, Timur Lang. No sooner had al-Hihi come in that he started telling him about the second part of the dream (omitting any mention of the first).

"In this dream I had, Hammu, the strangest thing happened. My mind is still reeling! I saw myself in a Mamluk city sitting with the mighty warrior, Prince Timur, ruler of the Mongols and Tatars. At some points I was discussing things with him, and at others I was negotiating. I can't remember the sequence or details any longer. By the way, I recall now that my own shaykh, Muhammad ibn Ibrahim al-Abili, that master of rational ideas—God have mercy on him—predicted that I would eventually get to meet this person who, following the example of his forebears, would ravage the lands of Islam with fire and destruction and crush its people in a reign of terror and tyranny. This all happened at the beginning of the seventh Islamic century at the hands of Genghiz Khan, and the situation worsened with his grandson, Hulagu Khan, the destroyer of

Baghdad. Now that same Tatar onslaught continues its onward march with another descendant, Timur Lang. All this is happening to us when barely half a century has passed since the Middle East managed to escape from the nightmare of the Crusades and the western regions from their massive defeat at the battle of al-Arak in 591. I can think of no better account of these terrors and disasters than that of Ibn al-Athir, even though he did not live long enough to witness its final destructive phases.

"As I'm telling you about my dream, Hammu, I can recall now that my meeting with Timur was one of those events that manage to tell us a great deal about the Middle East's unreasonable share of misery and disaster. The meeting, which was interspersed with a meal and truncated conversations, took place in an atmosphere fraught with fear and rumor. The only way I found to counter it was at times to murmur verses from the Qur'an, the chapter on the sea from Abu al-Hasan al-Shadhili, and at others, to recall the Mamluk victory over Hulagu Khan at 'Ayn Jalut.

"Dear God, disperser of accumulated darkness, granter of dashed hopes, I pray You to lighten the burden of what is to come and, in the measure of Your great kindness, to turn my dream into a source of comfort for me and Muhammad's people. Amen!"

Like 'Abd al-Rahman, al-Hihi raised his hands to God as he repeated "Amen." The two men recited the *Fatiha* of the Qur'an and then in a powerfully spiritual atmosphere, performed some intercessions.

"Master," said al-Hihi as soon as they had finished, "I have a request to make."

"Fine, Hammu, say it with no hesitation."

"Ever since I met you, I've wanted to invite you to a meal in my modest home. But I've never dared broach the topic for fear of disrupting your work or interfering with your desire for seclusion. Barely a day has gone by during the first half of last month without Umm al-Banin insisting that you spend the Sha'ban celebration with us. I kept on refusing on the grounds that you were extremely busy and preoccupied."

"That is the night of innocence. Invite me, and I'll certainly be there."

"So then, my every hope is that we'll celebrate your return from the pilgrimage in my house and at my expense."

"In your house for sure, but only on condition that the expenses will be paid by those who've been blessed by their participation in the pilgrimage."

"If there's anyone to share my joy that you'll be honoring me in this way, then it's Umm al-Banin. She'll be shouting for joy and starting preparations for the sweets this very day!"

'Abd al-Rahman put a purse of money into al-Hihi's pocket, even though the latter made every effort to stop him. They then talked about the seven previous nights of dictation.

"I am hereby entrusting you, Hammu, with my dictated thoughts. If I return alive from the pilgrimage, I'll look them over carefully and make a few additions. If I should happen to die while I am there, then publish them as they are, along with this letter of mine by way of assent and verification."

"You will return to us, Master, as a devout pilgrim, hale and hearty. If you in turn should discover that I've passed away, the papers will be where Umm al-Banin keeps her jewelry hidden."

"God willing, you'll live longer than you expect, so you can be protector and treasure to your wife."

There was a knock on the front door. Sha'ban stood up, greeted the knocker, and announced that the cameleer was at the door. 'Abd al-Rahman leapt to his feet and went to his room to put on his travel clothes. When he came back and went out of the front door, he found al-Hihi and Sha'ban squabbling over who should help the cameleer load the camel and tether the baggage. No sooner had the hour arrived to join up with the caravan going to the Sinai port than 'Abd al-Rahman hugged first al-Hihi and then Sha'ban, telling the former to check on the house from time to time and the latter to take good care of Umm al-Banin when she went on her walks. As al-Hihi helped 'Abd al-Rahman mount the camel, he whispered in his master's ear, reminding him of his promise to pray that Umm al-Banin might have a child, all in order to satisfy her insistent demands.

And with one gesture 'Abd al-Rahman signaled to the cameleer to set out on foot toward their destination, while with another he bade his two friends farewell.

Between Falling in Love
and
Operating in the Shadow of Power

Ibn Khaldun relaxed by living close to the River Nile. He liked listening to female singing and consorting with the young. He married a
woman with a reckless brother who was reputed to be mixing with
unsavory company and thus fell into a pit of corruption. That, at any
rate, is what I read in *The Judges* by Jamal al-Din al-Bishniti.

Ibn Hajar al-'Askalani,
Lifting the Load Regarding Egypt's Judges

In Cairo lives someone who loves me and whom I love (Ibn Khaldun).

Ibn Qadi Shuba,
Postscript to the History of Islam

The pilgrimage: from the port on the west coast of Arabia, to the
Sinai peninsula, then to Mecca via Yanbu'.

The pilgrimage, returning to Egypt from Mecca, passing
through Yanbu', Qusayr, and Upper Egypt.

The round trip took about six months. As I'll explain below, I
found myself perpetually lost in a sea of distractions and fantasies.

On the way there and back I was traveling between the tomb of
Imam al-Shafi'i and the graveyard by the Muqattam Hills when I
was stopped by a troupe of horsemen. Their leader addressed me in

faulty Arabic: "You greet al-Zahir, our lord. Is forgotten? Cameleer go to your house, you come with us to the royal household."

On the way back I asked him to postpone the meeting till the next day so I could go home, take a bath, and rest. But he refused, saying that I could do all that at the palace.

It was while I was riding on horseback with them that I suddenly realized how very absent-minded and distracted I'd become. I had no trouble determining the cause: my mind was totally preoccupied with thoughts of Umm al-Banin. She had even made me forget that I was obliged to go and present my salutations to the sultan both before leaving and upon my return. The thought of her had banished the mighty Mamluk ruler from my mind altogether. What it all meant was that she was beginning to have an undesired effect on my interior self and infiltrating her way into my heart and soul. But I can swear that my conscience in the matter was clear. My only motive was one of pure and innocent affection and a strong desire that my prayers should accord this woman the boon of childbirth.

Ever since my arrival in Egypt as a refugee, there had only been three occasions when I had managed to have a meeting with Sultan Barquq in the Ablaq Palace within the Jabal al-Ahmar Citadel. I had paid scant attention to the architecture of the place, merely muttering 'What opulence!' as I reminded myself that God alone endures. I can recall that during the course of those visits my eyes would open wide as I passed through the portal to the private mosque where prayers were performed. For a few moments I had just stared at the sheer elegance all around me—the elaborate marble paving on the floor and the gilded ceiling in the sultan's private section. I had also counted the colonnades around the courtyard. This time, however, I seemed to have the status of compulsory guest, so I had plenty of time to look at my surroundings more carefully and take in things I had not had the chance to on previous visits. That is exactly what I started doing, once, that is, the servants had finished bathing, powdering, and dressing me. I took a look at the food I was offered, and was then informed that the sultan could not give me an audience till after the noontime prayers on Friday, the following day. I would thus have to stay overnight in the citadel palace.

Resisting the urge to complain or ask questions, I made my way to the sermon mosque where I prayed the afternoon prayer and relaxed for a while. I kept out of people's way so as to avoid having people stare or leer at me. I was also anxious to avoid running into any of the manipulators who had managed to get me dismissed from my position as judge three years earlier. As soon as I became aware that there were a number of people pacing around me, I got up to leave. In attendance I found two servants who may have been members of the viceroy's retinue. I informed them that I wanted to take a walk, so I set off with them following a few meters behind.

I now strolled my way through halls and courts, some high, some low. At times I was looking at the outside of palaces in black and yellow stone; at others, lofty domes appeared, all green and yellow; at still others, garlanded balconies that jutted out various distances and gave on to interior courts or gardens. Many were the jewel-encrusted doors that maybe led to the sultan's arcade and assembly rooms, or to the harem's entrance, or else to vaults where secrets were kept. With every one that I passed, I quickened my step in quest of some space where I could relax. I thought I found what I was looking for in a wing of one of the palaces; I sat down to rest in a broad room that was open to the gentle glow of the setting sun. The light was filtered through panes of copper-colored glass in various shapes and reflected in the mirror of the marble floor, on the walls, and the lofty ceiling decorated with precious stones, shells, gold, and lapis lazuli. The arches and columns too displayed their own share of spectacular beauty in the patterning of their lines and their gypsum filigree.

I asked the two servants to whom this palace belonged. They muttered something I didn't understand, and one of them went away for a moment. He came back with a man wearing an open mantle and a huge turban that almost covered his eyes. He greeted me respectfully and introduced himself. He was clearly an Egyptian, and informed me that he served as the official translator in the palace and *ustazdar*, meaning that he supervised the affairs of the scullery, the carpet store, the cellar, and other aspects of the sultan's private quarters. I asked him the same question I had posed to the two servants, and he replied that it had formerly belonged to one

of the amirs in the musicians' corps, but now it served as a guest
house for distinguished visitors.

"Tonight, sir," he went on, "you are such a guest. Is there anything I can do for you?"

As a way of passing the time I asked him to tell me about the
materials used to build the first citadel. His response came as a
confirmation of what I had anticipated.

"Ever since Qaraqush built it for Salah al-Din the Ayyubid,
Sultan al-Nasir Muhammad ibn Qala'un the Mamluk constructed
walls, towers, and the Ablaq Palace, and Sultan al-Zahir Barquq—
whose reign may God prolong—decided to use it as a residence, the
building materials and the various additions have been quartz crys-
tal and granite from Upper Egypt and limestone cut from the
Muqattam Hills."

Tapping a wall, I could not resist muttering to myself that the
Muqattam Hills had already been stripped bare, and now they were
making it even worse! Both before and after these slaves had come
to power in Egypt, they had revealed through their architecture the
extent of their nostalgia for their original Turkestan homeland.
They were determined that their buildings would resist the ravages
of time.

"Can I do anything else for you, blessed pilgrim?" the man
asked.

"Send someone to fetch my burnous from the citadel bath and
show me to my bedroom."

He gestured to a door at the back, and I followed him down a
long hall at the very end of which was another door with a servant
standing outside. He ordered that it be opened and invited me to
enter my bedroom for the night. He urged the servant to take good
care of me and wished me a good night's sleep.

Every single court and residence in this citadel was of wide pro-
portion; the concept of constricted space was totally unknown there.
The room I was in would be big enough for at least two families
from Fustat. It was several meters larger than my own house, and
was lavishly accoutered and furnished. As I sat down on a bench, I
could imagine Umm al-Banin entering this room and uttering cries
of amazement and wonder; I could see her touching the bed and

weeping as she explained that even in her most extravagant dreams she had never envisaged anything to match the softness of the counterpane and silk pillows or to match the splendor of the furnishings. I could imagine myself comforting her by saying that this was civilization flat on its back like a flagrant prostitute. Such opulence was a harbinger of a culture and people that were utterly corrupt.

I heard someone at the door asking to come in. The servant entered with my burnous over his shoulder and a tray of food in his hands. He put them down on a table and went to open a balcony window. With a smile he gestured to the outdoors before withdrawing once again. I walked over to the window. "Yes indeed!" I told myself, "he was right to direct me over here. These beautiful sights, stretching away as far as the eye can see, deserve much care and attention. What intensity of emotion, what loveliness!"

I took a rug and the tray of food over to the balcony and sat there, looking at the choice of food and staring out at the spectacular view, all in the gentle glow of the early evening.

You know, Umm al-Banin, if I direct my gaze to the northeast of the river, there is al-Mu'izz's Cairo spread out across its swampy ground, its minarets all yearning in the direction of the great al-Azhar mosque and the tomb of al-Husayn; its gardens, quarters, and streets; its nine gates opening onto the canal and the River Nile; its lofty white buildings behind Salah al-Din's walls; many edifices still standing in spite of the ravages that decay and disruption have wrought. Then, Umm al-Banin, if I turn and look to the southeast, there is Fustat, a city the Arab conquerors would never have bothered to build if it weren't for the doves that laid their eggs on 'Amr ibn al-'As's tent in Fustat.

The serenity I am feeling tonight is just a small part of what 'Amr himself—peace be upon him—must have felt.

Fustat is the place I love. To how many companions has she offered a refuge in abodes that time has worn away? How often have destructive hands roamed over her and piles of refuse accumulated in her confines? She has now become a haven for riff-raff and indigents, people who eat beans and peeled chickpeas!

There is Fustat, the place I love, spread out in front of me, with its houses, ancient mosque, baths, bazaars, and promenades, all bunched close to the Nile, with the islands of Roda and Giza close at hand on the other bank. Even closer than Fustat is the mosque of Sayyida Nafisa, the mosque of Ibn Tulun, and the Elephant Lake.

Anyone who can gaze out on the sights that I see has to feel a sense of enormous pleasure!

By this time night was falling. With it came a cool breeze, presaging the appearance of the stars in the night sky and lights. The entire spot where I was sitting was suffused with a gentle serenity. I had no idea how long it had lasted until I heard the call to evening prayer. I immediately stood, performed my ritual ablutions, and prayed the proper number of prostrations. Once I had finished, I went back to the balcony, wrapped myself in my cloak, and lay down. With that, I let sleep have its way, but not before I had recited to myself some lines of poetry that suddenly occurred to me:

When night clothed me in its apparel,
it was a young man in pain that donned it.

"Prayer is better than sleep, sir." That was the wake-up call I heard through the door of my room. I woke up with a start, and found myself on the silk bed. I allowed the owner of the voice to come in. My sense of shock disappeared when he told me that he had been worried about my catching cold, so he had carried me from the balcony to the bed. The exhausting journey had, no doubt, sent me into a deep sleep and made me lose all consciousness. The servant placed a breakfast tray in front of me and laid out some white robes. Reminding me that the Friday noon prayers would be happening soon, he went out and closed the door.

I leapt out of bed and went to the bathroom. After completing my toilet and washing, I hurriedly performed the morning prayer. I was especially anxious to have everything done before my appointment with the sultan. On the dressing table I spotted a container with toothpicks, a brush, and a jar of kohl. I started putting on my new clothes: a brocade kaftan and woolen mantle with green lining. I left the headcloth and cope to one side, and made do with cleaning my teeth and sprinkling my body and beard with rose water. Tying the turban around my head, I yelled for the servant. He came in with a thurible full of sweet-scented incense which he put down in front of me and left there till the smoke began to dwindle. I now tied the burnous round my shoulders and suggested we leave.

So there I was, about to enter the sultan's presence, perfumed to the hilt and decked out in a finery that was not my own; almost as though I had been transformed into someone else. I prayed, "Dear God, give this day a happy outcome, and shower me with Your pardon and triumph!"

The servant went on his way apace. I tried valiantly to keep up and kept snatching glances at the servants and soldiers in the court-yards and stables or standing at various gateways. Once he had escorted me as far as the congregational mosque, he left me to join all the other people going to prayer and make my way to a point close by the mosque's mihrab. My ritual ablutions were still valid, so I made a point of hurrying so as to avoid the possibility of being assaulted by any of the criminals that I had either slapped or thrown in jail while I was the Maliki judge in al-Salihiya. It was only with great difficulty that I managed to make my way to the front row close by the sultan's private prayer space. People stared at me, showing a mixture of respect and curiosity. Some of my acquaintances in the administration or the coterie of intellectuals came over and congratulated me on having completed the pilgrimage; my expressions of thanks took the form of embraces and as much cordiality as I could muster. The last of them was the military commander, or *dawadar*, Yahya Qutuz, who whispered in my ear that his master intended to accord me an audience in his reception room just before noon. Just then it was announced that the exalted sultan, al-Malik al-Zahir, had entered his prayer space. Everyone stood up and bowed in his direction. There were so many armed men shielding him from the congregation of worshippers that he was scarcely visible. "Praise to Him who makes the manumitted slave into a sultan," I said to myself. "He who makes whomsoever He pleases into a monarch, even were he to be a well-marked slave."

Once everyone sat down, the preacher, all dressed in black, mounted the pulpit which was draped in two black flags, the symbols of the 'Abbasi caliphate. Taking a sword from the muezzin who announced the call to prayer, duly followed by the other muezzins, the preacher greeted the congregation and recited the hadith: "If you are talking to your companion on Friday while the imam is preaching, then listen instead. You have been in error." This served as a prelude to the preacher reading from the prepared text normally used during Friday prayers. However, the obligatory mention of the 'Abbasi caliphs was significantly truncated, while prayers for the success, support, glory, and empowerment of the sultan were elaborate, almost as if the sultan were beset by a variety of dangers and a host of foes. Once he had finished and somewhat hurriedly led the prayers, he gave the people his farewell greetings. The sultan and his entourage departed, and people began leaving in droves.

I stayed where I was till there was some more space. Looking to left and right I spotted the *dawadar* waiting for me to stand. I got up and went over, and he ordered a slave to accompany me to the *darga*.

The *darga*, you ask!

After crossing a stone staircase and lengthy courtyard via a gently tiered stairway, I came to realize that this *darga* was a large space where people with an appointment to see the sultan would await permission to enter. I took a deep breath, fondly imagining that here I was, right next to the huge colonnade in the Ablaq Palace and that the hour of my deliverance was at hand.

I sat down on a bench by an iron window through which could be seen part of the sultan's stables. I could only imagine the well-coddled lifestyle the horses and camels enjoyed with all their servants, grooms, and doctors. One well-known fact about this Mamluk dynasty, as well as others like them, was that making a big display of stables was a source of enormous pride. Every ruler was anxious to outdo his predecessors by expanding them and making plans for still more enlargements, whether it involved workhorses from Barqa or more resplendent Arabian stallions. This window also provided a glimpse of the Citadel's large square, with soaring fountains, lofty palms, and fruit and sweet-basil trees. When I took a closer look, I even spotted a private playing field reserved for sultans and their coterie to one side.

So, here in this *darga*, with its vaulted roof, lofty pillars, and marble floor, here is where mankind has to wait for admission to the presence of the one who has the power to authorize salary increases and taxes or to cut them off; someone who can release people or have them strangled, one who may question but never be questioned. His long arm extends everywhere, taking and giving as he sees fit. He has eyes in every nook and cranny, and he alone is both ruler and overseer.

This waiting room is like the way of life itself. You're left standing behind the walls, while the lord of the state kitchen forces you to mark time by the beats of your own heart. It leaves you feeling distraught, shattered, and utterly impotent, trying to remain patient as you swallow your anger along with your spittle. The point of it all is to make you doubt both who you are and why you're there: you start to think about what it was you said that was inappropriate or what mistake you might have made. The tissue of rumors about you has turned into a veritable volcano of royal aggravations, then full-scale disasters.

If the postulant in attendance is wealthy, he should use some of it to purchase means of defense and prestige from the sultan. Otherwise he'll end up deprived of his entire wealth and sitting naked and bare-headed on the floor. The waiting person who comes from the intellectual sphere should not expect to use his scholarship in order to give himself airs or as a means of interceding on his own behalf; otherwise he'll be told that his knowledge is so many piles of wastepaper, and he can go away and sit on them. If this postulant happens to make a living by sword or pen, then he needs to cultivate an entrepreneurial approach. He needs to work out a way of reconciling an aspiration to hold an office above that of other people with the absolute requirement that he devote his attention totally and slavishly to the sultan with both tail and wings completely clipped; otherwise, of all people, he is the one whose head is the quickest to encounter the executioner's axe.

As the time crept toward later afternoon, I began to get tired of all this waiting and started looking at the faces of people passing by, sitting down, and waiting. Just like me, they all looked completely fed up with hanging around and guessing when their turn would come. Some of them were undoubtedly amirs and holders of high office, while others were merchants, poets, detectives, and murderers, all united in being slaves to salaries and boot-licking. They were all looking after their own interests with quaking heart and shaking hand, trying their level best to get more but forever scared of losing what they already had; it almost seemed as if on the one hand they regarded their possessions as being as valuable as their own eyesight and children, while on the other they were scared of them like some plague or evil personified. Under this particular regime more than others, the sultan neither confides nor trusts. His practice is to use a totally individualized method of turning the wheel of fortune or deprivation, something involving procedures that do not exclude treachery and death as means of dealing with people who had expected to find refuge in his shadow.

Fortunately for me, I didn't know a single one of the people waiting, nor they me—even though certain heads bowed in my direction from afar, no doubt acknowledging my judicial garb, that being the usual way I look to government personnel and its other denizens.

Once time started to weigh on me like lead, I went over to the chief guard and made it clear that I would really like my audience with the sultan to be hurried up. He gave me a withering look and led me to understand that he was deeply offended by my remark. I should wait my turn even if it took days.

The arts of being sultan are many, and the means of putting people down are no less numerous. Anyone given the honor of meeting the occupier of the throne will inevitably feel a sense of diminished respect and personal self-esteem; he feels an overpowering sense of insignificance. This is best effected by making people wait for ages until their shoulders sag and their backs are bent. At that point the best thing to do is to bend low and give up.

In order to fend off this growing sense of humiliation and contempt I developed a strategy of my own. I sat up straight, closed my legs, and cleared my throat. Staring up at the ceiling, I started putting a gloss on my particular virtues while dismissing any enumeration of my faults. I recalled that I had been treated with tremendous respect. In my own approach to the forthcoming meeting I chose to place the Circassian sultan within his own frame of reference, one removed from all the trappings of the sultanate and monarchical rule. As a result, he emerged as a slave who would have been bought and sold before being manumitted. It had only been by purest chance that he had then managed to seat himself on his throne. I imagined this exemplar of the sultanate, named Barquq, staring at me with his bulging eyes and asking me the question that he had been keeping for me: "During your pilgrimage, what was it that you prayed for on my behalf?" In my mind I started concocting a whole chorus of entreaties that I had framed in rhymed prose, the majority of them culled from things I had omitted to say about him when I was serving as professor and judge.

What brought me back from these mental ramblings was a voice calling out my name and rank, with instructions to proceed. I immediately gathered myself together and headed toward the door. Escorted by two slaves, I made my way through and reached a small hall lit by a number of candles. I was greeted by someone holding onto the dividing curtain, called the *hurdadar*. He started embracing me in a most peculiar fashion and rubbing my body with his hands as though searching for weapons or the like. It was only when I made clear my annoyance that he stopped. Such extreme caution and security measures have now become a normal procedure with the Mamluks—heaven help us all!

Suddenly the curtain was pulled back, and my name and rank were called out twice. The man gestured to me to follow him into a large arcade, punctuating his steps with bowings as he did so, while for my part I bowed slightly in the general direction of the sultan who was seated on his throne. The arcade was of the kind I had come to recognize in this huge palace, with windows looking out onto the stables. As was usual on occasions such as this, al-Zahir Barquq was surrounded by a cohort of amirs and scribes who were standing, while behind him were arrayed yeomen, guards, and retainers.

The sultan gestured to me to take some things from his food table, so I did so, choosing just a little of what was available. I chewed and swallowed it all as fast as possible, then washed the traces of meat, cheese, and sweetmeats off my fingers. I was then invited to step forward and did so. He greeted me in his usual fashion by banging his sleeve on my shoulder and asking in Turkish how I was. In reply I expressed my profuse thanks and my great pleasure at seeing him again, going to enormous lengths in acknowledging my gratitude to him as the great provider and sustainer, the all-powerful shepherd of his people. The pupils of the sultan's roving eyes looked moist and sleepy, as though he had been spending some of the time while I was waiting for an audience with him having a delicious nap or else consorting with a group of women from his harem. With those same two eyes he pronounced me blessed for completing my pilgrimage.

"So what precisely did you pray for on our behalf," he asked, "in these times when dark clouds are gathered and strife and unrest are raising their ugly heads again?"

Overcoming my sense of panic, I contrived an utterly artificial response: "My lord, may you be pleased, between Safa and Marwa, on Mount 'Arafat, in every holy place and on every occasion, I prayed that you be granted victory over your foes and power to implement your plans and projects. I yelled: 'O God, Answerer of Prayers, bolster with Your glory "Sultan al-Zahir, the mighty, the powerful, great leader of federations and peoples, inspirer of all kinds of glory, very sword of God unleashed against the infidel foe, source of mercy for his servants administered with a gentle care." With Your great power, O God, enable "the lord of crowns, thrones, and pulpits, of lofty arcades, palaces, and colleges, the monarch, supported by sharp-edged swords, pointed spears, and pens that suckled their glory from the inkwell's cradles." O Lord, bring under Your protection "the Commander of the Faithful, and acquaint him with the fruits of Your care in what he receives and dispenses; in this world, provide him with a happy outcome and in the next, the joys of those who dwell in paradise. O Lord, make good fortune his constant companion and glory his confidant. Be his protector and helper as he carries out his duties toward Muslims. Let them learn that his days will be long and his rule will be everlasting."' Later in the ceremonies, I proclaimed: "'O God, in the sacred name of Your Prophet, Lord of the Messengers, I beg You to protect our sultan against the adversities of fate and to grant the realms of Islam the boon of his standards, spears, and swords. Provide him with comfort in himself and his children, in his entourage and grandees, his own coterie and his people as a whole." Amen, Amen, O Noblest of Answerers, O Lord of the Universe.'"

As I finished, I raised my hands in prayer, whereupon the sultan and the entire assembly followed suit. All the while, I kept saying to myself, "O Lord, You know full well that throughout my pilgrimage I was only praying for Umm al-Banin. I beg You to pardon this lie of mine and to take everything into account when the account is to be reckoned."

Barquq now sat on the ground in front of his throne and made me sit beside him on his rugs and cushions. "Everyone's straining to listen to us," he whispered in my ear, "and everyone's eyes are watching carefully."

"Fine, blessed pilgrim," he went on out loud. "You prayed for me in various ways, but it's still the case that dark clouds have gathered. Strife and unrest are raising their ugly heads again!"

"O God," I replied in a whisper, "Creator of Punishment and Preserver of Order, please grant that Our lord may be protected against covert plots and terror; expose to the clear light of Your day all agents of intrigue and revolt. O God, grant Our lord protection against those who are sick at heart and bent on trouble, against the deeds of all wolves, dogs, and accursed bastards. O God, bring down Your wrath on all who harbor hateful thoughts, agents with seditious tendencies. O Lord, let their guile be their downfall and grant us victory over their demons. Amen!"

The sultan duly thanked me and charged me with praying a great deal on his behalf during my own devotions. He also thanked me for giving him advice as to how to tame the Maghrib—such a recalcitrant horse—and then bring it firmly within his fold. That said, he leaned over toward me.

"Before you left on the pilgrimage," he said, his eyes half-closed, "you had an amanuensis who sat with you during your retreats and took dictation based on your erudite comments."

Taking advantage of his sudden silence, I answered his comment with its implicit question by saying that indeed I had used al-Hihi as my amanuensis. I went on to extol his qualities and his complete lack of guile or suspicion.

"Well," the sultan interrupted with words that came as a shattering blow, "he's dead. May you live long!"

"Out of regard for the respect we have for you," he continued as he made to stand up, "we have given orders that he is to be buried in the Mamluk graveyard. 'Verily we belong to God, and unto Him do we return!'"

With that I stood and received some further pats from his sleeve in gratitude. The *ustadhdar* was told to take care of me, while the muezzin announced the call to afternoon prayers.

The sultan now left the arcade surrounded by his retinue and followed by various officials as he made his way to the mosque. I joined this throng, making full use of it to protect me from the pain in my joints that would afflict me every time I heard some terrible news or witnessed a distressing scene. The pain I felt this time lingered much longer because it was especially severe: that Hammu al-Hihi was dead and thus Umm al-Banin, his wife, was now a widow. O God, we beg You to show us Your mercy!

Once the afternoon prayer was over, the *ustadhdar*, chief yeoman, and some of his guards escorted me to the gate of the Citadel where two servants were waiting, watching over a splendid gray mule equipped with saddle blanket, mantle, heavy bridle, and polished saddle. Handing me a document to sign, the *ustadhdar* told me that the mule was a gift from the sultan. I asked him to express my profound thanks to the sultan, and then he left. With that, the yeoman came over and congratulated me on completing the pilgrimage and on the gift I had received. He then proceeded to astonish me even further by telling me something that made my pain and sense of disorientation even worse. "My dear judge," he said, "our police has learned that the house of your late amanuensis, Hammu al-Hihi, is currently being occupied by a young man with no papers. He claims to be the widow's brother. Were it not for the fact that the lady has testified to that effect and for the esteem in which yourself are held, we would have expelled him a few days after his arrival on Egyptian soil. The reason for that is that on more than one occasion our agents have encountered him in suspicious circumstances, consorting with all sorts of undesirable elements. We know for sure that he's a hard-core transvestite, a genuine scoundrel who shows signs of an unstable mind. So I'd suggest making sure that he behaves properly, or else we're going to send him back where he came from."

I nodded my head in agreement. What was I supposed to say now that I had just received yet another piece of shattering information? Helped by the two servants I got on the mule. Giving it a tap, I muttered, "It won't be with you that I find any consolation or comfort." With that I headed for my house, preceded by two horsemen and my own worries and fears. At the door of the house there was Sha'ban waiting. He hugged and blessed me. Once he had stabled the mule for the night, he followed me into the lounge.

"The baggage from your blessed pilgrimage is in your bedroom, Master," he said. "Every package is still sealed, just as you sent it."

I responded to the old man in a tone replete with affection and sorrow. "And I shall show you your share of it, Sha'ban, a gift from Mecca the hallowed. But first tell me, when and how did Hammu al-Hihi die?"

"The anguish on your face told me you'd already heard the terrible news. Hammu—God have mercy on him—died on the morning of the last Great Feast. He had suffered a stroke and was confined to chair and bed."

"And how is Umm al-Banin?"

"Not doing well, sir, and that's the truth, not well at all! Because of her husband's death, of course, but also because of one of her brothers who's causing her nothing but grief."

"Tell me about this disastrous youth. After sunset prayers you'll accompany me to al-Hihi's house so that I can offer my condolences."

"Not then, if you'll forgive me. Let's go after the evening prayers. At that point the young vagrant will be out till dawn spending time in dens of iniquity and vice."

I decided to follow Sha'ban's plan. When the moment was right, I planned to question Umm al-Banin about her brother. I spent some time in my bedroom checking on my baggage, then sat there waiting till it was prayer time and darkness would afford me the cover I needed. I was hoping to unclog my brain and lighten the oppressive load that all this new information had placed on me.

Ever since Hammu al-Hihi and his wife had come to Egypt, they had lived together in a tiny house in the Masmuda quarter. It was there that he had died of a stroke, leaving a wife with no means of support as far as I was aware. Once Sha'ban had announced my arrival, I entered through the doorway to be warmly greeted by Umm al-Banin and congratulated on completing the pilgrimage. Her words of welcome managed to drown out my own expressions of condolence and sympathy. She insisted that I sit in an empty reception room. I did as she asked, but took Sha'ban with me. When I asked about Hammu's illness, she sat on the carpeted floor close by my knees. With tears in her eyes she told me in fits and starts how Hammu had sensed the onset of death even before its actual arrival; she had had to endure bitter feelings of impotence and rage in the face of the inevitable.

"Doctors, amulets, sorcerers, we tried them all," she said, "but it was no use."

"The believer is tried, Umm al-Banin," I said, "the believer is always being tested. Better than weeping is a belief in God. *He who created death and life so that He might test you as to who is the best in deeds.*

"But let me ask you, sir, what is my sin that I should be left alone and destitute in a strange land?"

That made Sha'ban break his silence. "You're in a Muslim country, Ma'am," he said in a tone of harsh reproof. "Not only that, but you are under the care and protection of our Master until such time as someone may come and seek your hand, God willing."

Those words of Sha'ban seemed to have been a cue for Umm al-Banin to grasp my hands in hers and to start weeping. She keened in a variety of tones the like of which I have never seen or heard when it came to the expression of the most intense emotion and world-weariness. By God, the tears shed by this woman sitting in front of me seemed for all the world like hope after despair or rescue from distress! Their warmth and fervor were just like a drop of the water of life itself. Did I have the right to stop it or to withdraw my hand from hers? Absolutely not.

Some considerable time passed, with each of us under the sway of an irresistible force. For Umm al-Banin it was prolonged tears, and Sha'ban did his best to use his own silence as a way of putting an end to it. For my part, I was profoundly affected and resorted to such intercessions as seemed appropriate. Had it been possible to extend the occasion till night's end, I would not have resisted or made excuses. However, when a servant brought in a tray, I was reminded that the situation had its own protocols and emotion its proper limits. I withdrew my hand, and things returned to normal. Even so, as Umm al-Banin dried her tears, she urged me to try her coffee and sweetmeats, and paid some attention to Sha'ban as well. A serene silence now prevailed, which I broke from time to time with prayers, supplications, and a sip from my glass. I was anxious to hear all the details about Hammu's illness, but I kept suppressing the urge to inquire any further so as not to give his widow sitting beside me the opportunity to indulge in yet more sobs and weeping. However, in spite of my best efforts, she seemed able to read my mind and started telling me about Hammu's courage in the face of his predestined fate. Sha'ban in turn described how the funeral and burial had been well handled thanks to the help of neighbors and some of the sultan's own servants. Every so often, Umm al-Banin said, "And that's all thanks to you, sir."

The time came for me to question her about her brother, a young man about whom I had heard nothing but bad.

There was a moment's pause. "My family in Fez is fine, God be praised," she said all in a rush. "They all heard about my husband's death, but the great distance has kept us apart. The only person who was able to come was my brother on my mother's side."

"You have a brother on your mother's side? Where is he now?"

She looked seriously worried and lowered her gaze. "Sha'ban knows a lot about him," she said. "I've never liked or accepted this brother of mine. My family sent him here to share my misery. If only they hadn't done it! Tell him, Sha'ban."

"Tell him, you say? Tell him what? About his debauched behavior? About his threats to beat me up if I don't leave him alone? About his cross-dressing and pseudo-female mischief? His drunkenness and lewd dancing in brothels? The things I know are better said by you."

It was obvious that Umm al-Banin was too embarrassed to talk about a subject that transgressed all normal bounds of modesty and decency. I saved her the task of saying any more by asking whether she wanted him to stay or to leave.

"This wretched boy is a thorn in my side," she said. "All night I try to forget about him; all day I spend serving him with hand and cash. If only I could find some way of getting rid of him, sir, I would gladly donate all my rings and bracelets to the cause."

"Leave the whole thing to me. I'll make use of the law and regulations set by our noble imams to find a way of getting rid of him. For the time being, I'm going to leave you in God's tender care. I will see you next week after I have made the necessary arrangements and paid my respect at Hammu's tomb in the graveyard."

Umm al-Banin clutched at my burnous and requested that I stay for dinner, but I declined by claiming that I needed to rest. With that she disappeared for a moment, then came back with the pile of documents that she said her late husband had commissioned her to hand over to me. It consisted of the record of the dictations recorded during the seven evenings. I told her that Sha'ban would soon bring her the gift I had brought back for her from the pilgrimage. She started kissing my hand, calling down blessings on me, and begging me to remember her and visit her house. As we left, I heard Sha'ban saying farewell: "Be patient, Ma'am, be patient. Were I my master's age, I would marry you in accordance with the custom of God and His Prophet."

As I made my way out of the house, an old woman gave me a penetrating stare; from her looks she seemed to be leaping to conclusions about my visit to Umm al-Banin's house and raising a whole flood of tricky questions about my motives. God preserve us from prying eyes. God, Protector of Honor, be my witness that I only visited al-Hihi's widow to offer my condolences. My hand will only ever be extended to her in order to offer assistance. O God, if I gave her interests preference during my pilgrimage and allowed my mind free rein in thinking of her, You alone know the contexts of people's minds. You are forgiving and merciful!

For an entire month, days and nights passed. I stayed at home either correcting the section of my history on the eastern region or examining al-Hihi's transcript of my dictation and making the odd marginal note or addition. Once again I found myself surveying the ongoing flow of events and there from the inability of texts to examine and comprehend them from every viewpoint. The world, be it external or internal—and I may well have said this on some occasion—needs constant, ongoing research. I don't consider individual efforts aimed at coming to grips with it to be sufficient, nor do I approve of talk about the impossibility of error or confusion and the irrelevance of specialized knowledge and emendation. Religious scholars are indeed heirs of the prophets, as the saying has it. All well and good, but only on condition that they humble themselves before God and leave the gates of independent judgment open for the enlightening rays of truth and the additions provided by later generations of those who cherish research and wisdom.

Where Umm al-Banin was concerned, my researches were of a different kind, a situation where heart and powerful feelings were in charge. Opening my eyes every morning, I would find them still moist with the vision that constantly preoccupied my attention and attracted my deepest affection; and all that was quite apart from the way in which the image of her haunted my moments of distraction and daydreaming.

As the month passed, I went to visit her with Sha'ban every Friday evening. Gradually I found myself becoming her protector and benefactor, meeting her needs with the maximum degree of subterfuge and concealment. Every time I sat and talked to her, I could feel my sense of responsibility toward her grow stronger. A precious trust for me to take on, a priority on my agenda, these were the terms I used to describe her to myself.

During the course of my visit at the end of that particular month, I was eager to tell Umm al-Banin that the text of her complaint against her brother now contained signatures from witnesses as to his unseemly behavior and the harm he was causing her. In reply she told me that he was actually asleep in a neighboring house. That took me aback, and I was not sure what to do next. Leaving at this point would be a sign of cowardice, while staying might well bring some unanticipated and undesirable consequences. I asked my hostess quietly what she thought should be done. "Let's cut it off at the head," she whispered in my ear, "and let whatever happens happen." I gave the whole thing a moment's more thought, invoking brain and instinct in the process. I decided that my equivocal situation inside Umm al-Banin's house did not give me the right to take on the police's role when it came to defending her. Were I to do that, a whole scandal might erupt around me, one that would give rumor-mongers and pranksters the juiciest of tidbits to play with. Just as I was standing up to leave, I saw the reprobate coming straight toward me. "Who's this?" he asked his sister. He was indeed just as I had heard him described: effeminate in appearance and talking and gesturing just like a woman. He seemed drunk and ready for trouble. Umm al-Banin was understandably distraught, but it was Sha'ban who intervened. "This is your master, you rogue!" he said. "The friend of your late brother-in-law."

I headed for the door and went outside, closely watched all the while by a group of women headed by the old woman I referred to earlier. As I went on my way, followed by my servant, I heard the threatening words of the young man behind me: "Ah me, I'm sick!" he shouted. "But for that, I'd have made a public spectacle out of you."

All the following day I kept thinking about this incident. That night, after I'd prayed the evening prayer, I sat Sha'ban down in front of me and had him share some food.

"This matter with Umm al-Banin and her brother is reaching a crisis point," I said. "If I get involved, all sorts of rumors will start flying. What do you think?"

Sha'ban sat there in silence till he had emptied his mouth. When he started talking, it was as if he had been saving his words for some time in anticipation of the right moment.

"Sir, the rumors have been flying ever since your first visit. I've been keeping the various bits of slander and sarcasm from you so as not to upset you too much. The best thing I can see for you to do is to marry her."

"Marry her? Are you out of your mind? I'm almost sixty, and she's not even thirty yet. Does that make any sense?

"There are a number of reasons why it makes sense. Just consider: firstly, you'll put a stop to all the slander and abuse; secondly, you'll be able to exert authority over her disaster of a brother; thirdly and most important of all, the woman is very fond of you and respects you. At first she admired you, but now she loves you. Go ahead and ask me, I know exactly what she has told me and in the clearest of terms. By God, no one loves you as much as she does. As far as the difference in age is concerned, my Master is well enough acquainted with the life of Our Lord, the Prophet, to render that irrelevant."

Something else occurred to me too: if I married her, then maybe, with God's permission, I would be able to fulfill my dearest wish for children. That way I could guarantee that my prayers for the very same thing on her behalf would not be wasted!

She certainly deserved to have a companion; indeed, she was worthy of everything that is good. She could take the place in my heart that had belonged to my first companion in mind and virtue, my first wife who had been swallowed up by the sea along with my children. Sha'ban's words had made that much clear to me. I asked him if he was sure she would not reject my offer of marriage.

"Reject your offer?" he replied in amazement. "If it were not for the bounds of propriety, modesty, and custom, she would have come running to ask for your hand. My dear blessed pilgrim, put your trust in God and fulfill your religious obligations as the law stipulates."

Before doing anything else, I decided to settle the problem of Umm al-Banin's brother by doing something decent for him. My notion was that he was really a poor wretch in need of some sympathy and help. I asked my servant to bring him secretly to a place in the Qarafah graveyard close by Hammu's tomb. And one day, just before sunset, that is precisely what happened.

When I took a close look at his face, which was not made up this time, I could see for myself how downtrodden and desperate he looked, for reasons I did not know. He may have been a young man, but his body looked emaciated and his expression was one of total despair, the look of someone about to be hanged. Since I had previously had to deal with all manner of Arab tyrants and rogues and had sometimes even managed to win them over, I had assumed that it would be fairly simple for me to straighten him out. But this situation now seemed a lot more complicated. The young man was clearly disturbed and sick; there was no room for doubt on that score. Homilies about proper behavior would be no more use than entrusting him to the care of doctors specializing in psychological disorders. The worst crime of all would be to yell and scream at him or to chase after him like some rabid animal; that would only manage to extinguish the remaining vestiges of that light which burns inside every human being. The best way to keep that light burning and even improve its brightness was to nurture it carefully with kind glances and gentle words. Then maybe it would blossom and grow.

I asked the young man what his name was and how he was feeling. He responded in a clear, gentle voice. I questioned him about Fez and its inhabitants, and he replied in terse phrases. He outlined for me the rampant corruption and harsh existence that had led many young people to leave and other folk to develop all kinds of stratagems and uncouth behavior. He added that such circumstances did not exempt well-educated people like himself nor even professional tradespeople.

The young man clearly seemed a lot more relaxed, something that Sha'ban may have helped bring about. Seizing the opportunity, I broached the topic of marriage.

"What would you say, Sa'd," I asked him quite openly, "about the idea of our becoming related by marriage?"

"Related by marriage? Do you have a daughter you're offering me?"

"No! I'm the one who wants to get married. I would like your permission to marry your sister, Umm al-Banin. I'm asking you in front of the tomb of her first husband, my friend Hammu al-Hihi— God have mercy on him."

"Umm al-Banin has spoken about you, blessed pilgrim, with a good deal of pride and admiration, so much so that it scares me sometimes. If she'll accept you, all I can do is offer you my blessings."

"Fine. Then, God willing, we will execute the vows and then look for ways to improve your situation."

Clasping his shoulder, I slid a purse of coins into his pocket. His eyes gleamed with joy, and he kissed my shoulder. With that I left and headed for the stables, followed by Sha'ban.

The beginning of Rajab in the year 790 was a date that I shall record in liquid gold and tears of joy; a date in a blessed month, one in which I felt I had been born again to find Umm al-Banin living in my own house. I had obtained two witnesses to testify to our marriage and organized a very simple wedding feast in the company of close friends and neighbors. God Almighty helped make all the arrangements very easy; even Sa'd, her brother, calmed down and kept a low profile, as though he had come to terms with his own self.

In the light of this happy event, I have found myself in a state that I can only describe as being almost drunk on love. I am totally infatuated with my new wife and the aura she brings with her; infatuated with my own sense of vigor and well-being; infatuated with the signs of beauty wherever they appear—in the smiles of children, the singing of birds, the gentle breezes wafting over the hungry soul and the bodies of all mankind.

I am incredibly happy, O how happy!

So great is my happiness, that, if it weren't for my Maliki beliefs and a God-driven determination never to pronounce the word "I," I would abandon all restraint and let it take flight in a welcome to all people and things!

So great is my happiness that, if I were a better poet than I am, I would compose it on my beloved's breast as garlands of light and passion!

As the saying goes: "Live in Rajab, and you'll see a wonder!"

A wonder indeed is the way my entire existence has been transformed from its normal dullness and misery to circles of brightness and felicity!

A wonder indeed is the way time slips by like water between my hands!

A wonder indeed is that I no-longer feel any pain in my joints, as though I never had any problem!

A wonder indeed is the return of my bodily desires after a prolonged period when I simply withdrew and abstained!

I have no doubt whatsoever that the person responsible for all these miracles and others is a woman; she it is who has lifted the curtain and served as catalyst, flooding waters, and great gift. But for her, I would still be displaying all the symptoms of depression and mourning; my desires and rights in life would all be bottled up inside me.

For all my shyness and my efforts at keeping things discreet, Umm al-Banin noticed the change in my demeanor and health. She took great pains to make me happy, and regularly prayed behind me, thanking God for His creation and blessings. Every Friday we both went to visit Hammu's tomb and pray for his departed soul.

There was just one blemish that suddenly reared its ugly head to spoil the serenity of my new married life, and I did my best to contain and handle it in as amicable a way as possible. It concerned Sa'd, Umm al-Banin's brother, who reverted to his old iniquitous ways. According to the neighbors at his sister's former house, he turned it into a den of rowdiness and sex.

"I warned you, sir," Sha'ban said in a tone of disapproval, "that the rascal would forget all about his promises to reform his behavior. All your words, all your generosity, are no good. Whatever you do, Satan will always breathe his poison into that man's nostrils. I think the best thing to do is to return the house he's living in to its owner and seek the help of the doctors in the mental hospital."

Sha'ban's advice seemed sound, and I got Umm al-Banin to agree to it. That done, I decided that it was essential to avoid any kind of compulsion or violence. With that in mind, I planned the entire operation with all the skill I had acquired from the realms of politics and writing. The entire matter was more subtle than the finest flour, harder than combing a virgin forest. To start with, I persuaded Sa'd that for the time being he should spend some time being treated in the Ibn Tulun Hospital and assured him that he would be well looked after there since I was acquainted with the director and some of the doctors. That done, I proceeded to make the arrangements and handed out whatever bribes and 'donations' were needed.

O Lord, it is not right that I should be living a life of such joy and happiness while depriving this wretched young man of my help and generosity. Nor it is right that there should be so many deficiencies in the world and so much rampant egotism. Nor is it right that the fire of life should reach some people as coolness and peace, while the great mass of humanity feels only suffering and searing heat.

Were I a lot younger, I would want to delve deep into the study of the interior world of mankind. I would search for the hidden causes of disturbances and imperfections in the mind, and then devote myself to finding cures and therapies. Unfortunately, however, I have little to offer on the topic.

Six months went by after my marriage to Umm al-Banin. The latter half of that year represented a turning point in my life and my understanding. I came to know my Lord in the beauty of His creation, male and female. More than ever before, I used to yell out, "Life, Our Lord did not create it for nothing." I rediscovered Ibn Qayyim al-Jawziya's work, *Meadow for Lovers*, and delved into it with confidence. My only interest was making the lover happy and placing her between heart and rib.

So I'll say it: Even though I'm almost sixty years old, love and life are two facets of a single blood. Anyone without love is without life. This too: Love and prayer are like conjoined twins; if you don't cloister yourself with the one, you miss the other and lose out on God's favor and welcome.

Ideas like these had definitely occurred to me when I was with my first wife, but their impact and integrity were negatively affected by external distractions and the enticements of rank. Today, however, such thoughts have come to occupy center stage in all their glory.

So many matters and activities that I used previously to ignore or pass by I now find myself paying attention to: food, for example, drink, clothes, walks, and old buildings.

I now know the names of all the food and drink that Umm al-Banin prepares for me. They're all of excellent quality and, because they're beneficial and easily digested, they're much prized by me. When they're brought to me, all I can do is offer my thanks and admiration, since they clearly represent the best of this earth's fruits and a harbinger of those others in the Garden of Eden.

I have always been anxious to wear clothes that were fairly plain in both color and design. But when Umm al-Banin chooses them or sews them herself, the quality is measurably higher. What is more, she uses the nicest powders in scenting them.

Then there are the walks and buildings; O my heart, tell us your story, although words would probably fail us. Here too, my wife is primarily responsible because she loves to go out on walks. Needless to say, Sha'ban gets some of the credit too. I've discovered that she knows a number of monuments and buildings in Cairo and Fustat, many of which I had only heard of by name. When I asked her how she came to have seen so many of them, she confessed that, when Hammu al-Hihi, her first husband, had become sick, he had asked that they go on strolls as a way of relieving his depression. She had accompanied him, either trailing his wheelchair or else in boats or on mules. That's how she had come to visit Roda Island, and even Giza and the pyramids.

One day in the month of Shawwal, I went on a journey of rediscovery, seeing parts of Cairo through my wife's eyes. Wearing my burnous, I walked at a slow pace while my wife followed close behind wearing her Maghribi jallabiya and veil. No sooner had we left our quarter of al-Mahmudiya than she became the one walking ahead of me as though leading a horse. We went in one gate and out another, just as though she were going in the door of her home in either Fez or Cairo. We made a tour of Cairo, from Bab al-Faraj to Bab al-Mahruq, passing by Bab al-Qantara, Bab al-Futuh, Bab al-Nasr, and Bab al-Barqiya. At every one of these city gates we would look at a promenade, a famous quarter, a shrine, or a mosque. Then we made our way through al-Zahir's gardens. We were entranced as we took in the tall palms and azarole trees with their wonderful scent and birds chirping away. Myrtle, roses, eglantine, willow, jasmine, and many other gorgeous scented plants—we savored them all. The blooms were all open and radiant, providing light, dewdrops, bees, and butterflies to the delighted passerby; the best of them, said my companion, could only be seen in dreams—how true! Their colors and shapes grew in such rich profusion that the human imagination could only grasp their beauty in terms of a gift to mankind from their primary Giver.

Via the Turjuman and Baha' al-Din quarters teeming with people, we passed by a number of streets, markets, and stores before finally reaching the Mosque of al-Hakim. We stepped into a supply store, and I insisted on buying a length of cloth that Umm al-Banin chose, and others in the Beggars' Market and Bayn al-Qasrayn where at her request I bought a pomegranate. At a copyist's stall I inquired after an Egyptian copy of Ibn Hazm's *The Dove's Neckring.*

Every time my wife and I found ourselves caught in a crowd, she would lean over and say to me, "It's Gog and Magog!" To tell the truth, there were indeed so many people living and moving so close together that it was a real crush of legs; moving was so difficult, it was like the Day of Gathering itself. At that point, I began to get concerned and pulled my wife toward me; I was worried at the way passersby were looking at her and felt a bit on edge in case something unexpected happened. Fortunately only a few wayward eyes stared in our direction; they must have assumed that the woman at my side was my daughter or something like that.

I sat down on a small bench in front of the main entrance to the Mosque of al-Hakim; after the rigors of our walk I needed a respite. Umm al-Banin sat down in front of me telling me about her visits to the mosque with her late husband, Hammu. They had visited this mosque just as often as the Azhar, the shrine of Sayyida Zaynab, and the tomb of al-Husayn.

"Is it true," she asked me, "that this mosque was built by a tyrant?"

"Yes," I replied.

"Did he really stop women leaving their houses?"

"That and more. He ruthlessly destroyed people's lives, inverted the clock, and banned astrology and singing."

"By God, if I'd been alive during his reign, I'd have shown him how women from Fez do things. . . ."

I tried hard to suppress a hearty laugh, but was only partly successful, particularly when this woman from Fez went on to ask me in all seriousness, "This al-Hakim, the builder of this mosque, was he Barquq's father or grandfather?"

I promised to tell her when we got home. We continued on our way, while I muttered to myself that history and Umm al-Banin were clearly two diametrical opposites that would never come together. So I pray You, God, to keep her as innocent as she is and well rid of information about kings and eras.

On Bayn al-Qasrayn I showed my wife the big palace and the minister's residence and then pointed out the Salihiya College where I had taught three years earlier.

"I am really terribly ignorant, 'Abd al-Rahman," she confided as she leaned toward me. "You're laughing at me. . . . "

"God forbid," I replied. "I would never laugh at someone like you who is so eager to learn. What made me laugh in front of the al-Hakim Mosque was something quite different. My dear Umm al-Banin, the builder of that mosque was mentally ill and used to use his ever-changing moods and stories from old women as instruments of rule."

"Stories from old women?"

"Yes, he used to get all kinds of information from deep inside people's houses, most especially those of senior officials in the government. He was able to use the information the old women provided to find out all their reprobate habits involving eating and sex. They all assumed he must be some kind of sorcerer who could read the unseen."

My wife smiled broadly.

"That's what made me laugh," I went on, seizing the moment.

We made our way through alleys, squares, and markets till we reached Bab al-'Id Square; via Darb al-Salami and Darb Mulukhiya we reached the tomb-mosque of al-Husayn. Here I told my wife the story of al-Husayn's severed head, which affected her deeply. With that we went over to al-Azhar Mosque. Each of us went to the appropriate side to pray. When I came out, I found Umm al-Banin buying a pomegranate from an itinerant salesman, while a handsome young man kept hovering around her. That made me really angry. Without pausing to think, I grabbed the young man by the arm and told him to go away. He slunk away, but not before asking a hurtful question: "Are you her father? I'm prepared to ask for her hand in front of witnesses." Suppressing my fury, I went over to my wife. If it hadn't been for the number of people staring at us, I would have hidden her inside my cloak so as to avoid all the rude gestures that were being aimed in my direction. I scolded her for buying yet another pomegranate, when we had already purchased one before. She told me that for a few days now she had felt a craving for pomegranates; the sensation she felt was overpowering.

We arrived home safely and found Sha'ban anxiously awaiting our return. Removing my cloak and shoes I collapsed on the bench. Umm al-Banin disappeared inside for a moment and came out with a bowl of warm water. She started rubbing my feet in the water, something she had done for me regularly ever since we were married; she paid particular attention to ankles and toes. I had told her previously that, whenever my late wife had been cooking, resting, or taking a cure, she had regaled me with her own spontaneous remarks. So now Umm al-Banin proceeded to do likewise, adding some categories of her own, whose secrets she had learned from women in Fez, including telling jokes—'yarns' as we used to call them.

I asked Sha'ban to prepare lunch for us. He was delighted and took his time over it. I made use of the opportunity to convince Umm al-Banin that she should leave some of the household chores to my aged servant. Then he would not get bored with sitting around with nothing to do; that would make him forget the idea that we did not need him any more. Tyrannical regimes are bad in politics, I told her, and they are just as bad in household management. She relented and supported my position, promising to slow down a bit and take advice, something al-Hakim, the builder of the mosque, had never done.

I had to take a nap, and did so in the bedroom before the time came for afternoon prayers. While I was dozing, a thought occurred to me about incipient old age, the first signs of which I had glimpsed during our morning walk. On the basis of such early symptoms I came to the conclusion that it involved having one foot in the grave and the other in a state of patience; a gradual process of finding movement increasingly trying to the point of impossibility, all that accompanied by a distressing realization that it was actually happening. Death consisted simply in a confirmation of rigidity brought on by a lack of awareness of the body.

In order to keep pace with my wife and make her happy in intimate as well as public matters, I would need, as of today, to keep old age's clutches at bay and thwart all efforts launched by

decrepitude and weakness to gain control of my body. I would have
to follow the lead of old people who were fit and well, seeking aid
and sustenance from Him who is Eternal and Alive. O God, I
beseech You not to cover my head with too many gray hairs, nor to
weaken whatever strength of mind and body I have left!

Somewhat resentfully, I got up and joined my wife on the roof
veranda overlooking the Nile. She was sitting there modestly contemplating, all the while devouring a pomegranate and staring at her
stomach. When she realized I had come up, she told me somewhat
bashfully that she really wanted some pears and cake. I ask Sha'ban
to go to the closest market and get some. Just then she started crying like a baby. I asked her if she wanted some more fruit or sweetmeats, but she hid her face in her hands and seemed surprised that I
did not seem to realize why she was having these cravings. For a
moment she hesitated, but then stuttered out her wonderful news:
"I'm pregnant, 'Abd al-Rahman, pregnant!" I was so overjoyed that
I almost started crying too; I had never seriously thought that this
could happen.

"So you're pregnant, Umm al-Banin!" I said, hugging her to me.
"Have you made quite sure?"

"The signs are all there. I can tell and so can the midwife."

"*Pray to Me and I will answer you.* All praise and thanks to my
Lord!"

The kind of joy that I could now see making my wife cry was
something the like of which I had never witnessed before. I can offer
it as a definition of life itself. Life requires of us that we be willing
to accept it as it is and offer it tokens of generosity and happiness.
Joy and energy must win the battle against gloom and restraint.

Sha'ban came back with the things he had been asked to get and
a tray of coffee. I stood up and hugged him, whispering the good
news in his ear along with instructions to help Umm al-Banin
around the house. He was excited and offered me blessings, prayed
that she would have a safe delivery, then withdrew. I started sipping
my coffee, while my pregnant wife wiped the tears from her face
now smudged with kohl and bits of cake.

Ever since I found out about my wife's pregnancy, I've been
counting time in days, living a life of excitement and anticipation.

110

So worked up have I become at the thought of life growing inside my wife's womb that I have found neither the energy nor interest to keep up with events or follow recent developments, however significant they may have been and wherever they may have occurred. The process of waiting while an embryo changes from an unseen force into a visible reality is something that demands as much concentration as possible. During this waiting period I've occasionally had the chance to look over my papers with a view to editing and correction, adding a thought or note here and there by way of illustration or explanation. I've also been staying up a lot at night, performing the required prayers and reading extracts from Ibn Hazm's *The Dove's Neckring*, Ibn Qayyim's *Meadow for Lovers*, and Abu al-Faraj's *Book of Songs*. Most of the time I have been making preparations and feeling scared, listening to Sha'ban's advice and observing everything the man does. I have no doubt in my mind that he fully deserves to enter paradise without any further reckoning.

By the time of the Great Feast in this same blessed year, Umm al-Banin had entered the sixth month of her pregnancy and had thus passed the most difficult and risky period. We spent the feast day itself in the usual way. At noon we welcomed visitors from the sultan's retinue and Maghribi folk resident in Cairo who offered us blessings on this sacred day. The next day I went to visit some of our neighbors and indigent folk, before heading to Ibn Tulun Hospital to check on Sa'd and see if he needed anything. What a dire story I was to hear!

Everyone there informed me that my brother-in-law was in a terrible state. He had started refusing all food, having already refused to take his medicine or to say anything. I asked one of the doctors if there was anything he could do to cure Sa'd's condition. In reply he said that it was always difficult, and, when the symptoms were combined in certain ways, well nigh impossible, because everything was that much more complicated. I asked him what needed to be done. He told me that, till some kind of miraculous recovery might take place, what was needed was a program of forced feeding. Accompanied by two guards I went into Sa'd's room which was actually more like a prison cell or hermit's room. He lay there spreadeagled on the bed like a rigid corpse, staring up at the ceiling which was marked with blotches of dampness and paint. I sat down beside him and tried to get his attention, but without success. I gently pulled back the blanket and was horrified to see his body so emaciated, with protruding bones and limbs tied to the bed, exuding the stench of disease and sweat. I asked the guards why he needed to be restrained and was told that it was to prevent him trying to commit suicide again.

Good God, is it conceivable for a man to die in such dreadful circumstances!

Holding back tears, I leaned over Sa'd's prostrate form and asked him if he knew my name, but without result. Then I launched into a call for help, a plea, something that seemed to emerge from every bone in my body: "I beg you by God, I beseech You by all that is precious and dear, to let me know Your wishes."

I repeated this several times till I grew weary of it. Eventually the young man answered me in a quavering tone that sounded as if it was coming from the bottom of a well: "I want my share of light and open space, my portion of the sun's abundance and wings of darkness."

His reply sounded to me like Satan's own whisper or the ravings of a madman, but for the moment I held such notions in abeyance.

"How can I bring you those shares, Sa'd?" I asked.

He looked at me with eyes that were a picture of the profoundest despair. "Get me out of this prison!" he yelled with all the strength he could muster.

All questions and conditions become otiose in the face of someone who is on the very brink of collapse. Without even a moment's pause for thought, I promised that next day I would take him out of the hospital. I said I would fulfill my promise provided that he ate some lunch and let people administer some first aid. How relieved and happy I felt when I glimpsed some signs of relief on his face!

I told the guards to take off his restraints, and they did so, albeit with a certain hesitation. They then prepared some good food for which I paid generously. Once the patient had eaten the food with considerable difficulty, I asked the guards to wash him with soap and hot water. With that I kissed him and promised to come back as soon as possible. I headed for the door and went to the director's office.

"Is this supposed to be a hospital where people are cured," I asked in an aggravated tone, "or a collection point for the dead?"

"Calm down, sir," the man replied. "Wasn't it you who put the patient in our hands?"

"Yes, but that was so you could cure him, not destroy him."

"We have used every method at our disposal. What we've discovered is that he's completely out of his mind. He's a danger to himself and others."

"So he's sentenced to a life of total inactivity?"

"The public interest must come first. Keeping people who are liable to infringe it is an absolute obligation under law. Isn't that your area of specialization, Judge?"

"In my opinion the preservation of delegated interests does not under any circumstance require the killing of a human soul. But enough talk. I'll be back tomorrow to take my brother-in-law out of this hospital."

"Leaving is not as easy as entering, good pilgrim."

"What do you mean? I've paid the costs of his time here and more. Are you trying to stop me taking him away and saving him from an inexorable death here?"

"Steady on, sir! You can take him out, but only if you pay an indemnity in cash and sign a duly sworn statement."

"A bribe to get him out! How much?"

"Three thousand dinars for the former, and a thousand for the latter."

"Say: *Nothing will ever beset us unless God has prescribed it for us*. By the will of Him who tarries but never neglects, we can settle things tomorrow."

Quashing my anger I set out for home. Bribery and corruption on the way in and out, everywhere you look! A pox on all forms of organization that have to rely on such venality!

Umm al-Banin asked me why I was in such a bad mood. I decided not to tell her the whole story, not wanting to give her a shock in case it led to highly undesirable consequences.

During the night just before I went to sleep, I thought of asking my friends in the palace to get the indemnity for releasing my brother-in-law cancelled, but I soon abandoned the idea so as not to make the whole thing even more complicated and risky. There might be a lot of chit-chat and awkward questions to deal with, all of which would reflect badly on me.

Next morning I found myself thinking again about the idea that had occurred to me last night, namely of asking Shaykh Abu 'Abdallah Muhammad, the Sufi from Sale, and a follower of the Maliki rite, for advice; he and I together used to take care of legal issues for people from the Maghrib. In the early morning I made my way to his small convent, which was outside Cairo, close to the western canal. As soon as we had sat down together over a pot of bitter mint tea, I broached the topic without any preliminaries. In great distress I told him about the tragedy of Sa'd's life and let him know that in my view he was not acting of his own volition; any change in his condition could only come about through the will of God's pious saints.

For a moment he remained silent, then kissed me with a gleaming smile on his face, the kind of smile that makes it possible for one to endure any hardship and suggests that there can be a way out of any difficulty.

"Take it easy, Wali al-Din," he said, "take it easy. First of all, tell me about the government officials. How far have their personal cravings taken them up till now?"

I was surprised by the shaykh's interest in the people he was asking about. After all, government officials and religious shaykhs are two different species who rarely have anything to do with each other.

"They all seem to be fine, Shaykh Abu 'Abdallah," I replied somewhat tersely and with as much confidence as I could muster. "The truce between them all is still working, and their swords remain in their scabbards."

"That's not what I've heard. I don't know whether you actually don't know or don't want to tell me, but you should be aware that the atmosphere between Yalbugha al-Nasiri and Barquq is going from bad to worse; there's bound to be conflict between the two of them. You should start thinking which one of them you're going to back, which horse you want to win."

Umm al-Banin's pregnancy had, it would appear, distracted my attention from other matters, with the result that this Sufi shaykh knew more about world affairs than I did. But for the fact that I am forced to wander my way along the corridors of power, I would be extremely happy with the ways things are. I asked the shaykh why he was so involved in current events.

"That may be," he replied, "because I was born and grew up in Rigraga close by the sea, a region much affected by sudden changes in weather. The port is always full of ships except when the winter storms blow up. I can still picture scenes of the way the sea used to get roiled by the wind. Even the poor there separate into different groups and sects. In summary, some of them take Sufism to imply a complete denial of worldly things and mortification of the senses, while others choose to see it as represented by the generous hand of God Himself, standing alongside His servants, their necks outstretched to achieve the precious values of beauty, truth, and justice. God willing, I see myself as belonging to the latter group, not the former. Then doesn't religion involve rituals and behavior: some time for one, some time for the other? My day is spent on both aspects until I manage to encounter the visage of my Lord, the Generous and Mighty."

"Wonderfully said, Abu 'Abdallah. May you be blessed."

"Now tell me about the matter you're concerned about."

"It's about my brother-in-law who is somewhat deranged."

"Yes, in both the Maghrib and here I've seen patients in yet worse states than that of your brother-in-law. Here's the conclusion I've come to: such mental problems will never be cured by resorting to violence, isolation, or cauterization. You have to let the patient tell the story and reveal the agonies he is suffering. Once that is done, you need to nurse the condition with tender, caring words so that you can track down the thread that is tying the various biles and fumes together into a noxious mixture. Understanding is what's needed, that and nothing more. With God's aid that's the path to a cure."

I was anxious to make quite sure I understood what he meant. "What is to be done then, Abu 'Abdallah?" I asked.

"He shouldn't be either in your house or in the hospital. Instead he should come here to my convent. Along with my other students

I can teach him to fear God and seek His protection in his personal struggles. *As for the one who fears the station of His Lord and denies the soul its fancies, Paradise is the refuge*—the Lord of Mankind has spoken truly."

"My own hope in God Almighty and in you is great. But suppose the young man keeps on causing trouble and doesn't repent?"

"In that case, I'll recommend that you send him for a while to the Qalandariya Mosque outside Bab al-Nasr."

I was well aware that the adherents to that particular sect belonged to the Malamatiya movement, a group that considers itself liberated from all conventions regarding conduct and conversation and licensed to indulge in activities forbidden by both religion and custom. All of which made people shun and censure them. However, for the time being I refrained from questioning the shaykh's reference to them, preferring at this stage to show my delight at the offer he had made. I stood up and showered his head with kisses, while he asked God's forgiveness for such expressions and kissed my shoulder in turn.

The sun was barely over the horizon before I had removed Sa'd from the hospital on the terms stipulated by the director and left him in the care of the Moroccan shaykh—may God prolong his life. I also made Sa'd very happy by carrying out all the promises I had made.

I performed the evening prayer in the al-Azhar Mosque, then returned joyfully to my wife. She had been worried by my absence. Once she had calmed down somewhat, I decided to tell her everything about her brother. She was delighted to hear what I had done and blessed me for it, while I drew her close to me and felt her enlarged belly.

As I lay down to go to sleep, I felt a severe pain in my joints which affected my back. This time it was so bad that I was not able to hide it from Umm al-Banin, so I told her, all the while cursing the scars and wounds of political life. "We'll cure it with cups!" she shouted. She laid me on my stomach and brought out a small box from under the bed. Opening it she took out some cups, moistened them with kohl, filled them with translucent wax which she lit with a match, and put them on the places that ached. The warmth felt very good, and I asked for more until I felt very relaxed. While she was rubbing my back with aloewood oil, I must have fallen into a deep sleep, ever grateful to my wife.

On the tenth day of Muharram, 'Ashura' Day, I thought about accompanying my wife on visits to some Shi'i monuments. I asked her to choose between the shrines of Zayn al-'Abidin, Sayyida Nafisa, and Umm Kulthum. "In each one of them," I told her, "the government expects people to weep over the slaying or exclusion of members of the holy family, but the scent of musk is what lingers there the longest."

But Umm al-Banin—how sensible and calm she is—decided not to take me up on the suggestion for fear of exhausting herself or even bringing on labor unexpectedly when she was far away from the midwife.

"'Abd al-Rahman," she went on, "have you forgotten perhaps that I'm in my seventh month? My heart tells me that my daughter is going to be a seven-monther just like me."

"A girl you say? Who told you that?"

"Her gentle movements and the midwife's probings. What do you say we name her al-Batul, like my late mother?"

I hugged her to me and kissed her on the forehead. Not being a successor of those pre-Islamic people who regarded the birth of a daughter as a bad sign, I repeated to myself the words of the noble prophetic hadith. "Do not show your dislike for girls. They are precious companions."

"We're going to be happy with our baby," I said, "whether it's a boy or girl. We'll name this seven-monther whatever you like—thanks be to God who knows the world of the unseen!"

We ate breakfast. I decided to stay at home for a few days so as to be near Umm al-Banin when she was about to give birth and also close to my books and papers.

I now secluded myself in my library and started prioritizing my readings. I wanted to get things organized in my mind so that I could continue writing the chapter on the Mamluks for *The Book on the Lessons of History* and also my autobiography, *Information on Ibn Khaldun and His Travels East and West*. Research on the Mamluks, these erstwhile slaves who go on to become rulers, took up all my time. I even started using two authors at once, but only on points where they both agreed, all the while struggling to deduce significant ideas from the wealth of information and data about events. But no one should get the impression that my reason for working this way was to fill up time or because I felt the onset of old age. To the contrary, there were two major reasons. One of them is general: namely that future generations should be able to profit from another cycle in the long heritage of historical lessons. The other is more personal, and I must admit it here so as to avoid any ambiguity: I have this tendency to adjust my understanding of events to my own sense of self-preservation, as a kind of protective shield against an entirely futile end, be it slow or swift. It is something that never fails to hurl me headlong into the grinder of caprices and the arena of clashing swords. As a result, I either find myself banished and sent into the wilderness of exile, or else I'm cut into two pieces and my shoulders are dislocated. Here is the way I put it:

> Whenever politics becomes a craft used for deceitful purposes and an instrument for wreaking havoc and death, religious scholars should remove themselves from the scene to the maximum extent possible. That is what I have deduced from my own experiences in the Maghrib, and, ever since my arrival in Egypt as a refugee, I have detected the very same forces at work. Furthermore, I can say that the long arm of the Mamluk regime of this region has no rivals when it comes to the fierce support of both allies and mercenaries—something I term 'solidarity of convenience and clientage.' Once launched and enhanced, that phenomenon can easily rival other types of group solidarity in inciting one group to behave aggressively toward others and inflicting patterns of murder and sequestration. Religious scholars, even those who turn to the mystical path or resort to the apparently secure shade of neutrality and discretion, cannot avoid involvement in this crushing and destructive pattern of group identity, unless, that is, they are to go crazy or lose their minds entirely. When dealing with the ruler, the religious scholar has no alternative but to be either with him or

against him. Any third way is a lost cause. This is what I have
come to realize since I came to Egypt. It's for that reason that I let
the *atabeg*, Altunbugha al-Jubani, enroll me as a member of al-
Zahir Barquq's retinue so that this Mamluk sultan would include
me within the framework of his general protection and supply me
with salary and food. Whenever he throws his fits of kingly anger,
I am reminded of the fact that I am totally indebted to him for my
daily bread and the very fact that I'm alive. God is my witness
that, while I may be a part of this enforced indemnity, I have done
my level best to remain as aloof and cautious as I can. I have kept
my glowing encomia to a minimum and, to the extent possible, I
have steered clear of politics and not indulged in all its 'alarums
and excursions.'

This is my statement about the absolute requirement that one look
closely at the particulars of the regime currently in power, something that, as a matter of personal incentive, involves a consideration of my own future in the light of all this political turmoil.

The information that I have collected and the conclusion I have
drawn from it lead me to state that for people who find themselves
with their heads in the noose of this Mamluk regime, daily life is in
the hands of a totally unpredictable demon. Anyone who has lived
through circumstances in which banishment and execution have
become basic features of justice and law will know precisely what I
mean. Not even chess players, professional diviners, and *zir*
aficionados are safe. Disasters can strike when you least expect it,
and punishment and mercy alternate with each other like night and
day. You can be clobbered at random, and then you're pardoned
without warning. The entire situation is controlled by whim; say
that and you've got it. As you stumble on your way among blind
people with their sticks and a thick knot of binding ropes, your task
is to manage your life and see your path ahead as best you can. All
the while you are hoping and praying that your own star is somehow
in the ascendant and misfortune is currently preoccupied somewhere else.

I have written quite a bit to describe the visible side of the history of the two Mamluk dynasties, the Bahri and the Burji. As usual,

I've focused on the sultans, their appointments, depositions, raids, and conquests; on disasters and murders too, all interspersed with revolts and insurrections. Steering my way between the actual course of events and the murky area of suppositions, I have managed, through a lucky chance, to focus on a tangible element relevant to al-Zahir Barquq, one that has served me well when things have become especially trying. This particular sultan has tended to use mercy as a display of his power, and only to resort to violence in measured ways and after due deliberation. Unlike the tiger sultans, you'll only find him shedding blood when it is absolutely necessary. When he has won a victory, he tends to give back to his vanquished rivals their positions, salaries, and estates and only to impose a minimum degree of prison time or official reprimand. That's how he behaved, for example, with Baraka, his first partner in government who launched a revolt against him. He thought it was enough punishment to imprison him in Alexandria, where someone assassinated him without permission. It was the same with al-Nasiri, his deputy in Aleppo and the most dangerous of his rivals from the Yalbughwiya.

I have tried to understand the secret behind this particular aspect of his personality, and can only assume that it lies in the period before he became sultan. He is a manumitted slave from abroad who has lived a life of indigence and deprivation; he has known corruption, perversion, and imprisonment. Furthermore, he was one of the Mamluks involved in the murder of Sultan al-Muzaffar Hajji and his replacement by our noble sultan. Here's what I wrote about their brutal revolution in *Travels East and West*:

> They unleashed on the Egyptian people a series of outrages the like of which had never been seen since the establishment of the dynasty. Seizures, abductions, beating on doors of houses and baths so as to fool around with women, unleashing all conceivable kinds of debauchery and lust at every turn. Everyone was in a panic. The entire matter was taken to the sultan, and there was much praying and beseeching to God Almighty. The senior figures involved in the revolt held a meeting with the sultan and negotiated a cessation of their attacks. He ordered them to leave, then set his army and retinue on them with orders to capture them by

force. Within what seemed like the twinkling of an eye they were all taken prisoner; the jails were full of them. They were fettered and paraded round the city as an example. Most of them were dis-emboweled, but the rest were either exiled or imprisoned in distant parts. Then they released Barquq, who took over things, and Baraka al-Jubani, Altunbugha al-Jubani, and Jarkas al-Khalili.

Forgetfulness is the bane of all scholarship. It is thus essential that the person currently occupying the ruler's throne in Egypt be reminded of the past. That way, his image will be enhanced and the possibilities for the future will become that much clearer.

This Barquq, manumitted slave that he is, carries with him a criminal record that is chock full of vile and disgusting deeds. He is the champion abductor and rapist of women, even within the sanctuaries of home and baths!

This Barquq the Circassian has been imprisoned, chained, and paraded through streets and markets!

Like any major brigand or highwayman, his life has been spent gambling with death. Scoffing at dangers and disasters, he has always managed to escape through some miracle. It's as if he is not just one person, but many, as the term 'Circassian' suggests.

So then, he has emerged from the very pits of evil, from the ranks of foreign slaves, from the fraternity devoted to violence and rapine, to become Barquq, the sultan of Egypt today, one who is always ready to forgive and who shows both common sense and moderation in his mode of governing and the way he treats his defeated foes. It is almost as though he is trying to use such behavior as a way of cleaning the slate of his past crimes and his undesirable origins, all in the hope of dispatching to the Creator a stream of apologetic letters seeking His forgiveness. This is how I embellished the account in my *Book of the Lessons of History*, although I gave a more economical version in *Travels East and West*:

Thereafter Barquq took it upon himself to run the government, using threats, bribes, and familiarity as means of solving issues in its various subdivisions. He would make a point of balancing revenues with expenditures and putting clamps on the proclivities of

Qala'un's descendants in spending money on luxuries and indulging in grossly excessive habits until the stage was reached when expenditures were almost under control. As a result, the ruling class could not maintain its lifestyle. Barquq observed all this and looked for other ways to put an end to government wastage and reform corruption. This cause became his primary pretext for occupying the throne and using the title of sultan, in that the descendants of Qala'un had been so corrupted by luxury and had had such a negative effect on the regime, that the entire thing had degenerated into sheer vice and everyone involved seemed content with the situation. That is why he assumed the throne on the nineteenth of Ramadan in 784, taking the title al-Zahir.

I hid myself away until the end of Muharram. I kept studying and writing, checking and mulling things over, and making notes as I did so. At the same time, I made sure to take good care of my wife and listen from time to time to the sound of the baby moving around in her womb. Two days before the end of the month—a Thursday morning, in fact—I was concentrating on my writing when I heard Umm al-Banin scream for the first time, followed by other prayers for God's aid. Those screams, I told myself, are a harbinger of my family's future, and I rushed downstairs to her side, overcome with joy. I immediately sent Sha'ban to bring the midwife. Umm al-Banin was flat on the bed with labor well advanced; she was sweating and groaning as she clasped the sheets and pillow for all she was worth. I sat down beside her and held her hand so she would know I was there. I wiped her forehead with a cloth dampened with rosewater, saying, "O God who brings us out of all perils and agonies, grant her an easy delivery and keep her safe from the risk and shocks of labor. Grant, O Lord, that the baby may move safe and sound from the darkness of the womb to the light of life itself. O God, make things easy rather than difficult; release the child from the womb unharmed; and give us the bounty of Your blessings and boundless good health. O Merciful and Compassionate One!"

Within minutes the midwife arrived with her assistant. After greeting me, she asked me to leave. I went back to my office, but my mind was totally distracted. I kept saying "O Merciful God!" over and over again so as to dispel all the dire presentiments I kept having.

Oh and Oh again! The twists of fate! Dear God, I have suffered my share of them and more. Was it not more than enough when the Great Plague snatched my father and teachers away? Did You not strike me too hard when my wife and children were drowned at sea?

I don't know how long the time actually was that I spent, an emotional wreck, measuring the wait by the beat of my pulse. My entire brain felt as if it were chained down by dreadful chimeras and premonitions.

Then all of a sudden came the first signs of my release: a single sound followed by a baby's crying. Confirmation came when the midwife invited me in to look at my daughter and check that everything was fine. Beaming with the greatest conceivable happiness, I responded to her congratulations with profuse expressions of thanks. I leaned over and kissed Umm al Banin, offering thanks to God for her safe delivery and for our new daughter, al-Batul.

Umm al-Banin looked pale, and her hair was a mess. Her smiling face was a mixture of sweat and tears of joy. She looked as though she had just been through fierce combat but had finally emerged victorious. I asked the midwife to take good care of her, then left the room in response to the shouts of Sha'ban who was waiting outside. His eyes welling up with tears of sheer joy he hugged and congratulated me, then gave me a sealed letter which had been sent by messenger from the sultan's palace. I opened it and found it was a copy of a decree appointing me teacher of hadith at the Sarghitmishiya College. The decree had been dated—incredible to believe—more than two weeks earlier, but never mind . . . I hugged Sha'ban and allowed him in to see Umm al-Banin and our baby girl. Then I went and sat down at my desk. "Joy upon joy," I told myself with untrammeled delight, "like light upon light! This daughter of mine has already me the most incredible good fortune. *When Your Lord announced: If you show thanks, We will indeed increase it for you.* My Lord, through Your goodness and munificence I am the happiest of mortals. I am so grateful!"

I stood up and undressed myself so I could wash before prayer, but only after I had organized the major works on hadith on a shelf, prime amongst them being *The Smooth Path* by Malik ibn Anas, imam of Medina. Perhaps his would serve as the organizing text for the materials to be covered in my classes.

Once I had finished my prayers I headed for Umm al-Banin's room, but retraced my steps when I found her surrounded by women of all ages consuming sweetmeats and cups of milk and emitting trills of joy. I called for Sha'ban and gave him a sum of money to buy essentials including, of course, a ram for sacrifice on the seventh day. Then I sat down with Malik's tome and started preparing for the classes after the afternoon and sunset prayers at the new college to which I had been appointed.

The topic I selected was one for which I had obtained a number of licentiate degrees from my teachers in the Maghrib. It was not my intention either to take Malik's side or to lay stress on the fact that people in the Maghrib tended to imitate him and follow his teachings. What I had in mind was the fact that Egyptian students are much in need of elementary instruction in hadith; they really want a truly unusual imam who can transcend all the compromises and difficulties and use them all to bang on the wall. Ahmad ibn Hanbal said, "When you're talking about hadith, Malik is really 'the Commander of the Faithful.'" Before him al-Shafi'i had said, "If a hadith comes from Malik, grab it with both hands." So I planned the basic elements of the class in my head, trying to frame it in accordance with the clearest pedagogical methods. First, a biography of the author of *The Smooth Path* with details of his life and in particular the circumstances in which he passed on his learning—his bodily and mental fitness, his profound belief and devotion, and his good reputation among religious scholars and pietists. Second, a history of the book itself, taking into account its transmitters, the qualities of the different readings in accordance with the chain of authorities used. Thirdly (and lastly), the body of the text and its contents.

The women's cries of joy grew yet louder. In the meantime, all I could do was snatch a few bites of lunch, then head for the Sarghitmishiya school in order to meet the principal and lecture to the students. I told Sha'ban that, all being well, I would return home after the sunset prayers.

When I reached home later on, I rushed up to Umm al-Banin's room and found some women still there. I greeted them, and they responded before taking their leave; all, that is, except two, who made their way to the kitchen. Umm al-Banin looked as happy as could be, smiling and eager to talk, but covering her face with her hand whenever she felt shy or overcome by emotion. I checked on the baby and found she was nursing from her mother, half-awake and half-asleep. I stared at her for a long time, as though I had never seen a nursing baby before.

"Praise be to God," I said. "We have been blessed with the birth of a wonderful child. If you like, I'll name her al-Batul on the morning of the seventh day. Now you need to ask me where I went at noontime today. No, save your energy and let me tell you. Sultan Barquq has appointed me teacher in a major school near the Ahmad ibn Tulun Mosque that you know well. The appointment letter was delivered to me on the very morning of the day when this blessed child arrived. I gave my first class following the afternoon prayer. Ask me how it went—it was well received, and I had a number of compliments on it.

"I thank God for his blessings," she replied with a certain amount of effort. "I pray God to preserve you for al-Batul and her mother, to grant you success, and give you a position of prestige."

What pure sentiments those were, making their way straight to the heart where they were tokens of affection and beauty. I leaned over my drowsy wife and kissed both her and the baby, then headed for my office to get some sleep.

On the day of the ram sacrifice, I decided that I wanted an occasion that was simple and unassuming; in other words, without lots of guests, a band, or elaborate spread. I was not prepared to listen to people gossiping about my having a child at such an age or anything else connected with my personal life. The question of women invitees did not involve me, although I did suggest to my wife that she make do with just a few of them.

I thought about Sa'd, Umm al-Banin's brother, and sent Sha'ban to fetch him so he could share in our joy and I could check on his condition. A little before noon the slaughterer arrived. I slit the throat myself, intoned the phrase "God is great!" and named our child amid a female chorus of trills and cheers. Sha'ban outdid himself in offering a helping hand, spraying perfumes, and negotiating between slaughterer and cook. Sa'd, who looked fine to me, went around the house offering his help, seemingly unconcerned about sharing space with women.

So, everything went exactly as I had wanted. When everyone had eaten their fill and the poor had been given their share, I went to a room whose window looked out on the guest quarters. From late afternoon onward the house began to fill up with throngs of women visitors; I had no idea who they were or where they came from. And, of course, as with any occasion like this where a lot of women gather together, the devil made his appearance in the form of singing and dancing. However, my curiosity was such that I could not stop myself lending both ear and eye to what has going on. Women from the Maghrib and Egypt vied with each other to light up the scene with all kinds of dance and song and the various instruments of pleasure as well, in the form of drinking cups and food trays.

In the midst of them sat Umm al-Banin, smiling happily, showing off her new clothes and revealing the henna on her hands and feet.

I am aware, of course, that on such joyful occasions, women will frequently take some small amount of opium along with their tisane and sweetmeats. It gives them energy and inspires them to laugh and dance even more. Faced with such a custom, all a Maliki jurist like me can do is to entrust the entire matter to God Almighty and ask Him for mercy and forgiveness.

Just as I was closing the window in order to block out the sound of voices, I noticed Sa'd amid all the women; he was letting out trills of joy and dancing a solo in the middle of their circle with extraordinary skill. Rubbing my hands in despair, I told myself that this was one mistake I could not overlook. I instructed Sha'ban to ask the young man to come up at once and talk to me.

"So, are you a man or a woman?" I yelled.

Sa'd was taken aback by my question and paused a moment to recover his breath.

"Oh, Master," he said with very effeminate gestures, "what a question! If only you knew. You should leave it to Him who created and leveled."

"Now listen, you," I said, "beg God's forgiveness for saying such a thing!"

"Did God consult me about how I should be? He is the one who created me and put me together. Neither male, nor female; that's what He called me and left me somewhere in between. Can there be any worse hell than this?"

As the young man spoke, he kept crying and sobbing, as though trying to put his natural self and utter weakness into words. Feeling sympathy for his plight, I hugged him to me and told him to stop crying on such a joyful day. I asked him to go back and keep doing what he'd been doing, if he so desired. He went off happily, promising to go back to the mosque the following morning.

So here's something else I am consigning to You, O God!

For me, civilization involves either Bedouin in the desert or else the urban environment of cities. The ruler is either just or unjust. Flaws are either passing or endemic. In general terms, things are either possible or not. However, when it comes to the bits in between or even coexistence of opposites, as in the make-up of my brother-in-law, Sa'd, I have neither experience nor competence in such domains.

God granted me and my blessed little al-Batul yet another beneficence at the end of her third month: I was made controller of the Baybars Convent. I received the sultan's appointment just before the end of Rabi al-Akhir following the death of the late Imam Sharuf al-Din al-Ashqar.

This college was situated inside Bab al-Nasr not too far from Mahmudiya where I lived. What made this appointment that much more advantageous was that my enhanced monetary position enabled me to expand my collection of rare books and to buy essentials and even luxuries for the house. The salary I got as controller now afforded us a life of wealth, ease, and space. However, I was well aware that it was, almost inevitably, a short-term situation, one that could be terminated without warning at any moment, day or night, and in the twinkling of an eye.

And that is exactly how it turned out. Just a few short months after I had taken the position, warning signs of my imminent dismissal began to hover over my head. Faced with Umm al-Banin's delight with our daughter, I had to force myself to show a happy face rather than look miserable—all smiles instead of frowns. It would have been the worst of all crimes to erase the smiles from the faces I adored or to sully our family home with all my worries and gloomy predictions. However, my clever wife managed to guess what was going on in my mind. One day I was feeling particularly pessimistic because of the bad news I had heard concerning the mounting disagreement between Sultan Barquq and his viceroys in Aleppo and Malatya, the two amirs, Yalbugha al-Nasiri and Mintash.

"You look very worried, 'Abd al-Rahman," she asked me out of the blue. "What's it all about?"

I could think of no way to avoid telling her a bit about the current situation. But, in any case, discussing the situation with the most beloved person in the world might serve to lessen the tension I was feeling.

"It's the sultan, my dear," I said. "This time he's really in danger."

"What's that got to do with us? If one goes, there'll be another."

"It's more complicated than that. If Barquq goes, my positions in the school and college go with him."

"That's not certain. But even if it did—God forbid that it should—I could sell my trousseau and gold, along with all the extra pots and pans we have. With God's good help, dear husband, we would not die."

Trays and plates all inlaid with gold and silver, silk fabrics, superb furnishings, all of them luxuries that had come my way after assuming the controllership of the Baybars Convent. To be sure, selling it all might bring us enough income for at least a few months, in addition to which there would be my cash savings. Umm al-Batul's simple, yet eloquent words convinced me about food necessities.

"God preserve you," I said, "times of rebellion often bring with them all kinds of disturbances and mayhem. I can't guarantee that I myself will remain safe and sound."

"If things get very bad," she said, "we'll go back to Fez and live among our beloved relatives there. In any case, I long to see Fez again, with its gates, baths, fountains, and gardens."

We would be running away from a ditch all the way to a well. That's what I told myself but did not say as much to my companion, a woman who was forever thinking of my interests, showing me love and affection, and intervening whenever I felt desperately sad.

"The city has a wise ruler," I said. "The baby's crying, Umm al-Batul. Go to her."

There are in life certain situations when one has no choice but to turn to God. So, my good man, use your brain and turn things over to Him. Or, as Shaykh al-Rikraki once advised me: "Think carefully which horse you're betting on."

The clashes between the enemy brothers of Yalbugha got progressively worse as day followed day. Indeed, according to confirmed reports, what started as a series of skirmishes in the Damascus region turned into bloody fighting in the heart of Egypt itself, first on the outskirts of Cairo and then around the Citadel, itself a symbol of Burji Mamluk power.

From the end of Jumada al-Thaniya news from the sultan's side began to dwindle steadily as day followed day till eventually all signs of life in the homes of his retinue and officials disappeared. For that reason I found myself compelled to rely on the stories people told me. I would sift through them and adjust their contents in accordance with the conversations I was having in the Sarghitmishiya College, the Baybars Convent, and Shaykh al-Rikraki's convent—they being the circles to which I was confining my movements. That was how I managed to confirm that Barquq had disappeared and al-Nasiri and Mintash had taken over. The two of them had been reinforced by Turkmen and had captured the Citadel, where they had installed Hajji ibn al-Ashraf on the throne and named him al-Mansur. Thereafter I was also able to confirm that Barquq had surrendered himself in return for a pledge of security from Amir Altunbugha al-Jubani whom he had previously imprisoned in Alexandria but who was now an ally of the people who had overthrown him. According to what I could deduce from the reports, this pledge played a large part in saving the deposed sultan from what would otherwise have been a certain death. The amirs of the Yalbugha, under the command of Mintash, insisted on finding him, and it was then agreed that Barquq would be transferred to the castle of Kerak in southern Syria. There he would remain until things became clearer and the storm calmed down.

I could no longer manage to keep my worries hidden inside my own home; the clashes were simply too intense. Throughout the cycles of history there have always been episodes and crises during which it has been at least difficult, if not outright impossible, for one to simply stay out of the way and devote one's attention to scholarship and the delights provided by the good things of this earth. That applies especially to me, since I have regularly plunged feet first into the welter of politics and reluctantly set myself along a path where I can now see that, if things go to pieces and collapse, then so do I. The only difference has been when I've changed one allegiance for another and made adjustments in order to fit in with the dictates of temporary necessity and the shadows of victorious swords. Were I to be asked now why I choose to be buffeted by such storms, I would reply that it is because of the mother of my child, Umm al-Banin—God grant her peace. Our blessed little daughter, al-Batul, is now my prime resort, my antidote against the cruel whims of fate and events. Within the haven she provides I have found an abundance of ways to calm the soul and rid the body of its aches and pains. My most enjoyable times are those I spend receiving her tender care and attention and listening to her simple comments on the current events I share with her. Were it not for my worries about being the target of sudden surprises, I would cheerfully let things go their own way and retreat to the serenity of my own home. Then I could steer clear of all the news and concentrate instead on writing and reading, with only my gentle wife and smiling daughter for company.

In the second half of 791, I could no longer pretend to be out of the loop concerning the second chapter of the tragedy involving the Citadel and the Ablaq Palace. This time the tragedy's plot involved the previous rulers, since they disagreed as to whether Barquq should be killed or kept alive. It turned out that Mintash, who vigorously advocated the former solution, managed to outwit his opponents and had his two rivals, Alaldayn al-Nasiri and al-Jubani, imprisoned in Alexandria. To all appearances he had managed to grab control and was now running the government by himself.

I had never met the victorious amir, the former viceroy of Malatya, but the few tidbits I collected all depicted him as a man with a very short temper who had people killed without mercy and bolstered his arguments with the edge of a sword, a supreme master at the arts of intrigue and duplicity. It was my ill-fortune to witness these traits when I was forcibly taken from my home and family and conducted to the palace. Once there, I found myself face to face with the new puppet caliph, al-Mansur, along with judges representing all the schools of law, a few jurists, and senior army officers. While we were all standing there exchanging smalltalk, in marched Mintash armed to the teeth, followed by his *dawadar* and *jundar*. He gave us all a gruff greeting and then ordered one of the jurists to read out the text of a fatwa which posed the question: "Is it lawful to kill al-Zahir Barquq? The grounds are that he gave aid to the Christians by severing their allegiance to the caliph and sultan, and made war on Muslim armies."

Without resorting to any preliminaries, I gathered my resources and took the initiative in addressing Mintash.

"Giving judgment by fatwa, Amir, is a legal matter that demands serious thought. In order to reach a decision, we judges need tangible proof and eyewitnesses."

"Tangible proof and eyewitnesses, you say, man of law?" Mintah responded in a dry, arrogant tone. "Just ask the senior army officers here. If you're not convinced, then you can leave your books and the cosy environment of your house and enter the theater of war so you can see for yourself the way Barquq has favored the Christians over his Muslim brothers. If you're still not convinced, then Egypt has no more need of you or your legal opinions. After all, you weren't born here."

I said nothing, not because the man's words had silenced me but rather because I had assessed the dangers involved in responding, orders that I be imprisoned, or banished, or even killed. The chief judge, Badr al-Din ibn Abi al-Baqa' of the Shafi'i school, took advantage of a moment when Mintash went over to talk to his aides and came over. "Don't complicate matters, pilgrim judge," he whispered in my ear. "We'd better keep our real feelings to ourselves, or else we'll all be destroyed." He then took a pen from the *dawadar* and signed the document. All the secular and army judges did like-wise. When my turn came, all I could do was to add my own signa-ture, suppressing a choking sensation as I did so.

Everyone rushed out and went their own way, while Mintash watched people leave with a look of total disdain.

I must confess that all the way home from the palace I was afraid of being ambushed or shot at. I kept urging my mule to go faster and cover the distance involved as soon as possible.

"Cover me up, Umm al-Batul," I shouted, "please cover me up. I keep feeling feverish, then cold again. Prepare whatever potions you can and help me get better so I can remain alive and gauge what the future has in store for me. I'm enveloped in dark clouds; whether they're thick or scattered, it's all the same. In the end, I'm going to pay the price either for signing that document or for being reluctant to do so. It may mean prison or dismissal from my posts. All options remain open. How is the baby and how are you? For me, you two—so help me God—are the only things that are keeping me alive and fending off the fevers life brings. I feel as though I'm back at the early stage of my life. If it hadn't been for you, Umm al-Batul, and the fact that I met you, I would have given up. 'Here's my splayed out wreck of a body,' I would have told the impinging fates, 'pounce on it, destroy it, tear it to pieces, till only a thread of smoke remains—the thread of the spirit as it willingly and contentedly returns to its Lord.'"

From bedroom to kitchen my wife went to and fro preparing potions, listening to some of what I said and ignoring the rest. Sitting down beside me with her boxes and bottles, she started mak-ing me swallow concoctions and wiping my face and limbs with a cloth. She then placed a dampened band over my forehead and eyes.

"Now, 'Abd al-Rahman," she said, "you'll be able to sleep and stop your ravings."

"Those ravings, my dear, are the result of drawn swords and rivers of blood."

"Go to sleep, I told you, and recite Surat al-Nas that you told me to memorize."

"I hear and obey, my dear. I will indeed recite Surat al-Nas as many times as possible. And I will go to sleep, even though I'm still scared I'll be snatched out of bed by the Mamluks of either Barquq or Mintash. One group will drag me out into the desert. 'You can stay out here in the boiling sun, you fair-weather signer, you half-baked supporter,' they'll yell in my face, 'You can stay out here till you fry.' The other group will take me to their master who will vent his furious revenge on me: 'You can spend your days in the remotest of prisons, you endorser of false documents, you half-baked supporter.'"

From that infamous day, the twenty-fifth of Dhu al-Qa'da, when I signed the false fatwa, until the end of the month, I stayed at home. I kept praying and reciting the Qur'an as a way of counteracting the effects of a mental breakdown. With the beginning of Dhu al-Hijja I allowed myself to be tempted by the satanic desire for news and information. As the weeks went by, I started getting news from Shaykh al-Rikraki, the Shafi'i judge whom I've mentioned earlier, and some students of mine who had political contacts. Everything pointed to the fact that things were moving in Barquq's favor and that the noose was tightening around Mintash and his friends. The reason seems to have been—and God knows best—that the governor and people of Kerak remembered everything Barquq had done for them, so they sided with him and gave him their support. To their company were added some of Barquq's own Mamluks and some Bedouin troops as well. The deposed sultan was thus able to muster an army and march on Gaza. After capturing the city, he then proceeded to Damascus and laid siege to the city. Thereafter, days passed without any confirmable information, until the time when, like everyone else, I heard about the Battle of Shaqhab just outside Damascus, where Barquq's forces defeated the army of Amir Hajji and Mintash who had put him on the throne. It was confirmed that Barquq was solidifying his control over Syria prior to returning to Egypt where he would once again ascend the throne and resume his rulership of the country.

As Barquq was making his way back to Egypt, the people of Cairo heard that his Mamluks had been released from prison and had pounced on the Citadel where they had expelled Mintash's followers and, in anticipation of their master's return, gained control of the Ablaq Palace under the command of the Mamluk, Bata.

I have dozens and dozens of blank pages just waiting for me to find the time to write down the finer details of recent events in the history of this Mamluk dynasty to which I have been witness. However, I don't have the energy to retrieve them from my mind and memory. At this point, my life hangs by a solitary thread. It is one that the returning sultan can easily sever with a single blow of his sword since he is bound to take the dimmest possible view of the fact that I signed that false fatwa against him along with all the other judicial authorities. Is there any chance of reason getting the upper hand, or that maybe he'll take mitigating circumstances into account; the fact, for example, that the signatures were obtained under duress? The answers to all those possibilities must be left to God to decide and to the extent to which the sultan feels inclined to show mercy and forgiveness.

While waiting for the situation to become clearer and for decision day to arrive, I spent my days going from house, to mosque, to college, to school. I also found myself preoccupied with two other things: Maghribi documents on the one hand, and the composition of a poetic plea for mercy addressed to Barquq on the other.

Whenever I found myself with time to spare, I made my way to the Zuwayla quarter, which was near the one where I lived, or else I would meander my way around the Kitama quarter near al-Azhar Mosque or the Musadama quarter alongside the Elephant Lake. By now the Maghribi quarters in these various parts of the city have vanished, but they can still provide the historian with a reminder of the Fatimi 'Ubaydi dynasty, which relied on Maghribi Berbers for support just as much as the body does on its spinal column. The reason for my visits to those districts was undoubtedly a desire to smell the sweet breeze of my homeland and slake my intense feelings of nostalgia. Who knows, any time soon I might be forced to pick up and move back to Tunis or Fez.

I worked on the poem for Barquq at night. Next morning I would refine its phraseology and check on the rhymes. The poem was so full of hyperbole and entreaty that it weighed on my heart like a ton of lead. Poetry without any genuine feeling or buried fire is useless verbiage, no more. That much I have learned about every line I've composed throughout my life. This particular poem, with its very particular audience, found me powerfully aware of the unconvincing artistry and affectation I was using. I saw myself as sticking and patching verses together, letting things go their own way until such time as I felt like piecing them all together into some kind of coherent entity. Here's part of it:

My lord, when people think well of you
And your hands are guarantors of every wish,
Neglect me not; with regard to you
I have neglected neither pledge of love nor beautiful hands.
Keep me close by. Fate has been unkind,
Dispatching its steeds against me.
A foreigner has seen approval and ease combined
To inure him to sorrow and estrangement.

Just before dawn I leapt out of bed and filled a page with yet more verses for recital:

Our foes have crafted calumnies
Every one among them fatally flawed;
About me they have circulated bizarre falsehoods
Set up as snares to their own interests.
So accept our excuses. Today by the life of the sultan
We are begging you to accept them.
To confront the onset of days, accept the help of a foreigner
Who complains about the barrenness of his life.
Your neighbor is your guest, one who enjoys your protection;
And the generous man never neglects his guests.

These verses and others like them were the products of many long hours that I spent in the early morning. They so exhausted me that I felt totally wrung out.

Half way through the year 792 Barquq re-entered Cairo in triumph, to the accompaniment of all the trappings of pomp and victory. According to many accounts (some of which I gathered at the council at Hammam al-Sufiyya), Sultan Barquq had barely defeated Mintash before he got the judges to depose Amir Hajji. He then received an acknowledgment from the 'Abbasi caliph in Baghdad that he was indeed ruler of Egypt. No sooner was he restored to his position than he named his Mamluk, Bata, as his *dawadar*, then summoned the prisoners from Alexandria. After upbraiding them for their conduct, he restored them all to their former positions. Among those who were treated this way were al-Nasiri and al-Jubani who were re-appointed governors of Aleppo and Damascus respectively. I will not conceal the fact that these developments made me feel a lot better and suggested that things might work out well for me. The only thing that gave me pause was when I learned that a decree had been issued promoting Sudun to the position of viceroy in the sultan's office. As far as the post of controller of the Baybars Convent was concerned, I came to realize that my chances of getting it back were nil since Sudun harbored a special hatred for me because during my time as a judge I habitually opposed his corrupt requests. My dismissal from the Baybars Convent coincided with the day when I was summoned to the sultan's presence. He spared me nothing in his condemnation of the fact that I had signed the fatwa authorizing his deposition. He then let me go, but without even accepting my excuses.

When I returned home, I started hugging my wife and child as hard as I could. I felt as if I had just escaped certain death and slid my way out of Izra'il's clutches.

When night fell, I sat down to look over my apologetic poem, filling in blank passages, changing the order of phrases, and adding new lines. These are some of the new lines I added:

How is it that the college has been taken from me
When no crime was committed or misdemeanor?
Nay, it is a position I have worn with pride
Appointed by noble decree and duly draped gown.
I had hoped for another,
One that by its promise would be granted.
I used it as a base for future hopes,
Assuming its boons would be unending.

As I put the final touches to the poem, it occurred to me that it might be a good idea to send it to my old friend, Altunbugha al-

Jubani, viceroy of Damascus, and ask him to intercede with the sultan on my behalf. I concocted a few more verses on that theme, then sent it to Damascus in safe hands. After much waiting and procrastination, the poem—along with its references to waters returning to their normal courses and so on—seems to have done the trick. I found myself gradually forgiven by the sultan and returned to his grace and favor.

The Baybars Convent had been snatched away from me, but my income from teaching and the Fayyum farm was enough to meet household expenses. Actually, there was enough to allow my wife and I to take our daughter, now one year old, out for a stroll in the public park, to look at the rams butting and the cocks squawking, and even to watch the shadow play. God be praised for the boons He let us enjoy!

Poking one's nose into matters that are liable to occur without warning or forethought, getting involved in situations whose only function is to show one how little choice and how little discretion over his own future he has, these are just some of the many snares that may entrap those religious scholars who find themselves seduced by the attractions of politics. They have no experience whatsoever in the hothouse atmosphere of political life, nor do they possess the know-how needed to keep rulers at arm's length. Their only resort is to pack their bags and run from one ruler to the next.

Faced with such a situation, the only stratagem I use—and in spite of everything I continue to rely exclusively on reason—is to stay at home and stick to my books and writing. If I have to go out, it is only for some really pressing reason or else to visit my college or the houses of God.

Exhaustion! It creeps its way into my body and joints without license or permission. It moves ever forward, sure of its advance, enveloped in the ruthless onward march of time and the headlong clash of days. It falls into two separate categories: the first arises from the sight of endlessly repeated dross; the symptoms of the second reveal themselves in people who delve into the deeper levels behind events and the causes of change in a quest for hidden pearls and useful lessons. I wonder, have I now reached the culmination of both types at once?

I wrote that paragraph in the margin of one of the stack of papers that I filled over the past year and a half about the history of Mamluk Egypt. One evening at the beginning of the year 797 I was on the point of confessing to my dear wife that I felt really tired, but then I changed my mind and made an effort to look alert and happy. I was anxious to seem (to the extent possible) just as youthful and fond of life as my wife was. As I wrote on a piece of paper at the time, "I have no right to object to my wife's *joie de vivre*. She's well aware that my hair has turned gray, but it's not right to make her aware of the extent to which my veins and joints are showing signs of the wear and tear of old age. Dear God, if You have planned for me to die at this particular stage, then I beg You to make it quick."

My feelings of exhaustion during this particular year may well have been intensified by the fact that so many of my colleagues and members of the government died. Some of them were actually killed, including al-Jubani, al-Nasiri, and Mintash, all in Syria. Others fell ill and died, such as Shaykh al-Rikraki, and Chief Judge Ibn Abi al-Baqa', the Shafi'i. Still others died unexpectedly, such as some of the brigade commanders and Yahya from Sudan, the servant at the Hammam al-Sufiyya. There were many others as well.

"God grant them a just reward; every soul gets to taste death; verily to God do we belong and to Him do we return." I kept having to repeat these phrases of condolence to family and friends of the deceased.

"The last time I saw Shaykh al-Rikraki, Umm al-Batul," I told my wife, "I asked him as usual how Sa'd was. He told me that, now that he was living with the Malamatiya community, his moods were more normal. He then advised me to hope for the best and not ask too many questions."

I devoted several paragraphs to the circumstances surrounding the killing of Altunbugha al-Jubani. I included a sympathetic obituary as an acknowledgment of the kind role he had played in bringing about a rapprochement between the sultan and myself and of the fact that he had stood by me in hard times. I closed the passage with this sentence: "All I have seen in him is good, so I beg God to accord him the same." Nor was I content merely to write such things. I went in search of one of his sons, knowing that he lived close to the Elephant Lake. My purpose was to offer my condolences and discover the whereabouts of his father's tomb in Damascus. After exhaustive investigations I was able to track him down at the al-Khayyam tavern on the banks of the Nile, quite close to al-Luq, the quarter of lay-abouts and riff-raff. It was only after I had disguised myself as an Egyptian and made sure the room was dark enough that I ventured inside. Sitting down beside al-Jubani's son at a low table, I introduced myself and explained the reason for my visit. Even though he was clearly drunk, he managed to express his gratitude and respect.

"You ask me, sir, about my father's burial place," he went on. "I have no idea exactly where they buried him. I wasn't able to attend the funeral ceremonies; I don't even know if there were any. There was always a huge chasm between my father and me even when he was still alive. As for now, well. . . ."

He yelled to the waiter to bring over a carafe of wine and a cup of coffee.

"The permitted and forbidden: they're both available here, so, if you'll excuse me, I invite you to take your pick. Revered pilgrim, I cannot stand reproach and criticism, having received more than my due of both from my late father. In many ways, man has decisions made for him. Was it my choice to be Altunbugha al-Jubani's son, and thus be banned from politics and made to consort with ordinary folk? Did fate offer me counsel in polishing up the kinks in my career or dealing with the various trials life has thrown at me? I've had to make my way through life as best I can, like some fleeting shadow or passing cloud. In the world to come may God be forgetful and forgiving."

The young man sitting next to me had clearly been wronged. Gingerly taking the cup of coffee, I listened attentively to what he had to say.

"In the political arena, sir, the very worst disaster to affect a man is to die before other people."

I pushed my turban back from my forehead. "Who is there," I asked, "who doesn't die before others?"

"By 'other people' I mean enemies and those who oppose one's ideas and initiatives. I have no doubt that my father felt that his death was one such ignominious defeat."

I started fidgeting as a way of showing that I was about to leave the tavern, but the young man begged me to stay.

"Can't you stay here with a son of the people?" he asked. "What I've just told you is merely ephemeral nonsense. But what is more important then anything else is about to appear before our very eyes. Please stay with me for a while so you can watch and listen."

As long as the possibility of anonymity was still there, I had little choice. Furthermore the wine had not yet reduced him to incoherence.

There was suddenly a total silence in the tavern, even though it was packed with customers and filled with pipe smoke. The silence was broken by a singer behind a curtain whose nightingale voice was accompanied by the strings of a lute. The words of the song were Persian, from the *Ruba'iyat* of 'Umar al-Khayyam. My companion leaned over and told me that he was Persian on his late mother's side. Sipping his wine and sucking on his pipe, he kept swaying from side to side as the music inspired him.

For sure, I told myself, this invisible woman's lovely voice merits a place in the haven of passion, amid cascades of flowing delight. In such a sound resides the very definition of the ideal of sweet-tempered refinement. It has an enormous power to attract the spirit of the listener to life and the pursuit of beauty; of that there can be no doubt. The voice is warm and lush, dispensing beauty all around it. One can swear an oath that the owner of that voice is a paragon of beauty and an authority. In addition to those thoughts and in spite of my normal piety and Maliki beliefs, I allowed myself to be inspired by the passions of the moment in this space that seemed like some secret nocturnal garden. In my mind I pictured the singer's body in all its panting, white-hot nakedness. I could envision the very breath of her, the breath of youth, a captivating breath, one that had only to come into contact with wilting bodies in order to restore them. The soul that it entered was purged of all accumulated dross and misery. . . .

I allowed myself to chase after ever-regenerating fantasies. All my efforts at dispelling them, curses aimed at the duplicity of the devil and other temptations, were completely in vain.

My companion kept closing his eyes or staring fixedly into the void, mouthing blissful sighs at the sound of the singer's voice as she borrowed shapes and colors from the vocabulary of passion and tenderness. At this point the singer stopped for a while to recover her breath, and the lute played a solo.

"When it comes to the realm of politics," my companion said, "I have neither pass nor transit visa. I'm a child of the people. Even so, revered pilgrim, there's still life to be lived; there are perfumes, women, and melodies. But for the nightclub, life on earth would be unbearable. It provides a refuge for those who are lost and badly done by. Here I can distract myself from time's onslaughts and ever increasing despair."

For a moment he stopped his litany of misery, but then he picked up again. "If only you could see the body of our singer tonight, sir, you would be as convinced as I am that, by comparison, politics is a sick joke. A pox on Timur Lang and all enemies of beauty."

He downed the rest of his cup. "Don't you agree with me, sir," he went on, "that with this particular singer the *Ruba'iyat* of 'Umar al-Khayyam are as ravishing as can be? With her, the sounds emerge from her throat like so many pearls scattered around, like light upon light! With her the *Ruba'iyat* can teach me the alphabet of life and death; they prompt me to garner pleasure without delay. Pleasure comes from the very pulse of existence, the pulse whose impetus is the very moment itself."

The singer resumed her performance, and the tavern once again fell into an emotive silence. The whole place seemed to be swaying to and fro like a boat being tossed by waves, sleepy and intoxicated. I clung to my cup of coffee, avoiding as far as possible the probing stares of the revelers. By now I was getting very impatient and made every effort to be as inconspicuous as possible.

"Is it true, I wonder," asked my companion, "that this singer and all other young beauties like her will one day be food for worms?"

Then he whispered in my ear, "You're not really my companion, coffee-drinker, but rest assured that the only thing I'm drowning in my glass is my anxieties. Apart from that small slip, my hands are clean. They've never slapped anyone's face or been sullied by the blood of either human or animal. O Lord, I associate no one with You. Your radiant essence I adore only through Your bounty and forgiveness."

And, as the singer brought her song to a close, he joined in:

No pearls of righteousness do I enlace,
Nor sweep the desert of sin off my face.

And other voices inside the tavern sang with them:

Yet since I never counted one as two,
I do not quite despair of heavenly grace.

The curtain was now pulled back accompanied by a storm of applause. Wonder of wonders, I now discovered that the singer was not a woman at all, but a flat-chested boy with short hair.

"Don't be shocked, revered pilgrim," my companion said, "to discover that the singer is a transvestite. It's the singing and atmosphere that matter, not gender. But since you're such an astute judge, tell me, by God, what do you think of the *Ruba'iyat*'s eternal wisdom?"

I had to say something by way of reply, albeit briefly. "The genius of al-Khayyam," I replied, " lies in his uncanny ability to eradicate the contradiction between intellect and levity. His poetic talent is directly connected to his knowledge of algebra and astronomy. That's why his *Ruba'iyat*, at least in the translated version I have read, have a mathematical pattern that addresses itself to the spirit in the rhythm of 'To God alone belongs the power and might.' That way the passionate heat of their verse becomes cool and serene."

"Bravo, Master, bravo!"

"As for the ribald verses in the *Ruba'iyat*, I just swallow them like sour fruit and beg God for forgiveness."

"You can say such wonderful things when you are completely sober! Power to you, liberal and broad-minded sage that you are!

Now take a look at the flute player going up on stage. She's a genuine female, no question."

The woman now sitting on the chair, with a flute held between her fingers and its aperture to her lips, was indeed a woman; her clothes were those of a female, as was her stature and hair. Even so, I told myself that God alone knows the contents of people's hearts. What was most important was the perfect harmony between flute and player, so much so that you could imagine the one fusing with the other. Melody thus turns into a source of plaintive longing. A short while later, she was joined on stage by a drummer, violinist, and lute player. The lute player tuned his instrument to the right key, and they started playing. They were singing this *muwashshaha*:

> *Fresh are my wounds and the blood is splattered.*
> *My killer, dear brother, cavorts in the desert.*
> *They said: We will avenge you, but I replied: This is yet worse.*
> *The wounder shall heal me; that is a better plan.*

My companion unleashed a series of ribald sighs, then asked me what I thought. "This song is one of the best Eastern *muwashshahat*," I replied. "The poetry flows well, and the *basit* meter is properly used. Strophes and rhymes are flawless. But the performance is only average: it needs more instruments and better voices."

"Don't be so critical, Master! Just sit back and enjoy it."

The group now started singing:

> *When I knocked on the door of the tent, she asked: "Who*
> * knocks?"*
> *"One bewitched by beauty," I replied, "no thief or robber."*
> *She smiled, revealing a set of pearly white teeth.*
> *Drowning in the sea of my own tears I staggered back in*
> * disarray.*

The members of the group took turns reciting the two verses, each in their own way, then they were joined by a beautiful young man whom they let sing a solo while they accompanied him on their instruments:

> *Oh how long, how long have I loved your lashes,*
> *Yet you have no mercy, no heart that softens,*
> *So now, because of you, you can see how my heart*
> *Has become like a ploughshare in smiths' hands.*
> *Tears drop and flames leap high,*
> *Hammers fall to left and right.*
> *God has created Christians to be raided,*
> *But your raids are against lovers' hearts.*

This time I gave him my opinion without being asked. "That young man is from the Andalusian Maghrib for sure," I said. "Al-Jubani's son, did you notice how the singer put so much extra expression into the performance. *Muwashshahat* and *zajal*s are part of his regional heritage. The very best ones of all I have heard only in Fez and other places influenced by Andalusian culture."

As the troupe made its way off the stage to another storm of applause, I murmured:

> *Is the gazelle of al-Hima aware that it has enflamed the heart*
> *⸱ of a lover where it has made its dwelling place?*
> *In flame and lightning flash it behaves*
> *like the East wind toying with the firebrand.*

Once the stage was empty, someone piped up with the following anecdote: "When your favorite buxom wench comes to see you, tell her this joke. It comes from one of the two great authorities, either Ibn al-Jawzi, or else Ibn Qayyim al-Jawziya in his *Meadow for Lovers*: A wife and her husband had a falling out. So he started having sex with her a lot. 'God take you away!' she told him. 'Every time we have an argument, you come at me with a mediator I can't repel!'"

Everyone in the tavern let out a lewd guffaw. I realized that the level of debauchery was rising rapidly. As I was making ready to leave, a waiter leaned over and offered me a glass of wine—

compliments, he said, of some toffs in the tavern to the great Maliki legal authority, Ibn Khaldun. I stood up, told the waiter to take the glass back to its owners with clear instructions to the effect that I only take legitimate drinks. I said a rapid farewell to the astonished young man and hurried toward the exit. Behind me I left the dancer gyrating and soaring with every limb in her body.

"The tavern's your own place, revered pilgrim. Daytime's for legal affairs and teaching; nighttime's for enjoyment and deceit!" called the tavern owner.

I chose to ignore this leering suggestion and rushed away in the hope of safeguarding my reputation. Once safely out of the way and close to my house, I told myself that I had gone to the tavern to offer condolences, but I allowed myself to forget what the original purpose actually had been. Now my antics would be a free gift to my enemies, who would make a mountain out of a molehill. So, Umm al-Banin, for the remainder of the night you can be my covering and I yours.

The following hadith comes from Jabir via al-Khatib: The Prophet of God (may God bless and preserve him) said: 'Do not have sex before foreplay.' Well, it was clear that Umm al-Banin rejected both. She was extremely annoyed that I had stayed out till early morning. At lunchtime on the following day I had to invoke all my persuasive powers to convince her of the veracity of my account of what had actually happened the night before. In such matters it was intention that mattered, not missteps on the way. Even so, it was only when I had sworn a solemn oath that I had neither disgraced myself nor had sex with anyone that I managed to dispel the suspicions in her mind and persuade her to return to her normal smiling self. Actually I was secretly happy that she was jealous. I surreptitiously congratulated myself and thanked the devil for putting suspicions into her head.

One thing that the previous night's adventure did for me was to arouse my dormant infatuation with poetry. In the evening I now started spending many hours reading the *Mu'allaqat*, the principal collections of poetry—prime among them being the *Book of Songs* of Abu al-Faraj al-Isfahani, and the poetry of al-Mutanabbi and al-Ma'arri. But, every time I traversed the territories of these great texts, I became ever more aware of my own inability to compose poetry and my feeble talent on that score. I would make do with muttering to myself, "Everyone possesses the talents he has been given. I must content myself with what I have."

3

The Journey to Timur Lang, the Scourge of the Century

My revered shaykh—may God have mercy on his soul was Muhammad ibn Ibrahim al-Abili, a truly masterful intellect in his own right. Whenever I asked him about Timur Lang or discussed the Mongol chieftain's campaign with him, he would always reply, "He will soon be coming to our region. Should you live so long, you should certainly meet him."

Ibn Khaldun,
Travels East and West

Among the people eating was the chief judge, Wali al-Din [Ibn Khaldun]. All the while Timur Lang kept glaring at them. For his part, Ibn Khaldun was looking at Timur. Whenever Timur looked in his direction, Ibn Khaldun would lower his eyes. Once the stare moved elsewhere, he would look at Timur once again. "Great leader," Ibn Khaldun shouted after a while, "Praise be to God Almighty! With my very presence I have given honor to rulers of peoples; with my works of history I have revived eras that were left for dead; among kings of the Western realms I have seen So-and-So and So-and-So; I have met this sultan and that; I have visited the countries of the East and West; and I have consorted with rulers and deputies in every region. Even with all that, I acknowledge the boon that God has provided for me by keeping me alive and prolonging my existence in order that I may see one who is indeed a king in every way. In lawbooks about genuine authority, the role of kingship is evaluated by modes of conduct. If the food offered by kings is to be eaten to stave off perdition, then that which is now offered to us by our lord, the great commander, achieves that and more. It grants us all honor and prestige." That speech made Timur positively quiver with pleasure; he was almost dancing for sheer joy.

Ibn 'Arabshah,
Amazing Destiny Concerning the History of Timur Lang

In his spare time the master used to play with his little daughter; her favorites were tickling and playing horsey. One time, when he was getting ready to put her on his back, he suddenly realized to his horror that the worst thing that could possibly happen would be for his wife and child to be exposed to some danger. Thereafter, as he was busy studying and writing, he kept asking himself whether there could possibly be any danger worse than that posed by Timur ibn Chaghatay ibn Genghiz Khan. From Turkestan and Bukhara beyond the River Oxus, terrifying stories kept arriving about the brutal raids he had been conducting for the past seven years—as far as the gates of Baghdad itself! Had he not been forced to return to his homeland to put down a rebellion, Baghdad would certainly have faced the very same fate it had suffered at the hands of Hulagu Khan's hordes a century and a quarter earlier. People only sit up and take notice when confronted by imminent danger. But, as far as our historian was concerned, by far the most serious danger at that time was the brutal and rampant tribal spirit among the Tatars. As day followed day, he became ever more aware of the need to investigate their background and the reasons behind their strength. He regarded a Tatar attack on Mamluk territory as an unstoppable certainty.

History is like a maze. Its paths twist and break off; leave one and you are bound to land on another. For anyone who decides to investigate it in detail, death is the only respite. These thoughts went through our master's mind as he made ready to study the general history of the Mongols and that of the king, Timur, in particular, all with the goal of gathering and sifting information, then writing a narrative in accordance with the intellectual demands of living history.

Preparation implies reading books and documents about Tatar tribes and peoples. Whenever the events involved approached the present day or were in some way relevant to it, there was also a need to resort to oral testimony (and its verification). For that very reason, 'Abd al-Rahman made a point of listening carefully to reliable personnel in the sultan's retinue and holders of positions involving pen and sword. His regular visits to the Mountain Palace and certain departments in the Ablaq Palace served to convince him that the majority of people were acutely aware of the Tatar threat; the vaguely looming quality of current information about Timur was merely the calm before the storm.

'Abd al-Rahman's own misgivings found a reflection in the expression on Sultan Barquq's face and the tone of voice he used: "I've summoned you here, great judge, to seek your opinion about a request that Bayazid, the Ottoman warrior, has sent to the 'Abbasi caliph who, as you know, lives within our dominions, namely that the caliph dub him 'Sultan of the Byzantines.' That way, he will be strengthened in his dealings with the Christians in his own lands and against the tyrant, Timur—may God eradicate him!"

Our mufti, 'Abd al-Rahman, could not help recalling the things he had already heard about the terrible letter Timur Lang had sent to Barquq, a letter so terrible that Sudun, his viceroy, had felt unable to read it out. The letter demanded that Barquq surrender; should he refuse to step down, Timur would eliminate his entire dynasty and descendants.

"I am currently preoccupied, my lord," the master told Barquq, "with an investigation of Tatar history, the very people your ancestors defeated at the battle of 'Ayn Jalut in 658 I will present the results of my research just as soon as it is completed. Meanwhile, with regard to a fatwa concerning Bayazid's request to be called 'Sultan of the Byzantines,' I can reply in the affirmative and confirm that it is in full conformity with shari'a law. The only people who could object to such a decision would be those who might wish to cause a rift between you and your natural ally, thus sowing dissension among Muslims as they confront enemies and tyrants."

Barquq gestured to his interlocutor to approach. He patted him on the shoulder as a sign of his pleasure and approval and then urged him to proceed with his research as quickly as possible. With that he allowed him to leave.

In mid-795, word began to arrive about Timur's activities; this time, the Tatar hurricane seemed much closer than before. Oral and written accounts harped on the fact that he had managed to gain absolute power after killing Qamar al-Din, the ruler who had opposed him. His raids had now added Isfahan, 'Iraq, Persia, and Kirman to his dominions. But the news that hit Cairo hardest was that Timur had entered Baghdad where his armies had wreaked total havoc on the city's people and cultural treasures. In spring of the following year, Ahmad ibn 'Uways the Il-Khan, the former ruler of Baghdad, fled from the city to Barquq's Egypt and begged him for help in expelling the Tatars from his kingdom. Barquq rushed to prepare an armed force to set out and confront the invaders. Meanwhile, cities like Tikrit, Diyarbakr, and Raha were all falling like ripe fruit to Timur's army.

What is it, one wonders, that gives the Mongols their overwhelming ability to crush whole armies and take over countries with such devastating force?

The first idea to strike the master was that, from a theoretical point of view, their sense of group solidarity was by far the most vigorous and powerful in this era, but to that he added an additional factor, namely that Timur was an extraordinarily brilliant strategist. All the information he had collected about this warrior confirmed that the secret of his continuing series of victories almost certainly lay in the way he planned his campaigns and chose his battlegrounds on the basis of geographical know-how and political espionage. Furthermore, he was a past master at using scare tactics and psychological warfare, making sure that rumors were continually circulating about the overwhelming force he possessed. This phenomenon was responsible for the rampant paranoia about his destructive instincts among the weaker elements in each kingdom. Horror stories were continually being relayed to political centers by post and columns of fugitives and runaways. A stream of news now arrived to confirm Ibn Khaldun's hunches and suppositions. Barquq reinforced his army with various contingents of mercenaries, but preferred to set up camp in Damascus rather than go out to meet the enemy. Timur decided to postpone the confrontation and to leave the Mamluks hanging around in a state of full alert; they would hear news about the terrible fate of people in Byzantium, Armenia, and the Kurdish fortresses. At the end of the war that never happened, the Mongols decided to leave Baghdad, and their commander returned to his bases in Qarabaq. Ibn 'Uways entered his king's capital with some Mamluk troops, and the sultan himself returned to Egypt neither victorious nor defeated. Only one year went by before yet more disturbing news circulated among government officials, to the effect that Timur had killed the most dangerous of his family rivals, Tughtumish. With that, everyone started arguing in secret and in the open about the possible reappearance of the Mongol menace.

For a while, news of Timur disappeared, but his gruesome image still managed to cast a dark shadow over minds and councils. Whether occasions were public or official, the talk was always of his atrocities, his diabolical cleverness, and his cruelty. In the al-Muqattam Citadel, the Sarghitmishiya College, the Hammam al-Sufiya, and other places, 'Abd al-Rahman would listen to the talk with a critical ear. Even though he attributed a lot of the sentiments to ignorance and lively imagination, he still came to the conclusion that Timur was indeed the clearest possible case of a powerful tyrant, not only because he managed to keep his reputation firmly in place but also because he was extremely successful at keeping everyone so scared out of their wits that they thought about nothing else. With these conclusions in mind, 'Abd al-Rahman came to believe deep down that Barquq had actually been very happy that his encounter with Timur had not taken place. He was even more grateful that the tyrant had not put in an appearance while he— Barquq—was up to his neck putting out the fires of rebellion started by al-Nasiri and Mintash.

At this particular moment everything that was happening served as a prompt, goading the master historian to blow the dust off the parlous discipline of historiography and sharpen his wits in order to better understand the present and contemplate the future. He decided that, as long as he possessed sufficient bodily health and patience, he should accept the challenge. The decision coincided with the completion of a project whereby he had reread the last part of *The Beginning and Ending* of Ibn al-Kathir, part five of *Goal of Desire* by al-Nuwayri, and the third part of the *History* of Abu al-Fida', along with certain biographies and the Mamluk chronicles of Baybars, al-Mansuri, Ibn 'Abd al-Zahir, Ibn Sayyid al-Nas, Ibn Daqman al-Misri, and others. As a result, he felt able to devote his entire attention to histories of the Tatars and Mongols, a subject where he felt his knowledge was particularly lacking. But man does not always get what he wants. In the process of trying to focus entirely on the major topic of the hour and the fin de siècle catastrophe, 'Abd al-Rahman found himself facing all kinds of difficulties in obtaining the necessary materials and finding the time to read them. This was particularly the case with letters and documents from the sultan which Sudun, his viceroy and a dogged foe of 'Abd al-Rahman, did everything he could to prevent him from reading. This lack of access to documents became much worse when Bata the *dawadar* was appointed viceroy in Damascus and then died there. There were also problems with languages: the most important sources on Tatar history were in Turkish, Mongolian, and Persian. Had 'Abd al-Rahman not been of such an advanced age, most of these difficulties could have been dealt with fairly easily. As it was, he managed through various convoluted methods to get hold of copies of the letters of both Bayazid and Timur to Barquq and of two works in Persian, Yazadi's biography of Timur, the *Book of Victories*, and the history of Ghazan Khan by the Il-Khan historian, Sharaf al-Din 'Ali al-Azdi. Beyond that, he commissioned his bookseller in Khan al-Khalili, his students, and his distinguished Turkish colleagues to get him the major source-works on the subject. As days and nights passed, 'Abd al-Rahman began to realize that the process of gaining any kind of mastery of Mongol history was like plunging into an endless swamp. There were countless tribes and peoples, their lineages were a complete jumble, and their lands were remote and impenetrable. The whole thing made him dizzy and gave him a bad headache. In his spare moments he would draw diagrams to illustrate this or that family tree; he would also use scraps of papers to make lists of famous names, places, countries, dynasties, and tribes. As all this became almost a habit, he realized he was involved in a world where names and things were utterly strange from every point of view. This was a world where the only way of getting to the bottom of things was to devote oneself entirely to detailed research. All of which demanded of 'Abd al-Rahman something he no longer had at his disposal, namely energy, passion, and enthusiasm. For that reason, the pages he wrote on the Mongols were bound to be at the very least modest, and on occasion weak and confused.

Barquq summoned 'Abd al-Rahman for a visit late at night at the end of Safar in 799 When 'Abd al-Rahman laid eyes on the sultan, he realized that the ruler's usual nickname, al-Zahir, 'the manifest', no longer suited him. His eyes looked dim, sunken in their sockets beneath his bushy eyebrows and straggly unkempt beard. Elsewhere on his body, signs of early aging told people in the know that he was so preoccupied with the Mongol threat that he could no longer relax or get any sleep; nights would consist of endless bouts of insomnia.

When a mind is as disturbed as was that of the sultan, neither medicaments nor the wise counsel of advisers serve any purpose. For that reason, he would summon such people to his chambers at night and bombard them with questions and requests for legal opinions until morning came. When 'Abd al-Rahman's turn came, the audience took place in the great arcade along with the Maliki judge, Nasir al-Din ibn al-Tunsi, Sudun, the viceroy who was thus responsible for arranging audiences and controlling traffic, and the *dawadar*, Yashbak, the recorder:

BARQUQ (his voice muted, his expression depressed): I have invited the two great Maliki authorities in our blessed realm for this audience in order to seek their counsel regarding possible action against the Mongol tyrant, Timur the Lame—may God thwart his actions and eradicate his line!

(With that, silence fell, interspersed with the occasional cough. Sudun took it as his cue to repeat what the sultan had just said, on the assumption that the two judges had not heard what the sultan had originally said. To all of which he added a request that they give their legal opinions in the most beneficial way possible. 'Abd al-Rahman now felt constrained to open the discussion, doing his level best to avoid looking at the viceroy who would undoubtedly be on the lookout for anything provocative.)

IBN KHALDUN: In my view, al-Malik al-Zahir Sayf al-Din is doing the best thing possible by consulting widely on the topic. Religious scholars are, as the saying goes, the heirs of the prophets. . . .

IBN AL-TUNSI (wiping the sweat from his brow): The Prophet—on him be peace—said, 'A scholar who uses his knowledge to provide benefit is better than a thousand other believers.' He also said, 'Knowledge is the life of Islam.'

SUDUN (interrupting): We already know these hadith and others as well. Our lord the sultan needs advice on action, not other matters.

IBN KHALDUN: The Best of Mankind said, 'Knowledge is a treasure-trove, and the key to it is questions. So ask your questions—may God have mercy on you. He compensates four types of people for it: the questioner, the teacher, the listener, and the one who loves them.'

BARQUQ (calming things down): I wish to ask Ibn Khaldun, our learned friend, about his views on the tyrant Timur and the best ways to make war on him.

IBN KHALDUN: Military strategy, my lord, is the province of soldiers and members of military staff; of that your own outstanding knowledge is an example. Where tyrants are concerned, I have spent a not inconsiderable period of my life investigating the secrets of their power and the reasons for their victories. The amount of material written on the subject is very little, but to the extent possible, I have been trying to collect evidence and to compare examples. I will be able to present you with a copy of my conclusions as soon as I have written them out and edited them.

BARQUQ: Time is very short, and events are forcing our hand. If we need to wait for ages before deciding anything, it will work against us. Leave the writing process to mature in its own good time. Give me the benefit of your advice now.

SUDUN: I'm afraid that the author of the *Introduction to History* is reluctant to give us his advice or feels unable to discuss the subject. He is the one who keeps talking about the inability of religious scholars to discuss political matters.

IBN AL-TUNSI (as though emerging from a stupor): 'To the effect that religious scholars are of all people the most removed from politics and its subfields,' section forty-two of the sixth chapter of Book One of *Diwan of Topic and Predicate*.

IBN KHALDUN: What I say there refers specifically to jurists involved in canonical political thought and philosophers of the ideal community. I'm not referring to religious scholars in their general public role. But even then, they have no possibility of investigating politics when some people decide to turn the whole thing into a directorate for conspiracy, obscurantism, and injustice.

SUDUN (aggravated): Let's forget about irrelevances and get back to the point!

IBN KHALDUN: What I've just said and will go on to say is precisely the point. I'm sure, my lord, that chroniclers have given you information about the ancestry of the Tatars and Mongols, people of the North. I don't need to remind you that their tradition of invasion and rapine goes all the way back to Genghiz Khan and has been replicated by his descendants, Hulagu Khan who sacked Baghdad, and now Timur whose hordes threaten all the countries and souls that lie in his path. I don't think I'm exaggerating when I suggest that this tyrant, Timur, is the most ruthless and dangerous of all the Mongols. The reason is that he makes full use of advanced knowledge and strategy in applying his overwhelming force. Any invasion he undertakes is not a matter of random selection or ignorance. He'll only set out once he's convinced that success is assured.

SUDUN: So, is it your view that our lord, bolstered as he is by his amirs and *atabeg* soldiers, is doing something other than that himself?

IBN KHALDUN: My dear viceroy, do not put words into my mouth. Sultan al-Zahir Sayf al-Din possesses God-given perspicacity and organizational skills. His actions and his respect for scholarship and those who practice it is clear enough evidence of that.

BARQUQ: Finish your portrait of the tyrant, Timur. You've made me want to know more.

IBN KHALDUN: Timur, my lord—and the name in Mongolian means 'man of iron'—has managed to seize the Banu Hulagu and Banu Dushi-Khan realms by virtue of rigorous discipline, something that grew and then flourished in his own tribe just at the point when it was dwindling among those peoples whom he has vanquished. That discipline is the rigor of the Bedouin in the desert, the very thing I observed throughout the Maghrib region, a powerful force that can easily overwhelm civilized dynasties with their penchant for luxury. His knowledge and strategies are considerable and diverse. Firstly, he is a Muslim. Not only that, but he has compelled the Chagatai to convert to Islam—all in order to pull the rug out from under Muslim peoples who kept calling for a war against him because he was a Magian and thus a polytheist. He makes copious use of informers and spies in various regions and inside palaces; no doubt, there are some in our midst here. Beyond that, his invasions cause massive destruction; he covers whole areas with piles of corpses and skulls so that the dire news will be spread abroad and cause maximum panic.

IBN AL-TUNSI (trying to keep up): The Prophet—on him be peace—said, 'People's fears have amplified my own strength, giving me a month's leeway' (as recorded by al-Bukhari and Muslim in their collections of authentic hadiths, the *Sahihan*).

IBN KHALDUN: But Our Prophet had a divine mission, one that he spread among rightly guided people by volition and among polytheists by fear. He never conquered through the use of tyranny or superior force, but rather by victory and miracle given to him by the One, all-powerful God. Timur, on the other hand, has only one mission: to destroy land and lineage. His only purpose is to sit on the thrones of the world's kingdoms.

SUDUN (in a provocative tone): So, learned judge, do you really see this lame Bedouin who alarms you so much being able to sit on this throne? Following your general dicta here, does the Burji Mamluk dynasty share the probability of the same limited lifespan as others?

IBN KHALDUN: The lifespan of dynasties is the same as that of every one; it's all in God's hands. Eternity is God's alone. The Mongol tyrant is now exclusive ruler of his people and uses conquered peoples in order to feed his own armies. The only thing that can destroy him now is precisely what destroyed tyrants in past ages, in Macedonia, Persia, and Byzantium: too many invasions, the disorder they bring, and lengthy supply lines between center and periphery. Anything else involves setting up fortifications and armed human shields to protect inhabited areas and cities that need not be impacted by the Mongol firestorm. Previous invasions of countries have often involved long-term strategies, not sudden incursions. The Mongols already occupy large tracts of territory. My lord the sultan should let them wear themselves out grabbing territories in the North and controlling steppes and desert wastes. There is no wisdom in our contesting their rapacious policy. The consequences of doing so may well be severe.

SUDUN (feigning shock): Heaven help us all! Is the judge suggesting we do not go out to confront the tyrant and prevent him wreaking death and destruction among God's faithful?

IBN KHALDUN: The Mongol invasion is exactly like a hurricane or earthquake; there are bound to be victims and destruction. In such cases the smart thing to do is to let them expend all their energy beyond established limits of security. Our lord al-Zahir Sayf al-Din's decision to set such limits in Syria was exactly right. He sprang to its defense when the time came, but went no further.

SUDUN: I don't see how any of this solves the principal issue before us. Do you think the tyrant will attack Damascus again and try to sack it, even when our lord prevented him last time?

IBN KHALDUN: My own opinion is that Timur will certainly return to Syria with an even larger force and greater determination. As usual he'll start with the weaker parts. In one isolated city he'll pile up a mound of skulls, then he'll set fire to another. Preparations will have to be made for such an eventuality, whether it actually happens or God protects us from such a calamity.

BARQUQ (fighting sleep): So now, revered judge, we've reached the touchstone of the entire matter. Apart from military preparations that are the province of our fearless generals, give me some advice about other covert factors that might facilitate (and indeed accelerate) our victory.

IBN KHALDUN (staring fixedly at Sudun): Firstly, my lord, by strengthening the domestic front. How? By applying justice, the mainstay of proper kingship. Bribery and graft serve to corrupt morals and values. Injustice is the sure sign of a civilization's imminent collapse. If the ruler treats his people fairly and respects them, they'll be much more inclined to respect and love him and fight on his behalf against his enemies.

BARQUQ (gesturing to his recorder to write it all down): Absolutely correct. What else?

IBN KHALDUN: Open up the treasury and spend money on sharpening the war effort and making the prospect of fighting a war attractive to desert warriors. At this point the viceroy may well ask me, 'Where does the extra money come from? The revenue sources are already known and will not increase.' In response, my lord, I must offer some very basic advice. Whatever happens, do not further oppress an already weakened people or impose taxes on professionals or farmers. Do not make people even more despondent than they already are or try to force developers to curtail their activities. The only places where you are going to find the necessary money and equipment is in the coffers of the wealthy, people who are living a life of luxury and ease. A portion of their money and property will suffice to build all the buttresses needed to repel the Mongol threat. If they don't cooperate, their money will vanish and so will they."

IBN AL-TUNSI: *Verily those who store up gold and silver and do not spend them in the path of God, give them the glad tidings of a dire punishment.*

SUDUN (exasperated): The notables and senior officials of state will spare nothing to insure our lord's victory and defend the throne. Ibn Khaldun: Words are confirmed and bolstered by actions. The best charity is that which comes soonest. So let no money be smuggled away, no heirlooms buried, and no documents forged or concealed. The situation is extremely grave. Anyone who fails to appreciate that will perish in his ignorance.

BARQUQ: And what else?

IBN KHLADUN: Exchange of gifts, my lord, exchange of gifts! They are the best way to cement relationships, and a downpayment on peace. In this particular circumstance, the most important gesture would involve the sultans in the Maghrib, chief among them being the Marini sultan. When you send him a letter, remember that he is extremely proud, as were his ancestors. It is a good idea to address him as 'Commander of the Faithful' so we don't have to face the same misunderstandings and alienation that happened between Salah al-Din the Ayyubid and Ya'qub al-Mansur the Almohad ruler.

BARQUQ: What happened between them— may God show no tolerance to those who give offence?

IBN KHALDUN: The Ayyubid amir sent the Almohad sultan a gift and asked him to dispatch his fleet to blockade the French off the coast of Syria. The initiative was a complete failure, but only because he did not insert the phrase 'Commander of the Faithful' into his official letter. That at least is what the chroniclers tell us. *And God knows the contents of men's hearts.*

BARQUQ: I wonder, Wali al-Din. Do you think I'll need Maghribi troops and equipment in my war against Timur?

IBN KHALDUN: When I first arrived in Egypt, I thought the people here looked as though they had just emerged from the Day of Reckoning. Today it's the same or even more so. As a whole they're either people of modest demands and expectations —that being the vast majority, or else highly cultured people spoiled by excess and luxury. They've become more cowardly than a group of women flat on their backs. That's why for defense and attack purposes you're going to need the army to be reinforced by warriors and mercenaries from neighboring Muslim countries. The Maghrib, with its Bedouins and Berbers, is a veritable goldmine for sturdy fighters ready for hardships and battle. In addition there are the horses that my lord is always eager to ride, animals that seem created for toil and conflict. Gifts and presents, they will prepare the way for the declaration of *jihad* and mobilization.

BARQUQ: This is another reason why I have summoned you here tonight, Wali al-Din. You are aware that five or more years ago I wrote to one of the Bedouin chiefs of the Maghrib a letter of request to his Marini sultan, Abu al-'Abbas. I charged him with the task of selecting some horses from his region and bringing them back to me here. I have no idea what has delayed him in carrying out the task. Today I am going to entrust the Mamluk Qutlubagha with the task of taking gifts of cloth, perfume, and bows to the monarchs of the Maghrib. I am relying on you to give him appropriate advice as to how to conduct himself.

IBN KHALDUN: My lord, accepting such an honor I regard as an obligation.

BARQUQ: Is there anything else we need to discuss on this matter?

IBN KHALDUN: Yes, there is something more I would like to say by way of conclusion. I would ask the recorder to note it down.

BARQUQ (still fighting exhaustion): Then by all means proceed, even though we stay up till dawn.

IBN KHALDUN: My lord, I have no detailed knowledge of the arts of warfare, but I am still of the opinion that any resistance to the Mongol attack may well require a cluster of skills either simultaneously or in sequence: attack and retreat; marching in ranks and phalanxes; advancing and fortifying redoubts and trenches. Furthermore, I think that you should not expect to rely on lines of lancers and archers, the pride of the Mamluk army. It will be much more effective for commanders and strategists to make use of Timur's most deadly and effective weapon, deceit and trickery.

IBN AL-TUNSI (eyes closed): In *The Prevalent Model*, Diya' al-Din ibn al-Athir says that the person with a trick is more useful than an entire tribe. The Lord of Creation and Victor over Polytheists says, "War is deceit."

IBN KHALDUN: As weapons, deceit and trickery only work properly when they're used by someone who is completely versed in the finer points of strategic planning and can thus benefit from the various categories of useful information they provide. That's why you'll find Timur always surrounded by the most-qualified experts in every specialty. He never enters a city without first getting to know its religious scholars and co-opting some of them to his team. For example, he dispatched some of them to Samarqand to look into rebuilding and decorating its monuments. He's done the same thing more recently in Raha, Tikrit, Aleppo, and elsewhere. My lord, if you would like me to prepare a document of the things that I think most important and urgent, then by all means entrust me with such a task.

BARQUQ: Indeed, I would very much like you to prepare such a document.

IBN KHALDUN: God willing, the chapters will follow a logical progression. We'll start by recalling the Mamluk victory over the Mongols at the battle of 'Ayn Jalut, the interest in Ibn 'Abd al-Zahir's version of the heroic tale of Baybars who defeated the Mongol invaders, and the command that it be translated into both Turkish and Tatar; then a chapter on Timur's retreat in the face of Sultan al-Zahir Barquq's advance and the dispatch of trustworthy spies and agents to infiltrate his army ranks and tribes. God alone grants success.

BARQUQ: Power to you, Wali al-Din, power to you! (Gesturing to Sudun.) Escort Judge Ibn al-Tunsi out. He has fallen asleep.

IBN AL-TUNSI (waking up): Heaven forbid! *Neither slumber nor sleep take him.* God's peace on my lord the sultan!

BARQUQ (gesturing to Ibn Khaldun to come closer): Bata, the person who has always protected you against the evil designs of Sudun, has died. Sudun's fanaticism is part of a long-standing obligation I have, as you well know. But, God willing, I intend very soon to appoint you chief Maliki judge in Ibn al-Tunsi's place, whether he's alive or dead. And there's something else I want you to know: I'm feeling weaker and weaker and I don't imagine that any attack on Timur's part will happen while I'm alive. It's far more likely to be during the reign of my heir-apparent, my son al-Nasir Faraj. I'm asking you now, Wali al-Din, to take good care of the boy; be a steadfast counselor and supporter. Now you can get up and leave. Just one prayer I ask of you as dawn breaks on this day, that I might sleep a little. (He embraces Ibn Khaldun.) Go in peace.

When Ibn Khaldun woke up at midday, he was greeted by the beaming smile of his wife. He was surprised that she did not ask him why he had been out most of the night, and invited her to ask him. She did so, but still smiling and without the slightest show of concern.

"There have been many deaths," she went on, "so I suppose you've been offering your condolences again."

He paid no attention to this sarcastic remark.

"No, not that," he replied with a frown. "I spent the night with the sultan discussing crucially important matters."

"With the sultan? How is he?"

"Not at all well, Umm al-Batul, not at all well."

"A sultan, and he's not feeling well. So what's a poor citizen supposed to say?"

So saying she went off to prepare the meal. 'Abd al-Rahman meanwhile sat there, thinking about the fact that his wife did not seem to be so jealous any longer and wistfully reflecting on the passage of time that was certainly not working in his favor within his own household.

As soon as lunch was over, the master played with this little daughter for a while and fell asleep by her side. When he felt a certain amount of renewed vigor, he went upstairs and spent many hours till the middle of the night composing the document he had promised the sultan and letters to be dispatched by the hand of Qutlubagha to the religious scholars in the Maghrib in which he was asking for their counsel regarding the Mongol menace and their attitude toward Timur. Next morning, he went back to the palace and was one of the most prominent participants in the departure ceremony for the sultan's mission. He gave the emissary the benefit of his best advice and suggested the most direct route to get to the kingdoms to the west.

Ah, the vicissitudes of time and events. Ah, the effect of time on the human frame! At the very end of 799, emissaries reached Egypt from the three kings of the Maghrib. There was a superb caravan loaded down with the most costly luxuries and expensive gifts. The most opulent and lavish gifts—truth to tell—came from the Marini, Abu

'Amir. The royal household grabbed the smaller items and made off with them, leaving for the sultan some magnificent horses with gold-encrusted bridles and saddles. The day when these items were displayed in front of him was a notable day indeed. 'Abd al-Rahman meanwhile was busy talking to the Maghribi emissaries either in the palace itself or in his own home. He made all the necessary arrangements for their stay, gave them a warm welcome, and did not lose a single moment in questioning them at length about the conditions of both monarch and people in their countries. He repeated the procedure when they all returned to Cairo after completing the obligation of the pilgrimage to the Holy Places. They stayed in the city for a few days to rest before embarking on the long journey back to their homeland, duly honored with gifts from the generous hand of the sultan.

Following the death of the Maliki judge, Ibn al-Tunsi, Barquq appointed Ibn Khaldun as his successor in the middle of Ramadan 801, thereby fulfilling the promise he had made earlier. The gesture was marked by a substantial level of welcome and praise in spite of the best efforts of rumormongers and slanderers. The sultan also turned down an offer from Judge Ibn al-Damamini to purchase the post for a sum of seventy thousand dinars. The newly appointed judge was extremely grateful to be reappointed to this position and announced his firm intention to apply the law with justice and in accordance with the shari'a as God wills. He now devoted himself to the new position, to such an extent that he would often bring food prepared by his wife to his judicial office: sweet pastries prepared Moroccan style, meat slices Egyptian style. Deep down the judge had the feeling that his nomination to this position was a kind of farewell gift from the sultan who was now unable to keep his exhaustion and illness a secret from anyone. Indeed, not even a whole month passed before Sultan Barquq went to meet his Maker, after arranging the succession for his children beginning with his eldest son, al-Nasir Faraj, whom he placed in the care of the *atabeg*, Aytamish. He had Caliph al-Mutawakkil, amirs, and judges all serve as witnesses to his will. However, what ensued was a series of revolts that left 'Abd al-Rahman fair game for any number of eventualities; there were variations, but the basic import was always one and the same. Aytamish, the young sultan's guardian, gets above himself; Tanam, the viceroy of Syria, who loathes him, declares a revolt; Aytamish's *atabeg*s revolt against their own master and encourage the young sultan to get rid of the noose around his neck. Events pursued their course, and 'Abd al-Rahman grew tired of trying to keep up with it all. It was lucky for the new sultan that the revolt only lasted a few months. He marched to Damascus and managed to do away with all the conspirators either by killing them in battle or having them strangled.

The process of consigning the sultanate to Barquq's descendants and consolidating their hegemony by massacring dissidents, that may best represent the import of Sultan Barquq's bequest to his heirs. It suggests that those heirs had learned from their father that the only way they would be able to rid themselves of the Mongol menace was by consolidating Mamluk ranks and fortifying their fighting spirit. But there was something about Faraj's personality that deeply troubled 'Abd al-Rahman. It was not his general lack of experience, something that obviously resulted from his youth. After all, intelligence and sound advice could solve that problem. No, the real problem was a bad case of snobbery that was made yet more reckless by drink. The huge difference between father and son in this regard was not one that was likely to disappear over time; it involved temperament, posture, and build. 'Abd al-Rahman had noticed this great difference first hand when he had accompanied the young sultan on his expedition to Syria to quash the rebellion against him. In notes made on the journey he had written: "Timur's rampage is certainly going to come, O God, unless some miracle happens and the reason for it is no longer valid."

On the way back to Egypt, 'Abd al-Rahman asked the sultan for permission to visit the holy places in Jerusalem that he had long wanted to see, but events and duties had conspired against him. That is how he came to pray in the al-Aqsa Mosque, the original place toward which Muslims directed their prayers and the third of the sacred shrines that God blessed. From it, the Prophet Muhammad—on him be peace—had undertaken his night-journey into the heavens. In this mosque the entire roof was open to God's firmament as was the rest of the sacred enclosure in al-Quds protected by the walls of Salah al-Din ibn Ayyub. In such surroundings 'Abd al-Rahman's five senses all seemed to be pulling him gently toward abstraction and transcendence; a throbbing, yet firm desire urged him to launch himself on a spiritual journey. Were he not married and tied to the ground, he thought to himself, he would stay here close to the spacious mosque, humbly worshipping God and reflecting as he walked from David's chambers to Job's oratory, Mary's shrine, and Zakariya's temple—peace be upon them all. As he visited the burial sites of certain prophets, the Dome of the Rock, the paddock of Barraq, the Prophet's steed on his night-journey, the tower where God spoke to Moses, and many other holy places, 'Abd al-Rahman felt suffused by a pure spirit of sanctity and enveloped in its radiant light.

This holy city is a symbol of something that occurs readily to the mind of any fascinated visitor. Here amid the three divinely revealed religious faiths stand the covenants of the word all combined. Within the broad context of the unity of God the beginning and end is peace. For that reason 'Abd al-Rahman decided not to go into the Church of the Holy Sepulchre built on the site of the crucifixion because it represents a breach of those convenants and a slander against the Holy Qur'an.

Having fulfilled all his obligations in the city of peace and radiance, 'Abd al-Rahman made his way to Bethlehem, where Jesus, son of Mary, grew up. There he touched the remains of the palm root and wrote as follows about the church there:

> A huge building on the site of the birth of the Messiah. There the Caesars erected a structure with two rows of stone columns, rounded and aligned, topped by images of kings and the dates of their reigns, duly arranged for whoever may wish to verify their translation at the hands of those familiar with their circumstances. This building may well be seen as a symbol of the rule of the Caesars and the splendor of their regime.

From Bethlehem 'Abd al-Rahman made his way to Hebron which lies in a gently shaded valley. In spite of its small size, the town is greatly valued because it contains the place of prayer constructed by Solomon the Wise. While there, 'Abd al-Rahman visited the grotto shrine of Ibrahim, the Companion of God, Isaac, Jacob, and their wives—the purest of peace be upon all of them. There he prayed not only the obligatory prayers but the supernumerary ones as well. In awe and reverence he descended into the grotto, overcome by emotion. Before saying farewell he cast an eye at the grave of Lot—on him be peace—and expressed the wish to bathe in his lake before long.

On the coast of Syria, by the town of Gaza, he recalled that it would soon be time to rejoin the sultan's retinue on its way back to Cairo. He therefore made do with a short prayer in the city mosque. After eating a sampling of its dates and grapes, he mounted his horse and set off along the coast, avoiding the Israelite wilderness as he did so. On his way a variety of thoughts occurred to him: that visiting al-Quds, just like Mecca and Medina, served to rid any doubting mind of the existence of the spirit; the five senses were left with an indelible trace of that particular dimension called the absolute. Another thought was that any visit to the city of light and peace, to the tombs of the witnesses to the unity of God and those of their wives, was only totally fulfilled in the company of one's beloved life-companion.

At the northern outskirts of Cairo 'Abd al-Rahman caught up with the sultan's retinue and accompanied him into the city while steering well clear of all the pomp and ceremony. When they reached the approaches to the Ablaq Palace, he rushed off home, eager to kiss his wife and daughter.

The master's hunches about the young sultan's proclivities toward intrigue and slackness proved to be correct. Toward the end of 802 there was a noticeable change in attitude toward him, all accompanied by abuse and defamation. All the while Sultan Faraj paid no attention and did nothing. His retinue set about organizing 'Abd al-Rahman's dismissal as judge and the sale of the office for hard cash to the totally unknown judge named Nur al-Din ibn al-Khilal; no one either objected or saw anything wrong with it. The accusation leveled against 'Abd al-Rahman was exactly the same as had been used when he had first served as a judge: being too severe in imposing sentences and punishments—or, to put it in terms closer to the reality of the situation, the Maliki judge refused to close his eyes and "take in the broader picture." What he was supposed to do was to put on a robe crafted by the new military and administrative authorities and accept bribes from their friends who were owners of livestock, farms, and estates. That was how he was to behave if he wished to stay in the good books of political, state, and financial officials. The whole thing involved adjusting God's laws in accordance with their private desires and interests. What God had explicitly forbidden was to be declared legal. He was to turn a blind eye to crooked sales practices, deceit, and graft, and to go easy on opportunists and monopolists and other types of fraudulent operators.

No, no, a thousand times, no! That is what 'Abd al-Rahman said to Aqbay, the chamberlain who was intriguing against him as hard as he could. And 'Abd al-Rahman went on to say, "By God, in whose hands lies my own soul, no sultan, however great his sway may be, will ever dissuade me from passing judgment according to what is right." Those were inflammatory and crushing words, and they made his enemies realize that things had now come to a head. They forced the chamberlain not merely to fire the judge but to throw him in prison in the Citadel for a week. During that time 'Abd al-Rahman was allowed to read and to receive his servant, Sha'ban, who brought him comforting news about his family.

"Everything at home is fine, sir. Your friends have told me what had happened. Never mind, I told myself, I'll have to tell your wife that my Master is the guest of the sultan."

"That's fine, Sha'ban. Tell my wife that I'm the sultan's guest, and no one knows for how long."

While in prison 'Abd al-Rahman thought less about his own circumstances than he did about the cracks that were appearing in Egyptian military ranks and the ever- increasing advantages for the Mongol invasion. The sultan was very young; now he was aware of exactly how young! A plaything in the hands of evil cliques, only emerging from one crisis to fall into another. Those religious scholars who were both intelligent and well-meaning had neither role nor authority against the political power of clashing ambitions and intrigues. It was better to stay in prison than to be turned into a bridge for the exploitation of thugs and con men.

At the end of the week 'Abd al-Rahman was ordered released from prison and confined to his house. One of the walls in the prison preserved for posterity a line of poetry composed by its illustrious occupant:

On earth the noble man finds a retreat from wrong;
In it is a refuge for one who fears hate.

Barely had 'Abd al-Rahman hugged his wife and daughter before he squelched his anger by saying loudly, "This time, Umm al-Batul, we must leave this benighted country. Egypt is no longer a place of refuge from wrong. The Maghrib is my homeland, and it remains so even though it may have treated me badly. The voice of the Maghrib inside me keeps telling me to come home. Fez is wait-ing for us. Pack up our bags and make ready to leave."

His wife trilled three times in sheer delight. "Where do I start?" she kept saying as she paced around the rooms. "Sha'ban, help me!"

The old servant looked sadder than a raven. "Worries are half the burden of old age, sir," he said, "With your departure, my old age has finally arrived for good. The happiest days of my life have been spent in your service. How can I stand the thought of your leaving?"

'Abd al-Rahman had no idea how to talk to his faithful servant. He gave him a distracted look full of affection, but left it to his wife to come up with the right reply.

"You're one of us, Sha'ban. When we go, you can come with us."

"For me, Umm al-Batul," Sha'ban replied, "the world's bound-aries stop at Fustat and Cairo. Even when I was in the prime of life, I've never left my homeland. How can I possibly do it now when my back is bent by old age? If you have to leave, then do it slowly and deliberately out of kindness to me."

'Abd al-Rahman immediately set about calming Sha'ban down. He told his wife to think about the idea and to take things slowly. With that, he went up to his study to read and write.

The next day, 'Abd al-Rahman received a visit from the *dawadar* Yashbak al-Sha'bani. After welcoming him warmly, he told his visitor that he intended to return to his homeland, saying merely that he longed to go back. However, his visitor immediately revealed the reason for his visit.

"Wali al-Din," he said, "I've just spent more than a month in Syria, keeping track of news about Timur. I've been consulting with the amirs and also with the viceroy of al-Ghiba. If I'd been in Cairo, no one, not even the sultan in person, would have been able to harm you. Aqbay, the chamberlain, is stupid and dishonest; his only virtue is that he sided with Faraj during the recent revolt. As soon as I got back to Cairo and heard you'd been put in prison, I immediately went and told him about the documents I had written down when you had met with his father, the late Sultan Barquq. That made him shed bitter tears. He has asked me to apologize to you on his behalf and to offer you a Maliki teaching post at the endowment of Umm Salih. Then, so help me God, if Aqbay were not already heading for a downfall, I would ask that he be ordered to beg your forgiveness and to walk from the chamberlain's office on foot, just as he made you do when he summoned you."

'Abd al-Rahman burst into a smile.

"May God reward you well, Yashbak," he said earnestly, yet humbly. "God bless you for all your efforts on my behalf. Walking, I would remind you, is healthy exercise, warmly recommended by doctors and physicians. For old people like me it has well documented benefits. The primary damage resulted from the type of prison I was in before you returned from Syria. In my view there are two types of prison: one is an object of pride, the other a source of humiliation and degradation. I savored the first type when I was young. I served two years in prison in Fez during the reign of the Marini sultan, Abu 'Inan. The second type I have had to endure for totally unjust reasons at the beginning of the reign of a sultan who is still a minor and whose father I had served loyally. But let's not waste time talking about a trial that many people hoped would totally humiliate me, but now they've been proved wrong. I survived it in one piece, all because I spent much time contemplating the Mighty and Infinite One and the collected wisdom of India, Greece, the Arabs, and the Persians. I gave my memory a free hand and opened the gates to the spiritual inspiration of the mystical path. The Sufis of Islam gave me the benefit of their choicest moments. Al-

Karkhi was watching over me as we both intoned: 'Sufism involves grasping genuine truths; despair what is in mortals' hands.'"

"What about the new post you're being offered, Wali al-Din?"

"I do not need it. Tell them to sell it off as they did with my judgeship. The state treasury needs all the money it can get for the war against the Tatars. Beyond that, the Maliki rite has now become an orphan in this land of Egypt, rendered irrelevant by the corruption of centuries-old customs and spurned by the influential and wealthy classes. But tell me, Yashbak, what news of Timur?"

"Very bad, very bad indeed. Timur has occupied Anatolia and destroyed Siwas. Today he's making his way across Syria toward Damascus itself. The situation is dangerous, Wali al-Din, and extremely critical. In my role as *dawadar* and army marshal I've advised the sultan to send his army to Damascus to prevent it falling into Mongol hands. Damascus is in effect our easternmost gateway. If it falls—God forbid—Egypt is wide open to the final catastrophe. Several army commanders share this view, but not the majority of them. The entire situation now is marked by dithering; I'm doing my very best to get things changed, so help me God! I've suggested to Faraj that he take judges with him in his retinue, with you at the very head of the list."

"I'm grateful to you for your consideration, but my age no longer permits me to travel long distances."

"The place we're heading for is not far away, Wali al-Din. No one is going to view your non-participation with any sort of compassion or understanding. Take the next two days to think things over carefully. That's all the time you have before the middle of the month of the Prophet's birthday; that's when we're scheduled to leave. Once you've made up your mind, let me know."

That said, the *dawadar* got up to leave and bid 'Abd al-Rahman farewell with a great deal of affection and respect.

When 'Abd al-Rahman brought up this subject with his wife, there was much wailing. Umm al-Batul begged her husband to stay by her side. War, she said, was for soldiers. How was he supposed to explain to her that he longed to meet the Mongol lord and talk with him? How could he convince her of the significance of the coming battle and his desire to witness its different phases? All his eloquent phrases came up against her simple, naïve expressions of concern. He reminded her that she was bound to obey him. In response she threatened that, if he left them and went to war, she would take their daughter back with her to Fez. It was eventually left to Sha'ban to bring the dispute to an end. He was the only one who knew how to calm Umm al-Banin's worries and persuade his master to treat his wife gently.

Many were the hours that 'Abd al-Rahman spent thinking about the attraction he felt toward the Timur phenomenon, in spite of all the dangers and hardships involved. Lying in bed he decided that, if he were to travel to Damascus as part of al-Nasir Faraj's retinue (assuming that it actually happened), his motivation would not be a desire to support the Mamluk dynasty but simply his own intellectual curiosity and an eagerness on his part to be an eyewitness. Once the era of the Rightly-Guided Caliphs had come to an end, any notion of legitimate hegemony had been sheer fancy and pretense. It had all been activated on the tips of swords and spears. Only people willing to be duped by professional manipulators and genealogical trickers would ever be taken in by it. He had said as much many years earlier, and he continued to weigh its validity as he observed the 'Abbasi caliphate today, in all its feeble finery, being preserved by the Mamluks in fancy cages. There would be times when he felt that aspirants to monarchical rule need no longer be either white- or yellow-complexioned, neither round- nor slanty-eyed, just so long as everyone claimed to be a Muslim and to be protecting its essence and sanctum. So then, here he was, ready to travel to the very frontiers of raging conflict with neither weapon nor cause, on his way to assess the heat of history in one of its more troublesome byways; going with the primary intention of providing a portrait of the conflict and plotting its course on the chart of cataclysms and transformations in kingdoms and thrones.

On the day when the army was to march (which, after delays, turned out to be the third day of Rabi' al-Akhir), 'Abd al-Rahman kissed his wife and daughter goodbye and hugged Sha'ban. He asked his faithful servant to take care of the family for him. That done, he went up to the Citadel where he was warmly greeted by Yashbak.

From the sultan's personal stable he was given a splendid Maghribi mule decked with a gold-embossed saddle and jewel-encrusted bridle. Yashbak presented him to al-Nasir Faraj along with the other judges, then placed him amid the horsemen and walkers who were heading for Gaza on the seashore.

The journey from Cairo to Damascus, which took them by Shaqhab under Mount Ghabaghib, proceeded largely in silence, a quiet that was tinged with a good deal of fear and caution. The generally gloomy atmosphere kept being fed with news of the Mongol army as it made its grisly way through one region after another as far as Ba'albakk on its way to the Mamluk fortress in Damascus.

'Abd al-Rahman questioned Yashbak about the commanders' strategy for the campaign against the Timurid army. He was told that it involved defense of the city; defense and nothing but defense. The plan was to make Timur give up any idea of attacking or occupying it. He explained the time factor, something that, if properly planned, would work in favor of Faraj's army. Damascus was a fortified city impregnable to spearmen. Inside the city there were enough provisions to withstand a lengthy siege.

A war like no other! No marches, no clashes with the enemy, rank on rank; no plain where the opposing armies would encounter each other in a clash of arms and men. A war of waiting, 'Abd al-Rahman called it, and of rapid sorties. No winners and no losers. It might well last long enough for the Mongol leader to lose patience and turn his mind to other targets. Either that, or else he might lift the siege completely and retire to his bases.

For the first few days in Damascus, 'Abd al-Rahman devoted his attention to his students in the 'Adiliya College where he was staying. He started teaching them classes on the four schools of Islamic jurisprudence, but had little success in keeping their minds focused on the subject. Once it became clear that they were all totally preoccupied with events inside Damascus and news about the Mongols to the exclusion of all else, he agreed to answer their numerous and varied questions about issues of *jihad* and present-day history. He responded to their concerns as best he could with the knowledge God had given him. The most astute students asked him about the possibility of the Egyptian army repelling the Mongol menace; why the army commanders had decided to defend only Damascus rather than other cities in Syria. They were eager to know about the fate of the Syrian people should Mamluk forces suffer a defeat and return to Egypt. 'Abd al-Rahman's answers all stressed the competence and bravery of the Mamluk cavalry and infantry, while at the same time suggesting that the students make preparations for all eventualities and emergencies. Needless to say, he could read in their anxious expressions all the worries and concerns of their families and relatives. For that very reason, he made a determined effort to keep his own personal opinions to himself, namely that Timur was considerably stronger than al-Nasir Faraj and his forces, and not merely because of larger numbers in terms of equipment, but also superior military acumen and tremendous group spirit. 'Abd al-Rahman was convinced that ever since Barquq's death, the innate ruggedness within the Mamluk body-politic had been in a steady state of decline. However, in the current situation he was well aware that any public expression of such views would be foolish and irresponsible.

Toward the end of his first week in Damascus, 'Abd al-Rahman happened to be sitting in the courtyard of the Great Umawi Mosque. In such a holy place he was deep in thought, a habit he had developed during the course of his first fleeting visit to Damascus in the company of Sultan Faraj when he was putting down Tanam's rebellion. Some people sitting close by asked him if he had decided to leave the city if it were subjected to the kind of plunder and bedlam visited on both Aleppo and Hama at the hands of the Mongol invaders. He responded that all pious judges were an integral segment of the populace; they would stick with the people through thick and thin. Every day 'Abd al-Rahman was plied with a number of questions from worshippers in the mosque, and he did his best to respond, drawing a good deal of comfort and pleasure from such a spectacular mosque in which he was happy to pray and in particular to lead the Maliki community's devotions by the prayer niche of the Companions. Every afternoon he enjoyed participating in the purificatory reading, accompanied by voices sweet enough to be those of angels.

As the following week began, 'Abd al-Rahman headed for the copyists' market accompanied by a young boy whom Yashbak had appointed to serve him. He purchased the paper, ink, and pens he needed, then went to the book stalls close by Bab al-Jayrun to look for manuscripts of works about Byzantine, Jewish, and Persian history, and that of other peoples as well. These were regions the gist of whose history he had obtained from the history of Ibn Jarir al-Tabari but which was insufficient to meet the requirements of his own research. He went to the book shops in the ancient part of the city and poured over various books on the topic he had identified during the course of his earlier visit mentioned above. After several hours of such searching, 'Abd al-Rahman realized that his mind was too preoccupied with the current war atmosphere. He could not concentrate enough on the matter at hand and the details involved. He decided therefore to pay a copyist to make copies of as much as possible so that he could take it all back home with him to Egypt.

On Tuesday of his third week in Damascus, 'Abd al-Rahman paid a visit to a shrine between Bab al-Jabiya and Bab al-Saghir. He prayed for mercy on the dead, and paid particular attention to the names of those whose tombstones he could read: Bilal, Ka'b al-Ahbar, Umm Habiba, and her brother, Mu'awiya ibn Abi Sufyan. As he was about to leave, he found his path between the graves blocked by an old man, naked save for a loincloth; his face was wrinkled, his head bald, his beard scraggly; he was toothless, and his bones protruded as though he had just emerged from a grave himself.

"You have prayed for all of them," he said addressing 'Abd al-Rahman, "but not me. I am 'Uways al-Qarni. Follow me, sir, and I'll show you my grave."

'Abd al-Rahman frowned at the old man, hoping to drive him away, but lost his balance and fell to the ground, almost as though he had had a bad turn. The old man wiped 'Abd al-Rahman's hands and rubbed his chest. With that, 'Abd al-Rahman asked the man who he was and why he insisted on living among the tombs.

"That young man's a rogue," he replied. "He tries to attack me when he knows that I'm even weaker than his own faith. Young people today no longer feel the slightest sympathy for old folk like me. I've already stated my name, sir. Don't you know it? I lived in the time of the Prophet—on him be peace. I never saw him—more's the pity! Yet he envelops me and is ever close to me. Here's my throat; it caused me to die of choking, whereupon I was forever consigned to this place, condemned to be the very last of the dead."

"And what is your function, saint of God?"

"I guard the tombs against pranksters, defacers, pissers, and plunderers."

"And what can I do for you, saint of God?"

"Pray over my grave and convey my greetings to the Lord of Creation on the day you meet Him."

'Abd al-Rahman could see no way of avoiding tagging along behind this strange figure to an antechamber in the tomb. The old man claimed his grave was in a cave that could only be entered by skinny individuals who had eaten nothing for hundreds of years. With that he said farewell and disappeared into the cave, leaving 'Abd al-Rahman and his servant boy in a state of shock. They were even more surprised when they saw the very same man crouched in the top of a lofty palm-tree by Bab al-Maqbara, weeping and yelling 'I see the mosque as an eagle with broken wings! I see its dome shrouded in gloom! Will Damascus have its last rites?"

When 'Abd al-Rahman reached his house, he found Yashbak and the chief judge, Burhan al-Din ibn Muflih the Hanbali, waiting for him. He welcomed them warmly and told them about the strange man in the graveyard.

"There are lunatics like him in all the graveyards and some of the public parks as well," Yashbak replied. "But I've something more serious to ask you about. The soldiers are demanding that alcohol be declared permissible, the rationale being that it will relieve their boredom and compensate for being away from their families. The army judge has invoked the argument of temporary benefit to the public interest in registering his approval. His expressed opinion is that it's better for them to blow their minds once in a while rather than start a riot or make excessive demands for money or provisions. The Shafi'i judge claims to be sick and exhausted and has taken a non-committal position. The Hanafi judge has also adopted a lenient attitude, citing the laws of necessity and the benefits of beer drinking. However, our Hanafi colleague here has stated emphatically that the entire concept is illegal; indeed he's gone so far as to issue an opinion that all vines should be dug up and destroyed.

Ibn Muflih was a man in his forties, with a thick black beard and a warm, open face. 'Abd al-Rahman had met him before in Cairo. He had found his colleague to be agreeable company and knowledgeable about his legal school, being widely read in matters sacred and secular.

"Yashbak," said Ibn Muflih, "I'm going to state in front of our learned friend, Wali al-Din ibn Khaldun, that if strict adherence to the law is indeed 'commanding that which is right and forbidding that which is wrong,' then accept it and rejoice in it! God's own text declaring alcohol forbidden is totally explicit; there can be no ambiguity whatsoever. Our Prophet—the purest of prayers be on him—declared: 'Alcohol is the mother of all debauchery and the most grievous of sins. Anyone who drinks alcohol has abandoned prayer and had sex with his mother and paternal and maternal aunts.' This hadith comes from al-Khatib by way of Anas ibn Malik. Is that not so, Wali al-Din?"

"Indeed it is, Burhan al-Din."

"Regarding my opinion about pulling out vines, in the chapter devoted to rooting out evil God has declared wine, its drinkers, its manufacturers, its merchants, all to be repugnant. Those who protest that Jews and Christians living in our midst are permitted by their laws to drink wine forget that they are only permitted to do that inside their own homes and not in public places within the dominions of Islam. Isn't that right, Wali al-Din?"

"Indeed it is, Burhan al-Din."

Yashbak realized that the two judges were in agreement on the matter. He decided it was not worth asking any more questions, so he said nothing for a moment while he thought things over.

"Yashbak," said 'Abd al-Rahman, anticipating his thoughts, "you've asked me to give you my frank opinion. If you recall that the reason why I was dismissed from my position as judge was because I was applying the law and imposing punishments too strictly, then you could have worked out for yourself what my verdict was going to be. Any decision by jurists to legitimize soldiers' alcohol consumption on the grounds of temporary public interest is rendered totally invalid in law by its consequences. By analogy such a licence could be compared, for example, with legitimizing fornication, bribery, and all other types of debauched behavior. It's also rendered invalid on grounds of mental processes and the need to keep the mind alert and awake against the ravages of drunkenness and negligence. That is particularly the case in situations involving mobilization and war. Aren't such opinions the correct ones, Burhan al-Din?"

"Indeed they are, Wali al-Din."

"God Almighty has said, '*Do not come to prayer in a state of drunkenness.*' In my view *jihad* is a form of prayer. *Prepare as much force and string of horse for them as you can.* God forbid that such preparations involve carousing and head-bashing amid the vats of the mother of all evils. I am well aware, of course, that the army judge and the infantry commanders have a very low opinion of judges who follow the orthodox line. But, for heaven's sake, Yashbak, tell me what they're going to do! How are they going to succeed against the Tatar armies marching toward them from Jabal al-Shaykh and the West? Tell me, please, how is wine drinking supposed to help them when they find themselves in skirmishes against the enemy or making preparations for a great victory?"

Yashbak was a little taken aback. "Wali al-Din," he said, feeling the need to defend himself, "you know me well enough, so you're already aware of what my answers will be. You know that I'm not in charge of the war, but rather responsible for giving the sultan advice and counsel. I'm trying to reconcile the conflicting views of the commanders and amirs. I do whatever I can. For example, I was one of the minority who favored digging trenches around the approaches to Damascus; I also joined them in pushing the sultan to order the cavalry contingents to attack the Mongols at some particularly dangerous spots. And I've done other things too, but there's no need for me to boast. But there are also many people working against me here, and they have Sultan Faraj's ear too. I've managed to make sure that most major government officials came with us to Damascus; that way there would be no scope for conspiracy back in Cairo. However, now they're all indeed here, and doing their level best to bring me down by blackening my name with the sultan. That's the way war is, Wali al-Din. We need men like Qutuz, Baybars, and Barquq, God's mercy on them all. But what we have is Barquq's young son . . ."

Burhan al-Din seized on these words, as though they had given him a golden opportunity to say what he wanted. "The problem with the sultan is not that he's only thirteen years old," he said, "but that he's so irreligious. I'm well aware that a bottle of wine is never far from his side as he moves from the Citadel, to the square of the Dome of Yalbugha, to the Ablaq Palace. I'm well aware that he's so drunk that his cheeks are already on fire before he ever takes a look at the military situation or issues any orders. Small wonder then if the army asks for wine vats to be opened, since people usually follow the lead of their monarchs—as the saying goes."

'Abd al-Rahman rubbed his hands together in despair. "That's what has led me to ignore all news about army quarters and the sultan's personal situation! We judges have the right to know about goings-on, Yashbak. Otherwise, how are we supposed to issue opinions and give wise counsel?"

"The fact that al-Nasir Faraj and his retainers are drunk is no secret to anyone, Wali al-Din. He's permanently drunk. I get the impression that it serves to calm him down, since he seems constantly terrorized by the thought of being murdered, either by the Mongols or else the amirs who are constantly intriguing against him. I'm scared to death of these conspirators and agent provocateurs who keep slinking away from us here in Damascus and going back to Cairo. If the sultan sees that the number of people withdrawing is getting any larger, I think it's very likely that he'll decide to return to his capital city."

"Why doesn't he stop them going back to Cairo?"

"It's a vicious circle. Amirs convince the sultan that there's a conspiracy against him in Cairo, the seat of his power. So he allows them to leave, and they themselves then become the leaders of the rebellion."

For the first time 'Abd al-Rahman was now convinced, on the basis of the sincere tone in Yashbak's voice, that Timur would emerge the winner in the war against the Mamluk forces, whether he actually went to war or not. He asked Yashbak what new information there was about the Mongols.

"Reliable information only comes in fits and starts," he said. "What we know suggests that his army is no larger than ours in either equipment or size, although he does have an elephant brigade and ballistas. His agents inside the city are spreading all sorts of false information: they're saying, for example, that Timur plans to drown Damascus in a hail of incendiary bombs projected by long-distance catapults that only he possesses. The strange thing is that, when these agents are captured, they still stick to their story even if they're being tortured or threatened with death. We have twenty agents of our own, but that's all. No other Mamluk would volunteer for the job even disguised as monks or dervishes. Even when we tried to dragoon some of them, they threatened to defect and kill themselves before Timur's elephants tore them apart."

Burhan al-Din listened to Yashbak's report with considerable interest. "From your report," he said once Yashbak had finished, "I gather that the Mongol noose is tightening around our neck. I was preparing a whole series of fiery sermons to deliver to the Mamluk brigades in which I preach a spirit of courageous advance rather than sitting still, waging *jihad* instead of sitting on our hands. I was going to invoke Qur'anic verses and Prophetic hadith that would rouse men to action. But what's the use of such talk when corruption has sapped away all notion of traditional bravery and morale has sunk to the lowest possible level?"

"In spite of everything, dear friend, it's still the religious scholars' duty to inspire hope in people."

"Yes, and it's the duty of commanders and soldiers to fulfill their pledge to use every means to defend people. What's the use of an army that's crippled by fear and dissent? And what about generals who don't know the first thing about propaganda warfare? 'War is deceit,' as the Lord of Mankind put it. Timur operates on that principle in dealing with states and generals; he's both pioneer and genius in its application, and he uses it in spades! Yashbak, it's up to you and your colleagues to counteract his tactics and reverse the tide. If not, then heaven help Damascus, the Salihiya, and the Great Umawi Mosque in the face of Tatar terrors. The rivers of the city will run red with the blood of defenseless civilians, and the entire city will be pillaged and destroyed just as Aleppo and other cities were earlier. As the saying goes, whoever issues a warning is excused."

Yashbak now stood up, embraced the two judges, and spoke to them both before departing. "Waiting for deliverance from God," he said, "is a kind of worship. I'm keeping my eye on Aqbay and the infantry commanders. Everything is not lost, at least, not yet."

'Abd al-Rahman and Burhan al-Din were left facing each other, each one of them feeling a strong pull toward the other. A very special kind of mutual affection had developed between the two of them, and that made them want to spend more time in each other's company, if only to recompense for the occasions they had missed before. They prayed the noon prayer together, then sat down to eat lunch and chat. 'Abd al-Rahman learned that his Hanbali colleague was married to two women and had two children. He was astonished to learn that he had read the *Introduction to History* and many sections of *The Book of Exemplary Lessons* and that he knew Persian, Turkish, and even Greek well. What amazed him more than anything was the way Burhan al-Din was able to talk about schools of jurisprudence, Arabic poetry, biographies of kings, and national histories. It almost seemed as if he made a regular habit of strolling amid the bowers and meadows of knowledge without let or hindrance. In his discussions of a wide variety of topics with 'Abd al-Rahman he showed a great deal of critical acumen and good taste, and occasionally a truly exceptional degree of modesty. Whenever 'Abd al-Rahman chose to express his admiration, he would respond with statements like, "What God has taught me, Wali al-Din, is just a small part of the veritable flood of your own wisdom."

After taking a short nap, the two men went to the Umawi Mosque where they prayed the afternoon prayer together. They then went to visit some of the city's monuments, the whereabouts of which the Hanbali judge had prior knowledge. At one time he would refer to Damascus as 'the city of the two imams,' Ahmad ibn Taymiya and Ibn Qayyim al-Jawziya, and at another, 'the city of seven gates and rivers.' For the rest of the day, the two judges went to visit the Sufi cemetery where the two great imams were buried, then moved on to pass by some hospices, shrines, and markets in old Damascus and al-Salihiya. They made this tour on their mules and on foot.

The next day the two men decided to visit some parks, gardens, and sites by the rivers, places where the four elements of nature coalesced in exquisite ways to provide the visitor with the most beautiful and elaborate tableaux, all of which would be breathlessly described and explained by Burhan al-Din. Starting by the base of the citadel and following the bank of the River Barada they came to the famous district of al-Ghuta, and its hillock—complete with stream—containing the shrine to Jesus' cradle (on him be peace), then to the villages of al-Nayrab and al-Mazzah. Everywhere the two men looked there was water and greenery, and gardens and orchards one after another, and squares festooned with palm trees, all of them filled with varieties of birds. Crossing the Rivers Tura and Yazid they reached Jabal Qasiyun, place of ascent for the Prophets—peace be upon them all. They made do with a single shrine visit, to the birth-cave of Ibrahim, Companion of God, then descended the mountain once again to the city of al-Salihiya. There they ate in a restaurant before heading for a deserted house high up on one of the city's mountains, a house which Burhan al-Din said was owned by his brother who had disappeared two years earlier. He invited his companion to relax a little on the balcony before they both returned to Damascus.

On the balcony, 'Abd al-Rahman expressed his profuse thanks to his companion for everything he had seen. He then asked Burhan al-Din how he came to be so familiar with all the different districts in the Syrian capital.

"I forgot to tell you, Wali al-Din," Burhan al-Din replied, "that I'm a son of Harran, just like Imam Ibn Taymiya—may God perfume his resting place. I spent my entire youth in the Hanbali district of al-Salihiya before I moved to Cairo. For me, this small tour we've made today is a nostalgic revisit to the places I remember, vital segments of my very being. Were it not for the Mongol threat and our current state of mobilization, I would give you a much grander tour of every part of the city."

"And what about this brother of yours who's disappeared?"

"There are many stories circulating about him. The most probable—although God alone knows—is that he's living in Granada, rousing people to resist the Christians and save al-Andalus."

"If that's true, it's a wonderful thing he's doing. I'll ask my friends in Granada about him and, God willing, let you know what they have to say."

"While you're about it, ask them too about what's happening in the parts of al-Andalus that are left, our other great wound."

"Dear colleague, that particular wound is still bleeding, and none of the puny rulers of al-Andalus and the Maghrib has the ability to dress and cauterize it."

"From your masterful work of history, Wali al-Din, I've learned that the Almohad defeat at the Battle of al-'Iqab during the reign of al-Nasir in 609 presaged the end of any real possibility for Maghribi forces to recapture power in the fading light of once brilliant al-Andalus."

"That defeat was an act of revenge for the Muslim victory at the great battle of Hittin just over two decades earlier. Any hope of bringing al-Andalus back under the standard of Islam received its terminal blow when the Marini sultan, Abu al-Hasan, was defeated at Tarifah by the twin monarchs, Alfonso of Castille and Alfonso of Portugal, in 740. At one stroke, that defeat turned the Marini campaigns from *jihad* into short, uncoordinated raids. Now even the Banu al-Ahmar in Granada are keen to see them stopped, even if it means negotiating with the enemy forces."

"Those Banu al-Ahmar, just like all the other petty kingdoms, have neither minds nor guts. Ibn Sharaf has their number when he says, 'Using the term monarch in the wrong place is like a cat puffing itself up and pretending to be a lion.'"

"Dear friend, it was four decades ago that the ruler of Granada, Muhammad V, received me in the Alhambra Palace. Both he and his superb minister, Lisan al-Din ibn al-Khatib, spared absolutely no effort in welcoming and feting me. Thereafter he commissioned me to visit Pedro Alfonso in Seville, my own forebears' native city in al-Andalus. The purpose of the visit was to persuade the king of Seville to support the Granadan ruler in his war against his enemy, the king of Aragon. I was pleased, indeed keen, to accept the commission, not least because I was very worried by the possibility that the kingdoms of Seville and Aragon might see it as being in their best interests to unite, thus turning it into yet another regrettable episode in the Muslim history of al-Andalus. While I was visiting Pedro in Seville (whom his people dubbed 'the Cruel' and we named 'the Tyrant'), I saw from afar the mosque of Seville, which the Christians had converted into a church, and strolled through the gardens and along the banks of the River al-Wadi al-Kabir. Pondering the sad decline of Muslim rule in al-Andalus, I was over-come by profound feelings of melancholy and regret. At one point, Pedro the Tyrant obviously realized the way I was feeling (I had just returned from a visit to my ancestors' homes). In a typically gener-ous and regal fashion, he offered them all to me if I would agree to join his court. I declined his offer with apologies. In my heart of hearts I whispered in the ear of this cruel and debauched tyrant, so fond of war, money, and trinkets, that all the chattels of a life on this earth lived in his shadow were not worth a gnat's wing to me. God alone was the victor. . . ."

"My friend," said Burhan al-Din, "I've no doubt at all that the tyrant of this era of ours, Timur the Mongolian, will make you exactly the same offer, to go back with him to Samarqand in exchange for whatever your heart desires. And I'm equally certain that you will give him the same reply you gave the Sevillian tyrant."

"Islam has nothing to fear from Timur and the Mongols, Burhan al-Din. Like the Mamluks and many other groups, they have adopted Islam too, albeit in their own particular fashion. No, it is in al-Andalus that Islam faces its greatest threat. The Christians are constantly gain-ing ground, using their superior power and the knowledge we've passed on to them. Should they be victorious and gain control of the entire peninsula, they will not hesitate to kill Muslims and give them the choice of either evacuating en masse or else converting to Christianity. Beyond that even, they'll start harassing them at Maghribi coasts and ports. Dark storm clouds are rapidly gathering over Western Islam. O God, we beg Your forgiveness and mercy!"

Both men said amen to that, and then looked down at Damascus and al-Ghuta spread out beneath them, with light and shade alter-nating on the glistening rows of grasses, plants, and trees.

"As you well know, my friend," said Burhan al-Din remorseful-ly, "the walls of this city of Damascus are supposed to go back to a time just after the Flood. Whether that story and others like it is true or not, I still liken this city to an ancient tome, one of the most price-less books in the world, written on by Noah, Jayrun, Lazar—faith-ful Abraham's boy, Alexander of the Two Horns, kings of Byzantium, Muslim conquerors, the Umawis, and others. Is it con-ceivable for the Mamluks to leave this city totally exposed to debauchery, amputation, and burning, all at the hands of the Tatar Mongols? If Faraj and his army run away, Damascus will be left in the charge of religious scholars. In that case the city will have to be preserved and defended by using all the weapons of negotiation. Do you share my opinion on that, Wali al-Din?"

'Abd al-Rahman paused for a minute, abundantly aware of the significance of the question he had been asked.

"Should the sultan and his army withdraw," he said after a few moments, "I have no idea whether the senior administration will leave with him or stay to help protect the inhabitants of the city."

Burhan al-Din's expression showed the fire of determination. "I cannot stand in the way of a retreating army," he said defiantly, "but, by Him in whose hands is my very soul, I swear that I will not allow any scholar, doctor, or man of means to leave even if it costs me my life. You alone have the right to go, Wali al-Din, since you've been dismissed from your judicial post. Even so, I'm well aware that your sterling qualities will make you decide to stay here alongside everyone else."

"You're right, Burhan al-Din. If we have to negotiate with Timur, then it's religious scholars who will have to arrange things appropriately so that country and people can avoid disaster and mis-ery."

The looks that the two judges exchanged made it clear that they were in complete agreement on the matter. They stood up, embraced each other, then got on their mules to return to the ancient city of Damascus.

At the very beginning of 'Abd al-Rahman's third week in Damascus, he woke up early. He was eager for news. On the family front, he had heard nothing from Umm al-Batul in response to the letter he had sent two weeks earlier in which he had reassured her that he was well and promised to return to Egypt shortly. As regards the military situation, there was nothing new to add to his repertoire of information. This lack of news led him to improvise a class with his students in which he discussed information and the way people and history have a constant need for it. When he opened the class for discussion, the students' examples all spoke of the rampaging rumors and misgivings circulating among people in the city because of the psychological warfare being waged all around them and the excessive degree of taxation that had been levied on merchants and craftsmen. People of means and influence were purchasing travel permits to Egypt, the Holy Places, or any remote locations that would be safer. They asked their teacher for his opinions on their information, but he postponed his answers till he had had enough time to take into account everything they had told him in evaluating the focus of his lesson. He closed the class by emphasizing the benefits of eyewitness information in making a record of the major events of time.

Just before noon, 'Abd al-Rahman went to the postal tent in Yalbugha Dome Square in the hope of finding a letter, but there was nothing. He strolled through the streets and markets, staring at people's faces. Their expressions were even more despondent and grim than his own. Investigating their state of affairs more closely, he discovered that the garbage situation was becoming desperate. Individuals or groups of people were roaming the streets heaping insults on all tricksters and hoarders. Another group of young men kept wandering through the alleyways saying: "God, Merciful One, grant our lord the sultan victory!"

While 'Abd al-Rahman was absorbing these impressions of people and circumstances, two men dressed like dervishes blocked his way. While one kept looking all around him, the other said, "Sir, only poor and indigent people are left inside the city. You're obviously a learned and influential person. For two thousand dinars, we can either take you to see Timur, a great admirer of both religious scholars and lovers of luxury, or else take you somewhere else where it's safe." 'Abd al-Rahman was well aware that these two men could well be spies, so he gave them both a withering stare and then continued on his way to the Umawi mosque amid throngs of beggars and vagrants.

In every corner of the mosque people were reciting the prayer for mercy, asking for release and compassion. After washing and praying, 'Abd al-Rahman joined them in the recitation. He then went over to the Companions' prayer niche where prayers were led by someone of the Maliki rite. There he found worshippers preparing to conduct a funeral which people said was for the chief judge in Syria, Burhan al-Din al-Shadhili al-Maliki, who had been martyred during a skirmish between the Mamluks and Mongols. No sooner was the funeral finished than 'Abd al-Rahman sat in a corner of the mosque to rest his feet and frame. His mind was troubled by any number of conflicting ideas, and he suddenly felt the need to get together with his two friends, Yashbak and Ibn Muflih, so he could stay in contact and remove the veil of obscurity that he felt was clouding both mind and soul.

Yashbak welcomed the master to his residence in Yalbugha Dome Square with great affection and an optimistic mood. "Our situation vis-à-vis the Mongols has improved, Wali al-Din," he said. "Our last skirmish with them provided our cavalry commanders with a real picture of the Mongol army that is not based on fairy tales. The fighting lasted two whole days and finished yesterday. We engaged them with just two thousand horsemen in a valley a few miles to the west of the Dome. A number of men from their vanguard and main column were either killed, wounded, or captured. Left and right flanks were forced to retreat and take flight. We lost about one hundred soldiers. Among the victims you know was one of the Syrian judges, Burhan al-Din al-Shadhili al-Maliki, and the Maliki judge, Sharaf al-Din 'Isa was wounded."

Yashabk suddenly fell silent, as though he became aware of the way that his colleague's expression reflected a disdainful view of the significance of such a limited success in the context of a broader conflict.

"You should be aware, my friend," he went on, "that the decisive battle has not yet happened; true victory has yet to be won. Even so, I have to seize any light that I can, even though it may be just a glimmer. Our soldiers badly need to have their spirits raised and their mettle fired. Enthusiasm's what we need, Wali al-Din, enthusiasm, even if it means that we have to inflate the profits somewhat."

"Is there any other good news?"

"Sultan Husayn has come over to our side. He's claiming to have broken with his uncle, Timur. Am I supposed to regard that as good news? I'm keeping an eagle eye on him till I can be sure whether he's telling the truth or not."

"If I weren't so exhausted, Yashbak, I'd want to meet this sultan and some of the others prisoners as well. I could question them about Timur's intentions."

"They're all saying the same thing: every day Timur's situation is going from bad to worse. He's thinking of packing up camp and returning to his campaigns further north or even to Samarkand— which seems the most likely."

"But what if those stories are just a few of Timur's many tricks?"

"Wali al-Din, there are situations in which knowing what's the real truth is virtually impossible. Are we supposed to torture prisoners to make them talk, then torture them again to make them say what we want to hear?"

"That's not what I meant. I'm merely saying that we shouldn't rely solely on suspect information."

"You're absolutely right, my friend. As soon as certain amirs heard that Timur might possibly be packing up to leave, they were calling for us to return to Egypt. I spent much of the night with loyal commanders reminding the sultan and others who were eager to go home that Timur is a past master at such stratagems."

"The burden of years weighs heavily on my shoulders. But for that, my good friend, I'd be there at every battle, assessing the data for myself."

"God prolong your life, friend! We're much in need of you, but in the realms of knowledge and sound advice, not bloody conflict and the heat of battle."

"Bearing in mind my exhaustion and advanced age, your words are fair enough. Dear friend, I feel that I'm burning the last set of candles for my involvement in such things. The time is fast approaching when I'll no longer pay any attention to news, however significant it may be. It's the voice of life eternal that now beckons me."

"I've never known you to be so depressed, Wali al-Din. How are your wife and family?"

"I've not heard from them. There's been no reply to my letter."

"Give me a letter now, and I'll have it sent by carrier-pigeon. If you'd like to return to Egypt or to have your family brought here, just let me know."

"May you be rewarded for such kindness, my friend! Where is Burhan al-Din ibn Muflih?"

"That man's exercising *jihad* in his own unique way. He keeps going from one Syrian city to another, creating what he is calling 'defense groups' to protect land and people, then bringing them to Damascus. He is making plans and operating as if the Egyptian army is definitely going to leave Syria, in which case the final confrontation will be between the Mongols and the people of Syria."

"Were I his age, I'd be doing the same."

'Abd al-Rahman asked for some paper, wrote a letter to his wife, and sealed it. He stood up and handed it to Yashbak. The commander embraced him and went on to say that 'Abd al-Rahman should move into the citadel if he received notice to that effect.

For the remainder of Jumada al-Awwal, 'Abd al-Rahman kept getting news that boded no good. Students no longer came to class, and people—like rats in a basement—ran around in circles, seeking refuge in mosques, backalleys, and shrines. The soldiery involved themselves in an unusual and never ending sequence of maneuvers, watching the gates of Damascus, guarding the road to the citadel, and conducting patrols into quarters and streets.

Weather and atmosphere, physical and mental, turned oppressive, and the summer heat settled in for the season. The sun was a series of burning-hot metal bars that radiated their heat till the first part of night. Air, or what little was left of it, smelled foul and was mingled with the stench of rotting corpses. Even the clear blue sky was polluted by the black color of hovering crows, which made it look as if it were afflicted by a strange kind of flickering. The air was terribly hard to breathe. With such a disgusting cocktail of foul and noxious fumes it was a miracle it didn't burst into flames.

Was the Mongol hurricane about to descend on them all?

'Abd al-Rahman was turning over that very question in his mind when the mail brought him a letter. He assumed it was from his wife, Umm al-Batul, and that lifted his spirits. However, when he opened it, he discovered that it was actually from his friend, Ibn Muflih. He sat down and read his friend's words with considerable pleasure. In fact, it contained a very clear answer to the question as to whether the Mongol hurricane was about to descend on them. After the "In the name of God" and greetings, here is what Ibn Muflih had to say:

Dear Friend, I swear to God that the only thing keeping me away is that I have been traveling to Syrian cities, making every effort to form defense groups to protect land and people. I have only started doing this after receiving clear proof that the Egyptian army proposes to wash its hands of Damascus and leave its people to face the Mongol menace on their own without either army nor equipment. Every day that goes by sees the departure of this amir or that commander. I am almost certain that Sultan Faraj himself will soon join them, fearing for his own life at the hands of Timur and hoping to counteract the activities of conspirators in Egypt itself.

We have no alternative but to negotiate with the tyrant Timur. Had Imam Ibn Taymiya—God bless his spirit—been alive to witness our current plight, he would have authorized negotiation with the Tatar enemy as a way of avoiding the worst of his ravages and saving the blood of Muslims. In extreme circumstances, prudence is the most effective weapon for the weak and defenseless believer. God, the High, the Almighty, alone has the power and the might.

I envisage negotiation as involving face-to-face talks between our religious scholars in particular and Timur. Our principal task is to persuade the invader to agree not to harm civilians in return for receiving the keys to the city and the Citadel.

However, before any agreement is reached, Timur will insist on meeting with us religious scholars and judges, just as

*he did two months ago in Aleppo between the time when he
defeated the army and later destroyed its principal buildings.
All the evidence that I have been able to gather from people
who survived the assault on that city confirms how vicious the
Tatars are and how fond of trickery and deceit their commander is.*

*In any event, we must learn from the Aleppo case. During
the discussions that Timur had with the religious scholars of
the captured city, he asked them—according to accounts I have
received—a very difficult question: So which are martyrs, our
dead or yours? That kept everyone quiet for a while. Everyone
struggled to come up with an answer that would prevent what
would otherwise be guaranteed destruction. Eventually it was
al-Hafiz al-Khwarizmi, mufti of Aleppo, who saved the day by
pointing out that an Arab had posed the very same question to
the Prophet of God—on him be peace—who had replied:
'Anyone who has fought so that the word of God may be the
highest, that person is a martyr.' It is up to you, Wali al-Din,
to come up with a similarly authoritative hadith so that you
can expect to hear Timur react by saying, "Khub, khub"
(Good, good). In a word, the true Word is the basis for our
salvation. So help yourself avoid the worst possible outcome
and open in front of us the path of hope.*

*We are all relying on you, dear friend, to frame the discussion
with Timur because you are both a renowned scholar and a
clever strategist. Start now preparing for all the tricky questions.
Search through history for precedents and similar situations.*

*I am making ready for all eventualities, including the possi-
bility of Timur breaking all treaties and agreements. Along
with certain religious colleagues I am training a group of
young men in the techniques of street warfare. God is our
helper, and He alone has the power!*

For 'Abd al-Rahman this letter from Ibn Muflih served as a
wake-up call. As a result, he decided that the time had come to ver-
ify the real situation. It was the very beginning of Jumada al-Akhira.
He got out his mule and headed for some of the quarters close to his

house and to the citadel itself. The predominant color everywhere was dust: air, roads, animals, people. It was made even worse by the frequent skirmishes taking place to the west of the city. There was no let-up in the weather either, and the atmosphere was damp and foul. It almost felt as if the Mongol army had gained control of the snowy mountains and could prevent purer air from reaching the city and its citadel.

The expressions on people's faces made it clear that the only reason they were huddling together within the city walls was that they were too weak to run away and were scared to death at the thought of being brutally attacked. They all looked like maltreated animals, trying every conceivable contortion in an attempt to escape. They were hoarding food and water and leaving mounds of garbage in the streets that served as food for insects and stray animals.

When 'Abd al-Rahman stopped by the city gate known as al-Bab al-Saghir, he had no trouble with the guards in passing through; actually the chief guard happily conducted him to the office of the Citadel's commander, a man called Azdar. 'Abd al-Rahman was welcomed with a great deal of warmth and respect. As the result of a short conversation, he discovered that the commander was intent on defending the Citadel against Mongol troops even if the city of Damascus itself surrendered; he was quite fanatical on that point. 'Abd al-Rahman then raised the issue of his sense of loyalty to his lord, Sultan Faraj, and the fact that only those selected by the rich and famous would be allowed to seek protection in the Citadel. As the commander bade the judge farewell and placed a Mamluk at his disposal, he told him that the Citadel gates would only be open tomorrow morning, but that he was welcome to choose a tent for himself. "It is my personal hope," the commander said, "that you'll be with me when the crucial time arrives."

'Abd al-Rahman made do with saying farewell to the man, then got on his mule and allowed the Mamluk to take the bridle and proceed on foot.

There was not a great deal of flat space to be had in this lofty citadel, which commanded the heights and the rocky promontory. Everything seemed on the point of leaning over and rolling downward. There was so much movement going on that the whole place looked like a beehive or ants' nest. There were just a few houses, overlooked by a single well-sited mansion. Tents of all shapes and sizes were strewn over the terrain, sagging and flapping as they tried to afford protection from the heat and dust.

By a little after midday, 'Abd al-Rahman had settled into a small tent and performed his prayers. He had eaten a little bit as well, telling himself that, in time of crisis like this, one has to munch the odd scrap or two. He then tried to rest for a while, but it only helped his body. His mind kept churning away, beset as it was by all sorts of worries and misgivings. He was thinking as much about his own small family as he was about previous sieges that he had heard or read about. During the course of these musings he came to realize that any hope of his returning safe and sound to his family was entirely dependent on bringing the impending Mongol siege of Damascus to a conclusion. Such a conclusion would have to take the form of either a conditional or compulsory surrender of the city or else a successful use of resistance tactics until such time as the Mongols grew tired and the passage of time created dissension in their ranks. In that case they would pack up their camp and move their campaign elsewhere. The question was: could the people of Damascus stand the hunger that such a siege would involve, along with all the other miseries, overt and covert?

While his mind was wandering through the byways of memory in this fashion, with him only half-awake, he suddenly recalled an unusual event he had read about in a book on ancient Greek history, the name of which he had forgotten. It told how the army of the Peloponesian allies under Spartan command had been forced to raise the siege of Athens during the time of Pericles, all because they were afraid of being infected by the outbreak of plague inside the walls of the besieged city. Once he had fully recalled the story, he had an incredible idea. How would it be if the inhabitants of Damascus tried to fool the Mongols into believing that an outbreak of plague was spreading among the inhabitants of the city? He kept asking himself that question till he fell into a restless sleep, one that was interrupted by a series of terrifying, violent visions. He was woken up in the early morning by shouts to the effect that the Dome of Yalbugha was on fire, and the sultan and army had left. He rushed outside and found men scurrying around on their own and in groups, all saying the same thing. The news about the Mamluk army leaving could still be a matter of doubt, but the fire and columns of smoke rising from the men's homes and quarters was a fact that could be confirmed by the naked eye peering through the crenelated gaps in the walls.

'Abd al-Rahman sat down on a wide rock, read the prayer of mercy, and thought. With the first rays of the sun he stood up, went over to a lookout point, and asked the guard what he could see outside the walls. "There's nothing like seeing for yourself, Shaykh," the man replied. "Climb the ladder, stand beside me, and see for yourself."

Below the ramparts to north and west, lines of donkeys and mules were moving to and fro carrying loads, while columns of men and boys were busy digging trenches and filling them with scrap, straw, kale, and any other type of combustible material. In the distance there was a good deal of dust with horses charging about. The last of the fires were consuming the rest of the tents and catching the straw between the lofty palms; they reached as far as the banks of the Barada and other rivers.

"Who ordered the men to dig these trenches below us?" 'Abd al-Rahman asked the guard, who was a tall and sturdy youth.

"Not the Egyptian army; they've all left. Nor Sultan Faraj either; he's supposed to have gone too. The people who ordered these trenches dug were a group of fellow Muslims, authorized by the commander of this citadel."

"Do you happen to know Burhan al-Din ibn Muflih?"

"Do I know him? Who doesn't know the head of the Hanbalis in al-Salihiya? I'm sure he's with his lads, training them to fight and set traps. If you go down to the base of the citadel hill, you'll probably find him there."

'Abd al-Rahman thanked the guard, then went down the hill to look for his friend. He was sure that Burhan al-Din would have the most accurate information. He had hardly made his way through the west gate of the citadel and mingled with the trench-diggers before he found Burham al-Din without the slightest difficulty. Everyone knew him, as though he were a general or imam. The two friends embraced each other warmly. Burhan al-Din immediately started describing some of the armed contingents.

"We're doing everything we can, Wali al-Din," he said. "Everything else is left to the Great Organizer. Come to al-'Adiliya with us. We've an appointment with the senior administrators there."

The two men sat face to face in one of the houses of the deserted school, relaxing a bit and enjoying the quiet. They prayed the morning prayer together, then spent some time reading the Qur'an and reflecting.

"I received your last letter," 'Abd al-Rahman said. "I'd like to confirm with you now that the impression I got from it was correct. Is there no avoiding the Mongol attack now? Have the sultan and his army really withdrawn?"

Burhan al-Din looked at him in amazement. "My letter must have arrived late then! My dear friend, didn't you hear that the Mamluks have all fled? It was a full week ago they all left for Egypt under cover of night. Their last battle with the Mongols was a crushing defeat. Timur had fed them false information that his army was retreating in disorder, so the Mamluks dispatched some of their brigades to a valley specifically chosen by Timur. Once there, the Egyptians were crushed from every side by flame-throwers and the elephant corps."

"So where's Yashbak?"

"That courageous man managed to convince me that there really was a danger of rebellion in Egypt and asked me for my advice. I agreed with his opinion that he should stay with the sultan so as to bolster his regime and continue to advocate the defense of Syria. However, when he suggested that he take you back with him, I disagreed. My argument was that you wanted to stay with the judges so that you could negotiate with Timur as you had promised."

"You did well, friend, really well! Then what happened? In spite of my old age I can still bear hearing the rest of it."

Burhan al-Din smiled, as though procrastinating a little. The two men spent a short time in contemplation and silent prayer, then a group of jurists joined them, with a shaykh in Sufi garb at their head. They extended their greetings and joined the two judges. 'Abd al-Rahman was introduced to everyone there, although he seemed to have met some of them already. The chief judge, the Hanafi Mahmud ibn al-'Izz, made ready to begin the discussion as senior member of the group. At that point, the assembly was forcefully interrupted by the arrival of Azdar, the officer in charge of the Citadel, accompanied by his escort. He seemed very angry.

"Your assembly, gentlemen," he said, hand on sword, "is illegal and unacceptable to the sultan."

Burhan al-Din decided that he had no alternative but to face down the officer. "Firstly, Azdar," he said in a determined and threatening tone, "you are to salute these distinguished men with God's proper greeting. Then you can control your anger."

"No greeting is due to anyone who wishes to hand over the city to the tyrant."

"If you have received specific orders from the sultan, then show us the papers or else get the secretary of Judge Nasir al-Din Abu Tayyib who is here with us to witness them. If you really wish to protect the Citadel, then stay there along with your rich, influential friends."

"If you hand over Damascus—Heaven forbid!—you will be placing the Citadel in the direst jeopardy. You're well aware of that, Judge, and you all know as well that Timur has neither faith nor morals. He may give you a pledge of safe-conduct today, but he'll break it whenever he feels like it."

"Yes, we're aware of all that. And we're also aware that futile resistance to overwhelming military force is a brand of sheer stupidity, something that is certain to bring destruction down on our heads. The purpose of these good men gathered here is to persuade Timur not to harm people and to save the lives of unarmed civilians inside the city. If you have some other plan, then go ahead!"

"Stick to the high places, gentlemen. That's what an eagle with a broken wing does when it's surrounded by ravenous beasts. Our situation is exactly like the eagle's. Our only recourse is to stick things out to the bitter end. That's the only way that the enemy will give up, raise the siege, and go away."

After a moment's thought, 'Abd al-Rahman decided to say something that might calm Azdar's temper and lend support to Burhan al-Din's point of view.

"Okay, Officer," he said, "suppose Damascus were to fall after a period of resistance—God forbid—and the Mongols started pounding the Citadel with mortars from raised positions they'll construct. Would there be any other recourse besides negotiation?"

"I've thought about all the worst possibilities. After all, I'm a soldier and strategist. In my view, everything can be handled, just so long as the sultan comes back to fight the Tatars as soon as he has dealt with the rebellion in Egypt."

"That's pure speculation. If these judges had the slightest guarantee that Faraj would be coming back, they would be taking an entirely different approach to the situation," said 'Abd al-Rahman.

"If we resist to the bitter end, it will encourage the sultan to make every possible effort to rescue us."

"But just imagine that Timur takes the city by storm and enters through the gates before the alleged return of the sultan. What will the people in the city be able to do?"

"The Citadel is impregnable; it'll be our last resort. We have enough food and water stored for two months or more. That's more than enough time for help to arrive from the Egyptian army."

At this point, Burhan al-Din decided to raise the discussion to a new level in case some of the other jurists were swayed by Azdar's arguments.

"Gentlemen," he said, "the officer forgets the gruesome fate already suffered by many cities in Iraq and Syria without the Mamluks lifting a finger to help. Now he's trying to use speculations based on sheer fancy to convince us. Tell us, Azdar, if things get to a crisis point, will you open the Citadel gates to all the citizens who are scared for their own lives, even though they be poor and indigent?"

The officer stepped back a few paces. "The Citadel can't hold everybody," he stuttered. "In any case, Timur is not bothered with poor people. It's the affluent and influential folk he's concerned about. They're the people who need protection."

Hearing this reasoning, the shaykh of the poor quarters, a man named Shadid al-Din al-Azdi, leapt to his feet. "In matters of this world, you impious individual," he thundered in a tone that shook the entire building, "there is to be no distinction between God's souls."

Burhan al-Din seized the opportunity afforded by the clear consternation of the officer and his men and tightened the noose still further. "I have evidence, Azdar, which shows that you've been keeping for yourself a full third of all the wealth you're protecting."

The Hanafi Shaykh Ibn al-'Izz now broke his silence, aiming just one word at the officer: "Leave!"

It looked as though the officer might taking the order as a joke, but then the shaykh of the poor went right up to him. "My superior has told you to leave. So leave, or else I'll slap you in the face!"

With that, Azdar and his men backed away in some confusion and left. The Sufi returned to his position. 'Abd al-Rahman was utterly amazed by what he had just witnessed. He gave Burhan al-Din a questioning look and heard him say, "Gentlemen, our time is short. Azdar will undoubtedly set his men on us. Yesterday, when the great master Ibn Khaldun was not among us, we decided that I should take Shadid al-Din and go to see Timur with a view to getting him to agree to a guarantee of safety for homes and families in return for handing over the keys to the city. What we want and need is for us to come back with such a document. Should we be killed, then it's up to you to mobilize the local units while you wait for delivery from God Almighty. That's what everyone has already decided. What do you think, Wali al-Din?"

"It's an excellent plan, but I would request to accompany you to talk to Timur so I can collect more information about the behavior of rulers and the art of negotiation."

"You'll get to meet the great invader, Wali al-Din, provided the shaykh and I return from his tent unharmed. Our first trip there is simply to take the pulse. Our colleagues have chosen this colleague because he does not fear death and me because I know several of the languages the Mongols and people who serve them also understand. Now let's say the noon prayer and ask God for a successful outcome."

That same evening, Burhan al-Din returned from his encounter with Timur and met the judge at al-'Adiliya. He brought with him a guarantee of safe conduct and an oral request from Timur for the master to come and meet him. He noted that Timur had specifically mentioned Ibn Khaldun by name and explained the fact by saying that one of his retainers, 'Abd al-Jabbar ibn al-Nu'man, the Hanafi adherent to the Mu'tazili doctrine, was acquainted with many languages and knowledgeable about the most illustrious Muslim scholars in the East and West. The jurists all decided to accept the invitation and to leave at dawn the next day; they decided to gather by Bab al-Jabiya .

'Abd al-Rahman tried to get some sleep but he failed. Things turned from bad to worse when the college guard came and told him there had been a fight between Burhan al-Din's young volunteers and the Citadel commander's men in the Umawi mosque; staves and knives had been used. 'Abd al-Rahman got up immediately, closed the door of his house, and asked the guard to make sure the college door remained locked. Feeling a bit more secure, he started reading in the hope of passing the time and overcoming his worries. That was no better however, and things did not improve till he had spent the remainder of the night before dawn intoning one litany after another. He then performed his prayers and hurried to the meeting point.

Burhan al-Din was the first to arrive, followed soon after by the others. The judges discussed Azdar's defiance of their wishes and his threat to kill anyone who asked Timur for a document of safe conduct. They also discussed the fact that the chief Shafi'i judge, Sadr al-Din al-Munawi, had been captured by the Mongols in Shaqhab. Once again they asked 'Abd al-Rahman to wait for a day or two till things had become a bit clearer. He refused and insisted on being the first to be lowered down the walls. Burhan al-Din granted his wish with the aid of ropes and strips of cotton cloth. No sooner had he landed by Bab al-Jabiya than he was surrounded by soldiers and taken to Timur's Damascus superviser, Shah Malik. The man gave him a warm welcome, then dispatched him with his retinue to the khan's own billet. While 'Abd al-Rahman was waiting with considerable misgivings, he spotted a soldier dragging a half-naked man weighed down by chains. He had no doubt in his mind that this was the captured Shafi'i judge. A moment later he heard his name being called, along with his designation as Maliki judge from the Maghrib. He recited to himself two suras, al-'Asr ('The Epoch') and al-Sharh ('The Expanding'), adjusted his burnous on his shoulders, and entered the tent where Timur was sitting. As he set eyes on the man, he told himself that here was the incredible man in person, just as he had envisaged him! Slanting eyes, thick greasy hair, devilish beard, jutting forehead over a snub nose. His features and general appearance added to his general aura of cruelty and violence.

Timur, seated on his bed cushions, looked just like a lion in its den. His eyes took everything in, and he completely dominated the scene—including the plates of food that were laid out in front of him to choose from—before he turned his attention to all the Mongol groups hovering by the entrance like ravenous ghouls. 'Abd al-Rahman approached the bed and greeted Timur with head lowered. He was obliged to run his chin over the hand that was proffered to him. He then took his seat in the place indicated to him, and the translator was summoned. The man was introduced as the jurist, 'Abd al-Jabbar ibn al-Nu'man from Khwarizm, the Hanafi scholar whose name has already been mentioned above.

Timur's questions involved a systematic inquiry into every aspect of Ibn Khaldun's life: where from, when, why, and how. The answers were brief, and his descriptions of Sultan Barquq's beneficence toward him were especially prominent. 'Abd al-Rahman did however characterize the sultan's slaying of the Great Khan Timur's ambassadors as being one of his most flagrant errors. When the questions turned to the internal history of the Maghrib, its situation, cities, and peoples, 'Abd al-Rahman noticed that Timur's eyes began to sparkle with increased interest. Dramatizing his answers with gestures, the historian stressed the ruggedness of the terrain and the fortitude of its citizens. Even so, he was unable to divert Timur's attention from the subject. In fact, he listened as the translator proceeded to tell him what Timur was saying: "My lord is fascinated by a country that sits so nicely between two oceans and two continents. He wants you to write about it for him so it's as though he can see it with his own eyes, cross its borders, and envelop its plains and mountains beneath his feet." "To hear is to obey," was 'Abd al-Rahman's reluctant reply, to which Timur reacted with "*Khub, khub,*" and then invited his guest to eat the food in front of him. He ordered rashta, a favorite Mongol dish, to be brought in, and bowls of it were put in front of 'Abd al-Rahman. Standing up, he took several pieces, his hope being both to show his admiration

for Tatar cooking and to suppress the fear that he might be facing
the same fate as the Shafi'i judge whom he had seen being tortured.
He had recalled that some peoples of the North give people condemned to death a meal before they are executed. He only relaxed a
bit when Timur gestured to him to sit down and gave him some
inscrutable glances. 'Abd al-Rahman decided that the best way to
change the atmosphere was by launching into some totally contrived
panegyric statement. Here is what he said, speaking very deliberately so that the translator could follow and convey the meaning
accurately:

> May God support you! Here thirty or forty years have passed dur-
> ing which I have aspired to meet you. For you are the sultan of the
> world, the monarch of this earth. I do not believe that, since the
> time of Adam himself, a ruler such as you has appeared. You are
> not one to talk of matters at random. I myself am a scholar and I
> will explain what I mean: Strong rule depends on the solidarity of
> the community; the extent of authority depends on the existence of
> such a sentiment in abundance. Scholars past and present are in
> total accord that the greatest peoples in the world belong to two
> groups: Arabs and Turks. You are well acquainted with the Arabs
> and their rulership, how they came together under the banner of
> Islam with their Prophet. The Turks achieved the same through
> their rivalries with the kings of Persia. The way their king
> Afrasiyab snatched Khurasan from their hands is an indication of
> their quota of monarchical qualities. No one can match their group
> solidarity; no ruler on earth rivals them—neither Chosroes nor
> Caesar, neither Alexandar nor Nebukhadnezzar. Consider
> Chosroes, monarch of the Persians; but where do they stand in
> comparison with the Turks? Or take Caesar and Alexander, rulers
> of the Roman empire, where are they compared with the Turks?
> Nebukhadnezzar ruled Babylon and Nabatea, but where is he com-
> pared with the Turks? All this stands as proof of what I have just
> stated about this great ruler.

At first Timur ground his teeth and frowned, but then he let out
an abrupt laugh, which 'Abd al-Rahman took as a good sign. Timur

only resumed his former demeanor when his chamberlain informed him that the judges of Damascus were awaiting his pleasure in the tent outside. He ordered them to be brought in, then walked over toward them, dragging his clubfoot behind him. 'Abd al-Rahman followed behind along with the translator and mingled with his colleagues, focusing his attention on getting Timur to greet Burhan al-Din and Shaykh Mahmud ibn al-'Izz and talk to them both through the medium of Ibn al-Nu'man who was explaining things to everyone present. The gist of what Timur said was that he always appreciated the intelligence of religious scholars and looked forward to discussing matters sacred and secular with them. But such things were always better after a meal.

Timur went out of the tent and was followed by some senior officials. He took them to a tent where a feast had been laid out, mostly consisting of boiled lamb. Everyone ate as much as he wished. Some people communicated in whispers, while others used gestures. Timur sat there on his chair, eyeing everyone and urging those who were eating little to take more. From time to time someone outside the tent kept reciting:

Eat the feast of one who, if alive, would relay it to his family,
And, if dead, would meet God Almighty with full stomach.

When Timur made to stand up with the aid of his servants, 'Abd al-Rahman snatched the opportunity to go over to Burhan al-Din and ask him about the keys to the city of Damascus: had they, he asked, been handed over to Timur? He also asked about the disappearance of Shadid al-Din, the shaykh of the poor. He informed 'Abd al-Rahman that the shaykh was actually present, but had blended into the crowd like a tiny hair inside a cooking pot. Timur would not be demanding the keys at this point, but intended to wait till he could take the judges to the city gates where everyone could witness the official surrender.

Once Timur had stood up, propping his leg on a gold box, he gave everyone a piercing stare and identified someone behind them hiding by a tent pole. He shouted at him what sounded like angry orders. The translator came over to Timur: "The great leader orders the man hiding to eat." The man in question let out a cry that shook the whole tent and followed it with a ringing retort, "Tell him I will not eat." Everyone turned round in amazement and discovered that the man in question was none other than the shaykh of the poor, with his simple face, piercing eyes, and proverbial skinniness. He started countering Timur's threats by reciting, "As a Muslim I care not when I am to be killed; in whatever quarter my death belongs to God alone." Everyone was now convinced that the shaykh was going to die for sure. However, Timur rapidly calmed down and launched into a succession of phrases, punctuated by gestures and grimaces that swung from fiery expatiation to sarcastic rebuke. Once finished he sat down on his chair again.

"Praise be to Him, to other than Whom no praise is due!" began the translator. "He gives authority to whomever He wills and grants victory likewise. I have left your poor shaykh to his own devices; he can go where we wills. He is full of stuff and nonsense. Do you know why I spare such indigents my punishment? It is because the strand that connects him with life is thinner than a spider's web; such people care for survival not a jot. This shaykh who clings to my tent pole is one such person; indeed among their number he counts as one of the most stubborn and rigid. What's the point of cutting him in two when he's already like liquid or quicksilver? No, no! Spare me the world's hermits and all others who are weak in body or provision. Spare not just them but all others whose necks my swords wish to shun. Rather, give me sultans and grandees who rebel, people I encounter as foes during campaigns. I set my ravens on their heads before they are executed and force them to commit themselves to bloody conflict. The Circassian Faraj ibn Barquq is so afraid I might make him taste my punishment that he has run away. And you can pass on a message to his commander in the Damascus citadel: I will invade his domain like a roaring flood and crash of lightning and destroy this heretic's citadel just as I did previously to others. I intend to pulverize him in revenge for his stubbornness and arrogance and as a lesson to be learned by all such upstarts who choose to hoard silver and gold for themselves. That lesson is that their time is up. They can say farewell to all pomp and splendor and wash their hands of life itself.

"*O ye who believe, obey God and those in authority among you*—God the Mighty, the Wise has spoken truly. Obedience to me is a solemn obligation on all those whom I have conquered. I am what is ordained to be good; anything other than me is the opposite. This is the age of the Mongols, descended from the Chagatai, and no others. My rule is established in canon law and reinforced by the readings of astrologers in the heavenly firmament. Your own colleague, Ibn Khaldun, has confirmed these facts and confirmed for me what I know and all of you do as well. God preserve you all!

"Judges, if I have been sent to renew obedience to God through obedience to me, then why do people insist on defying me?

"Is the one who has invaded kingdoms and cities to be resisted?

"Is the one who has subdued peoples and communities to be resisted?

"Is the one who has bridled kings and sultans and brought down crowns and thrones to be resisted?

"The Mamluk Faraj and his army should have strewn my path with roses and jasmine. They should have thrown rice at me and sprayed me with perfume and rose water. They should have greeted me with dates and milk, with kisses and embraces. But instead, that manumitted slave has chosen the path of arrogance and loathing. When he came out to meet me with his army, we crushed them and sent them reeling backward; their deeds were *like a mirage in a depression which the thirsty man imagines to be water*—God the Devout, the Almighty has spoken truly.

"Verily it is our dead alone who are genuine martyrs.

"O God, make our martyrs dwell in Paradise!

"O God, shower them with the abundant rains of mercy and forgiveness!

"O God, prolong the life of our great lord, Timur, sustained by God!

"O God, strengthen his steps and grant him victory over the Mamluks and all other rebels! Amen! Praise be to God, the Lord of humanity!"

The judges all shifted in their places and took a deep breath. They felt as though they had just emerged from a trying examination, one in which they were supposed to don the armor of partiality and dissimulation, lift their hands in supplication, and go along with the prayers of the translator jurist, Ibn al-Nu'man, wherever they happened to lead. Burhan al-Din leaned over and spoke to 'Abd al-Rahman. "I notice," he said, "that, like me, you are eager to challenge certain details of what was just said. Maybe you noticed, as I did, that the translator added certain ideas of his own to the original. But in the present situation it's much too risky to say anything. So just pray to God that the tyrant's path will be removed from us."

By now the Mongols' shouting outside the tent had reached some sort of climax. Timur looked as though he were riding in a boat on top of it all, almost drunk from an excess of pride and delight. Then all of a sudden, with a single gesture of his hand, an abrupt and scary silence fell over everyone. After another gesture, he was put on a sedan-chair and carried away to his harem quarters. His official, Shah Malik, asked the judges to go back to Bab al-Jabiya ahead of the Great Khan and await his arrival there in the evening.

It was noon. Heat, indigestion, the mob of uncouth soldiery in the Mongol camp, Timur's explicit refusal to confirm his safe-conduct document, all these things served to make the judges feel almost giddy. They certainly did not feel like talking. As a result, each of them rushed back to his own house, hoping to get some rest before the appointed rendezvous with Timur on this nineteenth day in Jumada al-Akhira in 903.

Next to Manjak's tomb, close by Bab al-Jabiya, the air over Damascus began to reverberate to the beating of drums and the clarion calls of horns and bugles. The people in the city were thus notified of Timur's arrival at the city gates and his army's imminent entry into the city itself. The overwhelming atmosphere was one of fear and trepidation, something that was in no way mitigated either by the soothing sentiments of speeches and sermons or by talk of Timur's safe-conduct agreement. Most people were instinctively aware that the Mongols could not simply abandon their normally aggressive behavior at the threshold of Damascus and spare the surrendering city from their normal ravage and rapine. On the other hand, they also realized that any resistance coming from the Citadel was both an expression of ultimate despair and a gesture with death as a certain consequence. All people could do was to recite the prayer for mercy and then pray that the Mongol hurricane would not totally destroy the city along with all its people and produce.

Spurred by curiosity and a desire to witness the event for themselves, the people of Damascus gathered in the spot where Timur and his retinue were supposed to appear. At their head were the city's judges and dignitaries, decked in all the garb of pomp and respect. They felt bolstered by Burhan al-Din's slogan: "We are handing over the keys to the city, but not to our souls." The strident music still managed to scare people. All the while Timur sat in his pavilion, accepting greetings from those coming to see him and gesturing to them to take a seat. Once the gathering was assembled, a sudden silence fell over the proceedings. Shah Malik then demanded that the chief judge, the Hanafi Mahmud Ibn al-'Izz, appear before Timur. He then showed the judge a huge box filled with keys and conveyed to him the command that the symbols of the surrender of Damascus be placed inside the Mongol invader's box. At this crucial point in the ceremony, Burhan al-Din ibn Muflih stepped forward and bowed to Timur. Out of his sleeve he took a piece of paper and proceeded to read out loud so that everyone in the pavilion could hear. "Those pages also contain our keys," he said. "keys symbolizing our demand for a guarantee of safety. They contain the guarantee signed by the Great Khan, shepherd of Muslim souls, guardian of their womenfolk and possessions, Timur ibn Chagatai, the righteous, the upright." Judge Ibn Muflih then repeated his statement in Turkish (close to the Mongol's own tongue). Timur had not been expecting any of the judges to be so bold as to make such an impromptu statement in public, but even so he managed to keep his anger under control. He glowered at Burhan al-Din, then guffawed as he looked toward the rest of assembled company before gesturing to the judges to depart. As they left, Ibn al-Nu'man reminded them that from now on they would be obliged to deliver the sermon on Fridays and feast days in the name of the Great Khan, Timur the Magnificent. Ibn Khaldun was ordered to stay behind along with the notables of Damascus society so that they could discuss cutting off the water supply to the Citadel as a means of bringing about its surrender. Argument on the topic was long and inconclusive since there were various opinions on the subject of cutting off the water. Eventually Timur accepted a proposal from the translator that within two days the notables prepare a plan they could all accept and submit it to him. With that he allowed everyone to leave.

Once 'Abd al-Rahman had returned to his abode, he started worrying again because he had had no news of his family. He longed to return to his home in Egypt, but in the meantime he decided to be patient and prayed to God a great deal. He realized full well that the best way to rid himself of Timur was to respond to the latter's request for a description of the Maghrib. He therefore spent several days writing such an account, focusing on the ruggedness of the terrain and the steadfast qualities of its inhabitants. That way, he hoped he would be able to remove from Timur's mind any thought of launching a campaign against the Maghrib and adding its territories to the Mongol dominions further to the east. While he was busy writing this document, news reached him of the fall of the Damascus citadel after the Mongols had threatened to attack it with catapults, ballistas, flame-throwers, and other instruments of destruction, including—it was rumored—cannons. Certain judges also reported that the citadel commander had managed to escape and that Burhan al-Din had been arrested by the Mongols for confronting Timur over his demand for a share of tax revenues and because the people in the Citadel who had surrendered had been subjected to looting and murder. Barely two days passed before the judges brought even worse news: Mongol soldiers were mistreating the citizens of Damascus itself and confiscating money and property. The fires deliberately set by soldiers in people's homes and markets had reached the walls and roof of the Great Umawi Mosque and completely destroyed the eastern minaret.

"So Timur has broken his promise—may God rebuke him!" said Shaykh Mahmud ibn al-'Izz and those with him. "We must go to see him at once and complain angrily. 'Abd al-Rahman could only agree with them, especially since from the roof of the al-'Adiliya College he had been able to observe for himself some evidence of the destruction now being wrought on the city.

The delegation made its way swiftly to the al-Ablaq Palace where Timur had taken up residence. They asked his minister, Shah Malik, for a meeting with Timur, but without success. They then went to the office of his translator, Judge Ibn al-Nu'man, who welcomed them warmly, almost as though news of the atrocities in the city had yet to reach his ears. At this point the chief judge—in spite of his age and exhaustion—undertook to detail the outrages currently taking place in a tone full of anger and reproach. The Hanbali judge Shams al-Din Muhammad al-Nabulusi noticed that the translator seemed totally unconcerned and unaffected by the information, whereupon he yelled in his face, "Did we receive from your lord a document that guaranteed safety, or was it destruction? The Islamic religion is innocent of the Mongols and their deeds. *Those who transgress the statutes of God, those are the wrongdoers*—God who neither delays nor ignores has spoken truly."

Ibn al-Nu'man realized that he would have to say something, particularly since the judges as a group were obviously on the point of elevating the level of blame and rebuke to yet higher levels.

"Calm down, I beg you, esteemed judges, please calm down! I am already aware of the facts you are telling me. There is nothing I can do about it. But as a way of calming your fears, I will go beyond my authority and tell you things you either don't know or are ignoring. The kind of politics that follows the dictates of canon law and acts on its precedents only ever existed in the earliest days of Islam and in certain other brief periods. Secular politics, which is the most prevalent and forceful, is powered by the rites of conquest, control, and transferred interests. If you need the most complete treatment that sheds light on this subject, then ask your very own scholar, the historian Ibn Khaldun, about it. Now, in order to convey to you the import of my statement about the current situation, let me say—God support you all—that during the Great Khan Timur's campaigns, he has only ever operated on the basis of the conduct of great conquerors from the past. He will therefore give safe-conduct documents and sign agreements when temporary necessity requires that he do so; he will annul all such agreements and treaties whenever his own interests and those of his army so demand. If it is your view that, regarding what has happened in Damascus, the restraining factor of religion finds itself in a sorry state of decline, then it needs to be said that the reason for such a situation is that the logic of conquest and power has so determined. Such logic, gentlemen, requires that you be both aware of its existence and understand its import. You can then deal with politics as they actually are and not as they should be. You need to examine the subject not according to some idealized version that may exist inside your minds and dreams, but rather by reference to the nature of civilized society and the material elements in everything. Isn't that the case, Ibn Khaldun?"

'Abd al-Rahman felt extremely awkward, standing there between this very astute translator and his colleague judges. However, faced with such a difficult situation, he quickly decided to take the latter's side.

"Ibn al-Nu'man," he said, "the depiction of what is reprehensible is not in and of itself reprehensible. Talk about the nature of secular politics does not necessarily imply that as a consequence one should advocate them. Within the context of what you have termed 'the logic of conquest and power,' weakness in the restraining factor of religious devotion cannot serve as a pretext in any argument against such restraint. The blame rather attaches to the politicians of the country concerned and to people who allow themselves to succumb to ephemeral worldly desire and pleasures. But, for heaven's sake, let's stop indulging in the kind of discussion that in no way matches the gravity of the current situation and the outrages that people are suffering. Instead, why don't you talk to us about something we all consider outrageous and incomprehensible? If the Great Khan has achieved the conquest of Damascus, as he has done previously with other Syrian cities, then what possible logical reason can there be for breaking the agreement he reached? And how can anyone justify the outrages being committed against unarmed Muslims?"

Ibn al-Nu'man hesitated for a moment, then rubbed his neck. "If I am to respond to your comments, great scholar," he said, "it implies that this meeting of ours must remain absolutely confidential. Failing that, we'll all be dead. That's my absolute condition, gentlemen, if I am to suggest to you that the kinds of things you and I are witnessing are just a part of the evil deeds perpetrated by

Timur. As far as this khan-conqueror is concerned, actions such as those you are now witnessing have to be evaluated according to their utility with two purposes in mind. The first is that there's a secret pact between Timur and his colossal army, one that binds soldiers to him by ties of loyalty and victory in battle. In exchange he gives them a completely free hand when it comes to the money and property of conquered peoples. The second is that the khan never embarks on campaigns simply by fighting battles but by using rumors and tricks as well—especially by spreading terrifying stories. Timur's earthquakes and outrages have but one goal, to weaken enemies before he ever engages with them. Believe me, in the case of Damascus—with the exception of its citadel—he has ordered his soldiers to show restraint in their assaults on civilians."

The Hanbali judge, Shams al-Din, stood up. "Ibn al-Nu'man," he said, "everything you've just said is contrary to both canon law and logic. In any case, you can inform the Great Khan that we intend to curse him in mosques and homes and entrust his fate to God the One, the Powerful."

"My dear Judge," Ibn al-Nu'man replied, "such are your threats that I pity you and fear for your life and that of your colleagues. I certainly have no intention of translating it for the Great Khan. Fear God for your own sakes and show some forbearance."

The judges left the office and palace as quickly as possible. 'Abd al-Rahman stayed behind, anxious for some information about his friend, Burhan al-Din ibn Muflih.

"Your colleague Ibn Muflih's words really annoyed Timur," Ibn al-Nu'man replied. "He defied his troops and then refused to pay the full amount of tax. The khan ordered him kept in preventive detention in a safe place. But have no fear. He's in no danger as long as I'm with him. Now do you understand why I agreed with Shah Malik's opinion about not letting the judges have an audience with Timur?"

'Abd al-Rahman now headed for the Umawi mosque to see for himself exactly what had been destroyed. Inside people were putting out the last of the fires and removing the piles of ashes and refuse from the damaged cloisters and arcades. They all looked stunned, and their constant movement did nothing to hide their feelings. Once in a while one of them would ask out loud, "How can anyone who sets God's own houses on fire face his God?"

The historian sat down for a moment to contemplate the idea of Timur on the Day of Judgment. He envisaged him stating that he had not deliberately set fire to the Umawi mosque. It was just that the people who started the fire had no idea where it would end. 'Abd al-Rahman stood in a corner of the great mosque where strands of smoke were still drifting from time to time and prayed for a long time. He then returned to his house.

How to escape Timur's clutches? The question kept preying on 'Abd al-Rahman's mind; a tricky theoretical issue, since experience had long since taught him that only an absolute miracle could liberate anyone who becomes part of Timur's coterie. It was a habit of the khan to take scholars and trained professionals with him on his campaigns so he could use them in his favorite cities. He would also bring religious scholars along to enliven his councils and soirees with their learned discussion and banter. For his part, 'Abd al-Rahman, who had only joined Sultan Faraj's trip to Damascus with some reluctance, was now of an age when he no longer looked forward to the excitement of long journeys, even if it involved a journey all the way to Samarqand amid enormous pomp and respect. His exclusive and only desire was to return to Cairo so he could spend time with his family, friends, and books. But how could he express such a desire to Timur and get him to appreciate how strong his feelings really were?

He realized that a direct approach would not work; indeed it might well work to the disadvantage of both his own person and his goal. The only hope lay in a more indirect approach and some type of circumlocution, using all the devices of figurative language, simile, and allusion. Combined with all the necessary linguistic safeguards and rhetorical flourishes such methods might achieve the desired effect.

In his quest for means of escape, 'Abd al-Rahman decided to lay the groundwork for his flowery presentation by proffering some symbolic gifts to the Great Khan: a lavishly decorated copy of the Qur'an, a superb carpet, and a copy of al-Busiri's famous poem, *The*

Mantle Ode, along with some boxes of Egypt's famous sweetmeats. As he walked through the book markets, he became aware of the extent to which taxes imposed by the Mongols had destroyed the livelihood of so many merchants. "Their stomachs are bottomless," one of them told him. "Every time I feed them, they ask for more." "We've become their slaves in chains," another said. "We starve so they can eat. We suffer so they can have a good time." As 'Abd al-Rahman listened to complaints like these, all he could do was to recommend patience and promise that the calamity would eventually come to an end.

"My life proceeds through God's blessings. O God, let the paces of this faithful mule be enveloped in a process of release and rescue. O God, endow me with Your kindness. O Merciful and Compassionate One, clear the path before me and do not make things difficult!"

In the grand arcade of al-Ablaq Palace, 'Abd al-Rahman presented his gifts to Timur. He watched as the Great Khan got up from his chair and put the Qur'an in front of him. He then sat on the carpet and looked pleased with it. When 'Abd al-Rahman presented the copy of *The Mantle Ode*, he asked the translator to give the khan a few details about the work and its author. Lastly, he himself ate some of the sweetmeats to convince his host that they were safe to eat, whereupon Timur took some and swallowed them. He then gave 'Abd al-Rahman an inquisitive stare.

"Where's the report on the Maghrib, Wali al-Din?" the translator hastened to ask, putting the khan's expression into words. "Where's the report?"

"The report? Oh my!" replied 'Abd al-Rahman in some confusion. "However forgetful can one be . . . the report, yes indeed, the report. *It is only the Devil who has made me forget to remember it.* Here it is, straight from the warm inside of my burnous to the hand of the Great Khan."

Timur put the pile of paper on top of his hand as though weighing it. "*Khub, khub,*" he commented in a desultory fashion. He then addressed some remarks to the translator, the gist of which was that the text should be translated into Mongolian. 'Abd al-Rahman took a deep breath and waited for the appropriate point at which to say what was really on his mind. The senior officials in attendance were sitting by the door to the arcade, reacting to their leader's comments with gestures of support and approval. As they all watched, bleary-eyed, Timur, his mouth full of sweetmeats, started to make a speech involving much groaning, along with raising and lowering of his voice. Once finished, he ordered the grandees and commanders to leave. He then instructed the chamberlain to bring in two sturdy boys to meet the great scholar, Ibn Khaldun. The historian was told that these were Timur's sons, Miran Shah and Shah Rukh. They greeted him, then left.

When 'Abd al-Rahman made it clear that he was anxious to understand what Timur had said, Ibn al-Nu'man leaned over and translated for him: "What the Great Khan said with his voice lowered was that he was very upset to hear about the outrages to which Damascus and its citadel had been exposed. He was particularly saddened to hear about the fire that had destroyed part of the Umawi mosque. How could he not be affected when he had specifically recorded in his memoirs: 'I have made a great effort to avoid pillage and excessive force, because such deeds only cause famine and various other disasters that can wipe out entire races.' But what was he supposed to do when his specific instructions to his army to take a gentle approach were not always obeyed in the heat of the battle and the ravages that followed? If he forced his army generals to restrain their soldiers and forbid them taking spoils as the result of fierce battles in which they had risked life and limb, they might well cause him a lot of trouble. These were the rules of warfare; nothing could either prevent or change them. When the khan spoke out loud, it was to say that the Syrians had deserved the treatment they received at the hands of the Mongol army as punishment for the crimes they and the Umawis had committed against 'Ali and his two sons—may God sanctify their spirits."

Assuming that Ibn al-Nu'man's translation was accurate, 'Abd al-Rahman had not expected to hear such a statement from Timur. Seizing the opportunity he asked Ibn al-Nu'man to express his own criticism of the way the army had behaved in ways contrary to the laws of Islam and the spirit of Islamic conquests. However, the translator refused to translate any critical remarks for fear of the consequences. At this point a young boy of Arab appearance was brought in; he had a pale face and inscrutable gaze. The Great Khan muttered something about him, and Ibn al-Nu'man hastened to translate: "Since I have taken up residence in this palace, this boy has kept pestering me. He claims to be the 'Abbasi caliph of this era and demands that the caliphal throne in Baghdad be legally restored to him. I've consulted a few judges on the matter, and they've all dismissed the claim. But then I told myself I wouldn't make up my mind until I'd consulted the great historian, someone who's well acquainted with dynastic trees and other aspects of the case. So, Ibn Khaldun, I'm giving you a very important commission. It's a singular honor, something to make you forget all about the ravages that Damascus has suffered. Should I reinstall this young man who has come begging to me on his throne or not? This is a major issue, and I'm entrusting the decision on the matter to you. I will then carry out your decision."

It took 'Abd al-Rahman no time at all to determine that the issue was actually trivial. "I've written a great deal on the caliphate, O Great Khan," he replied. "Since the very beginnings of the Umawi caliphate some five centuries ago, I've come to regard it as an old, worm-eaten tree, retaining a mere smattering of its blessed aura, or else as an aged woman whose features evoke distant memories of a beauty long past and a vigor that exists no more. Today, more than in any previous era, the caliphate is a form with no meaning, a shape with no structure. Sultans make use of its legitimizing effects and adopt it as a kind of symbol and ensign. The ruler in this particular era who has latched on to it in the personage of the would-be caliph, al-Wathiq bi-Llah, is the Mamluk sultan Faraj. The institution resides in Cairo because it was transferred there from Baghdad by the founder of the Bahri Mamluk dynasty, Rukn al-Din Baybars, in about 660. The story of that particular sultan is very well-known. That is the extent of my knowledge about the current state of the caliphate. *Above every knowledgable person is the All-Knowing.*

Timur let out a terrifying laugh, then belched and spat in the face of the young boy kneeling in front of him. He started tweaking his ears and cuffing him on the neck.

"You fraud!" he yelled via his translator. "Did you hear the great scholar's verdict? Out of my sight with you, and forget about the caliphate! Make sure you never come back to me again with your requests for protection and thrones. Be gone. I don't like people pestering me. So, Ibn Khaldun, do you think I've done enough in response to your verdict? So help me, if you'd asked me to kill the boy, I would have done it. Is there any other favor I can do for you?"

'Abd al-Rahman's response was full of nostalgia and sadness. "In this land I am a stranger twofold. First, from the Maghrib which is my homeland and birthplace; second, from Egypt where my family lives. While I thrive in the shadow of your presence, I beg you to consider what grieves me in my exile."

"Say what you would like, and I will do it."

"My exiled situation has made me forget what I want. Perhaps you—and may God support you—may know what it is that I wish."

"Now that you have given me your verdict on the caliphate, how can I refuse you permission to return to your family? Since I'm in a good mood, ask me for any other desires you have."

"That you release Burhan al-Din ibn Muflih—may God grant you a good reward. Also that you give scribes and craftsmen in Damascus a safe-conduct document so that their lives and wages can be preserved."

"Your recalcitrant colleague will not be released until I leave this city. The document you can have."

'Abd al-Rahman expressed his profuse thanks to the khan and pronounced a number of prayers for his well being.

"They tell me," said the khan as 'Abd al-Rahman was about to leave, "that you ride a grey mule with a fine build. Will you sell it to me?"

"You want to buy it from me? Heaven forbid! If I had a whole stable full of fine mules and gave that to you, it would not be adequate compensation for your generosity and kindness toward me. Please accept the mule as a gift. Now I ask permission to leave so I can give the people of Damascus the good news about the safe-conduct document."

'Abd al-Rahman went to Shah Malik's quarters and collected the document with Timur's seal on it. He then went over to the horse pen by the palace gate but found no trace of his mule. He then understood that the walls of this place had ears and consigned the entire matter to God.

On Friday, the twenty-first of Rajab in the same year, 'Abd al-Rahman woke up early, intending to leave for Egypt as soon as possible before the khan changed his mind. He was still worried by the fact that he had received no news from Umm al-Batul and wanted to find out why. He collected his things together, then went to visit some judges and scribes. He handed over the khan's safe-conduct document, bade them all a fond farewell, then headed for al-Ablaq Palace on foot followed by his servant. Timur was seated in the sitting room surrounded by his two sons and retainers. The distinguished visitor hurried over to him. Timur whispered something in his ear that he didn't understand, so he asked the translator to help.

"It's obviously a woman who is responsible for your desire to leave us and go away. O Ibn Khaldun, how well I understand you and forgive you. I too have my wife in Samarqand, and we love each other. Her image is constantly with me. Neither campaigns, nor harems, nor all the women in the world can make me forget her. You and I are both almost seventy years old, and yet we both have room in our hearts for one woman above all others. Praise be to the ever-renewing Creator! Go then and take the quickest route to your destination. Here is a letter with my seal. You can use it to travel throughout my dominions. Should you one day find yourself with nowhere to go and wish to live under my protection, you can use it to come to my capital city. Here is my son, Shah Rukh. He is traveling to Shaqhab to find some spring pasturage for my animals. If you wish, you may travel safely with him. Whenever you meet sultans and amirs, tell them about me. And pray to your Lord for me that he may accord me the keys of this world and bliss in the next."

'Abd al-Rahman now exchanged an embrace with Timur, but said nothing more for fear of prolonging the meeting or venturing some unwise comments. He asked the khan's permission to head for Safad as the closest seaport, and it was granted.

On the same day, a caravan left, including some people for whom 'Abd al-Rahman's intercession with the khan had been effective; the majority of them were Mamluks in the secretarial professions. After one day's traveling, the company was attacked by Bedouin who stripped them of all their possessions and left them naked but for their trousers. It was in that state that they arrived at al-Subayba after two days of rapid travel. Having replaced their clothing, they headed for Safad and rested there for a few days. At that point, one of the boats of Ibn 'Uthman, sultan of Byzantium, arrived and transported them as far as Gaza from where they traveled overland to Egypt.

On the first day of Sha'ban, 'Abd al-Rahman parted from his travel companions and urged his camel-driver toward al-Mahmudiya, the quarter where he lived.

Conclusion

Once we reached al-Mahmudiya, I headed straight for my house on foot, without either burnous or possessions. After such a long absence I was longing to hug my wife and daughter. I knocked insistently on the door, and Sha'ban opened it. There he stood, mouth agape, eyes staring. He was so surprised and shocked he almost fainted.

I gave him the warmest of embraces as he welcomed my return and gave thanks to the Creator for my safe delivery. I asked him about my wife and daughter, but all he could do was keep saying, "A miracle from God! I have prayed to you, O God, to keep my Master safe from harm, and here You have brought him back to his family safe and sound! You have answered my prayer!"

"What about my wife, Sha'ban?" I insisted. "Where's my daughter?"

"It's hard for me to stand, Master. Please sit here beside me, and I'll tell you. When the Egyptian army returned to Cairo, the rumor spread that you'd been killed. 'The great polymath from the Maghrib has been killed by the Mongol wolf,' they all said. When your wife heard the news, her nerves gave way. Her brother—God curse him—convinced her to go back with him to her family in Fez. I blamed him for what he was doing, but he kept saying over and

over again, 'You've blamed me, old man, you've blamed me! Keep
on doing it, I love being blamed!' On the day they left, I tried to stop
them, but he was too strong for me."

"How is the little girl, Sha'ban?"

"Like all little girls of her age, she fell sick. All that encouraged
her mother to take her back to Fez to consult a physician there. But
I'm sure she's fine."

Now that I had returned, albeit bruised and battered, I had a host
of questions. However, I decided to postpone them till I was safely
reinstalled in my office and could think about the next move. Every
day I asked Sha'ban a few more questions; sometimes the answers
I got were useful, but, more often than not, they just led to yet more
questions. For more than a month I did not leave the house. The
only relief I could get from my misery was through prayers, intercessions, and continual supplications for relief from my worries.
Toward the end of the month, I started to get the better of my
depression, particularly once I had decided to make preparations for
a journey to Fez in search of my wife who had disappeared.
However, my plans on that score were interrupted by an unexpected
visit from one of Sultan Faraj's messengers. He came to tell me
about his journey to Timur in order to convey to him the Mamluks'
acceptance of the peace agreement. He also told me that, just before
the Mongols finally departed, Damascus and the mosque had been
set on fire again. As he was about to leave, he urged me, with a sin-
ister sneer in his voice, to accept a purse of money from Timur in
payment for the mule he had purchased from me. However, I refused
to accept the purse until I had consulted the sultan on the matter.

By noon on the same day I managed to overcome my weariness
and depression enough to make my way to the al-Ablaq Palace. I
needed to remove any shadow of suspicion of treason and bribery as
soon as possible and to nip any plots and intrigue in the bud.

While waiting for my meeting with the sultan, I asked the chamberlain—who was only recently hired—where Yashbak was and
learned that he had been appointed viceroy of Alexandria. So there
was yet more news to make a bad situation worse and lessen my
hopes of restoration to favor. When I went into Faraj's chamber, I
found him busy talking to his companions. I walked over and greeted

him. In a clearly audible voice I told him about the mule, the way that Timur had taken it from me, the amount of money in the purse, and my innocence of any malice in the matter. I asked that it be either returned to its owner or else registered in the treasury.

"No, no," replied the sultan in a drunken stupor, "it belongs to you." It was clear that he rejected the entire story and disapproved of the fact that I had used it as a pretext for coming to see him.

My relationship with this sultan will never be one of warmth and respect; the psychological barrier that separates us can never be bridged. But I no longer care about what goes on in the palace. My own sense of pride, my preoccupation with my own new situation, and other factors all combine to vitiate my need for all that. Thus it was that, when I received the purse, albeit with a deduction for the person who brought it, I praised God for releasing me from any incipient difficulties over this matter of the mule.

It was almost the end of Sha'ban, and there was still no news from Fez or Umm al-Batul. I was still extremely worried. For that reason, I wrote to the Mamluk sultan requesting his permission to travel to the Maghrib, merely pointing out that I longed to see my family and homeland. Unfortunately the response to this request took the form of a decree appointing me Maliki judge in Cairo for the third time. Into this new responsibility I read a desire on the sultan's part to keep me under the watchful eye of the Mamluk administration. All I could do now was to come up with some other way of escaping my situation. The best way I could think of was to insist on the strictest possible application of the law, a total rejection of applying two different standards, and an avoidance of any kind of recommendation or intercession when it came to dealing with cases and grievances. As a result, not even a year went by before I was dismissed from the position yet again. The position was sold to the person who paid for it in a kind of financial dog-fight, a man named Jamal al-Din al-Bisati, someone well versed in the fields of intrigue and bribery. Even so, I did not wait until my inevitable dismissal before trying another avenue of escape.

In Safar 804, I decided to write to the Marini sultan in Morocco, Abu Sa'id, even though I knew nothing about him because the

Maghrib was so distant and communication about events was so poor. I decided to concentrate on the threat that the Tatars represented and on making him aware of the need to remain on his guard against the expansionist ambitions of the man who had gained total control over the khanate and its dominions, Timur Lang the Mongolian. I recounted to the Maghribi ruler the period I had spent as an adjunct to the khan's retinue in Damascus, but avoided mentioning the fact that I had written for him a description of the Maghrib region. I then provided a short account of Tatar history, from the time when they launched a series of attacks across the River Oxus under their king, Genghiz Khan, all the way to his children who had divided up his widespread dominions in East and Central Asia. All these lands had also come under the control of Timur, son of Chagatai, ravager of peoples and lands, who had further expanded Mongol territories. In my document I compared the Tatars with the Arabs for their courage and Bedouin qualities of endurance, all with the aim of encouraging its primary reader to mobilize and toughen the Arabs of the Maghrib in readiness for emergency situations.

My aim in writing to the Marini sultan was not just to replicate my motivations in producing the earlier document for Timur. I also wanted to persuade the sultan to write a letter to Sultan Faraj requesting that I be allowed to return to the Maghrib. I had to find someone to deliver the letter, then wait to see what happened.

The letter was sent with a traveling merchant. From that moment, I waited for eight full months with no response or reaction from the Maghrib. Eventually I despaired of waiting and wrote once again to Sultan Faraj begging him to let me travel. Yet again his response was to issue yet another official edict appointing me Maliki judge. I accepted the position with the greatest reluctance so as not to annoy the sultan and completely sever every last strand of hope. This all happened in Dhu al-Qaʻda of the same year.

Like present, like past, water and water, this was the way I regarded my reappointment as judge: testimony, statements, mistakes, in never-ending succession, all accompanied by an increasingly sophisticated use of graft, fraud, and trickery. In such circumstances, how I longed to break my bonds and leave forever the whirlpool of corruption for another place where people could live a simpler life with their animals and land. Had I been younger and more vigorous, I would not have hesitated for a single second to take a boat or camel and travel long distances, taking in vast expanses and incredible sights on the way. But when old age strikes and you have one foot in the grave, all you can do is chew the cud while you wait or else react and object as you ride on the backs of fancies and dreams. For my part, I kept having disturbing nightmares. Whenever I woke up after them, my mouth would still be moist with the stirring words I had been uttering. There was one day when I managed to recall every detail about such a dream: I had been speaking to Sultan Faraj. He was totally drunk and weaving his way among his drinking companions. "You took me with you on a foul war and then you ran away. You gave me up for lost with your sworn enemy. As a result, when news reached Cairo that I'd been killed, my family was shattered. What do you have to say?" The sultan let out a vile laugh. "Old man Judge," he responded with a leer, "can anyone your age still be so in love? No doubt, your young wife has found herself another mate. Forget all about her and have a good time!" My dream finished with me saying, "God curse all wanton drunkards, you shameless and godless reprobates!"

At the beginning of Dhu al-Hijja, when I was most depressed, Sha'ban came up to see me with a beaming smile.

"Master," he said, "I hate seeing you so depressed and miserable. I realize that your wife's departure has affected you very deeply, but aren't you the one who has always said, 'Never despair of God's mercy'? During last year's pilgrimage season I asked a Maghribi pilgrim on his way back to Fez from Cairo to enquire after your wife and tell her that you are still alive and are longing to have her back. My network did not produced any results, but I'd like to try again with the pilgrims from Fez who are leaving here on their way back to the Maghrib. So write some letters to Umm al-Banin, daughter of Salih al-Tazi, and I'll see to the rest."

My expression managed to reflect some glimmerings of hope. Welcoming Sha'ban's idea, I kissed him and promised to write some letters.

I wrote just one short letter in a number of copies. In it I told my wife that I was still alive and employed and that my dearest wish was that she and our daughter would return to me. Sha'ban gave the letter to seven separate pilgrims and asked them to make a thorough search and carry out their mission to the full. I prayed to God to respond to my network of letters and bring about a happy outcome. Two months and more now passed with no news from the Maghrib. Meanwhile, I kept counting the time in heartbeats and upsets to my lifestyle. Neither my dismissal from the judgeship for the fourth time nor news of Sultan Bayazid's death in one of Timur's prison cages interfered with my patient waiting.

Rabi' al-Awwal of 806 came to an end, to be followed by Rabi' al-Akhir. Sha'ban tried to counter the effects of my rekindled depression with various promises and soothing thoughts, including a solemn promise to undertake the rigors of a journey—albeit after a two- or three-month wait—to bring my wife and daughter back. "Unlike you, Master," he would say, "I'm not involved in the sultan's court. It's up to me to perform this function as a sign of my gratitude to you for your generosity and kindness."

Sha'ban's genuine and kind offer touched me deeply and made me feel somewhat happier. With a certain amount of effort I forced myself to start reading books again, things that had been waiting on my desk for some time. I also made some additions to the dictated texts which my late amanuensis, Hammu, had written down during those seven nights, and some marginal notes concerning my correspondence with the late Lisan al-Din ibn al-Khatib and my journey to see the king of Castille, Pedro Alfonso, some four decades earlier.

At the end of Rajab in this same year, Sha'ban heard a gentle tap on the door at about midday. His heart in his mouth, he rushed over to open it. There, right in front of him, stood Umm al-Banin with her jalabiya, veil, and other familiar features. He could not stop himself from kissing her forehead and hands and yelling out her name in welcome and in thanks to God who had responded to his prayers. When he brought her up to my private quarters, they both found I was doing my prayers, so they waited till I had finished. However, I deliberately prolonged the wait till there was complete quiet and the only sound to be heard was me reciting my prayers. With that,

Sha'ban went to the kitchen to prepare drinks and sweets and get lunch ready. When he returned with his tray, I was still performing prayers and intercessions. Once I had finished, I started reciting some of the short suras from the Qur'an in an audible voice, and followed them with other litanies and prayers. At long last, I turned to face my wife.

"You did me wrong, my wife," I told her with tears in my eyes. "You believed all the stories about my death. You should have waited till my corpse was brought back. You should have planned burial rites in accordance with my station. You did me wrong, my wife!"

My wife leaped up and kissed my hands, then burst into tears. She asked Sha'ban who was on his way back to the kitchen to vouch for the fact that her brother had played a big part in her decision to leave. Everyone had assured her that people who fell into the Mongol monster's hands were sure to die. She went on to say that, as soon as she had received my letter, she had immediately made plans to come back here along with two families from the Fez nobility who were traveling to the holy places to perform the minor pilgrimage.

"And where's my daughter, al-Batul?"

"With my mother, revered pilgrim. When you left, her health deteriorated. Thanks to my mother's potions, she's much better now that she's in Fez. My closest friends advised me not to subject her to the rigors of such a long journey."

"But she has to come back. Without you and her this house is an unbearable wasteland!"

"It's the same with our home in Fez, O lord of men! No delight, no pleasure. I've returned so you can see me as you've known me. I've come to beg you, by our lord Idris, to come back with me to the city of that pious saint."

"That's very difficult, Umm al-Batul, and will require some thought."

After a period of silence, she told me she had promised the Fez families that she would be returning with them to Fez by boat from Alexandria at the end of Dhu al-Hijja. There were five months ahead, and that was quite enough to make preparations for the journey. For the time being there was no need to discuss the matter.

"From now till then," I said, "there's always God, the Wise Arranger. Sha'ban, bring in the lunch."

My faithful servant came in with lunch, all smiles and thanks to God. He spread it out in front of us and justified the amounts by saying that this was a festival day. I found my appetite again, a sure sign that my spirit had returned. I started asking my wife to eat and made an effort to erase all signs of annoyance from my expression. When I managed to smile for the first time, she went away for a moment and returned with gifts in the form of a burnous, prayer mat, rosary, and several bottles. I made do with taking the burnous, which was exactly like the one that was stolen from me, and handed the rest to Sha'ban with due thanks to Umm al-Batul for her kindness.

The remaining five months of 806 I devoted entirely to household matters; I worked on finishing them all as though I was going to die the next day. I sold as many of my possessions as possible, and used a legal stratagem to deed my house and its furniture to Sha'ban. I was equally anxious to satisfy Umm al-Batul's needs and turned every night I spent in her company into a night of all nights.

Every day I spent in the tender care of my wife, I struggled to rid my mind of the notion that my inevitable death was drawing ever closer. She never lost an opportunity to talk about our daughter and make me long for Fez and a life of ease there. When the time came for her to go back, I accompanied her to Alexandria. With many, many kisses, I said farewell, promising that I would join her in a few months. I then handed her over to the care of the noble families returning by boat to Fez.

In the first week of Sha'ban in the following year, just as I was putting the final touches to my preparations for departure, I heard that Timur had died. Even so, I did not celebrate. It was at precisely this point that I received a new decree appointing me judge for the fifth time. I had no choice but to accept, all in the hope that I would soon be dismissed. In fact, it was only about four months before I was indeed dismissed yet again. I gave thanks to God and wrote to tell my wife that I would soon be joining her.

At the beginning of Dhu al-Hijja my caravan of possessions—books and clothes—was ready to leave. I thought of asking the sultan for permission to perform the pilgrimage, my intention being to use the return journey as a way of heading quickly and secretly to the Maghrib. However, at this point the winds blew the wrong way, and my intentions were thwarted. I came down with a severe and totally unexpected illness that confined me to bed. The illness was very grave and had a terrible effect on my spirits which were already floundering in a swamp of misgivings and foul odors. But for Sha'ban who took tremendous pains to look after me, I would simply have given up and waited for the fates to make their judgment.

For the first five months of 807 I kept feeling alternately hot and cold, with permanent pains in my joints. The expressions on the faces of the few visitors I had made clear quite how ill I really was. On such occasions I said very little, but asked them not to spread word of my illness so that God could decide how to finish something that was already determined.

At the beginning of Rajab I received a letter from Umm al-Batul in which she reassured me that both she and our daughter were well and begged me to travel soon. Those sweet, impassioned words of hers were a kind of prelude to a stage when I started to convalesce. Ever so gradually, I started being able to wash myself for prayers and perform them at the right times. My appetite returned, and with it my desire to read. Had I been able to write, I would have noted down all the scattered, incoherent thoughts in my foggy mind about a world as envisaged by a tired and sick old man whose entire universe was bounded by his bed and house. All that was an incipient project that I thought I might compose some time soon, provided time came to my aid and God prolonged my life.

By the beginning of Sha'ban I could move about and even walk around the quarters close to my house. For an hour or two every morning, I used to walk through streets and markets, looking at people and objects with a kind of curiosity and longing, as though I were rediscovering them after a long, compulsory absence. Sha'ban would often accompany me to make sure I was comfortable and to give me whatever good advice was needed to ensure my safety.

When I felt strong enough, I went to see Faraj and told him of my desire to perform the pilgrimage and my longing for the noble Ka'ba and the holy places. But the drunken sultan gave a hearty laugh. "You're clearly unwell, Wali al-Din," he said. "I want to remove all your worries by reappointing you as judge. Through my generosity your health will be restored. Do not ask me for anything else." Had he not left immediately, I would have clearly indicated my unwillingness to accept the position and my longing to escape his clutches.

I was born seventy-six years ago, at the beginning of Ramadan, the month of fasting, the month when the Qur'an was sent down. This year, when the blessed month came round again, my illness returned even worse than before. I lost all taste for life and prayed to God to bring me close to Him. I begged for intercessions from his noble Prophet who spoke truly: 'When Ramadan comes, heaven's gates are opened and those of hell are closed.' As my death seemed ever more imminent, Sha'ban became more and more dismayed. I asked him to send my wife a letter that I wrote, requesting her to arrange my burial in the Sufi cemetery outside the Bab al-Nasr. Then I lay down on my bed, waiting for the arrival of the angel of death who would forever extinguish the residual warmth in my body; waiting too for the hand that would close my eyes with unique gentleness. . . .

This period of waiting starts with involvement, followed by a recondite, yet stunning plunge into the depths of folly and grief.

This is a wait for the jugular vein and all other pulses and pumps to be severed!

The process of dying, I can confirm, involves an end with neither doubt nor ambiguity. That confirmation comes from an internal voice, one that speaks from the midst of my muscles and limbs, using the language of separation and annihilation.

Ulcers on my legs, like ants, or rather bloody worms that crawl through veins and bones, making their way so, so slowly, and yet beneath the standards of rugged determination.

My head remains feverish; I know it well and its habitation.

The statement of faith before fate snatches me away unexpectedly!

So I muttered the statement of faith over and over again, interspersed with prayers for myself, my father, my family, and all my loved ones who will live on after me. I repeated these entreaties as many times as I could. I expressed the hope that Umm al-Batul, the sweet joy of my spirit, would happily join me in the Garden of Eden after traversing the narrow pathway safe and sound on the Day of Judgment. Then, once my mind started to close down and my tongue grew heavy, my own guardian spirit appeared to me and whispered in my ear, "Release me from these chains. . . . "

There is a vague blur in front of my eyes, and I realize that it is Sha'ban, whom my vision has transformed into a thin, ethereal being like smoke. I feel his presence as he leans over me, shedding a tear as he does so, or tries to feed me some light food. I feel him once again as he wraps my freezing-cold feet in woolen blankets.

Praise to the living God!

My entire life appears before my eyes as an amalgamated series of images, brilliantly lit and in sequence. When I look back on some of them in the light of theories about deserts and cities, East and West, sparks and ashes soon begin to fly. All that remains in my vision is a thick fog enveloped by smiling angels; they may well be the angels of mercy and understanding.

Praise to the living God!

Now the entire lower half of my body is falling apart in preparation for the advent of death. No doubt, it is anxious to liberate the spirit from the pit of decay and disease.

These drunken ravings are what emerges from an obsessive concern with the wait for the final breath or the last, great cry. As the wait spins ever faster and time settles into the great darkness, oh how nightmarish are the fearsome visions.

Seas on fire, hurling waves of blood and mire.

Glowering skies replete with winds and ashes, pounding the earth below with torrents of locusts, frogs, and lice.

Now all is confusion. My vision turns to iron.

Here now is Izra'il, the Angel of Death. He stands behind me, wearing a luminous garment whose folds seem like silken wings. He has not come to negotiate with me about death, but rather to urge me to set my sail and wash my hands of this lower world.

227

"Good man," he told me, "the years have exhausted you. You have long strived to reach your Lord. Now you will soon meet Him."

"When blood pours out of its veins," he asked, "does it ever return? Can fruit, once picked from the branch, be put back?"

"Impossible," I replied.

"You, then, are just like that fruit or blood," he said. "Put another way, you are like milk once it has left the udder. All it can do is disappear down the throat of whoever drinks it or else go sour till it evaporates."

"Since I am a graduate of this troubled era," I asked, "will you allow me to write my last will and testament?"

"It is not the right time," he replied. "You are like a hollow palm trunk, lying there on your bed paralyzed and subject to all sorts of gruesome visions."

All of a sudden the angel's voice disappeared. I begged God to sever the cord as quickly as possible.

Perhaps He who alone is eternal responded to my call. I saw myself making my way along a deep trench with many branches, byways, and dark spots. Having reached its end, I then saw myself plunging into a bottomless abyss possessed of total control over the forces of fusion and attraction. At its very bottom, twixt earth and dust, it had the power to restore the falling soul to its original clay. The only one to escape its depths was the soul that in its ascent clung to the rope extended by God from heaven to earth.

Glossary

Dates in the glossary are given in their Islamic (Hijra) form followed by their Gregorian equivalent.

'Abd al-Wadi: one of the North African dynasties during IBN KHALDUN's time, based in TILIMSAN (Tlemcen).

Ablaq Palace: the Mamluk sultan Baybars (d. 676/1277) ordered an ablaq (striped) palace of black and ocher to be constructed in Damascus. It was later replicated in Cairo by Sultan al-Nasir Muhammad ibn Qala'un, who was first chosen as sultan as a child in 693/1293, but then deposed and sent into exile in Syria; he reassumed the sultanate in 698/1299.

Abu 'Abdallah, deposed ruler of Bougie: IBN KHALDUN participated in a plot to liberate Abu 'Abdallah, the former amir of Bijaya (Bougie, formerly an important port, now in modern Algeria), and was imprisoned for two years by Sultan Abu 'Inan. For a short period, Abu 'Abdallah was restored to his dominions, but he was ousted by his cousin, Sultan Abu al-'Abbas.

Abu 'Amir: one of the Marini sultans in Fez who ruled for less than a year (799–800/1396–97).

Abu al-Faraj al-Isfahani (d. 363/967): Abu al-Faraj was the compiler of a large and famous collection of early Arabic poetry and song, *Kitab al-aghani* ('The Book of Songs').

Abu Hanifa al-Nu'man (d. 150/767): founder of the Hanafi school of Islamic law.

Abu al-Hasan al-Shadhili (d. 656/1258): born in northern Morocco, al-Shadhili became one of the most significant figures in the spread of Sufism. The Shadhiliya sect is named after him.

Abu Madyan (d. 594/1197): a renowned Andalusian mystic, he was born near Seville, but spent most of his life in North Africa.

Abu Sa'id: Marini sultan in Fez from 800/1398 till 823/1420.

'Adiliya College: this mosque–college in Damascus where IBN KHALDUN took up residence in 803/1400 was situated close to the citadel of the city and to the northwest of the Great Umawi Mosque.

Ahmad ibn Hanbal (d. 241/855): founder of the Hanbali school of Islamic law.

'Ali (d. 40/661): Muhammad's son-in-law and cousin, the son of the Prophet's uncle, Abu Talib. His appointment as the fourth caliph was the cause of the first great schism in Islam, creating the subdivision of the community into Sunnis who supported the Umawi dynasty and Shi'is who believed in the validity of 'Ali's claims.

Almohads *(al-Muwahhidun)*: the religious movement founded by Ibn Tumart that, after his death in 524/1130, became the ruling dynasty in North Africa and from 541/1146 included parts of al-Andalus as well.

'Amr ibn al-'As (d. c. 43/663): one of the most renowned commanders of Muslim armies during the early days of Islam, who was in charge of the conquest of Egypt. Legend has it that when a pigeon landed on his tent in the FUSTAT area to the south of modern Cairo, he took it as a portent and ordered the construction of the mosque that still carries his name on that site.

'Antara and Sayf ibn Dhi Yazan: these are two heroic figures whose exploits are the subject of lengthy popular sagas, traditionally performed in public by storytellers.

'Ashura' Day: tenth day of Muharram, a day of fasting for Muslims, this day has particular significance in the Shi'i calendar, being the day in 60/680 when Muhammad's grandson, al-Husayn, was slain at the Battle of Karbala.

atabeg: regent or tutor to a prince of the ruling family, a term that came into use when the Saljuq sultans took over civilian and military control of Baghdad in the eleventh century. If the ward of the *atabeg* died young, the regent was entitled to marry the ward's mother and thus become a ruler in his own right.

Atabeg Altunbugha al-Jubani (d. 797/1395): a close friend of IBN KHALDUN, he was a holder of a number of high offices during the reign of SULTAN BARQUQ. Following the failure of the rebellion led by YALBUGHA AL-NASIRI and MINTASH, BARQUQ appointed al-Jubani as governor of Syria. It was al-Jubani who interceded with the sultan to get IBN KHALDUN restored to favor after he had signed the legal opinion authorizing SULTAN BARQUQ's deposition.

'Ayn Jalut ('Goliath's Spring'): location of a battle in 658/1260 at which a large Mamluk army crushed a smaller force of Mongols, thus halting their advance to the south and west.

Aytamish: commander-in-chief of the army in Cairo, he was appointed special guardian of the young Sultan Faraj following SULTAN BARQUQ's death. The appointment was vigorously opposed by TANAM, the viceroy of Damascus.

Bab al-Jabiya and Bab al-Saghir: the Jabiya gate was in the western portion of the city walls of Damascus. Bab al-Saghir (the 'Small Gate') was in the southern portion of the walls.

Bab al-Jayrun: a gate in the eastern wall of Damascus, close to the Umawi mosque.

al-Bakri and Yusuf ibn Tashufin: not a great deal is known about al-Bakri who appears to have lived in the thirteenth century and to have been a biographer, writing a life of the Prophet Muhammad among other works. Yusuf ibn Tashufin (d. 500/1106) was one of the illustrious leaders of the Murabitun, the Berber dynasty known in English as the Almoravids, who ruled over North Africa and Spain until they in turn were placed by the ALMOHADS.

Battle of Arak: in 591/1195, the forces of the Castilian king, Alfonso VIII, were defeated by the Muslims under the command of Yusuf ibn Mansur.

Battle of al-'Iqab: a battle fought in al-Andalus in 608/1212 (also known as Las Navas de Tolosa), in which the Muslims were defeated by a Christian force led by Alfonso VIII of Castile.

Battle of Tarif: the sultan, ABU AL-HASAN, after securing a naval victory in the Straits of Gibraltar, invaded Spanish territory. Following a defeat at Tarif (also known as Rio Salado) in 740/1340, he was forced to retreat back across the strait to Morocco.

Bayazid I (d. 804/1403): the Ottoman sultan who made major inroads into Europe (including a victory at the Battle of Kosovo). However, following his defeat by Timur Lang, he was imprisoned and executed.

Baybars Convent: built by Sultan Baybars (704/1305), this convent *(khanqa)* had been established as a religious endowment *(waqf)* for Sufis. It was clearly a source of considerable revenue for IBN KHALDUN, something he missed greatly when he was dismissed from his post following his involvement in the judicial justification of SULTAN BARQUQ's deposition (see ATABEG ALTUNBUGHA AL-JUBANI).

Bayn al-Qasrayn: literally, 'between the two palaces,' one of the principal thoroughfares of Old Cairo, made famous more recently as the title of the first volume of Naguib Mahfouz's renowned trilogy of novels about Cairo between 1916 and 1944 (the English translation is entitled *Palace Walk*).

beautiful names *(al-asma' al-husna)***:** in the Qur'an, God is described using ninety-nine separate epithets, termed 'the beautiful names.' It is very common for Muslims to name their children *'Abd al-* followed by one of these epithets. Ibn Khaldun himself is named 'Abd al-Rahman—Servant of the Merciful.

***Beginning and Ending (al-Bidaya wa-l-nihaya)* of Ibn al-Kathir; *Goal of Desire (Nihayat al-'arab)* by al-Nuwayri; *History (Tarikh)* of Abu al-Fida':** three important works by scholars of IBN KHALDUN's period. Ibn al-Kathir (d. 774/1373) was one of the most famous historians of the Mamluk period; al-Nuwayri's (d. 732/1332) work is a literary compendium on a large variety of topics; Abu al-Fida (d. 732/1331) was an Ayyubi amir and also a historian.

al-Bukhari and Muslim and the *Sahihan*: al-Bukhari (d. 258/870) and Muslim (d. 261/875) are the compilers of the two most authoritative collections of accounts of the Prophet Muhammad (hadith), known as *sahih* ('authentic').

Burhan al-Din ibn Muflih (d. 804/1401): The chief judge of the Hanbali school of law in Damascus (other sources name him Taqi al-Din, not Burhan al-Din). He was later appointed chief spokesman of the deputation (of which IBN KHALDUN was also a member) that went to meet Timur Lang on behalf of the citizens of Damascus.

Castle of Ibn Salama: this castle gives its name to a town in the Oran region of present-day Algeria. IBN KHALDUN stayed there from 778/1375 until 780/1378.

City of Brass, Sijilmasa: The story of the City of Brass *(Madinat al-nuhas)* is a separate Middle Eastern narrative tradition that was added to the *Arabian Nights* at some point following its translation into French in the early eighteenth century. Sijilmasa, in the easternmost section of modern Morocco, was an important town on the trans-Saharan trade route.

dawadar: Originally the title given to the carrier of the ruler's inkwell, this position became during Mamluk times one of considerable authority. Among the functions performed by amirs who held this position were the selection of members of military expeditions and the supervision of tax collection.

Dawadar Yashbak al-Sha'bani: under SULTAN BARQUQ, Yashbak had served as state treasurer and had also been appointed one of Sultan Faraj's guardians. After suppressing the revolt of TANAM, the viceroy of Syria, Yashbak was appointed *dawadar*, or military chief, of Egypt in 803/1400.

The Diwan of Topic and Predicate (Diwan al-mubtada' wa-l-khabar): this is the second part of the title of IBN KHALDUN's work of history, *Kitab al-'ibar* ('Book on the Lessons of History').

escape after hardship: this is a particular theme *(al-faraj ba'da al-shidda)* that was popular as an organizing matrix for varieties of anecdotal narrative in the pre-modern heritage of Arabic literature.

al-Farabi (d. 339/950): renowned philosopher, known as 'the second teacher' (Aristotle being the first).

Fatimi 'Ubaydi dynasty: the Fatimi dynasty was founded by 'Ubaydallah who claimed descent from 'Ali. Moving to North Africa in the early tenth century, he established a base for the Shi'ite cause, beginning in Morocco and spreading eastward. In 358/969, Jawhar, the general of 'Ubaydallah's descendant, al-Mu'izz, entered FUSTAT. The Fatimi dynasty of Shi'ite caliphs remained in power in Cairo until 567/1171.

Fayyum: a depression and oasis filled with lush vegetation to the southwest of Cairo.

Fustat: taking its name from *fossata* (the Latin word for 'trench'), this is the oldest part of Cairo, to the south of the modern city.

Granada, Banu Ahmar: The Banu Ahmar gave their name to one of Islam's most spectacular monuments, the Alhambra (al-Hamra'—'the Red') Palace in Granada, Spain.

Great Plague: known in Europe as the 'Black Death,' bubonic plague struck Cairo and various places in the Middle East off and on throughout the Middle Ages.

Hafsi, 'Abd al-Wadi, and Marini regimes: these are the names of three of the dynasties who were continually intriguing against each other during the earlier part of Ibn Khaldun's career in the Maghrib region. The Hafsis (Banu Hafs) were based in Tunis, the 'Abd al-Wadis in Tilimsan (Tlemcen), and the Marinis (Banu Marin) in Fez.

al-Hakim (d. 411/1021): the Fatimi caliph who reigned from 385/996 to 411/1021. He suffered from a mental disorder, and his caliphate was characterized by the large number of extraordinary decrees that he issued—he declared night to be day, closed public baths, forbade Egyptians from going on the pilgrimage to Mecca, and so on. While it appears that he was assassinated on the order of his sister, Sitt al-Mulk, a group of his devotees fled to the mountains of Syria. Known as the Druze, they believe that al-Hakim is in fact in occultation.

al-Hallaj: one of the most famous figures in the history of Sufism (Islamic mysticism). After being convicted of heresy for proclaiming the phrase *"Ana-l-haqq"* ('I am the truth') during an ecstatic trance, he was executed in 309/922.

Ibn al-'Arabi, Ibn Sab'in, Ibn Qasiyy: three of the most controversial figures in Maghribi Sufism. All three were born in al-Andalus. Ibn al-'Arabi (d. 638/1240), author of *Fusus al-hikam* ('Bezels of Wisdom') and *al-Futuhat al-makkiya* ('Meccan Conquests') is the most renowned of the three (his tomb in Damascus is still a site of pilgrimage); Ibn Sab'in (*Budd al-'arif*, 'Temple of the Knower') was born in Murcia and died in Mecca in 668/1270; Ibn Qasiyy (*Khal' al-na'layn*, 'Removal of Sandals') participated in intrigues during the time of the ALMOHAD dynasty and was assassinated in 546/1151.

Ibn 'Arafa (d. 803/1401): MALIKI JUDGE and imam of the mosque in Tunis who successfully intrigued to have IBN KHALDUN removed from his position at the court of SULTAN ABU AL-'ABBAS, resulting soon afterward in the historian's departure for Cairo.

Ibn Battuta and Ibn Juzayy: Ibn Battuta of Tangiers was one of the most famous travelers in Arab-Islamic history. Setting out on the pilgrimage to Mecca, he traveled between 725/1325 and 750/1349 and eventually reached as far as China. Following his return to his native city, he made a further trip to Niger. He died in 779/1377. Ibn Juzayy was his amanuensis.

Ibn Hazm of Cordoba (d. 456/1064): renowned Andalusian jurist and poet, who also wrote Arabic's most famous essay on love-theory, *Tawq al-hamama* ('The Dove's Neckring').

Ibn Khaldun (732–808/1332–1406): His full name was Wali al-Din 'Abd al-Rahman ibn Muhammad ibn Muhammad ibn Abi Bakr Muhammad ibn al-Hasan. He was occasionally also called 'al-Hadrami,' a reference to his family's purported ancestry in the Hadramawt region of Southern Arabia. In this novel, the historian is called both Ibn Khaldun and 'Abd al-Rahman, and is also addressed by his peers as Wali al-Din.

Ibn Qayyim al-Jawziya (d. 751/1350): a jurist and theologian of Damascus, he supported the doctrines of his contemporary, TAQI AL-DIN IBN TAYMIYA. The *Rawdat al-muhibbin* ('Meadow for Lovers') is one of the most famous works on the topic in Arabic.

Ibn Sharaf (444–533/1052–1139): a renowned figure, poet and philosopher, at the court of al-Mu'tasim ibn Sumadih (d.

484/1091), a member of the Tujibid dynasty who ruled from Almeria in Spain.

Imam al-Shafi'i (d. 204/820): founder of the Shafi'i school of Islamic law.

Information on Ibn Khaldun and His Travels East and West (al-Ta'rif bi-Ibn Khaldun wa-rihlatihi gharban wa-sharqan): IBN KHALDUN's most significant extant works (all of them mentioned during the course of this novel) are 1) his work of history, *Kitab al-'ibar* ('Book on the Lessons of History'); 2) *al-Muqaddima* ('Introduction to History'), the theoretical preface to the history; and 3) *al-Ta'rif bi-Ibn Khaldun wa-rihlatihi gharban wa-sharqan* ('Information on Ibn Khaldun and His Travels East and West'), an autobiography.

Islamic calendar: The Islamic calendar is lunar rather than solar. It is dated from the hijra (emigration) of the Prophet Muhammad from Mecca to Medina in the year 622 of the Christian era.

'Izz al-Din ibn al-Athir (d. 630/1233): historian and author of *al-Kamil fi-l-tarikh* ('The Complete Work on History').

al-Jahiz (d. 255/869): one of Arabic's most famous scholars, al-Jahiz wrote on a vast number of subjects in the form of essays and anthologies and was also a major contributor to the development of an Arabic prose style and critical writing.

Kinana tribe: a confederacy of tribes in Arabia, whose territory was in the neighborhood of Mecca.

Luqman: a legendary figure in Arabian lore, noted for both his longevity and a collection of fables attributed to him.

Maghrib: word in Arabic meaning 'the West.' While today it is used to refer specifically to Morocco and, in broader terms, to Morocco, Algeria, and Tunisia, in IBN KHALDUN's time it referred to the general region to the west of Egypt.

Maliki judge: IBN KHALDUN had judicial authority within the Maliki school of law, one of the four principal schools of Islamic jurisprudence (the others being the Hanafi, Shafi'i, and Hanbali). This school was named for its founder, Malik ibn Anas, the author of a renowned early work of law, *al-Muwatta* ('The Smooth Path'), which IBN KHALDUN utilized in his teaching.

Mamluks: Mamluk is an Arabic word meaning 'slave.' The Mamluk dynasty that ruled Egypt, eligibility for which involved being born a slave and then manumitted, is subdivided into two periods: the Bahri period, 648–791/1250–1389, and the Burji period, 784–922/1382–1517.

al-Mas'udi (d. 345/956): a famous historian, whose major work is *Muruj al-Dhahab* ('Golden Prairies').

Mawlay Idris: this is the name of an important shrine close to the Roman site of Volubilis in Morocco. It is named for Idris, a descendant of the fourth Caliph 'Ali who fled to the West and established himself in Morocco. He died in 175/791.

mihrab: the niche in the wall of a mosque that indicates the qibla (direction of Mecca).

Mintash (d. 793/1393): one of the two primary leaders of the rebellion against SULTAN BARQUQ (791–792/1389–90). His full name was Amir Tumarbugha al-Afdali. Before the rebellion, he was serving as viceroy of the region of Malatya. Like his co-conspirator, YALBUGHA AL-NASIRI, he advocated executing the deposed SULTAN BARQUQ. However, while AL-NASIRI was restored to his former positions after being pardoned by the restored sultan, Mintash continued his revolt in Syria.

mosques of al-Azhar and al-Husayn: These are two of the most famous shrines in the old city of Cairo. Al-Azhar was built for the SHI'ITE FATIMI dynasty in the tenth century A.D. The mosque of al-Husayn (Muhammad's grandson), situated across a square from al-Azhar itself, is one of the holiest shrines in Islam and is believed to house al-Husayn's relics.

Mu'allaqat: the renowned collection of the longest odes (collected in groups of seven or ten) from the tradition of pre-Islamic poetry. They were collected during the early period of Islam and have since then served as the major yardstick for Arab poetic achievement.

Mu'awiya ibn Abi Sufyan (d. 60/680): the first caliph of the Umawi dynasty (41–132/660–750), that assumed the caliphate following the Battle of Siffin and established Damascus as their center of authority.

Muhammad ibn Ibrahim al-Abili: IBN KHALDUN's revered teacher in Tunis, an authority on philosophy and metaphysics.

Muhammad V and Lisan al-Din ibn al-Khatib: Muhammad ibn al-Ahmar (d. 793/1391) was one the rulers of GRANADA, a member of the Nasrid dynasty. Lisan al-Din ibn al-Khatib (d. 776/1374), one of the most famous literary figures of his age, served as his chief minister.

al-Mutanabbi (d. 354/965), al-Ma'arri (d. 449/1058): two of the most famous poets in the Arabic literary heritage.

Mu'tazili doctrine: the rationalist movement, questioning principle of predestination and the uncreatedness of the Qur'an, that became official belief during the caliphate of al-Ma'mun (d. 218/833).

The Path to Eloquence (Nahj al-balagha), The Epistle of Qushayri (Risalat al-Qushayri), Sufi Categories (al-Tabaqat al-sufiyya): the names of three significant works concerning Islamic beliefs: the first is by al-Sharif al-Radi (d. 406/1016) and contains texts attributed to 'Ali, the cousin of Muhammad and fourth caliph; the second is a treatise on Sufi beliefs by al-Qushayri (d. 465/1074); and the third is a categorization of Sufis compiled by Muhammad ibn al-Husayn Sulami (d. 412/1021).

Pedro Alfonso (d. 770/1369): often known as 'Pedro the Cruel,' he was king of Seville. It was in 765/1364 that Muhammad the Fifth of GRANADA and his minister, Ibn al-Khatib, sent IBN KHALDUN to parley with the king.

***The Prevalent Model (al-Mathal al-sa'ir)* by Diya' al-Din ibn al-Athir (d. 637/1239):** this is a famous literary compendium, in which the qualities of both poetry and prose are considered side by side.

Qala'un: the fifth of the Bahri line of MAMLUK sultans, he ruled from 678–689/1279–1290.

al-Qamhiya College: founded by SALAH AL-DIN (Saladin), it was the college to which SULTAN BARQUQ appointed IBN KHALDUN as teacher of MALIKI law in 786/1384.

Qayrawan: one of the most important garrison cities *(amsar)* that were built as part of the Islamic expansion across North Africa to the west in the seventh and eighth centuries. The city (in central Tunisia) is still famous for its superb mosque.

Qubbat Yalbugha: a small shrine to the south of the city of Damascus constructed by Yalbugha al-Yahyawi in 746/1345.

Rigraga: the river in Morocco that flows into the Atlantic between the cities of Sale to the north and Rabat to the south.

Riyah tribes: a powerful group of tribes descended from the Banu Hilal whose emigration from Arabia to North Africa is the subject of the famous Banu Hilal popular narrative saga. In IBN KHALDUN's time, they were centered around the city of Constantine (in contemporary Algeria).

Salah al-Din (Saladin), the Ayyubi, and Ya'qub al-Mansur, the Almohad: at the time of the Crusaders' siege of 'Akka (Acre) in 585/1189, Salah al-Din sent a letter to the Almohad sultan, Ya'qub ibn Mansur (d. 595/1199), requesting the support of his fleet. At first, the request was refused, but later Ya'qub did dispatch some vessels to support him. Salah al-Din was also the founder of the Citadel in Cairo.

Salihiya College: the college on BAYN AL-QASRAYN from which IBN KHALDUN operated as chief judge of the MALIKI school of law in Cairo.

Sarghitmishiya College: this college had been founded as a religious endowment *(waqf)* by Amir Sayf al-Din Sarghatmish.

Sayyida Zaynab: a mosque–shrine in the southern part of the old city of Cairo named for Zaynab, the granddaughter of Muhammad and sister of al-Husayn.

Shah Malik: one of the leading Mongol amirs, he was appointed viceroy of Damascus by Timur.

Sudun: Amir Sudun al-Shaykhuni was supervisor of the BAYBARS CONVENT and did not sign the fatwa approving the deposition of SULTAN BARQUQ, something that IBN KHALDUN reluctantly did. Thus, when BARQUQ was restored to power in 792/1390, Sudun was appointed viceroy in Egypt. IBN KHALDUN's dismissal from his position at the BAYBARS CONVENT followed soon afterward.

Sultan 'Abd al-'Aziz: Marini sultan in Fez (d. 774/1372).

Sultan Abu al-'Abbas: a member of the Hafsi (Banu Hafs) dynasty in Tunis, he was responsible for the restoration of the dynasty to power after the invasion of the Marini dynasty of Fez (748–750/1347–49). He ruled from 748/1370 to 772/1394.

Sultan Abu al-Hasan: father of SULTAN ABU 'INAN, Abu al-Hasan ruled as the Marini sultan in Fez from 731/1331 to 752/1351. A disastrous naval expedition was primarily responsible for his downfall at the hands of his own son.

Sultan Abu 'Inan: Marini sultan in Fez from 752/1351 to 759/1357, he assumed power after deposing his father, ABU AL-HASAN. Abu 'Inan gave the young IBN KHALDUN a court position as secretary in 757/1355, but later imprisoned him when he supported the attempt by ABU 'ABDALLAH, the amir of Bijaya (Bougie), to regain his kingdom (759–760/1357–58).

Sultan Abu Salim: Marini ruler in Fez from 760/1358 to 762/1360. He appointed IBN KHALDUN as *al-nazir fi al-mazalim* ('examiner of grievances').

Sultan Barquq: al-Malik al-Zahir Abu Sa'id Barquq (784–801/1382–99), the Circassian Mamluk sultan who often sought IBN KHALDUN's advice and appointed him to several important positions as both teacher and judge.

Sultan al-Muzaffar Hajji, murder of: a reference to the political turmoil in 783–784/1381–82 that accompanied the removal of the last of the Bahri line of MAMLUKS and their replacement by SULTAN BARQUQ, the founder of the Burji line.

al-Tabari (d. 314/923): the most famous of the annalist–historians in the early Islamic period. His monumental history, *Tarikh al-rusul wa-l-muluk* ('History of Messengers and Kings') has been translated into English.

Tamazight: the preferred term for the indigenous North African language often known as Berber (a term that, like the analogous 'Barbarian,' is regarded as an insult by its speakers).

Tanam: also known as Tanbak al-Hasani al-Zahiri, he was viceroy of Damascus. SULTAN BARQUQ's will stipulated that AYTAMISH be appointed guardian to the young Sultan Faraj, but Tanam managed to engineer a meeting of a council at which this provision was overturned. AYTAMISH refused to accept the decision, and a period of conflict ensued.

Taqi al-Din ibn Taymiya (d. 728/1328): a renowned Hanbali theologian who was doggedly opposed to forces of innovation within Islam. Throughout his life, his beliefs caused him continuous problems with the judicial and political authorities, and he spent many periods in prison. His influence on Muslim orthodoxy has been enormous and long-lasting.

Tashfin, Abu Zayyan, 'Abd al-'Aziz: the names of three Marini sultans, who ruled from 762–763/1360–61, 763–767/1361–65, and 767–774/1365–72 respectively.

Tilimsan (Tlemcen): a city now in Algeria, formerly an important center of power for the 'ABD AL-WADI dynasty, now renowned for its schools of what is still termed 'Andalusian' music.

'Umar ibn al-Khattab: the second caliph of Islam, who was murdered in 23/644.

al-Wadi al-Kabir: river in Spain now known by the Spanish name Guadalquivir, which is derived from the Arabic.

Yalbugha al-Nasiri: Viceroy of Damascus and army commander during SULTAN BARQUQ's reign, he was one of two leaders (along with MINTASH) of a rebellion against the sultan (791–792/1389–90). Even though Yalbugha al-Nasiri joined MINTASH in recommending that SULTAN BARQUQ be executed, the sultan, once restored to power, forgave him and even reappointed him commander of the army that set out to fight MINTASH in Syria.

Zayn al-'Abidin, Sayyida Nafisa, and Umm Kulthum: Zayn al-'Abidin (d. 93/712) was the son of Muhammad's grandson, al-Husayn; Sayyida Nafisa (d. 209/824) was a descendant of al-Hasan, also Muhammad's grandson; Umm Kulthum was Muhammad's daughter by his first wife, Khadijah, and was later married to 'Uthman who later became Islam's third caliph.

al-Zaytuna, al-Qarawiyin, al-'Ubbad, al-Hamra': the names of four famous architectural monuments within the Islamic domains: the Zaytuna mosque is in the old city of Tunis; the Qarawiyin mosque is the oldest university institution in the world, having been founded in Fez, Morocco, in the mid-ninth century; the al-'Ubbad was a mosque-college in Tilimsan (Tlemcen) founded at the site of the tomb of the renowned Sufi divine, ABU MADYAN; and the al-Hamra' (Alhambra) Palace in GRANADA was constructed as the palace of the Banu Ahmar and remains one of the glories of Islamic architecture.

zir: a cleansing ritual, frowned upon by orthodox religion, involving dancing, trance, and invocation of spirits.

Bibliography

Fischel, Walter J., *Ibn Khaldun and Tamerlane*, Berkeley: University of California Press, 1952.

———, *Ibn Khaldun in Egypt*, Berkeley: University of California Press, 1967.

Harakat, Ibrahim, *al-Maghrib 'abr al-tarikh*, vol. 2, Casablanca: Dar al-Rashad al-Hadithah, 1984.

"Ibn Khaldun," *Encyclopedia of Islam,* 2nd ed.[CD-ROM version], Leiden: E.J. Brill, 1954– .

Qur'anic References

Above every knowledgable person is the All-Knowing . . . (12:76)

And faces will be submissive to the Living, the Eternal; and whoever brings injustice will have failed . . . (20:11)

And God knows the contents of men's hearts . . . (8:43)

As for the one who fears the station of His Lord and denies the soul its fancies, Paradise is the refuge . . . (79:40–41)

Do not come to prayer in a state of drunkenness . . . (4:43)

God will never oppress even a tiny atom . . . (4:40)

He who created death and life so that he might test you as to who is the best in deeds . . . (67:2)

It is only the Devil who has made me forget to remember it . . . (18: 63)

Like a mirage in a depression which the thirsty man imagines to be water . . . (24: 390)

Neither slumber nor sleep take him . . . (2: 255)

Nothing will ever beset us unless God has prescribed it for us . . . (9:51)

O ye who believe, obey God and those in authority among you . . .
   (4:59)

Our Lord, You know that which we hide and that which we pro-
   claim . . . (14:38)

Pray to Me and I will answer you . . . (40:60)

Prepare as much force and string of horse for them as you can . . .
   (8:60)

Say, O people, act in accordance with your station. I am acting, and
   you will know . . . (6:135)

Those who transgress the statutes of God, those are the wrong
   doers . . . (2:229)

Verily those who store up gold and silver and do not spend them in
   the path of God, give them the glad tidings of a dire punish-
   ment . . . (9:34)

When Your Lord announced: If you show thanks, We will indeed
   increase it for you . . . (14:7)

Women are clothing for you, and you are clothing for them . . .
   (2:187)

Modern Arabic Writing
from the American University in Cairo Press

Ibrahim Abdel Meguid *The Other Place* • *No One Sleeps in Alexandria*
Yahya Taher Abdullah *The Mountain of Green Tea*
Leila Abouzeid *The Last Chapter*
Ibrahim Aslan *Nile Sparrows*
Hala El Badry *A Certain Woman*
Salwa Bakr *The Wiles of Men*
Hoda Barakat *The Tiller of Waters*
Mourid Barghouti *I Saw Ramallah*
Mohamed El-Bisatie *A Last Glass of Tea* • *Houses Behind the Trees*
Clamor of the Lake
Fathy Ghanem *The Man Who Lost His Shadow*
Randa Ghazy *Dreaming of Palestine*
Tawfiq al-Hakim *The Prison of Life*
Yahya Hakki *The Lamp of Umm Hashim*
Bensalem Himmich *The Polymath*
Taha Hussein *A Man of Letters* • *The Sufferers* • *The Days*
Sonallah Ibrahim *Cairo: From Edge to Edge* • *Zaat* • *The Committee*
Yusuf Idris *City of Love and Ashes*
Denys Johnson-Davies *Under the Naked Sky: Short Stories from the Arab World*
Said al-Kafrawi *The Hill of Gypsies*
Edwar al-Kharrat *Rama and the Dragon*
Naguib Mahfouz *Adrift on the Nile* • *Akhenaten, Dweller in Truth*
Arabian Nights and Days • *Autumn Quail* • *The Beggar*
The Beginning and the End • *The Cairo Trilogy: Palace Walk*
Palace of Desire • *Sugar Street* • *Children of the Alley*
The Day the Leader Was Killed • *Echoes of an Autobiography*
The Harafish • *The Journey of Ibn Fattouma* • *Khufu's Wisdom*
Midaq Alley • *Miramar* • *Naguib Mahfouz at Sidi Gaber*
Respected Sir • *Rhadopis of Nubia* • *The Search* • *Thebes at War*
The Thief and the Dogs • *The Time and the Place*
Wedding Song • *Voices from the Other World*
Ahlam Mosteghanemi *Memory in the Flesh* • *Chaos of the Senses*
Buthaina Al Nasiri *Final Night*
Abd al-Hakim Qasim *Rites of Assent*
Somaya Ramadan *Leaves of Narcissus*
Lenin El-Ramly *In Plain Arabic*
Rafik Schami *Damascus Nights*
Miral al-Tahawy *The Tent* • *Blue Aubergine*
Bahaa Taher *Love in Exile*
Fuad al-Takarli *The Long Way Back*
Latifa al-Zayyat *The Open Door*